ZERO *at the*

A KATHERINE DRISCOLL MYSTERY

BONE

Mary Willis Walker

D0348617

W🌐RLDWIDE®

TORONTO • NEW YORK • LONDON
AMSTERDAM • PARIS • SYDNEY • HAMBURG
STOCKHOLM • ATHENS • TOKYO • MILAN
MADRID • WARSAW • BUDAPEST • AUCKLAND

For my father,
a lifetime devotee of the fine art
of reading in bed

ZERO AT THE BONE

A Worldwide Mystery/June 1993

First published by St. Martin's Press, Incorporated.

ISBN 0-373-26122-5

---★---

A SUDDEN CHILL

She heard a footstep at the open door and said, "Okay, Iris. I'm coming." But she didn't turn around until she heard a noise that sounded like some heavy coils of wet garden hose hitting the floor just behind her.

She spun around on her knees and caught a glimpse of the two shining dark coils, already unwinding. She had just enough time to note the beadlike texture of the black inverted triangles.

Bushmasters.

Then the lights went off.

The door slammed shut, throwing the room into total blackness.

The click of the bolt shooting home on the outside of the door entered her heart like a dull, cold arrowhead. From the frigid center an icy chill radiated out throughout her body, reaching down to the marrow of her bones.

Zero at the bone. Frozen. Iced.

---★---

Several of Nature's People
  I know and they know me
I feel for them a transport
  Of cordiality

But never met this Fellow
  Attended or alone
Without a tighter Breathing
  And Zero at the Bone

—Emily Dickinson

PROLOGUE

THE POINTMAN waited until dusk to take the hunk of rotting meat out of the toilet tank where he had hidden it three days before. Raising the dripping bag, he caught a whiff of spoiled meat through the plastic. Yes, three days in the heat was perfect for aging a beef brisket to just the right putrescence. Lucky this place smelled so bad no one had noticed the stench.

He tied the bag to the left side of his belt to balance the one on his right and padded to the lavatory door. He eased the door open and looked through the gathering darkness over Bird Lake, past the huge brick reptile house toward the Phase II section. Amazing how quiet this place was with visitors locked out and animals confined to their holding cages for the night. He preferred it like this. Only he, the pointman, was at large, free finally to do what had to be done.

A quiver of pleasure rippled from his scalp to his toes. This first one was going to be so easy. Too easy. After the years of anticipation, the act itself might not be enough.

No matter. Pleasure wasn't the point. Justice was the point. He had been training for this all his life and now, finally, the time was right. Nothing could go wrong. The time was auspicious—he liked that word—auspicious. It made his mouth water with anticipation for what was coming, the work of the night and dawn.

He stepped out into the open. The night watchman—that plump, pale, grinning fool—would be sitting at his station sipping coffee from his stainless-steel thermos. No sweat. No threat.

Wearing only black Reeboks, black spandex pants, and a black jersey, he moved soundlessly along the path. His good-luck piece, which had never failed him, even in the most desperate times, swayed on its cord under his shirt, stroking his chest, its scales catching a hair occasionally, like the caress of a woman with jagged fingernails.

As he neared the carnivora complex he sniffed the air, trying to separate Brum's smell from the rest of the animal odors. A full hundred yards away, the sharp acidic scent filled his nostrils. Brum.

It was the big male's turn to spend the night outside. He would be ready. Just like the pointman, it was Brum's nature to be ready for the kill.

"Opportunity's about to knock on your door, brother," he whispered, breaking from a walk into an easy lope. Approaching the high wire mesh fence that surrounded the quarter-acre exhibit, he spotted Brum, sprawled on his side, half-concealed behind an artificial boulder on the bank of the recycling stream.

As if he had been waiting, the tiger leapt to his feet and glided toward the fence on huge spongy paws. The last rays of the setting sun transformed each hair of his thick orange coat into a glowing electric wire. As he walked his nose seemed connected to the bag at the pointman's waist by an invisible thread of scent. When he was a few feet from the fence, the tiger stopped and hissed through his yellowed fangs.

The pointman jumped the guardrail to approach closer to the high fence. "Smell good, don't I, Brum-boy? You ready for me? You better be." He pressed his palm against the fence and felt a ripple in his groin when the tiger rubbed his body along the other side of the fence, dragging his coarse fur against the pointman's skin.

Seeing the tiger at twilight like this, against the backdrop of grass and trees and rocks, it was easy to imagine away the fence and picture Brum as a wild tiger. A solitary hunter in the forest at night. Senses honed by hunger, forced by the void at his center, the tiger would scent the prey and his stomach would shudder at the smell of warm blood pumping beneath thin skin. He would hold a crouch, listening, his small rounded ears twitching. Here the pointman laughed aloud, remembering he had read that Indonesian hunters shaved their nostrils because they were certain tigers could hear a man's breath rustling through his nose hairs. He believed it. Brum would hear every breath, every blink, every tremble. And slowly, silently, eyes riveted on the prey, he would creep into range.

Then would come the best part, the part the pointman had imagined so often, asleep and waking. He saw it now: the cat launching his body into the air, hooking his claws deep into the flesh of the right flank, pulling the shrieking prey to the ground. And then . . . the tiger's teeth knowing just what to do. Like a guillotine falling, his four yellowed saber teeth clamping shut on the throat, cracking the neck. Merciful and elegant. Maybe too merciful.

While the pointman stood dreaming, Brum paced the high fence, staring at the bag. When the man started to walk again, Brum glided along beside him, only thin strands of wire separating them.

At the door concealed behind the fake rock wall, the pointman reached inside his jersey for the cord around his neck. His good-luck piece. He pressed his thumb against one of the sharp fangs until a single drop of blood beaded up. Then he gripped the whole rattlesnake head in his fist and held it tight for a few seconds.

He pulled his keys from their secure place inside his pants and unlocked the door, his breath coming faster now. Inside the keepers' area, he relocked the door, nodding at Brum's empty holding cage.

His hand trembled as he unlocked the door to the tiny closet-sized room where it would all happen. He stepped inside and locked the door behind him. Good zoo procedure. Always.

He smiled.

Then he sat on the floor of the tiny room, his back propped against the wall, and studied the steel door leading out to the exhibit. It was several inches thick, locked and bolted, with an observation window at eye level. The window was made of heavy wire-reinforced glass, two and one-half feet square—just big enough—he'd measured carefully.

He sighed with pleasure and untied the two plastic bags from his belt. He worked out the knots in the first bag and reached in to pull out the brisket. The slimy feel on his fingers made him grunt and the stench prickled his sinuses. It was intolerable. Simultaneously he sneezed and heaved the offending bloody slab against the metal door. It hit with a smack and fell to the floor.

The pointman couldn't hear him, but he knew for a certainty that Brum was there, right on the other side of that door, probably with his nose pressed to the crack underneath. "Hungry, big boy? You cats like your meat at blood-heat, don't you? Well, just wait and see what I have for you. It's what you've been wanting all your life."

From the other bag, he took a pair of soft cotton gardening gloves, a piece of beef jerky, and a brand-new pair of wire-cutters.

With his front teeth he grabbed the jerky and pulled hard to rip off a piece. He could take his time now. He had all night and very little work to do.

He wanted to make it last as long as possible.

ONE

IT WOULD BE Higgins, that wretched pug, yipping his way into her dreams.

Through closed lids, Katherine Driscoll felt the first light filtering through the east window of her bedroom. If she kept her eyes squeezed shut, maybe she could regain that blessed state of unconsciousness for just a few more minutes.

But no. The other boarders were joining in now—first the ancient basset hound with her basso-profundo baying. Then Jack Reiman's German shepherd with his wolflike howling, and then the rest, sixteen of them at last count, all joined the cacophony. And the peacocks from their roost on the kennel roof screeched their accompaniment.

She crossed her arms over her eyes and pulled her knees up tight. Always before, the entire eleven years she had lived in this house, she had relished getting up in the morning. She loved the rosy color of the early morning light. She loved feeding the animals and planning her schedule for the day. She loved being her own boss.

But not now. God, how could she cope with everything? The problems were too much. After all the years of coping alone, finally, just too much. Chaos was closing in on her.

She rolled over on her stomach and buried her head in the pillow. What was it she had been dreaming? If she kept her eyes closed and her mind empty, she might recapture one thread of it, and that thread she could grab on to and use to pull up the rest of the dream. If she could only have a few more minutes of peace.

Awake, there was that long list of dreads to face up to.

Listening to the edge of pain in Higgins's incessant yapping, she allowed one of the minor dreads to float to the surface—Higgins. His owners, two elderly sisters who were her closest neighbors and best boarding customers, were returning from their annual trip to Europe. Today. They had sent Higgins a postcard from Rome promising to fetch him on their way home from the airport. There was a postscript for Katherine reminding her to make sure he got plenty of exercise.

Oh, God.

She could visualize their reunion now. The two hulking sisters would arrive in their yellow Cadillac, their faces puckered up, ready to ask if their little Higgins wiggins had had a nice visit with his Aunt Katie. But instead, they would look at their beloved pet in horror and demand to know what had happened to him. And then she would have to explain the bizarre business of the garbage bag and the beer bottle. They were going to be horrified. Well, could she really blame them? When they were paying twice the going rate for Higgins to have extra-special, personal attention.

Katherine groaned.

Now that she had admitted one of the demon-dreads, the others seeped under her eyelids with the morning light and began to swarm the inside of her head. Her body clenched in defense.

But then a single sound made the muscles relax and the demons flee: Ra's nails clicking on the bare oak floor. Eyes still closed, she listened to the dog's approach—the heavy breathing, the jingle of his tags; then his moist, pungent breath tickled her face and his cold nose poked into the hollow of her neck. She inhaled the warm earthy odor of him and reached out her fingers to bury them in his thick coat.

Finally she lifted her head and opened her eyes. Taking his head in both hands, she kissed the golden retriever on his long muzzle and swung her legs out to sit on the edge of the bed. He rested his head on her knees and gazed up with wide-set almond eyes. She sighed with pleasure at the weight of the big head.

"Dual Champion Radiant Sunrise's Amun-Ra—son of champions, sire of champions—need to go out for a tinkle, baby?" she said.

In response, the dog lifted his head and pranced in place, his signal from puppyhood that he wanted to go outside. Katherine rose and padded barefoot toward the kitchen, with the dog high-stepping beside her.

She measured some coffee into a filter and plugged in the percolator. While she did it, she glanced out the window across the yard to the kennel—twenty-five rectangular dog runs under a long shingle roof. Her boarders were pacing their enclosures, impatient to be fed. Higgins, still yapping, was hurling his plump body against the chain link. Katherine hoped his stitches would hold.

She slipped her feet into a pair of old moccasins, opened the door for Ra and went out after him into a clear October morning. The sun was already heating up; it would be a warm fall day, perfect for taking the new black Lab to the pond to work on some water retrieves.

She surveyed the pasture behind her house; the switchgrass was dotted with Viguiera goldeneyes and sunflowers. Even now she took pleasure in her isolation, her privacy, in not being able to see another house from where she stood. She loved going outside in the morning in her nightgown, working alone in tattered shorts, answering to nobody. It made all the sacrifices worthwhile.

The twenty acres surrounding the house, from the rural road to the west as far as the creek on the east, were hers, all hers, what she'd always wanted. A piece of Texas. A home she had worked hard to create for herself. And a business that had made her comfortably self-sufficient. Until last year.

When the dogs saw her approach, they began to mill furiously around their narrow enclosures. She called out to them. "Okay, you beasts. Calm down. Breakfast's coming."

She entered the shed at the end of the kennel and began to set out seventeen plastic feeding bowls. From a huge garbage can full of Science Diet Extra, she dipped varying amounts into sixteen of the bowls. First she put down a bowl for Ra, who had been dancing around her feet as she made the preparations. Then she delivered the food two at a time, opening the cage doors with her elbows, sliding the bowls in as she greeted each dog by name.

Higgins was last, since he was on a special diet that took some time to concoct. For him she mixed two cups of Canine CD Maintenance Life, "for the older dog," a quarter cup of oat bran, a thyroid pill, two Ascription tablets crushed up for his arthritis, and some garlic compound for his coat—just as Hester and Judith had instructed. She turned her head away as she opened his door so she would not have to see the shaved gray skin with the long jagged cut in his rotund flank and the fifteen stitches the vet had used to close it. She rubbed his silky black ears without looking at him once. When Joe arrived, she'd ask him to apply the antibiotic salve to the wound.

As the dogs ate, she dragged the hose from cage to cage, filling the water containers, fortifying herself with the familiar routine. By then the cats, all four of them, were winding around her ankles mewing. She dipped into a smaller garbage can of dry cat food and spilled a tiny portion into each of their four bowls. "This is all you get, guys. No complaints. The rest you have to earn yourself. Go out and catch those damned snakes the way you're supposed to. And you, too," she called out to the pair of peafowl on the roof.

This comforting morning ritual over, she and Ra walked back to the house. When she heard Joe's old Chevy pickup in the driveway, her stomach gave one huge churn. How was she going to pay him? She was already a week behind and he lived close to the margin. It wasn't fair to keep him waiting. She had a responsibility to him.

The dreads were back in full force.

"Can't put it off any longer, can I, Ra?" she said.

Well, she'd sit down and look at the numbers one more time. Maybe an idea would come to her, a solution. Sure. And maybe the bank would decide to forgive her loan. And maybe her rich uncle would die and leave her some money. And maybe Higgins's cut would heal up before noon. And maybe her life would return to normal, as it had before all this trouble.

Back in the kitchen, Katherine poured herself a cup of coffee and slouched into the chair at her desk where she did her paperwork. For several minutes she sat unmoving, staring at the shoebox full of unpaid bills, last week's registered letter from the bank topping off the pile. Her coffee steamed untouched in front of her.

Finally she took a sip to fortify herself, opened the lower right-hand drawer of the desk, and drew out that other letter—the one that had come on Friday, plunging her into a weekend of inner turmoil such as she hadn't ever experienced as an adult. After reading it several times in disbelief, she had stuffed it in the drawer and slammed it shut so hard the knob fell off. For forty-eight hours, it had alternately drawn and repelled her. She had resisted its gravitational pull, making a wide berth around the drawer every time she passed it. Until now.

Just feeling the paper between her fingers kindled an angry flush of heat in her chest. Goddamn him. Why now? How can he think I would ever respond to this? The man must truly be insane.

Coffee forgotten, she spread the letter out on the desk and looked at the four careful folds in the yellow legal paper. Without reading the words yet, she absorbed the handwriting. Done in black ballpoint, it was big, bold, aggressively slanted and looping—the handwriting of a man who could drive his wife and daughter away and then ignore them for thirty-one years. Her anger burned higher; the flames leapt from her chest up through her neck into her cheeks, scorching the skin from the inside. God, the contempt she felt for that man was beyond words.

Taking two deep breaths to get her through it, Katherine read the letter once more.

37 Wirtz Ave.
Austin, TX
512-243-9080 (Home)
512-338-6712 (Work)

October 11

Dear Katie,

You'll probably be surprised hearing from me suddenly like this, after so long. But I heard you were having some financial difficulty and I have a proposal to help you out.

Katie, sorry I missed your birthday. Every year when October 2 rolls around I think about you and what a cute little girl you were. It's hard for me to write this, real hard. I hope you don't hold against me the things that happened when your mother and me were having our difficult times. Now you are an adult yourself you understand these things. Anyway you probably don't remember much since you were so young at the time, only a baby really.

About your problems, Katie. I don't want to discuss this in a letter. It is confidential, but I want you to know the full amount you need is available in cash immediately so there will be no foreclosure on your property. What you would need to do in return is something only you can do. It would not be difficult for you, I'm sure. You might even enjoy it. So if you could come to Austin SOON, in the next few days, we could discuss it. It is really in your best interests to come, so I hope you'll let bygones be bygones. These are hard financial times in Texas and it is good if families can help each other out.

I hear you are the best dog trainer in central Texas. That makes me real proud and doesn't surprise me at all since our family has always had a way with animals. Remember Pasha? What a good watchdog he was? Be sure to remember him just in case something should happen to me.

I'm still at the zoo, have been all this time. Never really regretted it. For the past eight years I've been senior keeper in charge of the large cats. I'd love to show them to you.

I was sorry to hear your mother died.

You are my only living relative in the world since my parents died two years ago (both in a six-month period) and my sister, your Aunt Julia, died last December. Of course, I don't count your mother's family as mine since we have been divorced so long.

Your Dad,

Lester Renfro

P.S. Please keep this receipt and key in a safe place for me and bring them with you when you come to Austin. I'll fill you in on everything then.

P.S. #2 No need to let anyone else know about this.

Katherine felt the flames engulf her face and lick at her brain now, her head swelling with the heat. Like a dragon forced either to breathe fire or explode from the heat buildup, she jerked up from the chair and began to pace circles around the kitchen, puffing little bursts of hot air from her cheeks.

It was almost like an infantile rage. Yes, she felt like a baby beginning to choke from fury. But why? This was so extreme—not something a realistic, independent woman should feel. She had gotten over this thing with her father long ago.

I might be surprised to hear from him after all this time, he says. Uh-huh. It is a bit of a surprise to hear from a father who hasn't even recognized my existence for the last thirty-one years. "Let bygones be bygones," he says. Uh-huh. Sure. It's as easy as that. Families can help each other out in hard times. Oh, yes. Good idea, Lester Renfro. He hopes I don't hold what happened against him? Well, he's right about one thing: I *was* too young to remember. But, oh, how I wish I could remember!

Katherine stopped pacing and pressed her hands to her hot cheeks. She had no memories, none at all, from her first five years. It was as if the time in Austin when the family was together had never happened.

She knew only what her mother had told her, again and again and again, as if in the telling she could exorcise her anger: "Don't expect anything from your father. Ever. He's a crazy man, a certifiable maniac. We dropped his name so we never have to hear it again or have anything to do with him. Ever."

Leanne had certainly kept that vow to her death.

But in spite of the stories told and retold, for years Katherine had not accepted the idea of her father as maniac and tyrant. It hadn't felt right to her and she had yearned for him.

Throughout her childhood, she had waited and hoped and fantasized about what it would be like when he came to claim her. She remained faithful to the idea of the father who would come to rescue her and help her. She had a recurring fantasy of his taking her to work with him at the zoo. She'd help him feed the animals and clean up and make the rounds. He'd see how good she was with animals and he'd say she could be his number-one assistant. It had been a sustaining vision during difficult years.

Ridiculous.

What a fool she'd been. But by the time she was fourteen she had finally accepted reality. Her mother was right. She realized he wasn't ever coming and she didn't even care anymore. It was the most important lesson, one she would never forget: She had only herself to depend on. And that was all right with her. She loved being on her own. And she'd done pretty damned well.

Until this bad economy. And she sure wasn't the only one caught by it.

"A man like that shouldn't be allowed to walk the earth," Katherine said aloud, waking Ra, who was snoozing at her feet. "The son of a bitch just assumes I'll come running. Never. I'd die first."

She began to pace again, in quick, furious steps around the small kitchen. When she got back to the desk, she forgot about the open drawer and walked right into it, whacking her left shin against the sharp edge. The impact dislodged the white knob again and sent it rolling under the stove. The hell with Lester Renfro. Let him stuff his financial help.

She leaned over and looked at her throbbing shin. A red knot was puffing up right on the bone. She sat down, fighting back tears, and returned to a question that had nagged her all weekend: How does he know I'm in trouble? How does he know I'm a dog trainer? How does he know my address?

It was more than passing strange. She was not in touch with anyone in Austin and her mother hadn't been either for several years before her death last year. So how did he know?

From the still-open drawer she drew out the envelope the letter had come in. From it she removed the key and the small square of paper he had sent along with the letter. She held the key in the palm of her hand and examined it for the first time. It was a small round-headed brass key. On one side it was blank; on the other, the word ABUS was engraved in small capital letters, and under that, "Germany."

The pain from the bruised shin seemed to absorb her anger for a moment. She closed her eyes and squeezed the key tight. The metal felt warm; it had taken on the temperature of her skin. My father touched this key. He put it in the envelope and sent it to me. It's important to him. It unlocks something he wants me to have. Something he thinks could help me.

She looked at the tiny receipt. At the bottom it said, "Lamar Boulevard Self-Storage, 1189 Lamar Blvd., Austin, Texas." It also said, "$23 received on October 11, 1989, for unit 2259 for one month."

This was so bloody melodramatic. If he had money he wanted to give her, why didn't he just send her a check, not make her come begging to him. You wouldn't keep money in a storage unit, anyway, would you? And what was it he had in mind for her to do? Something that only she could do. Ridiculous. Anyway, how could a zoo keeper accumulate enough money to help her out of this mess? Did he know she needed more than $90,000?

She opened her hand and stared at the key again. Well, it was possible. Maybe those relatives of his who died left it to him. Or maybe he'd been thrifty and saved it over the years. It was just possible that he had enough.

She shook her head violently. Christ, what a fool she was! The same credulous child who kept expecting him to come. Why was she even dignifying this with her attention when she had important issues to deal with? She tossed the key onto the desk. It hit and bounced off to the brick floor.

With the sudden noise, Ra leapt to his feet from a deep sleep, as if it were a gunshot. He was ready to go to work.

Absently, she rested her hand on the familiar bony ridge down the middle of the sleek head as she leaned over to pick up the key. She slipped it into the envelope and stuck it back in the drawer. Her stomach contracted as she caught sight of the box of unpaid bills. "Oh, Ra, who could even imagine a situation where we might lose everything we've worked for? It's just not possible."

The dog looked up at her and began to prance in place.

"Okay." She picked up the notice from the Bank of Boerne. "Don't worry. Today's the day. I'm going to do whatever it takes—beg, borrow, or steal. Since I've already borrowed, I guess it's time to beg."

She picked up her cup and took a sip of coffee. It was stone cold. She set it down again and looked at her watch. "Two hours until my appointment at the bank, Ra. Just enough time to put that new Lab through his blind retrieves.''

She looked down at him and tried to smile, but her lips trembled with the effort. "Someday we're going to look back and laugh at all this, aren't we, baby?"

TWO

By the time Katherine pulled her Wagoneer into the parking lot behind the one-story redbrick building that housed the Bank of Boerne, the white blouse she'd just put on felt damp. She turned off the engine and checked her watch. Five minutes early. One fat drop of sweat rolled slowly from her temple along her hairline.

She'd faced adversity before. Often. But this time was different. She loathed the idea of asking for help. It made her cringe just to think about it. And that she should have to ask George Bob Rainey made it even worse.

She pulled from her bag the letter and notice of sale that had arrived by registered mail six days before. She turned the engine back on so she could have some air-conditioning while she reread them.

It was bad news.

The worst.

She was three months behind on her mortgage payments. "In monetary default," it said. *Default*—an ugly, accusatory word. The bank was forced to accelerate the loan so her entire balance of $90,899 was due immediately. If she did not make her payment by Tuesday, November 7, her property would be auctioned off on the east steps of the Kendall County Courthouse at 11 A.M.

Only twenty-two days from today!

The bank's attorney was posting the property and kennel assets for foreclosure on the bulletin board at the courthouse, and if she could not meet her commitments, it would go on public sale.

That phrase—"If you cannot meet your commitments"—stung her hard. She had always taken pride in meeting her commitments head-on. Hadn't she always met more commitments than other people? When she was growing up, her mother had often seemed helpless and lost—more the child than Katherine. Hadn't she taken care of things alone at home during her mother's absences? And hadn't she managed to do well in school, too? Hadn't she put herself through college? Hadn't she built a profitable business from the small beginning of raising and training a few golden retrievers?

And when her mother got cancer two years ago, hadn't she, Katherine, taken over and paid the enormous hospital bills that her mother's tiny trust income couldn't pay? And all this on her own. The only help she had ever asked for had been this bank loan to buy her house and land. She had met her payments on time every month for eleven years. Until the medical bills and the downturn in the economy had sabotaged her.

Yes, she could go on and on about commitments.

As a matter of fact, that's just how she saw herself: an independent woman who had always met her commitments. God, it sounded like an epitaph. She visualized it written on her tombstone: "Katherine Anne Driscoll. She met her commitments." Somehow she didn't like the sound of it as the summary of thirty-six years. Joyless.

She looked down at her watch again. Three past eleven. She hurried into the bank feeling hot, awkward, and pretentious in high heels and a straight skirt. Trying to look like I don't need money, she thought. Trying to look proper.

As she entered, she saw George Bob Rainey across the lobby and felt the usual rush of embarrassment his presence always brought out in her.

He walked toward her beaming, his face even fuller and more boneless than when she had seen him two months before. "Kate. Good to see you. Good to see you." He seized her hand and pumped it up and down several times. Priming the pump to get money out of it, Katherine thought. I wish it were as easy as that.

"Come on into my inner sanctum," he said, steering her with an open palm on her back, something Katherine loathed. Especially now when her back was probably a little sweaty from the tension. When I was paying my mortgage on time, she thought, I could have shrugged his hand off. But not now.

The door of his office was mahogany with gold letters on it: "George Bob Rainey, Vice President."

He opened it and steered her in. He gestured to a small straight-backed chair that was dwarfed by the huge desk. A supplicant's chair. Perfect. She perched on it, adjusting her straight skirt to cover her knees.

"Well, Kate, you're looking good, girl. Still seeing Johnny Rhenquist?"

"Uh, no. Not lately." She was determined not to give him any grist for gossip over her broken engagement. "How's Major?"

George Bob Rainey eased himself into the big burgundy leather executive chair with a low grunt. "Oh, mean as ever. A real pistol. We still have to muzzle him when guests come to the house. Hell, he took a chunk out of Charley Holbein's leg last month. Damn dog. I pretty near beat him to a pulp after that. I should've done what you suggested years ago and had you train him. I'm afraid it might could be too late now."

Katherine thought it had been too late even five years ago, when he had brought the huge German shepherd, then a puppy of eight months, to one of her group obedience classes. The dog was high-strung and aggressive toward the other dogs, and George Bob had refused to correct the behavior. She'd had to ask him to leave the class. She'd also had to reject the repeated leering advances he'd made over the years. Each time she turned him down, he'd clucked and said it was too bad she wasn't a good sport like her mother.

The problem was this was a small community. He knew Leanne's reputation and he never let Katherine forget it. Whenever she was around him, she felt an undercurrent of shame and a need to prove herself businesslike and sexless—the exact opposite of her mother.

George Bob was looking down at the open folder in front of him on the desk. In an instant, his face was transformed, from genial host to no-nonsense banker. This new man looked up at Katherine with his eyes slightly narrowed, his thin lips sucked back into his mouth. He was ready to get down to it.

She put the letter on the leather desktop and slid it across the wide expanse toward him. "I got this last week. It was a real shock."

He glanced down at it. "Yes, ma'am, I know. Looks like we got a real problem here."

Katherine took a deep breath and began as she had been rehearsing it in her head. "When I was in two months ago to talk about this, I told you my business was down, just like everyone's around here, but that it was improving—slowly—and that I had plans for increasing my profits, if I could have some more time."

She saw that his jaw was opening. He was about to interrupt, so she rushed on with the rest of her speech. "You said I could have a few months to work it out. I haven't had enough time, and I can't pay it all at once, but I am in the process of...working it out. I have some better ideas in mind. I can get an outside job; I can lay Joe off to save on overhead. If you could bear with me on this for just a few more months, George Bob, I will pay everything I owe. I've always been a good customer, paying right on time for eleven years.''

Katherine found herself breathing hard after this speech, not because it was more words than she usually spoke at one time, although it was, but because of her profound resistance to saying them. It was too close to begging. And she could hear herself what bluff it was. The truth was she was just stalling for time; she saw no way she could pay off the debt in this lifetime.

He leaned forward and folded his hands in front of him. ''Kate, it's no longer a matter of just curing the default. Since the loan has been accelerated, you owe the full ninety-one thousand dollars.'' He didn't even have to look down at the folder for the number, Katherine noticed. He was loaded for bear. ''Now I don't want to be discouraging here. I know what a can-do sort of gal you are, but let's us look at some serious possibilities here. Have you tried to sell the place?''

She looked down at the backs of her hands. They were gripping her knees so tightly the bones and veins stood out in relief. ''Not really. But I had a realtor look at it and she said I'd be lucky to get a hundred thousand for the whole thing, including the extra ten acres. That's less than I paid for it. She also says it would take a long time to sell it in this down market.''

He shook his head slowly, sadly. ''This is the hardest time for real estate I ever did see. Who ever would've thought this would happen?''

George Bob had lowered his voice to funereal tones. Katherine's heart slowly contracted. This was certainly his worst-news voice. ''Now, Kate, we want to work with you on this, but we have a responsibility to our shareholders and our depositors to see that these loans get paid. If they don't get paid, we are responsible to make the most we can out of the collateral. Unfortunately, it's just like the notice says.'' He picked it up and pushed it back across the desk to Katherine. ''The loan committee has decided that we will have to foreclose on this property if you can't figure out a way to pay what you owe by November seven.''

''That's only three weeks away. How can I figure it out in three weeks?'' Her voice was in danger again of rising to a whine. She clenched her jaw to stop it.

''Kate, let's get serious. You've got some family in Austin could help. I know from your mama that you've got a rich grandmother. Hell, you're one of *the* Driscolls. Why don't you call them and ask for a loan to get you over this bad hump? That's what I would do if I was you."

She shook her head angrily.

He continued. "If it was up to me, I'd give you as much time as you needed, but it's not up to me." He gestured to the office next to his, the president's. "We don't like to take over properties. That's not the business we're in. But the powers that be say we got to collect on these real estate loans or do the best we can with the collateral."

For the first time he looked down at the open folder. "Says here in the loan agreement your collateral is the twenty acres, house, kennel building, and the assets of the kennel."

"Other than the runs and some dog-training equipment, there aren't any kennel assets," she said, fearful of the next shoe to drop.

"Oh? It says here those champion dogs, big retrievers you breed and train—they're part of the assets, the collateral assigned to the bank."

Her breath got ragged. "Oh, I sold the dogs months ago to help pay the mortgage. They went into the May and June payments."

"Did they? That must've been real hard for you. How about that big one rides around in the car with you, the one that wins all the field trials?"

"Ra?" Her voice sounded thin, even to her own ears. "But no one would consider him part of the kennel assets. He's . . . my pet. Just happens to have won a show or two."

"Charley Holbein says that dog is worth twenty thousand in stud fees alone. Says it's the best field-trial dog he's ever seen. Now come, Kate. I know how it is to get attached to critters, but this is business." He pronounced it "bidness."

Katherine had never before known what it meant to feel faint. She gripped the edge of his desk to keep panic at bay.

He looked her straight in the eye. "Anything I could do for you on this, Miss Kate, I would do, but the committee has made a decision. They think the value of the property will continue to sink, so giving you more time would likely just delay your agony, and increase the loss we'll surely take on this."

George Bob stood up. He was dismissing her. It was all over.

There must be more she could say to stop this. Katherine opened her lips to protest. But she didn't utter a sound because she knew it would come out as a whine. And she had taught herself never, never to whine.

Finally she found a neutral voice. Still sitting, she said, "So that's it? I have until the seventh of next month?"

"'Fraid so." He looked at the calendar open on his desk. "Twenty-two days from today." He looked up at her. "We go back a long way and you've been a good customer, Kate. I sure dislike having it turn out like this."

"Me, too," Katherine said in a small voice that was humiliatingly close to tears. She stood up and let him usher her to the door. Before passing through, she stopped for a final try.

"George Bob? About the dog—Ra—he really is a pet. The only reason he's won some field trials is that he and I get on so well . . . you know, we have good rapport. He wouldn't work well for anyone else. It wouldn't make sense to foreclose on a dog, would it?" She tried to laugh at the idea, but the sound that emerged was more like a whimper.

The banker kept his business face in place, but he draped a heavy arm across her shoulders. "I know this is real hard, but that animal is a valuable asset. I'll present it to the committee, Kate, but I can't make no promises." George Bob liked to slip in a double negative every so often to show that he was a good ol' boy at heart, even though he was a banker.

WHEN KATHERINE GOT BACK to the car she was shaking, her torso damp with cold sweat. She climbed in quickly, wanting to lie on the floor and pass out so she wouldn't have to feel what she was feeling. It was fear, panic. Things were out of control, swarming in on her, and she was powerless to stop the momentum.

She rested her forehead against the hot steering wheel and pictured her house—the two old yellow wing chairs flanking the stone fireplace in the living room, her books neatly organized in the shelves; the cool white bedroom with the tall pecan trees shading the windows; the wood-and-brick kitchen. In her mind's eye she saw the pasture behind the kennel in the morning light. Ra was loping through the wildflowers, his plumy tail carried high on the breeze.

Not only was she about to lose her home and her business, but she was probably going to lose Ra, too.

When a car pulled into the space next to hers, she sat up straight and searched her purse for the key. She began talking to herself: "Am I just going to lie down and feel sorry for myself? Let these bankers ruin my life? Hell, no. This is not like me. I've had hard times before and I've always gotten through them. I don't have to accept this."

She started the engine and revved it a few times to fortify her courage. She would fight back.

KATHERINE WAS SO stunned she forget to put the phone down until it began to buzz at her. Then she let her head fall forward and pressed her fingers hard into the base of her neck. Her lawyer had just finished reading the loan documents. There was no recourse, he told her, but to come up with the full $91,000 in the next twenty-two days. In response to her question about Ra, he'd said there was no question that the dog was part of the kennel assets. Too bad, he'd commiserated, but there it was.

Then he'd asked the same question George Bob had asked: "Don't you have some family who could help out?"

She'd glanced down at the drawer containing the letter.

"No," she'd said into the phone. "No family."

As she massaged the tight cords in her neck, she thought about it.

No family.

Her mother had always impressed on her that they had no family except one another. Whenever Katherine had brought up the subject, Leanne had sat her down and reminded her that they were alone in the world. Katherine's father was a maniac they would never see again. And her grandmother, Leanne's mother, had disowned them forever when they moved to Boerne, had warned them never to come crawling back to her for anything. Leanne's father had died when Leanne was sixteen and her only brother, Cooper, was nothing but a toady, always currying his mother's favor.

"My mother's a greedy, selfish, unforgiving woman," Leanne would say. "A spoiled, indulged woman who inherited a fortune and vowed never to give a penny of it to us. Anyway, we would prefer to starve to death rather than go groveling to her for anything."

Then Leanne would flash her dazzling smile and say gaily, "Anyway, the two of us are a family, aren't we? We're happy as we are, sufficient unto ourselves."

Sure, Katherine thought, sufficient until the next man came along. Thank God all that was over and she didn't have to feel that abandonment anymore, now that she was grown up. But now, today, with these problems weighing her down, she felt strangely like that child cooking her own dinner, not knowing when her mother would come back.

Katherine stood up from her desk and looked out the kitchen window to admire the billowy clouds in her big sky. Family? Who needed it!

She heard the purr of a car pulling up to the kennel, then the slamming of doors, and the high twangy voices calling. "Yoo-hoo, Kate, Joe. Higgins, where are you?"

Oh, no! The sisters Kielmeyer, come for their dog.

She looked out the window. There they were, dressed in their usual floral traveling outfits and sensible shoes. They had known her when she was a girl, before she had decided to call herself Katherine instead of Kate. They were old friends and usually she was delighted to see them, but today she didn't know if she could face them. Would it be better to let them see Higgins first? Or to rush out and try to explain everything before they saw the damage? But it was too late now. They were already bearing down on the kennel.

Katherine called her dog. "Come on, Ra. You had something to do with this. Let's face the music together."

THREE

JUDITH HELD THE squirming Higgins on the shelf of her ample peach-flowered bosom. To a stranger it would look as if she were squeezing the life out of the little dog because his bright pink tongue dangled from his squashed-in black face. But Katherine had never seen him with his tongue in.

As Katherine walked across the lawn, Ra ran forward to greet the women. Politely, he sat at their feet to receive his accustomed praise. Hester, the smaller sister at two hundred pounds, and the more talkative, leaned over and rubbed his ears vigorously.

Ordinarily Katherine would be delighted to see them back, but not today. "Welcome home," she said. "As you see, we had a problem while you were gone. But Dr. Burris says he will be fine." She watched their faces apprehensively while she spoke. For ten years Higgins had boarded with her when the sisters were out of town. Since they traveled for four months every year, and since they paid double the usual rate for Katherine and Joe to give special attention to Higgins, he was a major and dependable source of income.

Both of them were staring at her, waiting. Katherine had never seen them look so severe, their sagging faces set into stony silence.

"It happened Tuesday—a freak accident," Katherine said. "He was out running with Ra. You know, exercise to keep his weight down, as we talked about. First Ra would chase Higgins, then Higgins would chase Ra." Katherine was pleased to note that both sisters looked a little softer at the vision of their darling playing with a friend.

"There was a garbage bag waiting for Joe to put out at the curb. Ra jumped over it when Higgins was chasing him and Higgins tried to jump it, too. But you know his legs are shorter and he didn't make it and landed right on top of the bag. There was a broken bottle in the bag that cut him through the plastic."

Katherine's eyes started to fill with tears when she described it. The scene had been awful—bloody and dominated by pitiful yips of pain. Best they didn't hear about that. "It was a very long cut.

Well, you can see that, but fortunately not too deep. I know you both have a great deal of confidence in Dr. Burris, and he knows Higgins well, so we took him into San Antonio, to Dr. Burris's house, since it was after office hours. He disinfected it and put in fifteen stitches."

Now Hester had taken Higgins from her sister and restrained him in her arms so she could study the long jagged cut with the black stitches. Her forehead was squeezed down over her eyebrows.

Katherine stopped to catch her breath. She still had no idea what they would do—drive away and use another kennel in the future? Spread the bad word among their numerous friends? Report her to the Humane Society for neglect?

There was silence as the sisters absorbed the news and explored the injury with gentle fingertips. Finally Hester spoke. "How did the little fellow behave during this emergency?" she asked, pressing her crinkly, powdered cheek gently against the dog's injured side.

"Oh," Katherine said, "he was splendid. After the initial shock, he was very brave, lay quietly in Joe's lap so he could hold a towel to the cut to stanch the bleeding. No complaining at all."

Both sisters smiled at their dog.

"I feel so bad about it," Katherine said, discovering as she spoke the words how really bad she did feel. "Higgins and Ra have always played together when Higgins is here and . . . well, this was a bad accident. He's due at Dr. Burris's the day after tomorrow to have his stitches removed. The cut seems to be healing well. Oh, and there's an antibiotic salve to put on twice a day." They both nodded at her. "It will leave a scar, he says."

Hester handed the dog back to her sister. She approached Katherine, stretched her arms out wide, and wrapped them around her. "It must have been dreadful for you, Kate. You're so fond of him. And then to have to worry about how we would feel when we saw him. He can be so clumsy sometimes, just a knucklehead really."

Judith said, "You must let us reimburse you for the vet bill. Dr. Burris doesn't come cheap."

"Oh, no," Katherine said. "That's my expense."

"Well, we need to collect his things and get this boy home," Judith said. "Did you have a chance to work on his manners, Kate?"

"Yes, before the accident we did. Put him down a minute and I'll show you."

Judith deposited Higgins on the ground gingerly. He stood there on his short bowed legs, his tongue protruding, his corkscrew tail curled tight against his fat rump. Katherine moved to stand directly in front of him. In her gruff dog-training voice, she commanded, "Higgins, sit." Higgins immediately dropped his rear end the three inches to the ground.

Both Hester and Judith let out a squeal of surprise.

"Good boy," Katherine said. "Higgins." She waited until she established eye contact with the dog. "Down." Higgins thought for a second longer than she liked, and pushed out his short front legs so he was lying down.

"Oooh, good boy," Hester said. "Kate, it's wonderful. I don't know how you do it. I wish we'd asked you to train him sooner. It just never occurred to us that he could be trained. He's always been so... opinionated about things."

When Joe had loaded all Higgins's toys and his bed into the trunk of the Cadillac and Judith had written a check and tucked it into Katherine's shirt pocket, Hester hefted herself in under the wheel. Judith climbed in next to her with Higgins in her lap. "Oh, it's so nice to be home," Hester said through the open window. She looked at the fields of wildflowers and sighed. "I don't believe there's a place in all Europe as beautiful as your place, Kate."

Katherine was surprised by a surge of tears welling up like a force of nature, as if from an underground spring.

"Oh, my dear, what have I said?" Hester wailed.

Katherine couldn't speak. She held up her hand—a request for time to gather her composure.

"Come sit in the car with us for a minute so we can talk," Judith said, reaching behind her to open the back door of the Cadillac. Katherine got in obediently.

"I'm going to give us some air." Hester started the engine, rolled up the electric windows, and turned the air-conditioning on full-blast. The sisters both swiveled their heads toward the back seat, waiting.

Katherine sat for a long minute with her head down. She was not accustomed to telling her problems to anyone. It was always better, she'd found, to keep them private. But for the first time in her life, a swell of emotion was threatening to overwhelm her. She finally found her voice and began to talk. Once started, she couldn't stop.

She began with her morning visit to the bank and the impending foreclosure.

"That George Bob Rainey should be ashamed of himself," Hester said. "He could give you some more time. He's probably got himself a buyer interested."

Katherine went on to tell them what the lawyer had said about Ra being part of the collateral. She even told them about the letter from her father and how she felt about it. They were a perfect audience. They listened attentively, nodding and making little cooing noises at the worst parts, asking questions only occasionally for clarification.

By the time she'd finished, Higgins was asleep in Judith's lap, making wet snuffling noises with each inhalation.

"So," Hester said, "in three weeks, the bank will take your house, your land, and your business, including Ra, if you don't come up with ninety-one thousand dollars."

Katherine nodded.

"And your father has offered you the cash you need to pay off the loan, but you hate him for his past neglect so you refuse to go collect the money. Do I have it right?"

Katherine said, "But he never even—"

Hester interrupted. "No, I know he didn't. Kate, our father was the son of a bitch to end all sons of bitches, wasn't he, Judith?"

Judith nodded so vigorously her tight perm loosened.

"And you know what? I enjoy the money we inherited from him all the more for it. When we go to Rome and stay at the Ritz, I like to think of that cheap, surly bastard sweating it out in the oilfields for the money we're spending. He beat us just to keep in practice and he used to complain that his life would be better if girls were all drowned at birth. Should we turn down his money because he mistreated us? Hell, no. All the more reason to take it and enjoy it. Kate, you get in your car and drive to Austin now. Let the bastard pay to ease his guilt. Tell him he can begin making it all up to you by saving your dog from foreclosure."

Katherine had stopped crying. It felt as if there had been a major shift in the earth's surface and suddenly she were viewing it all from a different place. Why hadn't she seen it from this perspective herself? It made perfect sense. Why should she suffer for his deficiencies as a father?

Both of the sisters were studying her expression. When they began to chuckle, Katherine realized she had a smile on her lips. "Okay," she said. "I'll go."

"That's very good," Hester said, clapping her hands.

"Will you call us, Kate, and let us know what happened?" Judith asked.

Kate opened the door and climbed out of the car. "Absolutely. Be sure to have Higgins practice his sits and downs. Next time he's here we'll work on down-stays. He could use that."

When she shut the door, Higgins woke with a start.

Judith propped him up on his haunches and waved his paw in Katherine's direction as they pulled slowly out of the driveway. Katherine waved back at him.

A GROWING ELATION swelled her chest. She tried to contain it. After all, this was not going to be some big emotional reunion. It was a business transaction. She was going for the money.

She called out to Joe, who was hosing down the kennels, "Joe, can you hold down the fort for me this afternoon? I've got to drive to Austin."

Joe dropped the hose and pushed his abundant black hair back from his forehead. "Okay, but I don't take out that big Doberman while you gone. I don't even put a hand in there to feed him. Not me."

She could barely contain her desire to get on the road. "Tanya can stay in today. I'll be back tonight." She started to walk backward as she gave instructions. "You remember that Jack Reiman is picking up Gunner at six. His bill's on the desk. Don't forget to give him a flea dip and make him all pretty."

Joe nodded in his usual long-suffering way. "Yeah, I remember. He be ready. When do I get paid?"

Katherine pulled out the check Judith had tucked into her pocket. To the three-hundred-dollar boarding and training fee, Judith had added another two hundred, a sum that more than covered Dr. Burris's bill. Katherine breathed a sigh of relief. "Tomorrow," she called back to Joe. "After I deposit this check. Okay?"

She looked down at Ra frisking at her heels. "Okay, Ra. We're going to Austin to surprise my father. Out of the mists of the past I am going to appear full-blown, Athena-like, in front of his eyes. We're going to let the bastard pay his dues. Oh, yes, Ra. The sisters Kielmeyer are right. It is about time."

It was one o'clock when Katherine saw Austin's pink granite capitol dome on the horizon to the north. The drive had taken just one hour. In ten minutes she could be at the Austin Zoological

Gardens in Zilker Park. She could see her father, talk with him, touch him. After thirty-one years. The idea made her feel shaky. She needed just a little more time to get mentally prepared.

She decided to make a quick side trip—the clandestine drive she had made so many times before. It wouldn't take long.

That first time, when she was sixteen, she had looked up the address in the phone book, her hands trembling with excitement when she found the name: Driscoll, Anne Cooper, 1007 Woodlawn.

And today, just as on that first trip, her heart quickened as she exited Mopac onto Windsor and entered the posh old Enfield area, turning onto Woodlawn. The houses got bigger, older, richer. She slowed down, studying each house, feeling, as always, alien to the opulence of this old neighborhood, as if she were a transient who would be stopped by the police for loitering where she didn't belong.

She came to a stop in front of the largest house on the street, a stone mansion with slate roof and leaded glass windows. Not a beautiful house, like some of the others on the street, but solid, massive, ageless, speaking of money and permanence—qualities she had never known.

This was her grandmother's house. Still was, according to the most recent Austin phone directory.

The first time Katherine had driven by the house twenty years ago was the day after she got her driver's license. She had talked Leanne out of the beat-up old station wagon, saying she was just going to drive around San Antonio. But instead she'd driven directly to Austin, where she stopped at a gas station to look in the phone book and got a street map. Then she'd found her way here, to this stone mansion, and sat outside looking at it, just as she was doing now.

She had first gotten the idea of going when she read in the *San Antonio Light* that Anne Cooper Driscoll had received an honorary doctorate from the University of Texas for her many contributions to the quality of life in Texas, especially to the Austin Zoo. The newspaper picture was of a perfectly groomed, handsome woman of sixty, smiling in her cap and gown. That had been twenty years ago. Now Anne Driscoll would be over eighty. She might even be dead.

Katherine rested her head back on the seat and watched the lacquered oak front door. In this house, this mansion, her mother had grown up. Katherine could understand how miserable it must have

been for her to have to live in the small rundown house they had
occupied in Boerne, to work as a saleswoman at Joske's, and to
raise a daughter on her own. In this house, her mother had lived
in luxury until she eloped with Lester Renfro.

The story Leanne told and retold was of herself, the indulged
daughter of a rich family, being seduced at eighteen by a handsome zookeeper she'd met while doing volunteer work at the zoo.
She'd given up everything for him, gone against her family and
social class to marry him. Then he turned out to be a violent and
evil man. She had tried to make it work, but finally she had been
forced to leave him in the middle of the night, taking five-year-old
Katherine and fleeing Austin. Lester Renfro had not only driven
them from the city of their birth, but he had caused an irrevocable
split between Leanne and her mother and brother, who had washed
their hands of her.

Katherine wasn't sure if the story was true or not. It was hard to
know with her mother. But no one had ever made a more complete break with the past than Leanne Driscoll. After leaving Austin, she had never returned, not even to pack her possessions. She
never again saw her husband or her mother or her only brother.
She had slammed shut the window and pulled down the shade on
her past.

The problem was it had slammed the window on Katherine's
past, too.

She looked at the leaded windows of Anne Driscoll's house. The
draperies were pulled closed. The silent house gave nothing away,
kept all its secrets. Secrets. There were so many secrets in this family.

Katherine could understand why her grandmother had objected
to her daughter's marrying so young, and marrying someone poor.
But that happened in many families, and they didn't break with
each other forever over it. Leanne had always refused to talk about
it, but something had happened that created a break so total that
mother and daughter never saw each other again after Leanne and
Katherine had moved to Boerne. Katherine thought about her
grandmother, an old woman living alone in this immense house.
What could happen that was so bad that you would never want to
see your daughter and granddaughter again? She could not imagine.

She looked at her watch. It was after one-thirty. Time to get on
with it. Katherine took MoPac south. She crossed the bridge
spanning Town Lake and turned left into Zilker Park where the

Austin Zoological Gardens had been located for close to sixty years.

She had driven past the zoo often on her trips to Austin, but she had never entered. It would have been a natural thing to do. When she was in Houston or Dallas, she always went to the zoo. But she did not want to make even a gesture toward a father who had made no gestures to her.

To her surprise, the parking lot was almost full—on a Monday afternoon during the school year. The zoo was doing great business.

She let Ra out for a brief run before leaving him in the car with the windows open.

As she walked through the entrance gate, she stopped and looked up, transfixed. On top of each gatepost was a huge stone elephant balanced on one leg on a stone ball. She gasped in recognition. I know those elephants. I loved them. He lifted me up over his head so I could touch their trunks. We walked across that wooden bridge and watched the birds along the creek.

She paid her six-dollar adult non-member admission at the window and picked up a map. Crossing the wooden bridge over the creek, she felt a sudden rising panic. What should she do first? She could just go and look for Lester, but she wouldn't even recognize him. What if he wasn't pleased to have her appear here so suddenly? Maybe this meeting should have been more private—at his house perhaps. Maybe she should have called ahead.

She glanced down at her khaki shorts and old Nikes. At least she should have changed her clothes. He hadn't seen her since she was five. What would he think? Her mother had been so beautiful, so meticulous in her grooming. Would he expect that in her? Be disappointed that she was a different kind of woman?

She walked slowly past the large flamingo display and the snack bar, looking for a ladies' room. She found one behind the snack bar. When she emerged five minutes later, her hair was brushed, her face washed, and she had applied some light lipstick.

To give herself time to recapture her resolve, she paused in front of a wooden bulletin board: TODAY'S ZOO NEWS. Next to it, in a huge cage, labeled "Parrots of the World," vividly colored birds squawked and spread their wings as a spray of mist rained down on them from the top of the cage. She ran her eye down the listings of recent births, public feeding times, and "Meet the keeper" demonstrations. A large handwritten note proclaimed the imminent arrival on breeding loan of a female white rhino from the Frankfurt zoo, the birth of a spider monkey, and the hatching of a clutch of thirty-nine king cobras. Thirty-nine! Katherine shivered and turned away.

She walked back over the bridge to the administrative office. She would ask for him in the office. They could call him, so he'd be expecting her. Give him a little advance warning.

The offices were tucked behind a stockade fence near the gate. She entered a room throbbing with noise and so jammed with people she could barely push her way in. Men and women with cameras and microphones sat on the sofas, leaned against the walls. They all held notebooks and tape recorders. Several uniformed men surrounded the reception desk. Surely, Katherine thought, this is not all for the birth of some king cobras. For the rhino, maybe.

Sideways, she worked her way through the crowd to a desk where a young woman with a long blond French braid was talking on the telephone with her hand pressed against her other ear to shut out the clamor of the room. Into the phone she shouted, "I can't give you that information," and slammed it down.

Katherine leaned over the desk and said, "I'm here to see Lester Renfro. Could you call him and tell him he has a visitor?"

The woman opened her mouth wide, then snapped it shut with a click. "Is this some sort of joke?" she asked, staring at Katherine.

"A joke? No," Katherine said. "Why?"

She noticed that the uniformed man leaning against the next desk watching her closely was an Austin policeman.

The woman reached across her desk for a folded newspaper which she offered to Katherine. "Here," she said, tapping a finger on a picture at the bottom of the front page, "this is the afternoon edition of the paper. Just came out."

Katherine saw a photograph of the massive broad head of a tiger. The caption underneath said, "Brum, the Siberian tiger that killed his keeper this morning at the Austin Zoo."

Katherine took the paper and braced one hand on the corner of the desk. The article accompanying the photo was headlined, "Tiger breaks window, kills Austin Zookeeper."

She had to read the article twice before it registered.

AUSTIN—*A five-hundred-pound Siberian tiger smashed through a glass window early today, dragged a veteran Austin zookeeper into the animal's display area, and mauled him to death.*

Lester Renfro, sixty, apparently was walking through a service corridor when the tiger broke through a 2-1/2-square-foot, quarter-inch-thick glass-and-wire mesh window and pulled him outside to a natural-habitat area, Austin Zoo director Sam McElroy said.

"We are uncertain at this time just how the accident happened," McElroy said. "There were no witnesses to the attack."

The tiger, a five-year-old male named Brum, was isolated after the attack, but will not be destroyed, according to McElroy, because it is a member of an endangered species.

Renfro, a zoo employee for thirty-seven years, had been senior zookeeper in charge of large cats since 1978. Previously, he had worked with reptiles and small mammals. He is the second worker killed at the zoo in its fifty-six-year history.

A reporter standing next to Katherine had been reading the article over her shoulder. "Pretty grisly," he said. "They won't say yet whether the tiger snacked on him. Really that's what everybody's here for, to get in on the autopsy information. The director is holding a press conference in a few minutes."

Katherine leaned against the corner of the desk.

"Ma'am?" the policeman said, "could you give us some space up here for the news conference? We're about to start and we need to clear this area out."

Katherine didn't hear him the first two times he asked. She was thinking about timing and that hers was possibly the worst in the world. Thirty-one years. And on the day she decides to come see her father, he gets killed by a tiger.

Damn him. The fires of rage began to fill her chest again. God damn him to hell. Typical. His last act in the world was to let me down.

Again.

FOUR

KATHERINE ELBOWED her way through the crowd to the back of the room. She needed to be alone, and she needed to lean against something solid. In a hallway just outside the main room, she found the only available surface to lean on—a doorframe leading into the men's room. There she braced her shoulder and tried to exhale the anger that was mushrooming inside her, but it clung to her lungs like a coating of napalm.

Goddamn. This is so frustrating. Now I'll never get a chance to tell him how angry I am, how long I waited for him. As soon as you start to depend on anyone in this world, they leave, or die. I suppose I should feel sad. I should feel sorry for him dying a violent death like that. But I don't. Not at all.

She reached a hand into her shoulder bag and rummaged around until she touched the cold metal of her keys. She found by feel the small brass key she'd added to her ring before she left home. It was the one Lester had sent her. She closed her fist tight around it, until its sharp edges bit into her palm. What about the money now? What about whatever is in storage waiting for me? That's what I came for. God, I hope he wrote it all down.

The men's-room door swung out suddenly, cracking into her bent elbow. Sharp shooting pains coursed through her arm. She moaned and pulled the throbbing arm in tight against her chest. As though the tears had been lined up waiting, they broke through and trickled down her cheeks.

A tall man with shaggy black hair filled the doorway. His zoo uniform was rumpled and covered with dark stains. He glanced down to see what he'd hit. "Oh. Was that you? Sorry," he said as he came through, his hand making a quick pass over the front of his pants. "Sorry."

He did a double take when he noticed the tears on her cheeks. His swarthy, unshaven face turned serious. "Was it as hard as that? Your elbow, huh?" He reached a big hand out to touch her shoulder, but when she shrugged away, he dropped it into his pants pocket. "Will it be okay?" he asked.

Katherine nodded furiously to get rid of him.

"Well, sorry again," he repeated, backing away. "But that really isn't a good place to stand, is it?"

He moved only a few steps away to join two other men in dark-green zoo uniforms who were standing in a huddle with the secretary with the long braid. The four of them put their heads together in animated whispered discussion. They stopped talking and snapped their heads around to the front of the room when the door to the director's office opened and three men emerged. The man in the middle raised his hands for silence and got it as the reporters turned their cameras on him. Flashbulbs flickered.

"Ladies and gentlemen. Thank you." He was a wiry, kinetic man of about fifty, with a huge head of thick white hair. He wore a faded blue workshirt, red knit tie, and khaki pants. Two grim-faced men flanked him. One, short and stocky as a fireplug, wore a shiny dark suit. The other, Teutonic-looking and stern, with a gray-blond crew cut that showed his scalp, was dressed in a crisply ironed zoo coverall.

The group noise faded to a murmur.

Katherine cradled her aching arm and leaned back against the doorframe, keeping an eye on the group in front of her. They were clearly zoo employees, so they must have known her father. She wondered what they had thought of him. The men's uniforms all had zoo-emblem patches on their left sleeves and name patches she couldn't quite read over their right breast pockets. The young woman wore a khaki short-sleeved safari-style shirt and shorts of the same color and fabric, which showed off her muscular tanned legs to advantage.

The big man who'd come out of the men's room leaned down to her and said in a stage whisper, "This is the first time I've ever seen McElroy at a public function when he wasn't wearing an animal somewhere on his person."

The group chuckled conspiratorially.

"Don't knock it, Vic," the woman said. "It brings in the money. It will be fun to see how he manages to turn this into a fund-raising event."

"Oh, he will seize the day," said a tall, cadaverously thin man, who was much older than the others and had deep pockmarks on his cheeks and forehead. "If he doesn't reverse the cash-flow problem, he can kiss off this job. And McElroy loves the limelight too much to give it up easily. Somehow he will manage to turn this to his advantage."

They stopped whispering as the director spoke. His voice, clearly accustomed to speaking to groups, filled the room. "Most of you know me. I'm Sam McElroy, director of the Austin Zoo. It falls to me today to discuss some very bad news. You all know that early this morning one of our veteran keepers, Lester Renfro, was killed in a tragic and highly unusual accident. All of us here at the zoo are grieving for him."

He bowed his head for a moment to indicate grieving before continuing. "I'm going to share with you everything I know about the accident. It isn't very much because Mr. Renfro was alone at the time and, of course, the autopsy and police reports aren't complete yet. But here's what we have been able to make out: Lester—Mr. Renfro—arrived early for work today. He often did. That's the kind of worker he was. Starting time is six-thirty, but he was seen by one of the night watchmen arriving about six-ten. Apparently he entered the Phase Two zookeepers' area to feed the tigers. Since the last two days were fast days for the large cats, he would have wanted to feed them right away."

A buzz of excitement flared through the room. Several hands shot up. "Mr. McElroy—question, sir!" called one of the reporters, waving a notebook in the air.

"Please, gentlemen, ladies. Let me finish my statement and then I'll try to answer any questions I can." The buzz died down but hung in the air as a background hum.

"Apparently Mr. Renfro was looking through the observation window in the steel door that leads from the keepers' corridor to the outdoor display area when a Siberian tiger broke the window and dragged him through into the exhibit. The medical examiner's preliminary report, which Lieutenant Sharb has just shown me"—he gestured toward the very short man standing next to him—"indicates that Mr. Renfro died from a broken neck." McElroy glanced down at a page of notes in his hand. "Most of the ribs on the left side of his body were fractured. And there were multiple lacerations on his face, hands, and arms."

The buzz began to rise in volume again. McElroy raised a hand to quiet it down. "At seven-thirty this morning Hans Dieterlen, our senior keeper"—he gestured to the morose man who stood on his other side, legs apart, hands clasped behind his back—"stopped at the Phase Two building to confer with Mr. Renfro about a leopard they were planning to sedate this afternoon. He entered the building, using his own key, and called for Mr. Renfro. When he got no answer, he looked into the corridor and saw glass on the floor and one boot.'' McElroy paused here and the room was dead quiet. It was evident to Katherine that the director savored the telling of a good story.

"He stepped into the corridor, noticing glass shards hanging out of the window frame and Mr. Renfro's hat impaled on one of them. Just then the face of a tiger appeared in the window. Of course, Mr. Dieterlen left the corridor and secured the door. He radioed for help immediately, fearing the worst. In accordance with section three of our emergency protocol, he called for the shooting team.

"Only two of the five members of the team were on the premises at the time. Danny Gillespie was in the office when Mr. Dieterlen's call came in, so he was able to grab a rifle and get to the scene within four minutes. That's an excellent response time. The head of the team, Victor Jamail, was there five minutes later with a twelve-gauge shotgun. When they saw Mr. Renfro lying facedown in the outside exhibit and the tiger lying about fifteen feet away, they could tell it was too late. So they did not fire at the tiger. Instead, the two of them and Mr. Dieterlen used a fire extinguisher from the building to frighten the animal into its holding cage. They determined that Mr. Renfro was dead and called an ambulance and the police. And now you know just about all we know about the accident.''

Reporters started to wave their arms and call out questions to him.

The director held up a palm to stop the babble. "But let me say one last thing before you ask your questions. Mr. Renfro was working alone with the tigers even though we all know it is far better to work dangerous animals in pairs, the way we used to. But recent cutbacks in the city budget have forced us to reduce our staff and economize in this way. I can't tell you how much we all regret this.''

The zoo group in front of Katherine began to whisper again. The young woman reached up and patted the big man's shoulder, as if to console him for something. Then she smiled around at the men. "See,'' she whispered, "he's a genius. He did get the fund-raising in. And he saved you from having to speak to these vultures, Vic.'' The third man in the group remained silent, just shaking his head. He was a powerfully built man who had his short sleeves rolled up to reveal a string of tattoos on both arms, running from his bulging biceps down to his thick wrists.

Every hand in the room was up now, with voices calling.

"Mr. McElroy!"

"Sam."

"Lieutenant Sharb, question!"

"Please . . . over here."

McElroy raised a hand again. "Okay. Okay. Let's do this in an orderly way. Mr. Samuels, from the *American-Statesman,* let's start with you."

The bearded reporter shouted above the noise. "We don't want to be macabre here, sir, and there's no delicate way to ask this, but our readers will want to know whether the tiger ate some of Mr. Renfro." The room was silent for about twenty seconds. Katherine felt her stomach turn over very slowly. *Blood of my blood and flesh of my flesh.*

The director finally found his words: "Mr. Samuels. You understand that the autopsy report is not finished. I have said that there were multiple lacerations on Mr. Renfro's body from the attack. It is difficult to determine whether those injuries were inflicted in the initial attack or, um, later on. Next question to Miss—"

Samuels pushed his way to the front of the crowd and drowned out the director's voice. "Wait. I haven't finished my question. Lieutenant Sharb, let me ask *you.* Were there parts of the body missing? There are rumors flying that the tiger ate considerable portions of him. Is it true?"

The director looked down at the short policeman, who sighed and stepped forward. "Mr. Samuels," he said in a low, raspy voice, "it appears that the tiger may have ingested some flesh. Yes."

Flesh of my flesh.

Every hand in the room was up now. The noise level rose and Katherine felt the heat in the room rise with it. She pulled a crumpled Kleenex out of her bag and swiped at her wet brow. Samuels was jumping up and down now yelling, "What body parts? Has the tiger's excrement been analyzed?"

McElroy had to shout over the noise. "Okay, Miss James from *The Dallas Morning News.* Your turn. Go ahead."

A shrill female voice rose above the background noise. "This animal has eaten human flesh. Aren't you afraid that this tiger has become a man-eater? Shouldn't it be destroyed?"

The zoo workers in front of Katherine looked at one another and collectively rolled their eyes skyward. The tattooed man narrowed his eyes, stretched his arms out, and tensed his hands into a simulation of tiger paws. Then he pretended to creep up toward the

woman who'd asked the question. The group around him had to
stifle their laughter.

Sam McElroy looked at the woman as if she were a heathen to
be converted. "Miss James. Tigers are predators with one mission
on earth. They are born to hunt and kill. It's what they were created for. He was just being a tiger. No. We have no intention of
destroying him."

"But isn't it true that once a tiger has tasted human flesh, he
becomes an incorrigible man-eater? Won't that make him just too
dangerous to have around?" the woman shouted back.

The director bit off his words. "Tigers are very dangerous. This
tiger was born here at the Austin zoo and we have always known
he was particularly aggressive and dangerous. He is a real tiger. If
we are looking for blame here, Miss James, we need to look to the
engineer who determined that the glass in that window was thick
enough to withstand a determined five-hundred-pound tiger. We
ought to look at the city council members who voted to cut our
budget by a fourth this year so that our keepers have to work alone.
This is what we should be looking at, not blaming a tiger for doing what he was born to do."

Katherine was certain that he was right. She didn't want the tiger destroyed either. But she wondered how she would feel about
seeing him. It reminded her of an incident she hadn't thought of
in years. When she was in high school she'd had a part-time job
with a trainer who worked mostly with guard dogs. He had two
beautiful young Dobermans he was training. One day a group of
boys climbed the fence and tormented the dogs, who attacked and
mauled one of the boys almost to death. Before the ambulance had
driven away with the injured boy, the trainer had ordered the dogs
into a down-stay and, with tears running down his face, had shot
them both in the head. Weeping, Katherine had asked him why. He
had said because he wouldn't be able to look at them with pleasure anymore. She wondered if she would ever be able to look at
the tiger with pleasure.

She sprang to attention. A reporter was asking if the zoo was
worried about a lawsuit, if the safety procedures had been sufficient.

"No," the director boomed. "Our safety procedures are excellent, as good or better than any zoo in the world. There are more
accidents in zoos than you are aware of. The work is dangerous.
But the Austin Zoo has had only one other fatal accident in our

fifty-six-year history and that was more than three decades ago, way before my time. We have an excellent safety record."

A woman in front yelled out, "Why were you withholding food from that tiger, Mr. McElroy? It sounds cruel. If the tiger hadn't been starving, maybe this would never have happened."

The small zoo group had kept up a steady, whispered commentary on the questions. Now the thin older man hissed in a falsetto, "Poor, abused pussy cat. God, these bunny huggers piss me off. Maybe she'd like to go in the cage and comfort poor Brum. How do people get so ignorant?"

"Two fast days a week is standard practice at all zoos," the director said patiently. "The purpose is to replicate eating patterns in the wild so that our large cats do not become obese in captivity. It is not cruel in any way." He pointed at a man in the front row. "Yes. Next question."

"This is a question for Mr. Dieterlen, since he was there when the shooting team arrived. Mr. Dieterlen, I understand and support the reasons for not destroying the tiger now, but why didn't Mr. Gillespie or"—he glanced down at his notebook—"Mr. Jamail shoot the tiger when they first arrived on the scene? Mr. Renfro might still have been alive when they got there."

Hans Dieterlen took a step forward and looked hard at his questioner. When he began to speak, Katherine was surprised at the thick German accent. "Mr. Gillespie, who was first to arrive, is an excellent marksman. If there had been any reason to shoot, he would have shot." He stopped speaking and stepped back, apparently a man of few words.

"But, Mr. Dieterlen," the reporter said, "why have a shooting team if they aren't going to shoot in an emergency like this?"

Hans Dieterlen stepped forward again. "All zoos have shooting teams to respond in case of dangerous animals escaping and endangering the public. In cases of any threat to the public they are instructed to shoot without hesitation. But in this case there was no danger to the public and the harm had been done. It was clear Mr. Renfro could not possibly be still alive. You would have known it too if you had been there." He stepped back and leaned over to whisper something into the director's ear.

"Ladies and gentlemen," the director said, "we need to limit this to two more questions, please. Go ahead, Mr. Cannon. You're next."

"What about the calls and public reactions you are getting here at the zoo, Mr. McElroy? What seems to be the consensus in terms of whether the tiger should be allowed to live?"

"I have no idea, Mr. Cannon. We do not make decisions like this based on public reactions. Siberian tigers are an endangered species. It is against federal law to kill them. We couldn't do it even if we wanted to. Of course, we are already getting a great many phone calls. The usual mix: some sensible, some crank, some downright scary. Certainly some say the animal should be destroyed. I'm sorry to say we have had some threats against the tiger's life. That is why we have taken the precaution of removing all the large cats from exhibit for a while."

"Last question. You there, in back."

A deep man's voice said, "We've talked a great deal about the tiger. But how about Lester Renfro? What sort of person was he? Is the zoo planning some sort of memorial for him? Does he have a family?"

Katherine felt her body clench up.

The zoo group began whispering again. "Lester Renfro," sighed the big man who had hit her elbow. "The only family that's likely to miss him is Felidae." The others nodded sadly. Katherine studied their faces. Were they sorry he was dead, or did they just regret the disruption of their schedules? She was torn between listening to them or the director.

"A good question," answered the director. "Mr. Renfro was an exemplary employee. Devoted to his work. It was his whole life. He had been going to night classes, working on a degree in biology at the University of Texas, so I think a good memorial would be a scholarship fund for keepers who want to pursue higher education. He could have done many more lucrative things, but he chose to be a zookeeper. He was at the Austin zoo for thirty-seven years. He worked with reptiles and small mammals before he became senior keeper of the Phase Two unit, large cats." The director looked into space for a minute, seemingly in thought. Then he said with genuine conviction, "He really cared. He was an advocate for his animals. Uh, family? Well, he was a divorced man with no close family here, I believe. We were his family. The animals were his family. He died doing what he loved to do."

"And that's the truth. Amen," the thin man with the cratered skin whispered, speaking more to himself than to the others in his group.

The press conference was over. The three men turned their backs and retreated to the director's office.

Katherine moved away from the door of the men's room as men began to head in that direction. She tucked her shirt down in back and took a deep breath.

Animals were his family, huh? Well, he does have some family. Right here and planning to inherit whatever it is he had in mind for me and anything else I can get. I came here for financial help and I intend to get it.

Even over his dead body.

FIVE

As THE ROOM cleared out, Katherine tried to think ahead. She supposed she'd have to endure some sort of funereal folderol before she could get down to the money. That could take for bloody ever and she had only twenty-two days before the foreclosure. Was it possible for an estate to get settled in three weeks? Probably not. She'd heard it was a lengthy process.

And, oh my God, what if he hadn't written it down? What if there was no record of what he intended her to have? She had the letter, of course, but would that count as a legal document? And what about the key and the storage receipt? Should she wait, or go by herself and look?

"Be calm. One thing at a time, Katherine," she whispered to herself as she approached the secretary's desk. Right now she needed to identify herself and get on with the process, whatever it was. She pushed her hair behind her ears and cleared her throat. A name plate on the desk said, "Kim Kelly, Assistant to the Director."

Kim Kelly was engrossed in conversation with the man who'd hit her elbow. Perched on the corner of the desk, he was saying, "But I went to all the trouble of clearing my schedule so I could go along. She may need sedating. I thought he'd want me to go."

"So would I, Vic, but he said—" She stopped mid-sentence when Katherine cleared her throat for the second time.

"I need to talk to Mr. McElroy, please," Katherine said.

"You have an appointment?" Kim asked.

"No."

"He's in conference right now. I don't think he'll be available all day. Do you want to leave him a message?"

"I really need to see him now. I'm Katherine Driscoll, Lester Renfro's daughter. Would you please tell him that?"

Kim's round brown eyes got rounder and she shot up out of her chair. "Yes, ma'am, I certainly will." She walked into the director's office without knocking, closing the door behind her.

The big man remained propped on the desk, looking steadily at Katherine. His face was dark with several day's stubble of black beard and his coveralls were badly stained with stiff-looking spots that looked a lot like blood. She read the badge on the left side of his chest: "Vic Jamail, Head Veterinarian." He looked more like one of the maintenance crew, Katherine thought.

"Miss Driscoll," he said, "I certainly am sorry about your father. And your elbow."

Katherine nodded and looked away.

"You must think we're a callous lot going about our business like this, but we find this kind of accident difficult to—"

"No, I don't find you callous at all. I'm going about my business, too, Mr.—"

"Jamail, Vic Jamail."

The secretary, emerging from the office, interrupted him. "Please come right in, Miss Driscoll. So sorry about everything. I didn't know who you were when you came in before. So sorry." She stood aside to let Katherine pass through the door.

Pausing a moment to smooth her shorts in back, Katherine glanced back at the big man sitting on the corner of the desk, watching her. Technically, he wasn't smiling, but a knot in the muscles at the corners of his mouth and the glint in his black eyes made her certain he was laughing internally. She felt unaccountably irked by it as she entered the director's office.

The three men leapt to their feet from identical green leather club chairs. In the corner behind them on a wood perch, a large white bird raised a crest the color of apricots and squawked, "Hello. Hello."

No one paid any attention to it. Sam McElroy approached her with his right hand extended. "Miss Driscoll?"

Katherine nodded, trying to assume a gravity proper to the situation.

"I'm so sorry." He took her hand as if to shake it and then covered it firmly with his other hand, squeezing it tenderly in a long nonverbal message of condolence. His wiry, tensed body bent close to her and his tanned forehead crinkled with solicitude. "When I said Lester had no close family, I had no idea you were here. I meant he had no family living in Austin. You should have told me you were here. That...circus out there couldn't have been very nice for you. Forgive us."

He continued to grip her hand. His moist pale eyes, the hunching of his shoulders, and the way he cocked his head all conveyed sympathy. Katherine was convinced. She felt a sudden tightness in her throat. Real emotion from him was the last thing she had expected. It made her feel like an impostor.

"I haven't seen my father since I was five, Mr. McElroy, so you were right in saying that he had no close family."

He turned toward the other two men. "Miss Driscoll, this is Lieutenant Sharb from the Austin police, and this is Hans Dieterlen, our head keeper."

The policeman stepped forward to shake her hand. The arm he extended toward her was so short and thick it appeared to be a deformity, but as she studied the rest of him, she decided it was in perfect proportion. She had the most inappropriate wish to see what he looked like naked.

She tightened her lips and shook his stubby hand.

Before he spoke, he pulled a wadded handkerchief from his pocket and blew his nose into it. He looked down into the handkerchief with a frown as he spoke to her. "We've been trying to locate you, Miss Driscoll, but we just got your address about an hour ago from Mr. Hammond, your father's attorney." His voice was so hoarse and gravelly Katherine thought it must be painful for him to talk. "You must have been on your way from Boerne. We don't like to have people learn these things before we tell them."

There was a long silence. Katherine felt they were waiting for her to say something, but she didn't know what.

"How did you find out, Miss Driscoll?" Sharb asked finally.

"Oh. Just now, when I came in the office and asked to see…my father, the secretary out there showed me the newspaper."

"What brings you today, Miss Driscoll?" the policeman croaked. "After not seeing your father all these years?"

She was totally unprepared for the question. She felt she had blundered into an exam without even looking over her notes. Lester had asked for secrecy, but he was dead. "Oh, he wrote and asked me to come. So I came."

Without any warning Sharb emitted two rapid-fire sneezes, spraying a fine mist into the air. Without intending to, Katherine took a step back to get out of range.

Sharb pulled out the handkerchief again and swabbed at his inflamed nostrils, shooting a dark scowl at the bird. "Was he expecting you today?"

"No. It was going to be a surprise."

The director held out his arms to them. "Please sit down. Miss Driscoll, I'm sure you could use a little rest. Could I get Kim to bring you some tea or a soft drink?"

"No, thanks." Katherine sat in the nearest chair. It was wondrously comfortable, deep and engulfing, the cracked green leather aged and softened to perfection. She let her open palms rest on the arms so she could feel it.

McElroy and Sharb sat in chairs flanking her, but Hans Dieterlen stayed standing. He made a stiff bow in her direction. "Miss Driscoll, my condolences on your loss. Your father was a fine worker. He will be impossible to replace."

"Thank you."

He turned to the director. "I need to go now, Sam. I have just time to get to Dallas to complete the paperwork before the Frankfurt flight arrives."

"Oh, yes. Our visiting femme fatale. Go on, Hans. Thanks for your help."

The head keeper made little bows to each of them and left.

"We have a rare white rhino arriving today," Sam explained, "on breeding loan."

Sharb kept his handkerchief pressed to his nose. "Miss Driscoll," he said, "what was the reason your father gave for wanting you to come see him? Was he in trouble of some sort?"

She hesitated. "No. Not that I know of. He just wanted to talk, I guess. Get acquainted."

"Is there any other family, or are you it?" he asked.

"I'm it. My father wrote that his sister, Julia Renfro, died last year, so I guess I'm the only relative left."

Sharb nodded. "You guess," he said under his breath and began coughing.

Katherine felt dislike welling up in her throat for the little man.

Sam McElroy looked at him as if he just that moment had noticed his distress. "Lieutenant, would it help if I had King Tut"—he waved toward the bird—"taken out for a while? I hate to see you suffer."

Sharb shook his head in short irritated jerks. "No. No. It wouldn't make any difference. The dander's everywhere. I'm going anyway." He stood and faced Katherine. "If you could come downtown later, Miss Driscoll—just some formalities, as next of kin. And a few more questions." He reached in his jacket pocket and pulled out a card which he handed to her. "At five? I'll be back in the office by then."

"Okay," she said.

"Just show them the card at the desk," he said. Noticing Sam was about to rise, he held out a hand to stop him. "It's been a long day. Stay where you are, Mr. McElroy. I'll talk to you tomorrow." The minute he had risen, the bird began to flap its wings and shriek, "Bye-bye, bye-bye!"

"Tut, quiet!" the director barked in the bird's direction. This caused a raucous increase in volume that made Katherine want to cover her ears.

The policeman looked back as he walked out the door, shaking his head in dismay.

Sam McElroy leaned forward in his chair and looked directly into Katherine's eyes. "Miss Driscoll, *anything* we can do to help, just let us know. Will you do that?"

"Yes, thank you. What do you think is my next step here?"

"Well, you need to see Travis Hammond. He was your father's lawyer, so he'll know just what to do. I believe your uncle, Cooper Driscoll, will help with arrangements. So you'll want to talk to him, too, as soon as possible.

"And we will do anything we can. You must know that I am beholden in many ways to your family. I'm talking here not just about your father. Living out of town, I don't know how much you know about your mother's family's contributions to the zoo, but the Driscoll name is almost synonymous with the zoo. Coop Driscoll is our current board president, and your grandmother was one of our founders and continues to be our most generous benefactor. We owe your family a great deal. And now this." He waved a hand in the air as if the accident had contaminated the very atmosphere of the room.

Katherine was startled to find herself suddenly a member of a powerful family that habitually received this sort of special attention. It felt unaccustomed, undeserved, but there was something nourishing about it. She found herself taking a guilty pleasure in it. And she wondered how far she could go in making demands.

"Mr. McElroy, I'd like to see where it happened," she said. "And the tiger, I'd like to see him."

The director looked at the ivy-covered stockade fence out his window for several seconds, then back at Katherine. "Fine. We'll go now."

"Thank you. Then I think I'll drive over to the attorney's before I go to see Lieutenant Sharb."

The director sprang up easily from the chair while Katherine had to struggle to extricate herself. People rising seemed to stimulate the bird. It began shrieking and pumping its wings up and down, propelling pale-peach feathers and gray fluff into the air. "What kind of bird is that?" Katherine asked.

McElroy was hooking a walkie-talkie over the back of his belt as he walked toward the door. "A Moluccan cockatoo. Damned nuisance, but I'm attached to him. Kim, I'll be over in cats for the next half hour. Please call Travis Hammond and tell him Miss Driscoll is here and that she'll be coming over to him in about forty-five minutes."

As they headed across the footbridge spanning Barton Creek, Katherine admired the free-flying native birds along the banks. Oh, yes. She remembered this place. She had been here before and she had loved it.

The director talked and walked at the same rapid-fire pace. Katherine had to walk briskly and listen attentively to keep up. "We opened late this morning," he said. "First time in the fifteen years I've been here. We're open every day of the year but Christmas, and always on time. But it was so traumatic getting here to this...terrible news. We've put the big cats, all of them, inside. I'm afraid we may have to keep them off exhibit for a long time. The calls have been hair-raising, even worse than usual. Tomorrow the letters will start."

He looked hard at Katherine. "I don't know where you line up on this, Miss Driscoll, but your father would have snorted at the idea of destroying an animal in a situation like this. He knew the job was dangerous. Keepers get hurt and even killed, no matter how careful they are. Everyone in zoo work knows that. It just happens sometimes."

As they passed an area where bulldozers were clearing rubble from what looked like a building site, he waved an arm to the workmen and said, "Here's where our new small-mammal house is going. It'll have one of the most advanced nocturnal sections in the world." He looked at Katherine. "Some of the funding comes from the Driscoll Foundation."

He waved a hand to the row of enclosures on the right and pointed to a gangly blue bird in the last cage. "That's our baby Goliath heron, first ever born in captivity." As he talked, he kept up a pace so rapid it was closer to a trot than a walk.

Katherine saw that promoting the zoo was so compelling a passion for him that he would be doing it in the middle of a nuclear attack. She found that kind of enthusiasm irresistible.

He picked up a plastic cup from the ground without slowing his pace. "Your father was a total professional in his job, the last one I'd expect to have an accident." He stopped to toss the cup into a trash can.

She took the opportunity of the rare silence to say, "Please call me Katherine."

"Oh, good. We like being on a first-name basis around here. And I'm Sam, of course. I want you to know, Katherine—this is difficult to say—that we regret this accident terribly, but I think you'll find the zoo safety procedures beyond reproach."

He's afraid I'll sue him, Katherine realized.

"Here we are." He put his hand on her shoulder.

They were approaching a large grassy enclosure, backed by what was supposed to look like a stone cliff but was clearly Gunite made to resemble rock. The rest of the exhibit was surrounded by a fourteen-foot-high green mesh fence with a one-foot lip at the top angled inward. A strip of grass separated that fence from a low barrier made of iron bars to keep observers away from the fence.

"This is the outdoor area shared by our two tigers. It was Brum's turn to be out here last night and Imelda's—the other tiger—to be in. Can't leave two adult tigers together unless they're mating, and even then it's risky, tigers being what they are."

Katherine glanced around the enclosure. Very pretty and natural with its grass and clumps of bamboo, huge boulders, a trickle of water simulating a stream. Then she noticed the door and she was hit with the reality of what had happened here. It was an inconspicuous gray door in the cliff, with a small window boarded over with plywood. The grass just outside the door was stained dark.

She wondered how long it took to be killed by a tiger.

They walked around the fence to a door in the back of the cliff. The director knocked on the windowless steel door. "We've assigned members of the staff to be here round the clock for a while—just in case." He looked at Katherine. "You going to be all right? We could do this another time."

"No. I'm fine," Katherine protested, wondering why her voice sounded so thin and far away.

Sam knocked again. In response came the clank of a big lock being opened. Then the door swung open.

A slight man in zoo coveralls stood aside deferentially to let them enter. A badge on the left side of his shirt identified him as "Danny, Cat Keeper."

The second Katherine stepped through the door and her nose twitched in reaction to the powerful stench of cats—urine and spray. Nothing like the odor of dogs, she thought. Far more aggressive and potent. She stifled the impulse to sneeze.

The director closed the door behind them and the keeper quickly locked it with his big key ring. "Thanks, Danny. This is Katherine Driscoll, Lester's daughter. I'm going to show her where it happened. Katherine, this is Danny Gillespie. He's been assigned to the big cats for the last several months, working for your father."

Danny glanced at her, shuffled his feet inside the knee-high rubber boots he was wearing, and gave a sheepish half-smile, keeping his teeth covered.

"You were on the shooting team," she said.

He lowered his eyes and ran a hand across the top of his wispy blond hair, trying to smooth it over the balding spot at the top of his head. "It was just too late to do anything for him, Miss Driscoll. I got there so fast, in just a couple of minutes, 'cause I was in the office when the call came in, but it was just too late." He looked up at her. His pale-blue, lashless eyes were magnified behind the thick glasses that made them seem elongated. She wondered if the swelling around the rims was permanent or if he had been crying.

"What made you so sure it was too late?" she asked.

The question startled them both. Katherine hadn't known she was going to ask it, and Danny blinked his eyes several times with the impact of it.

After a long silence, he said, "Well, he was all...oh, it was clear from the way he...you know, when tigers make a..." He stopped and looked at the director in desperation.

Sam stepped forward and put a hand on Danny's shoulder. "Danny, I know this is difficult, but some reporters at the press conference kept asking about it."

Danny sighed. "Oh." He looked at Katherine. "Miss Driscoll, I wish I could've gotten here in time, but the way he was lying, his neck was clearly broke, and the blood...well, it was just everywhere. I admired Mr. Renfro so much. He did such a good job with the cats and taught me so much. I've only been in cats four months, but I felt I'd found a home here." He shook his head apologetically. "I'm sorry."

Katherine looked away. They were in a white-tiled room with a drain running down the center of the floor. At the far end was a cage. Inside, an immense bushy-coated tiger lay on his side watching them with luminous yellow eyes.

"Well, there he is," said the director. "That's Brum. Five years old. Born here at Austin Zoo. Aggressive as all get-out from day one. What's he been like?" Sam asked the keeper.

"Pretty quiet, sir. We fed them both when the police finally left. And he ate pretty good. I've just finished hosing down the cage."

Katherine approached the cage slowly and stared at the cat, who stared right back at her. She'd never looked really closely at a tiger before. The bramble of black stripes framing his orange-and-white face looked like an inkblot, the same on both sides. If a psychiatrist asked her what the blot resembled, she would say the roots of some enormous plant. A man-eating plant, perhaps. The abundant quill-like white whiskers sprouted aggressively beside the pink nose. It was a beautiful face. Undeniably.

Sam approached quietly and took a firm grip on her elbow. "Do you want to see the rest?"

Katherine pulled her eyes away from the tiger and nodded.

Danny had unlocked the next door and was standing aside to let them enter. Sam preceded her in into a tiny closetlike room and stood with his back against the wall so she would have more room. The second she entered, she felt the horror of it. It was a gray concrete sarcophagus with a naked light bulb hanging from the ceiling. She flinched as she looked at the boarded window. It was impossible not to imagine what had happened here this morning: the sudden crash of glass breaking, the huge striped head punching through the window, the lightning-fast claws hooking into soft flesh. God.

When Danny entered the room too, the claustrophobia became too much. She pushed her way out. Until she saw this place, Lester's death had been a distant accident. Now it had come home. And she hated it.

She stood outside the door breathing hard, while the two men talked in low voices. "The police swept up all the glass," Danny was saying, "and took it away. Very thorough. They stayed for more than three hours."

He lowered his voice and spoke in reverent tones as if they were in some tiny roadside shrine. "But I don't understand it. He always said that ninety-five percent of safety on the job was locks. He wouldn't even be in here while Brum was still outside. He taught us always to secure the outside tiger into its holding cage before doing anything else. Always. A rule of his."

The director said, "It's hard to see. He was the most regular of men."

While the men talked, Katherine watched the tiger. He was on his feet now, pacing the cage, his lean hips undulating, his huge orange testicles swaying. He filled the cage with his color and vitality. Suddenly he reared up on his hind legs and rested his forepaws on the bars, brushing his head against the top of the cage. He towered over Katherine, glaring down at her. She stumbled a few steps backward to get out of his range of power.

She was embarrassed to note that Sam McElroy had left the anteroom and was watching her. She said, "Sam, I've got to go. I left my dog in the car for more than an hour. I need to rescue him and get to the lawyer's office."

As they left, Danny locked the door behind them. Sam walked her out to the car, giving her careful directions to Travis Hammond's office.

"And, Katherine," he said, "I want to repeat that anything I can do to help you, I want to do. Just let me know what it is and it will be done. Promise you'll let me know?"

She started the car, thinking of estates and wills. She was desperate to know if she could get what her father had for her in time to prevent the foreclosure. Would it be enough? Ninety-one thousand dollars? She took a deep breath. Well, she was about to find out.

As she pulled away from the zoo parking lot she looked in the rearview mirror at Ra, his ears blowing in the breeze from her open window. *It had to be enough.*

SIX

KATHERINE HAD BEEN surprised to hear that Travis Hammond was Lester's lawyer. He was the only person from her old life in Austin that Leanne Driscoll had kept in touch with. He had been a close family friend and attorney to three generations of Driscolls, and given the rancorous split between her parents, it was mystifying that her father would choose Hammond to handle his estate.

The office of Hammond and Crowley was in a tiny, low stone house on Guadaloupe Street. A historic landmark medallion with the profile of Texas glittering in stainless steel was affixed to the left of the door.

Katherine liked the interior instantly. It was sparsely furnished and cool, with white walls roughly plastered, and wide-planked pine floors, bare except for some Navaho rugs tossed at random angles. On the walls hung three black-and-white photographs—originals by Ansel Adams, she thought.

A very young receptionist wearing blue jeans and a faded workshirt was busy typing with two fingers at the keyboard of a Macintosh computer. When Katherine identified herself, she stood up and started to smile, but stopped herself, and instead said, "Yes, ma'am. Sorry to hear about your father. Please sit down for just a sec." She hurried from the room and slammed a door in the back. Before Katherine could sit down she had returned, with the old attorney limping at her side.

He was very thin and exquisitely tailored in a charcoal-gray suit. Above the snowy shirt collar and yellow paisley tie, his tanned, leathery face looked like a mask of tragedy. His mouth turned down at the corners, and his skin was a mass of brown wrinkles, like a peeled apple left out in the sun to dry. As he greeted her, a tic in his right eye convulsed all the muscles in that side of his face.

But his courtly Texas charm shone through. "Katherine Driscoll." He drawled the name out as he took her right hand into both his own. "Thank you for coming to see me. I can't tell you how devastated I am to hear about your father's accident. I would have called you right away, but I was in Lubbock and just got back to

Austin at noon to hear about it. Sam McElroy tells me you found out by accident. I'm so, so sorry about that. Forgive me.''

Katherine thought he really did look devastated. She wondered if that meant he had been close to Lester.

"Oh," he said, turning to his young receptionist, "this is my granddaughter, Susan Hammond, helping me out in the office while she decides whether to go to college or not. Hold my calls, please, Susie Q, so I can talk with Miss Driscoll."

"Okay, Grampa," she said, already back at her slow typing.

Travis Hammond took Katherine's arm and ushered her through the door of his office, taking care of her as if she were the frail one with a bad knee and a case of the shakes. He settled her on a beige camelback sofa and turned to close the door. The office, like the entry, was cool and simple, but she was jarred by the glassy eye of a huge deer head hanging on the opposite wall. It looked out of place in this civilized environment.

The lawyer turned and caught her staring. "Are you a hunter, Miss Driscoll? It's one of my great vices."

"Well, I train retrievers," Katherine said, "and I take them bird hunting as part of the training—duck and quail mostly, but no, I'm not really a hunter."

"That's a twenty-inch buck," he said proudly, his face relaxing for a moment, the mouth losing its arc of tragedy. "Got it last season when I went with your uncle, Coop, and that ol' boy fancies himself quite a hunter, but he didn't even get a shot off. Best trophy I've gotten in sixty-three years of deer hunting." He lowered himself into an elegant wing chair, crossed one thin knee over the other, and ran a trembling hand along the perfect crease in his pant leg.

"Miss Driscoll—" He stopped speaking when his eyes settled on her face, as if caught mid-thought by a recollection that dammed up the normal flow of words. The eye began to twitch furiously again.

Then he shook his head very slightly as if to dislodge an idea he didn't want to take root. Katherine wanted him to say it—what her face had made him think of. But he switched back to his smooth, courtly mode.

"Katherine," he said, "how difficult for you to lose both your parents in such a short time, less than two years."

Katherine hadn't thought of it that way. "I never really had a father," she said, "so it doesn't feel as if I've lost anything."

He flinched as if she had slapped him. Then he studied her face again and said, "I would have recognized you anywhere. I can see both your mother and grandmother in you. Have you been in touch with the Driscolls yet?"

"No. I haven't. I don't know if they'd want to hear from me," Katherine said, watching his face closely for a reaction.

He paused, gliding a shaky hand back over his fringe of silver hair. "Oh, I think it's time to let bygones be bygones. I believe Coop and Lucy, and especially Sophie, will want to see you. Your grandmother, I don't know about. I hear she's in a bad way. I usually go to see her, talk a little business, once a week, but Coop told me last week she wasn't up to my visit. She had a small stroke back in March, you know, and has been confined to bed. Coop says she's taken a sudden turn for the worse, another stroke, I believe, and she doesn't want anyone to see her like that. Such a proud woman."

"Does she still live in the house on Woodlawn?" Katherine asked.

"Yes. She'd been living alone there with just a daily housekeeper to do for her, but Coop says he had to step in and insist on a live-in nurse, given the deterioration of her condition." He gave one small chuckle. "She must be in bad shape if she's letting Coop have his way. Anne Driscoll is not a woman you insist to."

Katherine was surprised by the profound rush of disappointment she felt sweep over her. Too late. The saddest words in the language, and they seemed to be the story of her life. She was six hours too late for her father, and perhaps a week too late for her grandmother.

When she looked up, she realized the lawyer had been speaking to her. " ... and needless accident," he was saying. "Terribly painful for you, dear, but dreadful publicity for the zoo, too. I'm on the board, you know. Have been for thirty-nine years. I hate to see anything that might set the zoo back. Actually, you know, that tiger, Brum, was one of my personal favorites. Of course it couldn't have been your father's fault, either. Such a reliable, meticulous man."

"He was?" Katherine asked.

Travis Hammond leaned back and sighed. "Oh, my dear. That's right. You didn't know him at all. Hadn't seen him for...how long?"

"Thirty-one years," Katherine answered, feeling the full weight of each of those years.

He closed his eyes. "Yes. Since 1958. Such a long time. I first met your father when he married your mother. What a ruckus that caused! There were some stormy times there."

He opened his eyes to look hard at her for several seconds. "You may remember some of that bad business before you and your mother left Austin." He stared so long and directly at her that it occurred to Katherine he had been asking a question.

She shook her head. "No. I don't remember anything about that time, except maybe . . . today at the zoo I thought I remembered being there before."

The old lawyer was silent, looking up at the deer head on the wall. He seemed lost in thought.

She said, "I was surprised to learn you were my father's attorney. Because of your close relationship to the Driscolls, you know."

He came back to attention. "Yes. But I think your father held no animosity toward the Driscolls. Actually, I believe he went to see Anne on several occasions. I think they had buried the hatchet. But as for his coming to me for the will, he and I got to know one another well when I headed up the committee for the Phase Two building project, to house the big cats. We worked together on that very well, so it felt natural for him to come to me.

"He was a pleasure to work with, the steadiest, most competent of the keepers. He rarely missed a day of work and he often stayed all night with sick animals. Unpaid. Just for the love of it. He was a man so steadfast"—here the old man curled his long, trembling fingers into fists to illustrate—"if he said he would do something, then it would be done, even if it was long and difficult. Year in and year out, a man you could count on."

Katherine didn't want to hear this. She knew it would sound crass, but impatience drove her to boldness. "Mr. Hammond," she said, "I never knew my father, and I feel nothing toward him one way or the other. He never came to see me or . . ."

The old man surprised her with the passion of his reaction to this. He shook his head violently and grabbed both her hands, squeezing them in his thin dry fingers. He spoke as if he were pleading for himself. "Oh, Katherine, try not to judge so harshly. Sometimes we do things when we are young. We make mistakes that we regret so bitterly, but we can never—" He stopped himself abruptly. "Well, we wish we could change them, but we can't," he finished lamely and let go of her hands.

"Well," she said with a shrug, "my father wrote me for the first time last week. He said he had something for me, to help me out of the financial difficulties I've been having. Could you tell me how much? I need to know because on November seventh everything I own will be auctioned off if I don't come up with ninety-one thousand dollars."

The lawyer sat forward and opened his eyes wider in surprise. The tic in his right eye sped up. "He wrote that he had ninety-one thousand dollars for you?"

"He didn't mention an amount, just that it was enough to cure my debt."

He shook his head and, with a sigh, hoisted himself from the sofa and walked over to the simple wood trestle table that served as his desk. From a stack of folders he picked up the top one and brought it back to Katherine. He drew out a document and laid it on the low table in front of her.

Katherine held her breath.

"This is your father's will. I've just been reviewing it. Very simple. You are the sole beneficiary."

He did write it down! Katherine held the breath in to restrain herself from grinning. Things might work out after all.

"But I've just been talking with the bank, my dear. I'm afraid there's not going to be anything for you to inherit."

Katherine exhaled the breath she had been holding in a long sigh. Her stomach felt hollow. She hadn't eaten all day.

"Are you sure?" she asked.

"Yes. Unfortunately. I'll go over it all in detail with you, but the bank has frozen his assets. It's pretty clear that there's not even enough in his estate to pay off his creditors. So there's really less than nothing." He looked at her with his eyebrows squeezed so tightly together that a crevasse formed down his forehead.

"What exactly did he say in the letter?"

"He said he had the money to pay off my loan so the bank wouldn't foreclose on my home. He mentioned something I could do for him in return."

"What was that?" the attorney asked.

"He didn't say. He was going to tell me when I came to see him."

They were both silent for a minute. Then Katherine asked a question that had been on her mind ever since she had received the letter from her father. "Mr. Hammond, did you tell my father where he could write to me, or anything about me? I'm wondering how he got that information."

"Oh, I may have mentioned to him you were in Boerne. I kept in touch with your mother, you know. It would have been easy enough for him to get your address, I think."

Travis Hammond sat down next to her on the sofa and opened the file on the table in front of them. "Let me show you everything. I don't like being the bearer of bad news, but here we go."

Katherine sighed and settled back to listen. She was getting accustomed to hearing bad news.

WHEN SHE GOT OFF the elevator on the fourth floor of the Austin Police Headquarters, Katherine thought the day had brought more unpleasant surprises than her system could take. And it was only five o'clock. There was still time for more.

She caught sight of Lieutenant Sharb in a glass cubicle at the end of the hall. Now there was a man, she thought, capable of delivering endless amounts of bad news. He was typing at a computer terminal, so engrossed that he didn't hear her approaching. She stood in the doorway for several seconds before he looked up.

"Wait. Let me save this," he said in greeting. After punching some keys and grunting a few times, he stood up, rising only a few inches from his sitting height.

"Here. Sit down," he said, snatching a stack of file folders from a molded plastic chair.

He sat back at his desk and folded his hands in front of him. The rims of his small black eyes were red and puffy. "Miss Driscoll, I need to hear in detail why you came to see your father today."

She had had time to give this answer some thought. "Because he wrote me a letter asking me to come. I got it Friday."

"But why now? I wonder. He sure hadn't been in any great hurry to see you before."

Katherine gritted her teeth. There was no avoiding telling it. "He said he wanted to give me some financial help. I've had trouble with a loan at the bank in Boerne where I live and he said he could help."

"Got that letter with you?"

"No," she lied, trying not to grip her bag tighter as she said it. She had resisted telling Travis Hammond about the key and she didn't see any reason to tell this little man. It wasn't any of his business. Not until she had a chance to see what was there first.

He said, "You've just been to see Mr. Travis Hammond over at his office?"

"Yes."

He waited for her to go on, but she was silent. If he wanted to know something, let him ask for it.

Finally he said, "Well, you inheriting?"

She had a moment of confusion. "No. Yes. But there's nothing to inherit."

He nodded knowingly and opened a steno book in front of him. "Too bad. I wonder how he was planning to help you with that big loan if he was broke."

"How do you know it was a big loan?"

"Oh, from your bank. It's been posted. It's public record now, but we can get information like that from the banks anyway."

Katherine was breathless with shock. He'd been investigating her, prying. It was outrageous. The man was insufferable.

He picked up a ballpoint pen and clicked it in and out rapidly. "An amazing coincidence that you arrive at your father's place of employment only hours after he's killed—after not seeing him for thirty-one years. Don't you think?"

"Yes," she said, agreeing in spite of herself. "Yes, I do."

"Did McElroy show you the scene?"

"Yes."

He took a tiny plastic bottle from his breast pocket, tilted his head back and squeezed a few drops into each eye. He lifted his head and looked at her with eyes streaming. "Lemme ask you something. Do you really believe that a tiger reached through that little bitty window and drug a big man—one hundred eighty-five pounds of experienced keeper—through and killed him dead? Do you believe that, Miss Driscoll?"

Katherine was struck dumb. She felt her body temperature rising. "In case something should happen to me," said the letter. "Come soon." He'd had a premonition!

The policeman waited for an answer.

"It's hard to believe."

"Sure is."

"But you said to the press that the tiger killed him and may have—"

"Sure. The ME's first look-see was consistent with his being attacked by a tiger. But there were some...indications I found at the scene that the tiger may have had a little help from another species of animal. Homo sapiens, maybe."

Katherine was trying to hold her imagination in check. "What indications, Lieutenant Sharb?"

"Well, now, I can't tell you that yet, but"—he put a blunt fore-finger to his inflamed nose and mashed it to the side—"I have a nose for these things and this stinks as bad as that cat house over at the zoo." As if the mere mention of the cats were enough to set him off, he emitted a volley of violent staccato sneezes, spraying the desk and keyboard before he could find the crumpled handker-chief and apply it to his nose.

"Let me see if I understand this," Katherine said. "Are you saying this was not an accident? That someone fed him to the ti-ger? Is that what you're saying?"

Sharb shrugged his shoulders. "Murder maybe. Can't say yet."

Katherine felt rage simmering under her surface. "Why can't you tell me?" she insisted. "He was my father. I'm a taxpayer. I want to know what you've found."

He turned his hands up to heaven. "Policy, ma'am. As soon as we have something definite and my boss says I can release the in-formation, you'll be the first to know. So...who might have had a grudge against him? You have any ideas?"

Through clenched teeth she said, "Lieutenant, I didn't know him. I wouldn't even recognize him. I don't know who his friends were—or enemies, if any."

He nodded. "Well, we always look at family first. Playing the odds. Of course, you're all there is and we've already eliminated you."

"Why?"

"Because your man José says he saw you in Boerne at seven this morning. Time wouldn't have worked out."

"You've talked to Joe?"

"No, I've talked to the San Antonio Police, who've talked to him."

He reached behind him and lifted a box onto the desk. He pulled out a bunch of keys and a man's black wallet in plastic bags. "These are your father's effects. We're finished with them." He pushed a piece of paper and a pen toward Katherine. "You can sign here for them. The clothes we need to keep as evidence."

Katherine looked up at him instead of at the paper. "You aren't from around here, are you, Lieutenant Sharb?"

"Nah. I moved here from New Jersey coupla years ago. For my allergies." He shrugged. "Good Lord, from the frying pan into the fire."

He pointed to one of the keys. "That's the key to his front door. But watch yourself. He had himself one vicious dog. We had to subdue it to get in, but it's probably back on duty by now. Lord, the animals in this case are going to be the death of me.'' He looked up at her in mock surprise. "Oh, sorry. I didn't mean it that way.''

"You've already been to his house?''

"Sure. I wondered about a suicide note. Nothing there, of course. It was a dumb idea. Who ever heard of a suicide throwing himself to a tiger? Nah.''

Katherine signed the paper and dropped the keys and the wallet into her bag.

Sharb stood up. "Thanks for coming in, Miss Driscoll. How long are you planning to stay in town?''

"I don't know. Can we have a funeral? What about the body?''

"Oh, we'll want to hold on to that a while. We'll notify you. Where you going to be staying?''

"I don't know. Maybe I'll go back home tonight. I have a business to run.''

"Let José do it, Miss Driscoll. Stick close, where I can reach you, please. You'll want to hear about the autopsy and we'll need to talk again. So where'll you be?''

She felt the weight of the keys in her bag. "Oh, I'll stay at Lester Renfro's place tonight.''

He was already back at the keyboard. Without looking up, he said to her retreating back, "Remember I warned you about the dog.''

SEVEN

HE MUST HAVE moved after we left him, Katherine thought. This is not the house I lived in for my first five years. I don't know how I know it, but I do.

The bungalow at 37 Wirtz Avenue had been painted recently— a muddy brown with a tan trim. Katherine wondered if he had done it himself. She studied the house as she raised the back of the Jeep and extended her arm in the signal for Ra to leap out. After three hours of being cooped up, he exploded into the air as if he were heading for a water retrieve in a field trial, hitting the ground at a full run. "Hie on," she said, giving him permission for a run.

She watched him race to the end of the sidewalk, then called him back with a flick of her hand. While Ra sniffed the yard, she leaned against the tailgate and speculated: Was Sharb a total lunatic? Or might it be possible to arrange for a man to be killed by a tiger? She visualized the man all alone, arriving in the half-light of early morning to feed the cats he had tended for eight years, entering the tiny concrete room, looking up at the window. It might be possible. But the picture she conjured up was so ugly she shook it out of her head.

She decided instead to think about the end of her long discussion with Travis Hammond, what he called "the bottom line." Not a pretty subject either.

Her father owed $60,000 to First Western Bank on a second mortgage he had taken out a few years ago on his house, this bungalow in front of her. In this wretched real estate market, the house would likely bring less than $50,000. Since Lester had only $200 in the bank, the lawyer estimated that when the smoke cleared, Lester's estate would be in debt at least $10,000. No financial comfort for her there.

No life insurance.

No safe-deposit box.

Damn the man. Dangling the promise of salvation in front of her and then reneging on it.

When the lawyer had finally finished delivering his bad news, Katherine had considered telling him about the key and the storage receipt Lester had sent. But, in the lifelong habit of keeping her own counsel, she had swallowed the words. She'd take a look first, to see what was there, if anything. She could always ask for advice later if she needed it.

She put her hand in her purse and fingered the little key. Yes, it was solid—a real key. She closed her eyes and visualized a scene on the back of her lids. She locates the storage unit. She inserts the key in the lock—a perfect fit. She opens the door to find a roomful of thousand-dollar bills, stacks and stacks of them—her patrimony. She stuffs them into several grocery bags, loads them into her car, and drives straight to the Bank of Boerne. She walks into George Bob Rainey's office and tosses ninety-one of the bills onto his desk and walks out without saying a word.

She opened her eyes and dismissed the image with a shake of her head. Fun to think about, but it was a fairy tale. This was real life. If there was money hidden away, it would have to go to pay off Lester's debts. Commitments.

She jerked the keys out of her purse. Damn. It would be nice to be able to fantasize just once without commitments intruding.

Katherine took a few deep breaths to compose herself for Lester Renfro's house. It was easier if she thought of him as Lester Renfro rather than as her father. And, in fact, it was more accurate. He was no more than a stranger to her. The man had not been her father for three decades. She supposed she should be mourning him, but really, what was there to mourn?

Ra's avid sniffing of the yard and the wood steps of the front porch reminded Katherine there was a dog even before the barking burst from the house. A big dog, from the sound. Of course he would have a big dog. Like Pasha, the German shepherd they'd had when she was very young. He'd told her in the letter to remember Pasha.

Funny, she hadn't thought of him in years, but now she could picture him clearly—his large pointed ears and his soft, thick black-and-tan coat. Her first dog. Maybe... Oh, God, no. Katherine, you're losing your marbles. Dogs don't live for thirty-one years. And anyway—She had a flash of memory—Pasha died! He died the night we left Austin. I saw him dead on the bedroom floor. Strange, I've never remembered that before. I used to ask her about it, again and again—what happened to Pasha?—but Mother would never answer me. It was a secret. One of her many secrets.

She slammed the tailgate and approached the house. As she climbed the steps, the barking intensified.

"Listen to that, Ra," she said. "That's how a real watchdog sounds. You could learn a thing or two here." Ra's ears were triangled up and his tail lowered in anxiety. "Don't worry, you baby. One thing we know is how to deal with watchdogs."

As she inserted the key into the lock, the dog inside bayed frantically, nails skittering and scraping on the other side of the door. She turned the key until the lock clicked. Then, switching to that hard-earned voice she had cultivated over twenty years of training recalcitrant dogs—that menacing voice of absolute authority—she spoke two low, guttural words through the closed door: "Down, sir." The thud of a heavy body hitting the floor rewarded her.

"Good, boy. Stay." She pushed the door open very carefully.

It was an old black Lab bitch graying around the muzzle and wearing a red leather collar. She was panting in confusion and anxiety at not doing her job.

Katherine turned to Ra and pressed a flat hand toward the ground. He dropped into a down on the porch. She held up her palm to him to indicate he should stay and stepped over the threshold.

The house was dark and cool, all the draperies drawn.

Very slowly, avoiding looking directly into the dog's amber eyes, she approached, cooing a stream of constant endearments: "You beautiful old girl, good girl, doing your job. There, there, we'll be friends. Hungry, you old thing? Well, it's been a hard day. I bet you didn't like your run-in with Lieutenant Sharb either." She knelt and offered a hand to sniff. The dog extended a bright red tongue and licked her hand frenetically.

Katherine lifted the metal tag hanging from the collar and read it. "Belle," she said. "What a pretty name. I bet you'd feel better after a snack, wouldn't you, Belle?" Katherine stood and headed in the direction she knew the kitchen must be, allowing the dog to rise and follow her.

They passed through a room that had been intended as a dining room, but in the light from the open door Katherine saw that it had been used as a photographer's studio. The table pushed against the wall was covered with cameras and lenses and film and stacks of papers.

The entire wall space of the room from chair rail to ceiling was covered with photographs. All of them were black and white except for one section on the long wall opposite the window, where a burst of color caught her eye. She paused and sucked in her breath when she thought she recognized the subject of those color photos. But the black dog beckoned, whining and looking back at Katherine as she pushed through the swinging door to the kitchen.

"Okay, here I come." Katherine followed her into an immaculate white kitchen. The dog lay in front of a low cabinet and whimpered, staring at the cabinet door. "I don't even have to look for it, do I, Belle?" Katherine pulled out a bag of Alpo Dry and dumped a heap of it into an empty bowl on the floor.

Slowly Katherine walked back to the swinging door and pressed it open, surveying the photographs that papered the room. She reached out and flicked a light switch next to the door, flooding the room with fluorescent light. From all four walls, animals leapt out at her, filling her vision. Animals in zoos. Animals in the wild. Giraffes and rhinos, okapis, orangutans, gorillas, koalas, strange reptiles, exotic birds, hyenas, but above all, cats—big cats. Tigers, snow leopards, lions, servals, panthers, lynxes, and others she couldn't identify.

She was simultaneously eager and afraid to look at the color photos she had glimpsed before. Her eyes moved slowly around the walls until they came to rest on them. She could see from where she stood that they were all of one person—the same person over and over. She approached very slowly, her jaw open in amazement.

There were about fifty photos of her, some of her and Ra, her and other dogs she'd trained for field trials. A few of Ra alone. But mostly of her.

And they were beautiful. The best photographs of her she had ever seen or could even imagine.

From early childhood, Katherine had always hated seeing photographs of herself. They seemed unnatural, as if she were trying to be someone else, face frozen, body stiff and blocky. It was the visual equivalent of hearing one's voice for the first time on a tape recorder.

But these pictures . . . she couldn't take her eyes off them. They showed her as she wanted to look when she was feeling best about herself. In action. Doing what she did best. Dressed in the clothes she loved. Her face alive, catching the light.

For the first minute, the images of herself engrossed her so totally that the questions stayed at bay. The pictures had all been taken at field trials around the country. One series, her favorite, was taken in Vermont in October of last year, at the meet where Ra won his field-trial championship.

The largest photo, which had been blown up to ten inches by fourteen, was a close-up of her wearing a red ski sweater under her white handler's jacket. She stood in a field fiery with autumn colors, her left arm extended from the elbow, giving Ra a line to the retrieve. Her face was intent, glowing in the afternoon light, and her cheeks were flushed with the cold. It brought flooding back the feel of that day, that glorious day when everything had gone right, when Ra had responded to every motion of her hand as if she were casting him out to the exact spot for the retrieve.

Another photo was a close-up of her face in profile, so close she could see the tiny gold stud in her ear and the almost invisible scar on her upper lip.

Suddenly Katherine's legs shook under her, unable to hold her weight for another second. She sank slowly to the floor into a cross-legged sit, never taking her eyes from the pictures. Now the questions were flooding in.

Did he take these pictures?

How come she hadn't even been aware they were being taken?

Why so many?

As she glanced around the room, she knew for a certainty—she wasn't sure how, maybe from the consistent camera angles, or something about the vision—that all these photos bore the mark of one man. Lester must have taken them all. She was sure of it. That meant he had been there many times, close enough to her to take a picture as intimate as this. But why? And if he was there, why didn't he talk to her? She must have seen him many times at the trials and walked right past him without recognizing him.

A rush of hot pain gripped her neck and shoulders. Only a lover—or a loving father—would take pictures like these. Oh, God. Oh, God. She leaned forward and her bare legs were wet with falling tears before she even knew she was crying.

A cold nose poked in under her arm. Without looking up, she reached out and touched the sleek short hair of her father's dog. She leaned her head against the broad side of the old Lab and wept as if she were a five-year-old child. "I'm glad no one's here to see this but you, old girl," she murmured to the dog.

From the open door came footsteps and a woman's voice calling, "Now *that* is an incorruptible dog out—" The voice trailed off when Katherine jerked her wet face up toward the sound. She felt the shock of being discovered in a forbidden activity.

A tall woman wearing huge sunglasses stood in the door. She wore tight jeans stretched over ample hips and held an unlit cigarette in her hand. "Oh, I've come at a bad time for you," she said. "I could come back later." She leaned over toward Katherine. "Or I could stay and we could talk about it."

Katherine's chest heaved in an effort to respond, but no sound emerged.

"I know," the woman said. "I've done nothing but cry for the last six months and it's hard to cry and talk at the same time, but you can learn to do it. Here. I'll talk while you catch your breath."

She slipped the strap of a huge straw bag from her shoulder and let it thud to the floor. "I'm Sophie Driscoll, your cousin. I just talked to Travis, the old dear, and he said you'd probably be here, the police would give you the key. So I came to be family." She looked at Katherine's bent head. "Kind of late for that, huh?"

Katherine tried to dry her cheeks with the back of her hand. With her lowered head she gestured to the wall of photos. "I didn't know he had taken these. I didn't know he was there. He never even introduced himself."

Sophie slid her big sunglasses up to the top of her head and leaned over to study the pictures. "That's impossible," she said.

Katherine lifted her head, allowing her face to be seen in all its blotched and streaked vulnerability. "Really. I had no idea."

Sophie pulled a silver lighter from her jeans pocket and lit the cigarette. "Good Lord, this family. Lester could easily be as weird as the Driscoll side. I'm dying to see if someone like you who's been raised away from the influence"—she blew smoke out and waved her hand to direct it away from Katherine—"is as weird as the rest of us. I've wondered whether it's genetic or learned."

Sophie smiled down at Katherine, who was still sitting on the floor, stroking the old Lab and hiccuping. "But you look like family. You look like Gram. Lucky. Can I get you something to drink? A cigarette? A chair?" She snapped her fingers. "Some Kleenex?"

Katherine looked up at the broad face framed in frizzed ginger-colored hair, nodded, and laughed. Sophie turned and strode into the kitchen, giving the swinging door such a shove that it continued to swing violently on its hinges until she passed through it again with a roll of paper towels. She thrust them at Katherine, who tore one off and blotted her wet face.

"Sophie Driscoll? Cooper Driscoll's daughter?"

Sophie shrugged as if in apology. "Yeah. You're really out of the loop, aren't you?"

Suddenly Katherine wanted to be in the loop. And this woman could help her. "Did you know my father? I thought your side of the family didn't even talk to him."

"Oh, my parents didn't." Her voice took on a bitter, strident tone. "God forbid they should associate with a hardworking zookeeper. It will be fun to see how they maintain their superiority now they are poor."

Katherine sat up on her knees. "Poor?"

"Sure. Everybody knows my dad is close to bankruptcy."

"But I thought—"

"Oh, yeah, we used to be, and Gram still is rich. She's too smart to get into the trouble Dad did. But she won't help."

"But you *did* know my father?" Katherine repeated.

"A little. Just since I started working at the zoo part-time."

"Oh. Fill me in on . . . the family. I'm not even sure how many of you there are."

"Us. Not many. We're a dying breed, the descendants of Anne Driscoll. Unless you plan to produce some children, I think you and I are going to be the last generation. There's me and my father, and my mother, of course." She sighed. "I think it's time for a reunion. Why don't you come over tomorrow night and meet them?"

"Well, I'm not sure what I—"

Sophie interrupted. "Oh, shit. Just say yes and come. God, this family is stiff-necked. Now it's probably gonna take you twenty years to decide to forget your grudges and come to dinner."

Katherine stood up in one quick motion. "I don't have any grudges."

"Well, that would make you the only one." Sophie picked up her bag and slung it over her shoulder. "I have lots of grudges and I'd love to tell you about them now, but I've got my AA support group in ten minutes. I'd cancel, but they'd all say it was resistance. And I really need it. So we'll save the catching up for tomorrow. Okay?"

Katherine nodded.

"Around six. God, you probably don't even know where we live."

"No. I don't."

"Claire Avenue, 312. We're in the book if you forget or need to call." As she started through the door, she stopped and looked back over her shoulder. "Sorry about Lester and everything. I really liked him. See you tomorrow."

Katherine watched from the door as Sophie folded herself into a silver BMW. This was something totally new. A cousin. Family. Was it a good idea to go to dinner? Sophie's parents might not want to see her, probably didn't. Well, she would go whether it was a good idea or not.

A faint stab of guilt caught her in the stomach. Her mother would not want her to do this. She had made Katherine promise never to try to contact her family. But Leanne was dead. And there had to be some statute of limitations on these family feuds, didn't there?

She gestured Ra to come into the cool house and closed the door. The Lab got up from the hall rug and the two dogs sniffed each other for a minute. Then they plopped down close to one another on the cool brick floor in the front hall.

Katherine returned to the studio and studied the pictures her father had taken of her. They showed a woman so alive and absorbed that she was almost beautiful, the first time Katherine had ever thought herself so. That was what her father had seen and he had loved it from afar. Something had prevented him from making contact with her, but that something wasn't lack of love. Her eyes burned with the effort of holding back the tears. He did love her. All those years she'd yearned for him to come, he did love her. What was it that had kept him away?

She walked slowly to the door, as if in a trance, locked it, and returned to sit in front of the pictures. She gave up resisting and the tears began to flow again, stinging the skin of her cheeks as they fell. He did love her, and had wanted to do something to help her. Really that was enough, just knowing that. Somehow losing the house and kennel and even Ra didn't seem quite so devastating a prospect as it had. Her father had loved her and he had wanted to help.

When she was finished, it was almost dark outside. She stood up and walked around the house turning on lamps. She felt an absolute certainty now. Her father had promised money; it had to be somewhere.

And there was something he wanted her to do for him. She would discover what it was and she would do it.

EIGHT

KATHERINE'S FIRST IMPULSE was to jump into the car immediately and find the Lamar Boulevard Self-Storage, see what was waiting for her there. But she needed to take care of business first. If she was going to stay here tonight, she'd have to call Joe and cajole him into staying to take care of the kennel.

Before making the call, Katherine wandered through the tiny house, absorbing the neat feel of the small, well-ordered rooms. There was nothing ugly anywhere. It was sparsely furnished, but what was there was handsome and practical. It was a house organized around the interests of the occupant. The studio was set up for work. The small second bedroom had been turned into a library with a wide range of books on animals, photography, and some fiction. The only furniture in the room besides the bookshelves was an easy chair with a gooseneck reading lamp next to it. Later, she decided, she would go through the books more carefully, and spend some time in that easy chair.

In his bedroom, she sat down on the bentwood chair in front of his open rolltop desk, composing herself to call home. Her eye explored the contents of the cubbyholes at the back of the desk. In the first hole was a green plastic checkbook, a sheaf of canceled checks, and some bank statements. She pulled out the checkbook and opened it, aware of how personal an item it was.

She imagined someone going through her checkbook—the declining income over the past two years, the huge medical bills for Leanne, the balance close to zero right now. It would reveal a great deal about her life. She felt a smile creeping across her lips. Maybe she could come to know her father through his checkbook.

She flipped it open and paged through the check register to his most recent entries, written in the same bold, loopy handwriting as the letter to her. On October 2, he had made a deposit and paid some household bills, his last entries.

She looked back at September, his last full month of life and checked his deposits. It appeared that he was paid twice a month—$1119.50 on the first and the fifteenth. She ran her finger down the payment column of the register. He also paid his bills on the first and fifteenth. His regular monthly expenses—mortgage payment of $646.55 plus gas, electricity, and phone—added up to about $730. His only extravagance seemed to be a check written to Total Camera Mart for forty dollars.

So how come a man with such frugal habits has to take out a second mortgage on his home and dies in debt? Did he have some secret vices?

She pulled a pencil from the desk drawer and ran the eraser slowly down the payment column, working backward from October 2—through September, August, July, and then back through the rest of the year.

When she had finished, she leaned forward and began circling certain entries with the pencil.

Damn. With the exception of this month and last month, going back to when the register was started fifteen months ago, he had written a check for $1300 to Travis Hammond on the tenth of every month. Thirteen hundred dollars every month! No wonder he was in debt. That left him less than two hundred dollars a month to live on, after his fixed expenses.

What was the payment for? Why hadn't the lawyer mentioned it? It couldn't be for legal services, could it? She did some quick calculating. Over the last fifteen months, her father had paid out $16,900. That sure as hell wasn't the fee for drawing up the simple will Hammond had shown her.

She rooted around the cubbyhole to see if there were more old check registers, but she didn't find any. She opened the drawer and rummaged through the papers there. No check registers. She wondered where he kept his old banking.

Katherine leaned back in the chair and pressed her thumbs into the base of her neck. Why was her father paying a lawyer the lion's share of his salary for the last year? For what?

Well, she would certainly find out.

She picked up the phone, called information for Travis Hammond's number, and dialed it. It was the office number. A woman's tape-recorded voice said the offices of Hammond and Crowley were closed and would reopen at nine tomorrow morning. She could leave a message at the tone. Katherine left her name and her father's phone number, saying it was urgent Travis Hammond get back to her immediately. Then she stood and looked down at the checkbook lying on the desk.

There's something rotten here. Wait. Maybe the money was being invested for him. That's possible. And if he'd been making regular investments, that would explain his having enough cash to help me out now. But Mr. Hammond would have told me. Unless . . . she pictured the lawyer's troubled face. No. Impossible.

She sat down at the desk again and pulled out the canceled checks neatly arranged in one cubbyhole. She thumbed back to August and pulled out check number 5897. Dated August 10, it was made out to Travis Hammond in the amount of $1300. It was stamped "Paid." She turned it over. In the impeccable handwriting of one who grew up in an era when penmanship was taught, was written, "Pay to the order of account #340-980-43, Belton National Bank. Travis Hammond." Under that was stamped "Belton National Bank, August 15, 1988."

But why no check last month? Or this one? The tenth of October had passed almost a week ago. Just to make sure he hadn't written one and not recorded it, she went through all the canceled checks for September. Nothing to Travis Hammond.

I've got to talk to him right now. This is driving me crazy. I'll try him at home. She called information, but the number was unlisted. Damn. She'd have to wait until morning to find out about this.

She looked at her watch—eight fifty-five. Oh, my God, Joe! She still hadn't called him. He had been expecting her back by dinnertime. She couldn't put it off any longer. She picked up the phone and dialed. Joe answered on the first ring.

"Joe. This is Katherine. Sorry I haven't called, but things are crazy here."

"I heard from the police your father died. Sorry to hear it. I hope it's okay that I told them all the stuff they asked for."

"Yes. Of course, it's okay. Are things all right there?"

"Yup. Jack Reiman came and the Starks came a day early for Candace, so she didn't get her going-home bath, but they'll learn to call ahead."

"Yeah. Joe, I'm going to stay the night here. I have to do some things in the morning. Can you take care of things there? Why don't you get Rosie and Carlitos to stay with you?"

"Okay. But—"

"Your check. I know. I'll come home tomorrow and pay you. I promise. Okay?"

"Yeah, okay." He sounded like a peasant with centuries of oppression on his back.

"Would you call the Kielmeyers and tell them what happened, that my father's dead? I promised I'd call them. Tell them I'll call in the next few days, okay?"

"Yeah. Okay."

She hung up and grabbed the phone book from inside the bottom drawer. She looked up Lamar Boulevard Self-Storage and punched out the number. A gum-chewing voice answered on the fifth ring and told her they were open every night until ten.

Katherine looked at her watch. It was nine, exactly. She had an hour. She located the place on her Austin map, loaded Ra into the back of the car, and exceeded the speed limit getting there.

Lamar Boulevard Self-Storage was on the ugliest strip of road she had seen in Austin. Sandwiched in between a Pizza Hut and a discount furniture warehouse, the entrance was marked by a huge billboard announcing, YOU LOCK IT. YOU KEEP THE KEY. OVER 1800 SPACES. The gate in the high chain-link fence held a sign warning, GUARD DOG ON DUTY.

It was an enormous complex, covering many acres. Finding unit 2259 might take a while. As she drove past the office, a ramshackle trailer resting on cinder blocks, she decided it would be better not to stop and ask. Why? she asked herself. I'm just a daughter going to look at her dead father's effects. I'm not doing anything wrong.

On both sides of the driveway stretched endless expanses of identical long, low, flat-roofed, barracks-like buildings, constructed of concrete slabs covered by a pebble-like texture. Some had corrugated metal doors large enough to drive a truck through, but most had standard-sized gray-painted metal doors with hasps and padlocks. Just as she had envisioned.

The place was totally deserted and very dark. There was no moon; the only light was supplied by a 40-watt bulb hanging on a utility pole every hundred yards. She was glad Ra was with her.

After driving the length of the complex without finding the right number, she arrived at the back fence, fourteen feet high, with barbed wire on the top. The strip of dirt next to the fence was a dumping ground for old cannibalized cars and decrepit boats with hulls rotted out—a cemetery for dead machines.

She followed the fence until she reached a road running through the other side of the complex. So far she had passed buildings numbered 1 through 19 and seen no signs of life. It was a city of the dead, a ghost town.

She spotted building number 22 and turned into the shadowed alley running between 22 and 23. About halfway along, she located it—2259 was stenciled on the door. She stopped the car, turned off the engine, and searched through the keys on her chain until she found the small one. She held it between her thumb and index finger for a few seconds, warming the metal. For luck.

Before getting out of the car, she looked both ways down the long rows of locked gray doors. She had not seen or heard another living soul. "We don't like it here, Ra, do we?"

She climbed out and opened the back for the dog. "Heel. You stay right here with me." They approached the door. The lock was new and shiny brass. On it was engraved, "Arbus. Germany."

"Oh, Ra. This is it. Oh, boy." He wagged his tail wildly at the excitement in her voice.

Before inserting the key in the padlock, she looked up and down the long rows once more. The key slipped into the lock. A slight turn clicked it open. At the click she felt something shift inside herself. It was as if at that instant she had begun some secret collaboration with her father. It made her feel close to him.

She took the lock off, slipped the hasp, and hung the open lock back on the hook.

With her right hand she pulled the heavy door open, keeping her left hand on Ra's neck. When she felt his hair prick up and the sudden rumble shake his body, she leapt back from the opening, slamming her hip against the car. Ra held his ground, growling and leaning forward toward the darkness inside.

Katherine's whole body throbbed with her galloping heartbeat.

No. I couldn't have seen what I think I saw.

In the faint light from the bulb at the end of the row, she thought she had glimpsed a glittering animal eye and thick black-and-tan fur.

It had looked like a huge dog.

No way.

Ra was standing at ease now, waiting for her. When her pulse had slowed to a trot, she took two small steps forward and peered in again. "What is that, Ra?"

This time she knew it wasn't real. Real, but not alive. "God, that scared me. You, too, huh? What a pair we are, scared by a stuffed dog."

She stood at the entrance and studied it. The dog was a handsome German shepherd mounted on a wood platform, standing alert, ears perked up. The glass eyes were amazingly realistic. But why would someone do this? Sick. Was this Pasha?

He'd said something in the letter. Remember Pasha. What a good watchdog he was. Yes, a watchdog. I do remember. Pasha was a great watchdog. He made me feel safe. Something in the house terrified me and he made me feel safe. But safe from what? I can't remember.

Katherine looked back at the stuffed dog. It reminded her of the tombs of the Egyptian pharaohs—earthly treasures guarded by godlike dogs.

Katherine inched forward. "Let's see what treasures you're guarding, Pasha, if you are Pasha." She crossed the threshold into a room the size of a closet. On the floor sat three large cartons and a cheap metal file cabinet with two drawers. Katherine felt her whole body droop at the sight. She wasn't sure what she had been expecting, but this was not it.

She said aloud to herself, "What do you think people keep in these storage units, Katherine? Were you really expecting stacks of money?"

She approached the file cabinet and opened both drawers. They were filled with manila folders, but the light was far too dim for her to read the labels. She looked up at the ceiling. Damn. No light.

"Well, Ra, we've got our headlights, don't we?" She stepped back to the car, checking up and down the long row of closed and locked doors once more. No one. She started the car engine and turned on the headlights. They were not directed toward the closet, so she backed up and turned the car at an angle so the beams were aiming as close to the inside of the unit as she could get them.

Ra sighed and lay down in the open doorway while Katherine went to work on the files. Starting with the top drawer, she pulled out each file and examined the contents, holding it up into the light beam. The entire drawer was composed of magazine and newspaper articles about zoos, animals, and photography. He was a prodigious clipper—like her.

The second drawer contained old invoices and banking dating back to 1960. The man kept everything and organized it—like her. She rummaged through and located his check registers dating from July of 1988 back all the way to 1960. She held each one in the headlight's beam as she flipped through, pausing each time she came to the tenth of the month. There they were, payments of $1300 going back nine years, to June of 1979.

In May of '79, the check was for only $1000. She checked the deposit column and noticed that his paycheck deposits were smaller. As she went back through the years, the size of the checks diminished as the years receded, in direct proportion to his income. In 1960, when he was earning $7500 a year, he had been paying only $300.

But for the past twenty-nine years her father had been turning over almost half of his income to Travis Hammond. Why? And when did it start? The records stopped in 1960. What about before that? When she was a baby and the family was living together, had he been paying then, too? She stuffed the registers in her bag, wiped her sweaty face with her shirttail, and turned to the cartons.

She emptied them methodically. One was filled with envelopes stuffed with negatives and prints—all of animals. The other two were filled with old magazines—*Modern Photography, Zoo Management, Audubon, Smithsonian, National Geographic*—and paperback books on all subjects. After she had gone through them item by item, she repacked them hastily.

When she finished, she turned around to face Ra, still lying in the doorway. "It has to be here, Ra. Whatever it is. For starters, he sent me the key and receipt for safekeeping. Also, there's plenty of room back at his house for this stuff. He didn't need this storage space, but he's hidden something here for me, and he's left his old watchdog to guard it."

She stood up and wrested the top drawer out of the cabinet. Sweat began to drip down her temples. She lifted out the other one and tipped the whole cabinet into the light beam so she could examine the inside of the cabinet. Nothing. She lifted each drawer and felt the underside. Nothing. She tipped the cabinet back, resting it against the wall so she could look underneath. Nothing but a few pillbugs and spiders. She checked the rear of the cabinet before shoving it back against the wall.

"Well, shit, Ra. Where is it?" The dog didn't respond. He was asleep in the doorway. She stepped over him to get out of the stuffy closet for a breath of air. She looked at her watch. Ten o'clock. Closing time. One more look.

She stepped back over the sleeping dog, into the dark closet, and glanced around at the plasterboard walls and ceiling and the cement floor. Finally, her gaze settled on the stuffed dog in the dark corner, where the headlight beam didn't reach. She hadn't wanted to touch it, it looked so dusty. She hadn't wanted to look at it either. She wasn't sure why.

Now she examined its outline in the dark. How do they stuff dead animals? she wondered. Like the Egyptians, they probably take out all the insides first. So the body would be empty and they'd have to stuff it. That's why it's called stuffed! Stuffed with what?

She approached and rested a hand on the dog's croup. The dusty, dry fur and hardened hide didn't feel anything like the warm, muscular rump of a living dog. She knelt down and ran her hands up the back, neck, and head, down the chest, between the front legs, and along the belly. She stopped suddenly and moved her fingers back a few inches. There was something that felt like a welt under the fur. She explored it with two fingers. There was a slit in the belly running from between the front legs back to the groin.

Maybe this was the way stuffed dogs were made. No. The stuffing would fall out. Very gingerly, she inserted the tip of her index finger through the opening. She withdrew it immediately, thinking of the spiders underneath the file cabinet, then remembered she wasn't afraid of spiders and stuck it back in, farther this time. She felt only a void.

Slowly she moved back along the opening, wiggling the finger around until she touched something. It felt like the edge of a thick piece of cardboard. She tried to feel more of it, but her finger had knocked it away.

To locate it, she needed to fit her whole hand in. She inserted four fingers to the knuckles and pulled gently outward on one side of the slit. It widened easily so she could slip her hand in. She found it immediately—the edge of a thick envelope or a file folder. She could feel the edge, but she couldn't get a grip on it.

Sweat trickled freely down her hairline now. She withdrew her hand and wiped her face with her sleeve. Then she sat down to get a better angle up into the dog, resting her cheek against the musty dead fur. Using her left hand to enlarge and hold the opening, she inserted her entire right hand in past the wrist. The rawhide-like edges scraped the skin of her hand and wrist, but she pushed on until she located the object and was able to grab it. It felt like a big envelope.

But her hand was much bigger now, with it closed over the envelope, too big to pull through the opening. She used her left hand to pull and pry at the edges, gradually enlarging the slit, but still she could not get her hand out. The knuckles were raw and scratched from trying.

She refused to let go of the envelope. Her back was soaked with sweat and she was breathing hard with exertion.

The headlight beam suddenly wavered and a monster shadow flashed onto the closet wall.

She swung her head around and tried to leap to her feet at the same time, but her hand, caught inside the dog, jerked her back painfully.

"We're closing them gates now," said a gruff voice. "Di'n't you know we close at ten? Hey, how can you see anything in here?" He shone his light on her.

Katherine twisted her body around to look at him—a burly black man with a flashlight. "I was just fixing to release the patrol dog, girl. You lucky I checked first. He ain't like this one here." He waved the flashlight toward Ra, who awoke suddenly with the light on his face.

"Hey, you need help there?" He shone his light on the stuffed dog. "Je-sus, what that thing? Some stuffed dog? You need help there, lady?"

Katherine was twisted around facing him, arm pulled behind her. "No. No. I'm fine. Just finishing up with my . . . files here." She tried to smile. "Sorry I'm late. I'll be out in just a minute, okay?"

He reached down to touch Ra's head. "Okay, you finish up. I got to close them gates. So finish up."

"Yes, I am." Katherine had finally abandoned the envelope and worked her hand loose. It felt like raw hamburger meat.

"Peoples don't read that sign," the guard grumbled, walking away.

Katherine stood up. "Goddamn it, Ra, you're supposed to let me know when someone's coming! Bad dog, sleeping on the job. Well, what are we going to do now?" She looked down at the stuffed dog.

"Let's see if I can lift this thing." She bent over, reached her arms around the dog's legs and hefted. "Not so bad," she grunted, staggering with it out the door. She carried it to the open back of the car and hoisted it inside. Then she pointed for Ra to get in. He hesitated. "In," she commanded. The dog jumped into the back and sat as far from the stuffed dog as he could.

"Don't blame you," Katherine said, slamming the tailgate.

She got her purse from the closet, closed the door and put the lock back on.

A flash of panic coursed through her. Oh, my God, keys! She rummaged frantically through her bag. Thank God, there they were. She jumped in the car, locked the doors, and revved the engine.

The big guard was there to salute them through the gates.

Katherine's heart pounded with excitement. ''Oh, Ra, he did leave me something. I can't wait to see what we've got here.''

NINE

As if enacting some ritual of black magic to make the dead speak, Katherine waved her hand slowly over the twenty-one photographs and the six white pages. They had to mean something.

Sitting cross-legged on the floor of her father's studio, she closed her eyes and circled her head slowly, trying to relax the tension in her neck. The stuffed dog, eviscerated once more, lay tipped over on its side, pushed out of the way, under the long table. Both living dogs slept close by.

It hadn't been money, of course. But she hadn't really expected that it would be.

It was a message to her from her father. He had written "Katherine Driscoll" on the manila envelope. He had hidden it away and sent her the key and the receipt so she would be sure to find it if something happened to him. It was a secret communication from him to her, the only one they would ever share. Katherine was flooded with the desire to understand the message and carry out his intentions, if only she could figure out what they were.

After wrenching the large envelope from the cavity of the dog, she had spilled out the contents and spread them in a circle around her: twenty-one black-and-white photographs and six document pages—apparently copies of Austin zoo records concerning new animal acquisitions.

The photographs were all of animals being unloaded from huge vans, some in crates, some tied and hobbled. Katherine turned them over. On the back of each photo a date and a place were written in her father's handwriting. All were dated within the past three months and were marked with one of four names: Cloud Nine, Bandera; Circle Z, Fredericksburg; PLS, Lampasas; or RTY Ranch, Kerrville.

Katherine looked through them for the most recent ones, the four marked 10/2/89, just two weeks ago. All four had "RTY Ranch, Kerrville" written below the date.

Katherine picked one up and studied it. Four men were unloading a huge crate from a large van. Like the other twenty, it was not up to the usual standard of her father's wildlife pictures. It looked hurried, perhaps taken from a distance in insufficient light.

She picked up another. A striped antelope, large as a cow, with long twisted horns and huge ears, stood outside a crate. Katherine didn't know what the animal was called, but she was certain it was not native to Texas.

In another photo, a large goatlike animal with thick horns curling back into a semicircle over its neck was being released into a paddock. It had a long, flowing fringe of hair extending from its chin to its throat, chest, and down to its forelegs. It reminded Katherine of the three billy goats gruff. Again, she couldn't name it, but knew it was foreign.

The last picture dated October 2 showed three more large antelope-type animals standing in a paddock.

In other photos, she recognized a huge Cape buffalo, four wildebeest, and a pair of ostriches. There were several more varieties of horned antelopes she couldn't name, but she knew none of them were the native pronghorn antelope, white-tailed deer, or mule deer.

She was willing to bet these were African animals being unloaded at Texas ranches.

This was not so unusual. Katherine knew ranchers in the Boerne area who stocked their fenced areas with exotic animals and charged enormous fees for hunters to shoot them. It was a legitimate business. And a lucrative one.

She looked at the animals again and wished she knew more about African wildlife.

Then she remembered her father's library. She sprang from the floor and ran into the tiny second bedroom her father had used to store his books. His animal collection was organized into geographical sections. Out of the African section, she pulled a book called *A Field Guide to the Larger Mammals of Africa*. As she walked back to the studio, she leafed through the table of contents. If these photographed animals were African, they should be in here.

Stretching out on her stomach, she arranged the open book in front of her, with the photos of the striped antelope and the bearded animal right above it. She paged through the book, stopping at each illustration.

Midway through, in the section on Tragelaphinae, she found the big striped antelope. It was a bongo. Its habitat was central and west Africa, very rare now. In the last chapter, Caprinae, she found the picture that matched the bearded animal exactly. It was an aoudad or Barbary sheep, a wild sheep inhabiting the Saharan zone of Africa.

It was satisfying to be able to name them.

But so what?

Katherine shut the book and pulled the letter from her father out of the zipper compartment of her bag where she had stashed it. She reread the part that said, "What you would need to do in return is something only you can do. It would not be difficult for you, I'm sure. You might even enjoy it." What was he expecting her to do in return for the money? Something involving these documents and pictures he'd left with her name on them?

He'd intended to explain it all to her, but now he couldn't; she was on her own.

She reached for one of the sheets and studied it more carefully. The heading in bold type said, "Austin Zoological Garden Acquisitions." Under that were nine column headings: "Access No., ISIS No., Classif., DOB, Sex, Source, Paym. Fund, Acq.D, and Quar." The entries under those headings were printed in tiny, precise, accountant-like handwriting.

She wondered what the sheets had to do with the photos. Maybe the zoo had also acquired some of these same species. She pulled over the other five sheets and checked back in the book for the bongo's scientific classification. It was *Boocercus euryceros*. She ran her finger down the second column of the first sheet, then the second sheet. On the third one, she found it: (Access No.)M139744, (ISIS No.)11-2504, (Classif.)Boocercus euryceros, (DOB)6/3/85, (Sex)M, (Source)MFWAD, (Paym.Fund)ACDF, (Acq.D)10/2/89, (Quar.)21.

The zoo had acquired a bongo on October 2, the same day her father had photographed one being unloaded at the RTY Ranch in Kerrville.

So what?

If I knew a little more about the zoo, she thought, I might be able to figure this out.

She looked at the sheet again, intending to check for the Barbary sheep, *Ammotragus lervia*. But the tiny numbers and letters blurred and dissolved. She closed her eyes and felt the gritty friction of lids against bloodshot eyeballs. She put a hand to her face. The skin felt greasy and slack. God, she was tired. This had been the longest day of her life. She glanced at her watch—ten past midnight.

She needed to sleep a few hours and then come at this fresh. It was too confusing right now.

Slowly she rose from the floor, one aching joint at a time. She shouldn't lie on her stomach. It made the small of her back sore. Standing, she arched her back and groaned. She started to leave the papers and photos on the floor, but changed her mind and gathered them back into the envelope. He had gone to great pains to conceal these; so would she.

Both dogs struggled to their feet and padded behind her as she walked to the bedroom, carrying the envelope with her.

She lifted the mattress at the head of her father's bed and tucked the envelope between the box spring and the mattress. Then she collapsed on the white chenille spread. The last thing she heard was the dogs flopping down onto the floor next to the bed and the last thing she felt was the tufty pattern pressing into her cheek.

THE POINTMAN took his time to savor the moment. The morning air was brisk and invigorating. Yes, invigorating. Just mouthing the word made him feel renewed and powerful. Two days, two down. He was powerful, doing now what he was meant to do.

He looked around him at the old wood-slat blind on its spindly tripod legs, listing hard to the south. This was a world where he felt at home: country air and hunting. He'd like to have a ranch like this—a little place with some acreage and good hunting. When he finished this work, then, finally, he could concentrate on living.

He gazed down on the buck's antlers—ten sharp points. Perfect. "Practice makes perfect, sonny," his mother used to say. She was so right. Well, this one's for you, Mom.

The deer's huge dark eyes were wide open and already beginning to glaze over with white. The mouth was agape, with a trickle of blood oozing out onto the dirt. But that was the only blood. This part of it was very neat. The next part would get bloody; he'd need to get rid of these clothes, just as he had done with the others.

He leaned down and grasped the bases of the main antler beams and began to drag. Amazing how heavy in death these animals were who looked so light in life, as if they were subject to a different law of gravity. He tugged it a few inches at a time through the dirt, until the buck lay at the edge of the tree line. So it could be seen from the blind. Bait. It would draw the real prey.

Breathing hard from the exertion, he leaned over and caressed each of the five pointed tines on the left antler. It was the fighting tine, ten inches long and sharp as a skewer, that would do the job, he decided. He wished he could be around to see the faces of the cops or the game warden or whoever discovered this one.

After this, he would be half finished. Unless he added one more to the list. He had forgotten that there was one more person there. He might have to add her now that she was intruding herself. Really, it was fate. She was asking for it, putting herself in his path like that, reminding him of her role in it.

He looked at the neat bloodless hole where the arrow protruded from the deer's chest. He ran his eye up the shaft to the red plastic vanes, striated to resemble a feather, trying to decide whether to pull it out and get rid of it or just leave it there. He felt sour panic rising in his throat. It was childish and negligent that he hadn't thought that important issue out ahead of time. One of the reasons things had gone so well yesterday was that he had thought everything out, just the way his mother had taught him to do. "Always think of the consequences, sonny, think of the worst thing that could happen and plan for it."

He reached into his shirt for his talisman and held it, slowly squeezing, until the fangs punctured the skin of his palm. There. He felt better. It was fine. He was doing a good job. The first one had gone perfectly and so would this. He had right and justice on his side.

He could think about the arrow while he waited. There was time. He walked back into the trees and picked up his bow and quiver of arrows. "A good workman always cleans up his tools," he heard his mother say. He sat at the edge of the clearing with his back braced against an oak tree. The arrow could not possibly be traced to him. It had been purchased ten years ago in Waco. There was no way it could come back to haunt him. So it didn't really matter. It was just a—what was the word he had looked up the other day? Aesthetic. That was it. The question of the arrow was just an aesthetic matter. Would it look better in or out?

Now it came down to waiting, again. That was fine with him. He was a good waiter. He'd waited a long time for this.

THE DOGS WOKE HER at eight. She sat up in bed with a jerk.

My God, that envelope.

She leaned over and pulled it from under the mattress. If Lieutenant Sharb was right, if her father had been murdered, then the information in the envelope might have been the cause. And now she had it. Having it could be dangerous, really a police matter.

How come I didn't think of this last night?

I was just so tired.

She felt an unaccustomed flutter of fear under her breastbone.

Maybe I should run this over to Sharb right now and wash my hands of the whole matter.

She swung her legs over the side of the bed and pulled the envelope from under the mattress. She stared at her name written in big loopy black letters.

But my father didn't take it to the police. Why not, if my gut feel is right, and there is proof of illegal activities in here? He must have had a reason for keeping it to himself.

She ran her hand through her snarled hair. No, this is a communication between my father and me. There's no need to tell anyone about it yet. Anyway, things have always turned out best when I rely on myself.

Now Ra began to prance in place and Belle gave one sharp bark of demand from the doorway. Katherine stood up and stretched. "You're a tyrant, Miss Belle, you know that? Come on." She led them to the kitchen, filled two bowls with Belle's food and stuck them outside the back door, in the tiny fenced-in backyard.

Then she tried Travis Hammond's number, but his answering machine was still on. She left another urgent message saying she had to talk to him. She could think of no other way to find out about the thirteen-hundred-dollar payments than to ask him outright. When she tried to conjure up a logical explanation for why her father had been paying almost half his salary to an attorney for nearly thirty years, as far back as his records went, she drew a blank. It was incomprehensible.

She located a can of coffee and brewed a pot in her father's old electric percolator.

As she sat at his kitchen table holding a steaming cup, a surge of nostalgia gathered and swelled inside her chest, compressing her heart and lungs and her empty stomach, wringing them so painfully she had to set down the cup and wrap her arms across her chest. It was a feeling of longing for what had never been, for what she had only imagined. She wished above all else that her father were here now, to drink coffee with her. To talk about the secret pictures he took of her. To tell her about the contents of the envelope and what he wanted her to do with them. What could she do that no one else could? Had he had a premonition of his death? Did he feel threatened? Is that why he had urged her to come soon? Is that why he had sent the key and the receipt?

She leaned over and pulled the envelope from the counter. She laid the photos and documents on the table, one at a time, as if she were dealing out cards, and then studied them.

She focused on the documents and the headings at the top of the columns—not too difficult to figure out in the morning light: Access No., Classif., DOB, Sex, and Source were obvious; ISIS No. She had no idea about. Paym. Fund must be where the money to buy the animal came from. There were two separate sets of initials appearing in that column—AZSPF or ACDF. Surely anybody connected with the zoo could tell her what those were, but she'd have to be careful. They'd want to know why she was asking. Of the final two categories, Acq.D was certainly date of acquisition, and Quar. probably stood for the number of days the animal was kept in quarantine.

She turned all the photos face down and checked all the dates against the zoo records. The dates all matched up; each day a photo was taken, the zoo had acquired some animals. And for all those animal entries, the letters ACDF were written in the payment-fund column.

When the phone rang, she snatched up the kitchen extension, certain it was Travis Hammond finally returning her call. But a female voice said, "Hi, coz, this is Sophie. Just confirming dinner for tonight. Mother and Daddy are eager to meet you. You okay all alone there?"

"I'm not alone. The dogs are here."

"Oh, sure. The dogs. Well, is there anything I can do in the meantime to help you?"

"No," Katherine said. "Oh, yes. Do you have Travis Hammond's phone number at home? I've been trying to get him."

"Sure. Let me look here in Daddy's book." There was a silence. "Yes, here it is—538-9897. I don't think he keeps regular office hours anymore, so you might have better luck reaching him at home. See you at six, okay?"

"Yes. Oh, Sophie, where's a good place to shop for clothes? I didn't bring any with me, so I might buy some today instead of driving home."

She was silent for a moment, as if it were a weighty decision. "You'd like Scarbrough's, I think. Over at Highland Mall."

AFTER GETTING no answer at Travis Hammond's home number, Katherine called the zoo and made an appointment with Sam McElroy. He was going to be out of the office until five, Kim Kelly told her, but he could see her then.

Katherine put down the phone and groaned. More than anything in the world she hated to ask for favors. Well, he had asked—repeatedly—what he could do to help. She was going to take him up on the offer.

So she had a free day until then. She should drive home to pay Joe, check on the kennel, and get fresh clothes, but for the first time since she had bought the house eleven years ago, she didn't want to see it. Somehow it was easier to get used to the idea of losing it when she was away.

She felt like doing something irresponsible for a change. Yes, she would buy some new clothes to meet the Driscolls in. But first, there were commitments to fulfill.

She drove downtown and located the tallest bank building, one with gold windows and a parking garage. She entered the marbled lobby and rented a safe-deposit box. After making copies of the photographs and documents, she locked up the originals. As she left the bank, she couldn't explain to herself exactly why she had gone to the trouble, but it felt right.

She found the post office, wrote a check to Joe, and sent it overnight delivery.

Then she went shopping. She spent the afternoon alternately trying on clothes at the mall and telephoning Travis Hammond—at his office and home. He never answered and her frustration grew. The question of that thirteen hundred dollars a month paid out of a zookeeper's salary festered.

AT A QUARTER OF FIVE she walked through the elephant gates and entered the zoo's administrative offices. Kim Kelly, dressed in a long khaki shirt, white shirt, and high boots, sat at her desk filing some index cards in a metal box.

"Sam's not back yet, but I'm sure he'll be right along," Kim said, rising and opening the director's door. "Why don't you make yourself comfortable in his office, Miss Driscoll?"

As soon as the door was closed, Katherine jumped up and began to explore the office. The big desk was invisible under piles of papers and file folders. One wall was covered with bookshelves, sagging with books and magazines on animals and zoo management. Another wall was dense with framed photographs. She walked closer to examine them. Sam McElroy was featured with a variety of celebrities—a United States Senator, several Texas governors, Robert Redford, William Holden, a President's wife, and a few starlets she couldn't name. It was a celebrity job, and judging from Sam's radiant smiles in the pictures, he reveled in it.

The largest picture on the wall was of Sam and a slender white-haired woman in a zoo uniform. Each of them held cradled in their arms an infant gorilla in white diapers. From the newspaper picture she had seen years before, Katherine recognized the woman as Anne Driscoll. Her grandmother was gazing down at the tiny animal with wonder and delight in her eyes. It made Katherine yearn to know her.

Maybe she should go to see Anne, pay her respects. She would ask at dinner tonight if that would be a good idea.

Another wall was devoted to photographs of the zoo staff at work. Under each photo was a label identifying the subjects. She scanned the names for Lester Renfro. When she found it, she raised her eyes to a picture of a man sitting next to a lioness, his arm draped around her shoulders. She studied her father's high tanned forehead, dark eyes, and serious long mouth. She felt an impulse to take the photograph off the wall and slip it into her bag.

Looking through the other pictures, she was surprised at the number of familiar faces. She recognized the three men in the group next to her yesterday at the news conference. They were holding up a snake that appeared to be twenty feet long. Supporting the head was the rumpled, unshaven Vic, the head veterinarian. At the middle stood the emaciated man with the bad skin—ALONZO STOKES, CURATOR OF REPTILES, said the label. The tail end was held up by the muscular man with the tattoos—WAYNE ZAPALAC, REPTILE KEEPER.

She jumped and whirled around when the door opened. The director breezed in. His thick white hair was ruffled, as if he'd been running, and his cheeks were ruddy. He wore a plaid flannel shirt and the same red knit tie as yesterday.

"Sorry to keep you waiting, Katherine. I was off the grounds for a while. Showing birds of prey to St. Andrews's third graders." He collapsed into a chair and pulled a dead mouse out of his shirt pocket. He smiled apologetically as he laid it gently on the coffee table. A man with lots of charm, Katherine decided.

"Now. Sit down and tell me what I can do to help you," he said, fixing Katherine with a direct look.

Katherine sat in the same green leather chair she had sat in yesterday. It felt just as good.

A deep reluctance to do what she had planned was keeping her throat closed. He smoothed his hair down, waiting for her to speak. She took a deep breath and forced the words out. "Sam, I need a job. Right away. Starting tomorrow."

His expression changed, she thought, from solicitous to wary. But maybe she was imagining it.

"A job?" he asked, raising his thick eyebrows.

"Yes. A job here. I'm dead broke." This was absolutely true after her day of shopping. Her bank balance, after she had rented the safe-deposit box, bought clothes, and sent Joe his check, was reduced to $2.89. "I've had extensive experience with animals. I don't know if you know I'm a professional dog trainer."

"Yes. But that's a far cry from zoo work. Forgive me for asking, but didn't your father leave anything?"

"No. He was in debt."

"In debt? But he seemed to live so frugally."

"Yes. It's puzzling."

There was an agonizing silence during which Katherine struggled against the impulse to say, "It's all right. I'll find something else. Don't worry." But she held her tongue between her teeth and waited him out.

"Well," he said finally, "I don't think this would be a good idea for you—the associations, the constant reminder. Maybe I could help find you something else locally, if you'd like, with a trainer or kennel."

Katherine swallowed. Begging came hard. "You had asked if you could help and this is the one thing I need, Sam. I find I really am interested in zoo work—probably runs in the blood. Not just my father, you know, but my grandmother, and my uncle, and even my cousin Sophie's working here now," she reminded him. "I have to stay in town to settle things, but I'll need to eat." She gave a little laugh. "I've run a boarding kennel, so I know how to clean up after animals. I'll do anything you have." Oh, yes, I certainly know how to shovel the shit, she thought.

He rose from his chair in silence and walked over to his desk. He rummaged through one of the piles, trying to find something. "I want to do whatever I can for you, Katherine, but I don't want to hire someone and have them leave the week after we train them. I really think this isn't a good idea."

"I plan to stay," said Katherine, astonished at the lie. "My home is being foreclosed on and I have nowhere to go. So I'm planning to stay here." She cringed inwardly at the sound of her words. Pulling out all the stops now.

"There are several good training kennels in Austin," he said. "I bet we could find something right up your alley. Probably pays better, too, much better, given your experience."

She looked at him with eyes widened as big as she could make them. "I really want to be at the zoo, though. Sentimental reasons."

"Well," he said, pulling out a sheaf of papers and looking down at it, "the only thing we've got now involves handling reptiles, and most people don't want to do that. Anyway, it's a temporary job at minimum wage, no benefits. And Alonzo Stokes is a real slave driver. Believe me, this is a job you don't want." He looked straight into her eyes.

Katherine met his gaze and said in the strongest voice she could muster, "Yes, I do want it. It sounds fine. Reptiles. I can do that." She tried to smile her thanks. "Can I start tomorrow?"

He looked stunned. "Katherine, I don't feel I'm doing right by you here. If it's a matter of money to get you through the next few days, we can manage a loan of some sort. Or surely your uncle—"

Katherine interrupted before he could go any further. "No, thanks. What I need is the job and I'm ready to start."

He shrugged and gave a weak smile. "Okay. In the morning you can pick up a temporary uniform in the business office. But first you'll need to have an interview with Hans Dieterlen, our head keeper, as a courtesy to him. He likes to pass on all the hirees. Let me see if he's around."

He sat at his desk and picked up the phone. "Kim, see if you can get Hans before he leaves. I'd like him to stop in my office for a minute if he can." He put down the phone. "Anything else?"

Katherine wanted to ask about acquisitions and how they were handled, but her natural caution stopped her. If illegal activities were going on at the zoo, this man could be right in the middle of them. So she asked, "Do you have something I could read to familiarize myself with how the zoo operates, Sam? So I could get a little smarter about it quickly?"

He smiled and began rummaging under one of the stacks on his desk. "Our annual report to the membership would be a good place to start." He pulled up a brochure with a glossy picture of an orangutan on the front. Just then the phone rang. He answered and listened. "Okay. Thanks, Kim. Leave him a message to come talk to Miss Driscoll in my office at seven tomorrow morning. Would you do that?" He put down the phone and said to Katherine, "Hans is tied up now, but he'll see you tomorrow. You can work out the details then."

As he leaned across the desk to hand her the brochure, he said, "This will give you a good idea of how the zoo operates."

Just as she was about to take it, he flipped it over to show her the picture of a smiling man on the back. "But here's your best source of information. Your uncle's involved in all aspects of the zoo, and of course no one knows more about the zoo than your grandmother, but I'm afraid she—" He stopped there and shrugged.

"What?" Katherine asked. "She what?"

"Well, I haven't seen her for a while. I hear she's very ill, so your uncle is really the best source now."

"Yes. I'm going there for dinner tonight. I'll ask him." Katherine stood up and spoke her first honest words of the conversation: "I really appreciate this, Sam. Thanks."

"My pleasure. But beyond this, I can't help. You'll have to please Alonzo Stokes." He laughed and shook his head. "That's not easy."

Katherine studied the picture on the back cover as she walked out of the office. Underneath was a caption that began, "Cooper James Driscoll, Director of the Anne Cooper Driscoll Foundation and President of the Austin Zoological Society, the governing body of the Austin Zoological Gardens."

Something stirred in her memory. She read the rest of the caption. "The ACDF is a zoo endowment set up in 1950 by Anne Cooper Driscoll for capital improvements at the zoo and for the purchase of new animals for the collection."

ACDF! She pictured those initials written again and again in the payment-fund column she had puzzled over last night and this morning.

So. A foundation set up by my grandmother, run by my uncle, buys a bongo for the zoo on the same day one is unloaded at a private ranch in Kerrville. And my father finds that worth taking a picture of and hiding it away for me.

Now I am really interested.

TEN

Katherine sat slouched behind the wheel, studying the huge white brick colonial. Set back from the street and surrounded by ivy-covered oaks, it looked as though it had been there forever. The perfection of it ignited her sense of being an outsider about to enter some closed and enchanted circle of real Driscolls. She was about to have a job interview, only this one would determine whether she became part of the family or remained outside it.

Stupid, Katherine. Who cares?

She jerked on the handle and shoved the door open. *You've lived thirty-six years very nicely without being a member of this family, and you're only here today because you were invited. Don't make such a big thing of it.*

She slid down from the Jeep.

Walking up the brick path, Katherine was comforted by the sensual flow of silk against her hips and legs. She had no remorse over spending the last of her bank account on the expensive slacks and blouse. They made her feel tall and cool and independent, and right now she needed all the help she could get.

If someone were to ask her at dinner, "What are you doing to mourn your father?" she would have to admit that she had spent her first day of bereavement shopping. She smiled, thinking about it. It had helped. She felt better.

She stood in front of the dark-green door, tucked her hair back, drew a long breath for relaxation, and pushed the brass doorbell.

Sophie flung open the door and smiled admiringly at the new outfit. "You look much better than you did yesterday," she said. "Come on in. Mother and Daddy are anxious to meet you."

"Anxious" is probably the right word, Katherine thought.

Sophie walked ahead of her. She was barefoot, wearing a loose Mexican dress, emerald green embroidered in white, her wild hair held down by a matching band. They walked through an overdecorated living room with white carpeting so thick their feet left tracks in it, past a formal dining room with a mahogany table that could seat twenty, toward the back of the house.

She saw immediately that the front rooms were rarely used showrooms, an antechamber to the real house the family inhabited.

Sophie led her into an enormous paneled den stretching the entire length of the house. Thirty-foot cathedral ceilings with exposed dark beams and leaded lancet windows dwarfed the overstuffed furniture. A huge stone fireplace topped with the head of a Cape buffalo dominated one end of the room. This room, totally different in architecture from the rest of the house, had clearly been added on. It was designed to imitate an old English hunting lodge—an appropriate environment for displaying the master's collection.

Katherine raised her eyes and surveyed the collection of animal heads that populated the dark walls—hunting trophies from all over the world. The ubiquitous local white-tailed deer gazed down at her with glassy eyes, but they were overshadowed by more exotic game. There was a moose with a rack the size of a tree, a grizzly bear, several magnificent horned antelopes, and even a lion, mounted with his nose puckered in an eternal snarl.

She tried to repress the repugnance she felt for this display of death. After all, who was she to get moralistic about killing animals? All her adult life she had trained retrievers to hunt and in the process had shot countless birds. She was a hunter herself.

Nevertheless, as she looked around this room, she felt waves of contempt for the person who had killed and exhibited these glassy-eyed corpses.

Sophie saw her reaction and said, "Daddy's an incorrigible hunter." She shrugged. "Men. What can you do?"

A voice boomed from the far end of the room. "No need to apologize for me, little girl."

A large, vigorous man in his late fifties had entered and was striding toward Katherine with a jovial smile. As if I were a long-lost relative, she thought as she managed to return the smile. She extended a hand which he ignored in favor of enfolding her in a hearty hug. It seemed to last forever. She felt crushed, lost, smothered in the beefiness of his torso and the chemical smells of his deodorant and after-shave, and, under it all, the smoky smell of Scotch.

"There you are," he said, releasing her and stepping back to study her, "my niece, little Katie, grown into a good-looking woman. Last time I saw you, you were this high. It's about damn time we got acquainted."

Katherine struggled against her sense of being a different species from this man. She looked at the tanned face and sunken navy-blue eyes, the perfectly even white teeth, the slicked-back dark hair. This man was her uncle, a blood relative, her mother's brother. But it was like meeting a stranger. Without being aware of it, she had been hoping for an immediate sense of kinship, a blood tug that would draw her close.

She wanted to say something, but nothing that came to mind seemed appropriate for the occasion, so she smiled and nodded.

She was saved by the entrance of a petite blond woman in her early fifties who was doing everything possible to look like the University of Texas cheerleader she had no doubt been thirty years earlier. She began to talk the minute she entered the room. "So glad you've come to see us, Katherine. It's so good after all this time to meet you—though, as I was saying to Coop when we heard about this really terrible business yesterday, the circumstances are so tragic for your father and so unfortunate for the zoo." Her scarlet lips and thin, blue-veined hands moved in constant nervous flutters as she talked. "Dying in that way, after all his experience. So hard for you. It must have been quite a shock. Sam says you just happened to be there yesterday and found out by chance and I thought isn't that just the way things go."

On and on she prattled, without breath or thought, an ongoing stream of discourse, uncensored, unedited. Garrulousness was ordinarily something Katherine hated, but at that minute, it provided a welcome relief from the need to do anything but nod.

Finally Cooper Driscoll interrupted his wife. "Lucy, can't you get us something to drink? We'll sit down here and get acquainted." Obedient, but still talking, Lucy took their drink orders. Cooper wanted a Scotch on the rocks. Sophie asked for Perrier with lime.

Katherine hesitated when it was her turn. "Don't worry about me," Sophie said with a big conspiratorial grin in her father's direction, "I'm used to being around drinkers. It won't affect my iron resolve." Katherine took her at her word and asked for a glass of wine. It might help her loosen up and get through dinner.

Cooper Driscoll walked to what was clearly his chair, a large La-Z-Boy, upholstered to match the green fabric on all the other furniture in the room. As he settled into the chair, he lowered his eyes and said, "My condolences on your father. You just let us know what we can do to help." He let out a breath, as if he were glad to get that over with. "I never contacted you when your mother died.

I've felt real bad about that. We heard about it from Travis Hammond. He's kept me posted over the years about Leanne and you."

He sighed and said in a voice that sounded more like the voice from the real man inside all that jocularity, "I've thought about Leanne so often. When we were kids, she always kept the pot stirred, made life interesting. Too bad she turned on us when she left Austin. I've missed her." He shook his big head. "Now it's too late, too late."

Katherine knew how he felt. But she couldn't let his version pass unchecked.

"She felt you had turned on her," she said. "You and your mother."

He looked up, as if jarred suddenly out of a reverie. "No, ma'am. Certainly Mother was real mad at the mess she was making of her life back then. She was concerned it reflected badly on the family. She maybe felt that way for a while, but all these years it was Leanne who refused to see us."

Katherine looked down at her feet and, as if she were a bird looking down on earth from a great height, she saw the pattern of disrupted relationships in her family. This man missed his dead sister and had never made the hour drive to see her. Leanne, bitter to the death because her family had disowned her, had never tried to mend the rift. Anne Driscoll, a dying old woman, had made no moves to heal old wounds. And she, Katherine, perhaps the worst of all—pretending not to care about a father who loved her—it was all ludicrous and she didn't want to play her part anymore.

She glanced up. Cooper was speaking, back to his hearty tone. "Well, Katherine—is that what you're called now, or are you still Katie like when you were a little girl?"

"Katherine is fine."

"And you call me Coop, like everyone does. Uncle Coop doesn't sound right, does it, since we skipped knowing each other during your growing up?"

She nodded.

"Well, this must be real hard for you. I hear you came by the zoo yesterday to see Lester without knowing…what had happened. Did you have a chance to talk with him before that?" His deep-set eyes were totally encircled by skin so dark it looked charred.

"No. I didn't," she said, feeling the weight now of all those silent years. "I had gotten a letter from him inviting me to come, but when I got there he was dead."

"A letter? Giving you family news and such?" he asked.

Katherine seemed to be caught constantly unprepared. If only she knew whether she could trust this man. Then she could ask for help in deciphering the photos and documents. But it was safer to trust no one.

"He just asked me to come talk," she said.

"Sam says you hadn't seen Lester at all since you and Leanne moved away."

"Sam McElroy?"

"Yes, ma'am. He called last night, said you'd been in and might need some help taking care of things."

"Oh. Nice of him," she said, surprised.

"He said you haven't seen Lester all this time," he repeated.

"No," she admitted, "I haven't."

He smiled, showing every one of his dazzling teeth. "Well, I'd like to catch up and know all about you. I know you graduated from Trinity and I know you're a dog trainer with a successful business in Boerne, but that's about all I know."

"What Daddy means is you've done better than me," Sophie said. "I flunked out of UT after one semester and have never been off the family payroll."

Cooper protested in an injured tone that he didn't mean anything of the sort.

Lucy appeared carrying a silver tray with four glasses on it. She set it down on the massive oak coffee table in front of her husband and handed out the drinks, each with a small hand-stitched napkin. Katherine was glad to get hers, a huge crystal wine goblet full of ice-cold Chablis. Lucy had also brought a plate of mushrooms stuffed with cheese and spinach. Katherine slipped one into her mouth. It was heaven and boded well for dinner, which she hoped would be soon. She was starving.

When Lucy left again to tend to dinner, Katherine told them that his information about her business being successful was out of date. She told them about how she had started the business in high school when she worked for a trainer and made extra money by raising and training golden retrievers. When she had finished her wine, she told them about her financial problems and the likelihood that she would lose it all in less than three weeks. She told them about Ra and admitted she had come to see her father because he had promised financial help.

"Well, damn. I sure know how that feels," Coop said, leaning toward her and patting her knee. "We're getting snake-bit by this economy, too. I'd help you out if I had a pot to pee in right now. May I ask if Lester left you enough to make a difference?''

"No. Travis Hammond tells me he died in debt. So I'm puzzled about what he was intending.''

"No life insurance or anything?'' asked Coop.

"No.''

"Damned puzzling,'' he muttered. "What are your plans?''

"I'm going to work at the zoo, starting tomorrow,'' Katherine said. "I just talked about it with Sam McElroy.''

"Oh, that's great!'' Sophie squealed. "I'm there mornings, in the development office. We can have lunch. What are you going to do?''

"Menial stuff, I think. In the reptile house.''

Sophie rolled her eyes up and said, "Oy. Poor baby. Stokes is a Simon Legree. I've heard he has a fit if there's so much as a fingerprint on the glass of one of the exhibits.''

Cooper leaned forward in his chair. "That's what makes for a world-class reptile collection, little girl. We've got a second-class zoo here except for Alonzo Stokes's area. Folks come from all over the world to see his collection. Only zoo in the world to breed bushmasters with any success. If you want to learn the zoo business, you can't do any better than working for Alonzo Stokes, Katherine.''

Uncomfortable with so much talk about herself, Katherine felt compelled to ask him about his collection. He launched into what sounded like a canned presentation—stories he had told exactly the same way countless times. Each head in his collection had a story attached to it. He had hunted everywhere—Kenya, Botswana, India, Nepal, the Arctic Circle—but it seemed to Katherine he had learned nothing of those places except what could be shot there.

He stopped talking when Lucy automatically brought them a fresh round of drinks.

Sophie, who had been sitting on a zebra-skin rug with her head resting against the sofa and her eyes closed, took advantage of the lull. "How are things going?'' she asked, looking up at Katherine. "Is it pretty grim settling your father's affairs?''

"Well, I'm not sure. The police are keeping the body for a while, so I don't know about a funeral. I've been trying to call Mr. Hammond today to... get some things squared away, but—''

Coop interrupted. "You couldn't get him. I've been trying, too. But it figures. Deer season, archery only, opened yesterday. The ol' boy must be out at his ranch—he insists on no phone, so he can escape his clients, like me.''

During the silence that followed, Coop took a cigar from a box on the coffee table. He held it up to Katherine. ''Do you mind?'' he asked, already sticking it in his mouth. Katherine shook her head. She did mind, but it was his house. And she was trying to decide how to broach the next subject.

As he fired up a lighter and applied it to the cigar, she said, ''I'd like to see my grandmother while I'm here. I was wondering when might be a good time for me to visit her.''

Coop made quick, wet sucking noises as he drew on his cigar. ''This really isn't a good time for it, Katherine. She's not well at all now, and I don't know what kind of reception you'd get. At this juncture she's not up to any... upsets.''

''But Dad, she might like...'' Sophie began.

''You really don't know much about it, Sophie,'' he said sharply. ''You haven't seen her this past week. She's deteriorated.''

Sophie's fair skin showed a dark-red flush of blood under the surface. She lowered her head to hide the signs of embarrassment.

Katherine felt a rush of empathy for her—being rebuked like that. And she did not want to give in so easily. ''What's wrong with her?'' she asked, aware of how harsh the question sounded.

Cooper puffed on his cigar. ''Well, besides being eighty-one, she's had a series of strokes. It's left her with some paralysis on the left side. She's been in and out of consciousness this week, mostly out.''

When Lucy's voice crackled over an intercom to announce that Coop had a phone call, he got up from his chair. ''I'll take that in the office,'' he said.

As soon as he was gone, Sophie scooted closer to Katherine's feet. ''He tends to take over a conversation,'' she said softly, ''but later we can talk about the real stuff. He zonks out after dinner.'' She pointed at the empty glass sitting on the coffee table and rolled her eyes.

''I haven't always lived at home,'' Sophie said. ''This is temporary. I've just had a messy divorce. But I lived in Dallas while I was married to this shithead for ten years. You ever been married? Or lived with anyone?''

''No,'' Katherine said. ''I was close once, but he objected to dogs in the bedroom.''

They both laughed.

"Well, I'm taking a vow of celibacy from now on," Sophie said. "Celibacy and poverty—makes life simpler."

Katherine was wondering if dinner would ever come. She looked surreptitiously at her watch. It was eight-thirty, and she was accustomed to eating at six.

The call finally came. Lucy appeared in the door ringing a little silver bell. Katherine and Sophie followed her to a small breakfast area off the kitchen, where she had set an elegant table. Mirrored place mats and lots of silver reflected the light from five tall glass oil lamps in the center of the table.

Coop came in looking flustered. "Sorry, ladies. Business," he said.

They sat down at the table while Lucy brought in a platter with rosemary-scented beef tenderloin surrounded by little roasted potatoes and thin green beans. Katherine was ravenous.

"I hope you like it rare," Lucy said, adding a basket of cinnamon rolls and an open bottle of Beaujolais to the table.

"Yes. Oh, yes. It looks so good," Katherine said just as the doorbell rang.

"I'll get it," Sophie said, grabbing a potato and popping it whole into her mouth as she left the table.

Lucy began to cut succulent slices of the meat with a carving knife. Before she had a chance to serve it, Sophie returned breathless and flushed. "Katherine, a Lieutenant Sharb is here from the Austin Police. He says he needs to see you immediately on urgent business."

As she rose from the table, Katherine looked wistfully at the slices of beef tenderloin, her mouth still watering with hunger. That uneaten meal she would remember as the most desirable she had ever seen.

ELEVEN

KATHERINE'S HUNGER simmered as she waited for the policeman to get down to it. Sharb sat forward on the edge of a large easy chair, his face unshaven or shaved so long ago it didn't matter. One blunt thumb relentlessly ruffled the edges of the notebook resting on his knees while the other thumb snapped the button on the end of his ballpoint pen—in and out, in and out.

They were sitting in a dark-paneled room with the door shut. Sophie had called it the library when she ushered them in, but Katherine was still looking for the books. Other than a stack of old *National Geographics,* there wasn't anything that even resembled a book.

Long after Sophie's footsteps had faded away, Sharb remained silent, only his nervous thumbs showing any sign of life. If this was standard police procedure to make people talk, it was damned effective, Katherine thought. So uncomfortable was the silence, she had to hold her tongue between her teeth to keep from speaking. Did he somehow know about her trip to the self-storage place last night? Had he found out about the envelope her father had left? It was clear something new had come up.

Finally, as if he'd made some sort of decision, he gave the pen button one last big click and began. "Miss Driscoll, I need to know why you called Travis Hammond fifteen times today and left urgent messages on his machine."

Katherine was nonplused by the question. Something had happened, something bad. "What's happened?" she blurted out.

"Let me ask the questions. What was so urgent that you needed to talk to him about? And don't tell me it was routine matters in connection with settling your father's estate. I listened to your messages on the tape. You sounded angry and upset." He sat totally still now, hands at rest, the concentrated force of his attention on her.

She had to answer the question. She didn't want to because in the back of her mind lurked the fear that it might turn out to be somehow incriminating to her father. But the grim set of Sharb's black-stubbled jaw left her no choice. He was the law, however unappealing.

"In my father's checkbook registers," she said slowly, "I noticed that every month for the past twenty-nine years, as far back as I found records, he paid almost half his income to Travis Hammond. For the past five years that amounted to thirteen hundred dollars a month. I wanted to know what it was for."

Sharb allowed a sound, half-hiss, half-whistle to escape his lips.

"The canceled checks were stamped by the Bank of Belton, into an account there, endorsed by Travis Hammond," she added. "I called him to ask what the payments were for."

Sharb rested his pen on the notebook and ran a hand over his jaw, making a rasping noise. "We'll look into that as soon as the banks open in the morning. You have any theories about it you might want to share with me?"

Katherine shook her head. "What's happened, Lieutenant?" Sensing it was going to be unpleasant, she pulled her head in a little tighter to her shoulders, to get ready. She noticed that her hunger had vanished.

Sharb kept his hand cupping his jaw, partly covering his mouth as he spoke. "Mr. Travis Hammond was found four hours ago on his ranch in Kingsland by some deer hunters—legitimate ones, it's archery season, and they're licensed for it. He was impaled on the antler of a dead buck. Both him and the buck had been dead for many hours, probably since early morning. The hunters are being treated for shock. I've just come from there and I can't say I blame them." He shook his head. "Ugly scene."

He rubbed hard at the reddened lower rim of one eye as he looked at Katherine. "What do you think of that? Another animal gone berserk. Maybe it's the beginning of a general uprising, huh, where they're going to revolt and take over the world. What do you think?"

Katherine felt very cold. All that time she had been calling him, angry and demanding, the old man had been lying dead. She folded her arms around herself and saw behind her eyelids the frail old attorney making an impassioned plea for her not to judge so harshly the mistakes that others made when they were young. "He certainly wasn't killed by a deer," she thought. She was surprised when Sharb answered because she didn't know she'd spoken it aloud.

"No more than your father was killed by a tiger. I want a word-by-word description of your conversation with him yesterday. Everything. If he said it looked like rain, I want to hear about it."

Katherine repeated everything she could remember about the interview. Then she added, "He seemed very nervous, worried, anxious, but I don't know what he's usually like."

"Well, I should think he would be nervous after getting that note."

"Note?"

"Just like the one your father had in his hip pocket when he was murdered."

Katherine sat forward in her chair, her heart racing. "What note?"

"A warning note. It said"—he closed his eyes and recited—"'Lester, Put your house in order. Justice is nigh. An eye for an eye, a tooth for a tooth. Pointman.'"

"And Mr. Hammond had a note like that, too?"

He gave a nod. "Came in the mail about a week ago. His secretary, the little granddaughter, saw it when she opened the mail. She said he was indeed very nervous the last week. He may have destroyed the note because we haven't been able to find it."

He started to lean back in the chair, but discovered it was so deep, he couldn't do it and keep his feet on the floor, so he perched uncomfortably back on the edge. "Now, Miss Driscoll, if you got a note like that, wouldn't you go to the police with it?"

Katherine didn't answer. She was thinking of her father's asking her to come soon and wondering if the note had had anything to do with his haste.

Sharb prodded. "Unless you were up to something, huh? Is that what you're thinking?"

"Was there a date on the note?" she asked.

He shook his head.

"I was wondering if the note had anything to do with my father writing me to come to Austin. He stressed urgency." Again she was astonished that she had spoken aloud. Something about Sharb got her talking. Whatever technique he was using seemed to be working.

Sharb, for the first time, smiled at her, showing tiny, crowded teeth. "I was wondering that, too. And you know what else? I'm wondering if your coming has something to do with these events. After all, you arrive to see Lester Renfro, he's just been killed. You have a meeting with Travis Hammond, you call him on the phone, and he's killed. Is this just a coincidence? Are you bad luck—some sort of catalyst?''

Katherine instantly saw an image of herself arriving in town yesterday, brimming with anger and bitterness, so wrapped up in her own concerns she couldn't see past her nose. In spite of all her efforts to stop them, tears filled her eyes and spilled out. "I'm wondering, too," she said.

"Hey," he said. "Don't do that. I didn't mean to—just don't do that." He jumped to his feet and stood looking down at her. He pulled his handkerchief out of his breast pocket, looked at it and stuffed it back in quickly.

Katherine didn't know what was happening to her. She never used to cry, hadn't cried for years, and here she was dissolving into tears at any provocation. In front of strangers. She used the back of her hand to wipe her face.

He held a palm up to her. "Now, okay. Don't be so sensitive. I really didn't mean that the way it sounded. I meant I wonder why this is happening now, if your coming could have anything to do with it. But please don't do that."

Katherine looked up at him with wet eyes. It was surprising to see the effect her tears had on him. He didn't seem to be a man who would be bothered, but since it had caught his attention, she might as well get something out of it. She lowered her eyes and sniffed. "Please tell me the other things, about my father's...murder. You feel certain it was murder."

"Oh, yes. Oh, yes. It was." He held up a stubby forefinger. "Number one is the note. Someone—this pointman—has been threatening him." He raised his middle finger. "Number two is the wire. You know that the glass in the window was reinforced with wire. The window could have been broken from outside by a tiger, but the wire is another matter. It was cut absolutely clean. My man in the lab tells me even a tiger from Hell couldn't do that. Only a very sharp pair of wire-cutters."

He held up three fingers now and shook them for emphasis. "Number three is the traces of rotten meat on the inside of the door on the threshold. This one I'm real proud of 'cause not many of my colleagues would've been thorough enough to analyze the back of the door. Now McElroy and Dieterlen tell me the tigers are always fed in their cages. The food comes from the kitchen, they cart it in through the main door. It never goes into that little room. It would just never be there, so it wasn't the remains of zoo food. And four..." He looked up at her shyly, as if reluctant to tell her what four was, but then continued. "Four is that on your father's skin and clothes, even in his hair and eyebrows, we found traces of rotten meat, the same as on the door—beef, they think."

Katherine had never listened so intently in her life. She found she was actually leaning forward and turning one ear toward him.

He stopped his recital, but continued to hold the four fingers aloft. Katherine heard the heavy sound of her own breathing as she began to spin the story in her head.

"Now," he said, "can you make something of all that? Assume it was murder, just to humor me, and tell me how it could be done. You're an animal trainer. Must know something about animals, I suppose. Give me a scenario."

She nodded slowly and spoke as if in a trance. "The murderer picks a day when the cats had been fasting and are really hungry," she began.

"Good, good!" He smiled at her. "Go on."

"He or she somehow gets in early without being seen or stays all night. That wouldn't be hard for an employee, I think. He brings a piece of rotten meat to excite the tiger. He . . . rubs it on the door to keep the tiger right there. He brings wire-cutters." She paused, visualizing the tiger house, the tiny concrete room.

"Let's see. When my father gets there at six-fifteen, he...oh, hits him on the head or chokes him, or, if he's very strong, breaks his neck. Then, oh God, then he rubs the meat all over him and pushes him out into the exhibit. He breaks the window, using I don't know what, something heavy, but some of the wire won't give way. He's anticipated that, though, and he has his wire-cutters."

Sharb looked at her, nodding, his black eyes shining. "Just the way I see it." Then he lifted his notebook a few inches and slapped it sharply against his knee. "But why go to all that trouble? Why not just knock him off?"

"Well, in my father's case, he almost pulled it off, getting everyone to think the tiger did it."

"Yeah. But this deer thing—who would believe a man was gored by a deer? C'mon. Why go to all the trouble to make it look that way? Think about it: the nut'd have to go out, shoot the deer—it was shot with an arrow—then shoot the lawyer, looks like he was arrow-shot, too, right in the chest, then drag the deer to the lawyer or the lawyer to the deer, and then hoist the lawyer up onto the antler and stick one of the prongs, whatever you call them—I'm no hunter—into the wound of the arrow. Looks like that's what he did. Jesus."

Katherine was silent, absorbing it. Then she said, "You seem certain the same killer did both these."

He lifted his open palms and rolled his eyes up. "Hell, yes. Aren't you? Travis Hammond's granddaughter can't duplicate the threat note exactly, but when we showed her the one from Lester Renfro's pocket, she confirmed that the handwriting, the paper, and the sentiments were almost exactly the same on the one that came in the mail addressed to Hammond. Sure, the same man did these murders.

"And you know something, Miss Driscoll? He's a real evil son of a bitch. I know it. I have a foolproof technique for detecting them. You know how I do it? The hair on the back of my fingers stands straight up. Here. Look at that." He held out the back of his stubby hand for Katherine to examine. The thick black hairs on his fingers were standing erect.

"Causes a prickly feeling when I get into something like this." He looked down at his notebook for the first time, flipped the page and read for a minute, moving his lips slightly. "Let me ask you something else. What is the connection between your father and Travis Hammond? I know Hammond drew up your father's will and was handling his estate, but what else do you know about their relationship?"

"Nothing but what I've already told you. Mr. Hammond was the attorney for the Driscolls. He told me yesterday that he met my father when he married my mother, but he didn't really get to know him well until they worked together a few years ago on the committee for planning the new Phase Two cat exhibits."

"But if he's been receiving money for twenty-nine years, he was lying. There must be more to it," Sharb said.

Katherine nodded. "Yes. There must have been."

"We'll get on that right away. You can count on it."

"Oh," Katherine said, "this probably doesn't have anything to do with it, but my mother always felt very friendly toward Travis Hammond, really the only person in Austin she felt that way about. She kept in touch with him, until she got sick a few years ago."

Sharb nodded.

"Really I think my uncle, Cooper Driscoll, might know more about the relationship between Mr. Hammond and my father."

"Yeah. I plan to ask him about it when I finish with you. He had two calls on Hammond's answering machine, too. Big stick at the zoo, Cooper Driscoll, big stick all over town, huh? Though I hear he's had some financial setbacks of a major kind.''

"So I hear. I just met him tonight for the first time. Well, the first time since I was five.''

"Izzat right? Why's that?''

"There was a—well, I don't know what you'd call it—a rift, I guess, in the family when my mother and I moved away, not just a rift with my father, but with her family, too. And we just never saw any of them again after that.''

"Yeah. But why not?''

"Oh, the usual. I'm sure you see it all the time. My parents got divorced. My mother felt alienated and rejected by her family.'' Katherine squirmed in her chair. This was not something she liked talking about. And anyway, it was irrelevant.

"Yeah,'' Sharb persisted, "I've seen some real humdingers of . . . what do you call it? Rifts. But usually people get back together eventually with their families, their parents and brothers and sisters. But not your family. So what happened?''

Katherine felt suddenly pressured, and warm. It was stuffy with the door closed. "Well, I'm not sure. There was a fight.'' She lowered her eyelids and remembered: *I woke up in a sweat in the middle of the night. There was screaming and running. I was shivering, terrified of . . . something.* "My mother and I left my father,'' she said. *My mother, hysterical, weeping, grabbed me by the arm, dragged me out of the house, into the car.* "It was pretty awful, even thinking about it now. Everyone was mad at everyone.'' *I ran back to say good-bye. The dog, the dog I had loved and who had loved me in return, sprawled on the bedroom floor, eyes and mouth wide open.* "I don't know exactly what it was about. I was only five and I just don't remember.''

Katherine lifted her lids. "It can't matter now.'' That was more than she'd said about that time to anyone, ever.

When the phone on the table next to Sharb's chair began to shrill, they both stared at it until it stopped. Then Sophie came thudding down the hall and knocked on the door. "Phone for you, Lieutenant Sharb,'' she called, breathless, through the door.

"I got it,'' he said, picking it up. "Sharb here.'' He listened and said, "Good. A half hour more here. I need to talk to Mr. Driscoll, then I'll need to pick up from Miss Katherine Driscoll some canceled checks we need to look into tomorrow, at a bank in Belton. Then I'll be in. Okey dokey?''

He put down the phone and looked at Katherine. "Travis Hammond was killed with an arrow for sure. He'd gone out early to hunt, wanted to take advantage of the season, his wife said. Avid hunter. This will come out in the press tomorrow, Miss Driscoll. So will the new information about your father's death. You should prepare for the publicity. What are your plans?"

"I'm going to stay in Austin awhile, get things settled. And I start working at the zoo tomorrow," she said.

His mouth gaped open for a moment. "Why?"

"I need the money. You know about my financial problems in Boerne, and all my father left me was a couple of Lean Cuisines in the freezer, so I asked Sam McElroy for a job."

He began snapping his pen furiously for a minute. Then he said, "I wish you wouldn't."

"Why?"

He stuck his arm out toward her and turned it over so she was looking down on the back of his hand. The hairs between the knuckles still stood erect and, in spite of herself, she felt the prickle on her own hairless fingers.

"I can't explain it," he said. "I just wish you wouldn't."

TWELVE

WHY DID IT have to be snakes?

Katherine clicked the padlock shut and leaned over to scratch her ankle. Anything else she could at least tolerate. Anything in the entire world but these squirming, twisted, smelly vipers.

After thirteen days of working here, she still hadn't gotten used to their proximity. She felt constantly edgy and her skin prickled as if she were about to break out in a rash.

And it had been almost two weeks with no progress on any front. The only thing she'd accomplished was losing ten pounds she hadn't wanted to lose. Every morning she had awakened before dawn in her father's house and done the grim countdown: the number of days left until the foreclosure. Now there were only seven.

She stuck her key into the padlock on the next exhibit and sprang it open, then lifted it off the hasp so she could open the door a crack to peek inside. Beadlike dark scales glinting in the light, the two long bushmasters lay so intricately intertwined you couldn't tell which head belonged to which snake. They lay under a silk fern near the front of the exhibit. Good. The farther away, the better.

She shut the door softly so as not to attract their attention since they might be sleeping, but who could tell with creatures whose eyes were eternally open in a glassy stare. She reached into the canvas shoulder bag with the huge cloth gauntlet that protected her left arm past the elbow and pulled out a quivering white mouse. With her right hand, she squeezed the scissorlike handle of the long feeding stick to open the clamp and, holding her breath, stuffed the mouse in and let the clamp close slowly on its squirming body.

Most of the snakes ate dead mice, freshly killed by "cervical dislocation," as the disgusting Alonzo Stokes called it, grinning as he pronounced the words. But not these prized bushmasters. Hatched and raised personally by Alonzo Stokes's own hands, they were so finicky, he maintained, they could eat only living mice, stuffed right into their horrendous gullets. God.

She opened the door again and inserted the feeding stick with its trembling offering toward the larger snake, which raised its flat head at the mouse's approach and flicked its black forked tongue in the direction of the warm blood. She pressed the mouse right against the snake's sinister slit of a mouth, which opened slightly in response to the pressure. The mouth appeared nowhere near large enough to receive this adult mouse, but she'd seen the impossible happen before, so she persisted and watched the unhinged jaw open and open, until finally it gaped wider than the snake's own body. Inexorably, the jaws spread around the mouse. Suddenly the mouse stopped its shuddering and went limp. Probably shock, or the venom may have found its way to the small central nervous system.

She felt a ripple of repulsion start in her neck and undulate down her body. This was accompanied by the now familiar urge to scratch all over. It was almost instinctual, this fear and loathing she was powerless to control. She had thought it would wear off with exposure to the creatures, but it hadn't diminished an iota in the almost two weeks she'd been working in the reptile house. Oh, God, give me a vicious Doberman anytime.

When the mouse was firmly wedged in the gaping maw, she squeezed the handle of the stick to open the clamp and release the mouse, just as she had been taught.

She watched to be certain that the snake had firm control and was using its backward-curving fangs to move the mouse toward its esophagus before she withdrew the stick. Reaching into the bag for another mouse, she found she had been holding her breath during the procedure and had to gasp for air as if she'd been underwater. Panting, she shut the door and leaned her shoulder against the protruding white fiberglass box which formed the back of the exhibit. A sign on the door announced the correct antivenin in case of a bite, and a neon-orange sticker proclaimed: HOT! As if she could forget that these were highly venomous snakes, fully capable of inflicting a lethal bite, not just on a mouse, but on a full-grown human being.

To reassure herself, she glanced toward the big red emergency button that was to be pushed in case of a snakebite. She flinched in surprise when she saw Alonzo Stokes slouched against the refrigerator watching her. He gave a jerky thumbs-up with a nicotine-stained thumb and grinned. Under the cold fluorescent lights, the pockmarks on his cheeks looked like moon craters. She didn't smile back. God, the man must have had a world-class case of acne fifty years ago.

This was her first solo feeding after his intensive tutorial last week and, predictably, there he was watching, checking that everything was done perfectly for his darlings. Katherine thought she had known perfectionists before, but this man was fussy and demanding beyond anything she had seen. He oversaw every detail of what went on in the reptile house, even though he was a curator and most curators did not get into the day-to-day work of caring for the animals. But Alonzo Stokes personally trained all keepers, supervised the Tuesday feedings, checked the cage cleaning, even climbed in and scrubbed rocks to demonstrate how he wanted it done.

He had explained to her why the bushmasters merited this special feeding treatment. They were often fussy eaters, difficult to maintain in captivity. He said the day the first clutch of twelve eggs hatched in his office was one of the best days of his life.

Big deal. Snakes fucking. Disgusting. Just the sort of thing to excite the senses of an Alonzo Stokes. They even had their own special room in the back for breeding so they could have more space and privacy. A snake brothel.

She took a deep breath and reached into the sack for another mouse to feed to the smaller bushmaster. She opened the door and repeated the process, relieved that the snake opened its mouth and received the mouse readily and that the other one seemed totally involved in the slow and horrible digestion of a whole live mouse. That was the one good thing about feeding these creatures: at least you could be sure that a mouth stuffed with mouse could not attack.

As soon as she had withdrawn the feeding stick, she closed the door firmly, put the padlock back, and snapped it shut—a beautiful sound.

She turned to see if the curator was still watching. He was. No doubt to be sure she recorded on each snake's record card what she had just done—one of the many cardinal rules. She removed the gauntlet and held it in her teeth while she pulled a pen from her pocket and filled in the two large index cards on top of the exhibit box. Underneath the last entry she wrote the date and "1 A," indicating she had successfully crammed one adult mouse into each of the bushmasters. The classification of mice used on these cards made her ill: "F" was for "fuzzy"—a newborn mouse; "P" stood for "pinky"—a baby; "J" was for "juvenile"; and "A," for "adult." Somehow she was sure that Alonzo Stokes had come up with these classifications. It was the sort of thing that would amuse him.

She put the glove back on and looked up to see Alonzo's mouth twisted in what might be a smile in a normal person; but after a two weeks' exposure to his idiosyncrasies, she knew it to be a grimace of scorn. Wearing gloves was not recommended for working with snakes, he had told her. None of the other four reptile keepers wore them.

"They just make you careless and reduce your dexterity," Alonzo explained. "And they really don't give you much protection. Most of the snakes have fangs long enough to bite right through if they get the chance. And what about the rest of your body? Are you going to wear body armor?" Still, she felt the need to wear the one glove. It provided a layer, albeit an inadequate one, between the reptiles and herself. It kept her skin from crawling right off her body.

When she saw Alonzo turn and head toward his office at the back of the building, she exhaled and got on with the work.

The Gaboon vipers were the next charges in her new area of responsibility. She unlocked and opened the door to peer in at them. One was curled up in its hiding box; she saw the blunt tip of its tail protruding. But where was the other, the bigger one, the female? Her eye scanned the exhibit in panic. Sometimes it was hard to find even these big snakes because the exhibits were filled with rocks and artificial plants to replicate the snake's natural habitat. Ah! She drew back with a jerk when she saw the big one right under the door.

She knew that because the exhibit floor was a foot lower than the door, it was unlikely a snake could escape while the door was opened briefly, but still, when she saw the viper's broad flat head rising toward the opening, she panicked and slammed the door shut, holding it closed. God. Would she ever get over this fear? It was wearing her to a frazzle. Hundreds of times a day she caught sight of a snake and her body involuntarily tensed, ready to run for her life. Each time she'd hold her ground, grit her teeth and carry on. But where was it going, all that adrenaline that got released? It seemed to be accumulating as a sour bile in her stomach that had made eating almost impossible.

She pulled the list out of her shirt pocket and confirmed that the Gaboon vipers were to have one live mouse each, not force-fed.

Well, that was something. At least it gave the mice a sporting chance.

She reached in her bag and pulled out two squirming mice. Quickly, she cracked the door open, just wide enough, and pushed them through the narrow opening. The first one tumbled into the cage obligingly, but the second one, a handsome, nervous-faced piebald, had hooked its long incisors into the glove's empty tip above her index finger. She inserted the finger with the mouse hanging from it through the door and tried to shake it off, but when it let go, it lurched backward and fell to the floor just under the cage, hitting the ground running. She knelt quickly to retrieve it, but the mouse had scampered under the baseboard beneath the cages before she could make a grab at it.

Damnation. Well, it was gone. Nothing she could do about it now.

As she rose from her knees, she smacked her head smartly on the sharp corner of the exhibit door. Ow. Shit! Still open. She thrust the gloved hand up and slammed it shut. That's all I need on my first try feeding them alone—a mass escape. She stayed hunkered down in front of the cage feeling the tears fill her eyes as they did regularly these days. Her hatred for the reptile house was unspeakable. This had been the worst thirteen days of her life. All she wanted was to go home, but in another week there wouldn't be any home to go to, and she was no closer to solving her problems than she had been when she started here.

A deep voice above her head said, "How's it going, Katherine? Need any help?"

She looked up and was comforted to see Wayne Zapalac, one of her fellow reptile keepers. He had gone out of his way to be kind and helpful to her since her first day on the job—so kind that she was beginning to overcome her initial bias against his appearance.

"I just lost one of the live mice," she said. "It must be right around here."

With a quick knee-bend, Wayne squatted on thick, powerful thighs and surveyed the floor. He held a hand up to Katherine to keep her from speaking as he inched his way across the floor toward the incubator with the baby tree boas. His work boots made no sound at all. With a graceful lunge, he flew forward, shot out a hand under the incubator and came up with the spotted mouse in his fist.

"Wow," Katherine said, truly impressed with the capture. She opened the door a crack. "It goes in there," she said.

Wayne flicked it in easily, then opened the door all the way as he stood up. Resting his thick, hairy arms on top of the exhibit, he leaned over and gazed down into it, watching one of the vipers begin to stir and flick its tongue out. From wrist to bulging biceps his arms were covered with crude tattoos. She wasn't sure what the pictures were because she had felt embarrassed to look directly at them before. But now she could stare without his noticing. One was a scroll saying, "Semper fidelis," and another was a serpent coiled around a branch. Underneath it said, "Don't tread on me."

He looked up at her. "The feeding's a little rough first time, isn't it?" he asked.

"Yeah," she confessed. "I like the mice. Sometimes I feel like I'm feeding a higher life form—these bright-eyed mammals—to sustain a lower one."

He chuckled a low, from-the-belly sound. His neck was so thick that his head appeared to rest right on his sloping shoulders. "I know. Reptiles weren't my first choice either. I had my heart set on working with the big cats when I came here. Actually, it was your father who decided I really wasn't cut out for it. He thought my presence stirred the cats up—something about my energy. I was disappointed then, but he may have done me a favor. I've come to love some of these snakes."

The question erupted from her. "Why?"

"Why do I love them?" he repeated with a note of surprise in his voice. "Well"—he looked back into the exhibit, where both vipers were heading toward the piebald mouse trembling in the corner—"these guys because they're so beautiful. Haven't you noticed?" He gestured with his hand for her to join him. All his motions were graceful and gentle, she noticed, in spite of the bulk of his thick, muscled body.

She took a step forward so she could see in, too. He shook his head in wonder. "The pattern looks like an oriental rug, doesn't it? One that's very old and faded. The green and the violet are so soft and pastel they look like a watercolor painting, when the paint's all diluted and washy so you can see the paper through it." Katherine looked in at the big female and saw that it was true. Then she turned her gaze to Wayne, astonished at the sensibility couched in that loutish body. He was transfixed, staring at the vipers. It gave her a chance to study him. In profile, his blunt nose and heavy jaw had a simian look. A tiny diamond stud earring twinkled in his left ear. She estimated his age to be mid-thirties, or maybe older.

"And the head," Wayne continued, "broad and flat like a leaf, and those black triangles that point at that silvery eye. It's something you could never invent." He looked over at her to see her response.

Katherine smiled and looked again at the snakes. It would be very nice to be able to perceive them that way. She wondered if it was possible for her to alter her vision.

Wayne said, "I'm surprised Stokes is letting you do this so soon. I mean he has you working with his favorites when you've been here such a short time. He must have big plans for you."

"Probably wants to get rid of me in record time," she said with a smile.

"Oh, no, you've already outlasted several folks who've been and gone in a flash. One guy only lasted two hours, walked out and slammed the door when Alonzo told him to do a sex check on a mamba that had just been wild caught. You should have seen him run."

She laughed. It felt good to be relaxed enough to laugh, even for a moment.

Then she glanced back to the open door. The male viper had the piebald mouse cornered and was beginning the process of stretching his mouth around it. Katherine closed the door and secured the lock.

She pointed back at the bushmaster exhibit. "How about these? Can you work up any affection for them?"

"The bushmasters?" Wayne asked. "Oh, sure. They're magnificent." He used his key to unlock the door and opened it wide so they both could look in. The mice had disappeared into the snakes and were now visible only as bulges just behind the heads. "They don't have the subtle coloring of the Gaboons, but the raised beaded texture of the scales is nice and the size of them is awesome. They're the largest of all the pit vipers, the longest venomous snake in this hemisphere. This female is only about a seven-footer, but some grow to twelve feet.

"Did you know," he asked, "those little holes the pit vipers have in the sides of their heads are for receiving infrared heat rays? They can find a mouse and strike it accurately in total darkness. I think this was the species involved in that accident where the guy was killed. Stokes was here back then. That may be the reason he's such a stickler about safety and emergency procedures."

"He's a stickler about everything," Katherine said.

"Yeah, but on the subject of safety he outdoes himself. Didn't you have to study the bible and have a test on it?"

"The Emergency Procedures Handbook? Yes, all twenty pages. He gave it to me the first day and tested me on it the second. I have the steps memorized: number one, secure the snake; number two, push the emergency buzzer; number three, call 911 for an ambulance to Brackenridge Hospital; number four, check the cage door for the appropriate antivenin; number five, get said antivenin from the refrigerator; number six, lie still until the ambulance arrives. That's all there is to it."

"Unfortunately," Wayne said, "with these really venomous guys, if they nail you good enough it doesn't matter what you do; you die anyway. The head keeper at a zoo in the East died a couple of weeks ago from a saw-scaled viper bite. Forty years of experience and the best emergency procedures in the country and he died within twenty minutes. The venom just acts too fast if they get it deep."

Katherine felt her stomach undulate. "That makes me feel better," she said.

He looked up at her with a smile. "Sorry. I guess it's the kid in me. Maybe I still want to chase pretty girls with a snake and make them cry."

KATHERINE HAD BEEN counting the minutes to her lunch break. At exactly one o'clock she threw her glove into her locker in the keepers' dressing room, washed her hands twice, and rubbed on a perfumed hand cream. On her way out the back door, she waved through the glass of the service area to Iris Renaldo, the only other woman working in the reptile house, to indicate she was leaving. Iris saluted her in acknowledgment and went back to her job of harvesting fruit flies to feed the poison arrow frogs.

Outside, Katherine sucked the fresh October air into her lungs, trying to banish the reptile odor that seemed to cling to her nostrils even after work hours. Alonzo claimed that reptiles had no odor; there was odor only when keepers did not clean adequately. She scratched her head vigorously and headed toward the Phase II building. It would make her a little late to meet Sophie, but she had developed the habit of dropping in every day during her lunch break to see Brum for a minute. She wasn't sure why she did it, but it was the one thing that seemed to make her feel better.

Her general exhaustion these past thirteen days had been debilitating. After work each day she had collapsed into bed without any dinner and slept as if drugged until the alarm rang at six the next morning. Her desultory attempts to learn more about her father's photographs had uncovered nothing. She was no closer to understanding what he wanted her to do than she had been the night she found them. And Sharb was no closer to solving his murder.

She shuffled along the walk, her head down. For God's sake. Here I am, inside, in great position to learn things, and I get so exhausted every day, I can barely remember to ask questions.

She found herself walking past the dusty paddock that held the white rhinoceros, Teddy. She looked up briefly to watch him standing with his massive horned head over the stockade fence separating him from the female that had been brought in—Ursula, she was called, the great hope for some breeding action. All the keepers were making bets on whether Teddy would get it up when the time came. He certainly seemed interested, the way he was peering over the fence at her. Katherine stopped for a moment to look at the two prehistoric beasts, as monumental and low to the ground as tanks, their hanging folds of thick dried skin caked with mud and dust. But they were clearly eyeing one another with interest. What a mystery sexual attraction is, she thought, not for the first time.

It had been almost a year since she broke off with John Rehnquist and in all that time she hadn't felt even a flicker of interest in any man. Her capacity for it had probably atrophied. She was drying up, like Teddy's hide.

When she came to the now familiar gray metal door, she knocked loudly. "Coming, coming," the nervous voice said through the door as Danny unfastened the multiple locks.

"How's it going?" she asked, smiling at his tense face as he opened the door for her.

"Okay, I guess." He ran his fingers through his limp blond hair, slicking it back over the balding area. "But it's so dumb for me to just sit here all this time when I know how understaffed we are. I really think Sam is overreacting on this. No one's tried to get at these cats. Just keeping them inside for a while is enough. Maybe if you told him that, he'd listen, Katherine."

Katherine headed toward Brum's cage, annoyed by the whine that often crept into Danny's voice. It reminded her too much of her own tendency toward self-pity these days. "Why would it matter what I said? I'm junior to you here, Danny. Why don't you tell Sam yourself?''

He hurried to keep up with her. "Well, I did, kind of. But he's not going to listen to me. You're ... you know, you've got connections." He lowered his eyes. Behind the thick glasses, his eyes were magnified, the lashless lids large and fleshy.

"I'm just another zoo employee," Katherine said. "Believe me, I have no influence on anyone here."

With small fussy movements, Danny picked up a hose that was in her path and coiled it up hurriedly. He hung it on a hook on the wall and adjusted it so it made a perfect circle. "I've scrubbed every tile and drain and bar in this place. There's nothing left to do. I need to get back to work. I don't think I can stand being cooped up here much longer. Would you at least ask Alonzo if he'll request me in reptiles? I know you guys are understaffed over there and I'd really like to get some more experience with the herps."

He was right that they were understaffed and she had the aching muscles to prove it, but Katherine ignored him and turned her attention to Brum, who was lying on his side in the corner of his cage.

Danny persisted. "That guy with all the tattoos and the earring—Wayne Zapalac. He looks like the kind of guy who'd like to loaf around over here. Maybe he'd like to switch with me. You could ask him."

Katherine looked at Danny's earnest face. "The grass is always greener," she said. "He just told me he used to want to work with cats. But I think he's happy where he is now. And I don't think he's lazy at all."

She looked back at Brum and studied him as she did every day. His beauty was irresistible. "Hey, Brumble," she said, trying to catch his attention by moving into his line of vision. But he continued to stare listlessly into space.

"He's depressed," Danny said. "He needs to get outside for some fresh air and exercise. It's cruel keeping him confined like this. He's not used to it. This is how zoos used to be and how the bad ones still are. Animals cooped up in tiny cages, getting more and more crazy from the inaction." Danny leaned over and retied his tennis shoe, nervously jerking the laces tight, as if he were the one going crazy from the inaction.

Brum remained so still he could have been a stuffed tiger.

Katherine glanced up and noticed something she hadn't seen before. It was a metal plaque above the cage. It said,

In peace there's nothing so becomes a man
As modest stillness and humility.
But when the blast of war blows in our ears,
Then imitate the action of the tiger:
Stiffen the sinews, summon up the blood
Disguise fair nature with hard-favour'd rage.

—WILLIAM SHAKESPEARE

She read it over twice and said, "I never noticed that before. I like it." She looked at Danny. "That's advice we could all three benefit from." She turned to Brum and said, "Imitate the action of the tiger, Brum. Stiffen those sinews, summon up the blood."

"Katherine," Danny blurted, "this Lieutenant Sharb came to see me again to ask me questions. I wondered if they'd come up with anything new?"

"Not that I know of."

"They kept asking about whether Lester acted different the last few weeks and I didn't know what to tell them."

Katherine shifted her attention away from Brum. "Did he act different?" she asked.

"Oh, yes. And I told the police this. I didn't want to because I don't want to speak ill of the dead or make them think he was doing anything wrong, but he was a different man the last two months, excited and nervous most of the time. I felt sure something was going on in his life."

"You didn't tell me this. What did he do that was different, Danny?"

"Oh, he would leave me in charge here while he went off on some business of his own. Often. He'd even leave the zoo for long stretches on several afternoons. That was not like him at all, not telling me where he could be reached and leaving during work hours, not like him at all. And he took some days off, too, after years of never even taking his vacation time. Now don't get me wrong, it was okay with me; I like being alone with the cats, but it just wasn't like him.

"I even wondered if maybe he . . ." Danny looked up at Katherine from under thick lids. "This is why I didn't say anything to you, I wondered if maybe he had a girlfriend he was going to see or something."

Or maybe he had to take his camera and check out shipments of animals coming in, Katherine thought. "Maybe that was it," she said. "That wouldn't be so unusual."

"No. I was real shocked to read in the paper that the police suspect murder. But even though it's hard to think of anyone who would want to kill him, it's easier for me to imagine that than to imagine him doing something careless like going into the anteroom before securing Brum in his cage. That would just never happen. He was so careful."

"As fussy as Alonzo Stokes, do you think?"

Danny frowned, "He's pretty fussy, Alonzo, but I really don't know him all that well. When I first came to work here I was rotated into reptiles for two weeks once, so I know he runs a tight ship."

"Yeah. He sure does. Well, I'm late for lunch with Sophie. See you tomorrow, Danny." She smiled and gave him a little punch on the arm. "Hey. Stiffen the sinew, summon up the blood, okay?"

He tried to smile, but kept his teeth covered as if they were shy in the presence of company.

He went through the usual rigmarole of all the locks before she could get out into the fresh air again.

As soon as Katherine walked in the door of the little cafeteria, Sophie waved to her from a table against the far wall. Katherine smiled and waved back. She got a tray and went quickly through the line, grabbing a roast beef sandwich, a bag of potato chips, a chocolate brownie, and a Diet Coke. If she was going to imitate the action of the tiger, she needed a little protein.

Sophie sat with a blueberry Danish and a cup of coffee in front of her. She eyed Katherine's laden tray as Katherine unloaded it. "Good," she said. "I was beginning to think you never eat. How's it going?"

Something about Sophie gave Katherine the freedom to be honest. "Well, my feet feel bruised on the bottom, my home is a week away from being foreclosed, and I feel like screaming every time I see a snake, which is approximately a hundred thousand times a day, but other than that I feel great. How about you?"

"Oh, another day without a drink. Got all the mailers out for the koala opening. Had coffee with Vic Jamail, a short, romantic tryst at the African Plains snack bar. Unfortunately, all he wanted to talk about was you."

"Me?" Katherine felt a flush moving up her neck.

"Uh-huh. Wants to know why you aren't married, why you decided to stay in Austin, whether you like working the reptiles, what you're really like. The man is smitten, I think. And, Katherine, he cleans up nicely. You should see him in a suit."

Katherine laughed. "If he wants to know these things, why doesn't he ask me himself? This isn't junior high."

"Oh, sure it is. You don't really think things change, do you? He talked to me knowing I'd talk to you. Now you're supposed to indicate if you're interested so I can pass it back to him, so he can approach you with some confidence."

Katherine shook her head.

"Well, are you interested or aren't you?"

"I'm not."

"My Lord, think about it, Katherine—a man of forty who's never been married, has no kids, has a paying job and a car of his own, and I think he's got some dark magnetism. Who knows what passions lurk under that silent exterior? How can you say no to finding out about that?"

"I just have no interest right now. Tell him I'm grieving."

Sophie turned her hands palms up in front of her. "Okay. To each his own."

There was a silence while Katherine began eating her sandwich.

"So how's your investigation going?" Sophie asked.

Katherine stopped chewing. "What do you mean?"

"Oh, you know. You can't keep anything from me. This is Cousin Sophie you're talking to. You're trying to find out what happened to your father. And I don't blame you one little bit. I don't like mine much, but if something like that had happened to him, I'd want to find out, too." Her round blue eyes searched Katherine's. "So what have you found out? Spill it all."

Katherine smiled. "Nothing. Not a goddamned thing. I've been a total bust as an investigator." She took a deep breath. "Something I'd like to know about, though, Sophie, is the acquisition records for animals in the past half year. I'd really like to see them. Do you ever run across those when you're working in the office?"

"No. The records I see are on donors, the big givers and the little ones, so we can go after them to squeeze more out of them. We are insatiable in our need for money, as you will discover. The zoo donations and attendance figures have plummeted with the economy. But acquisition records—I think Vic keeps those."

"What about the Driscoll Foundation records, Sophie? Does he keep them, too?"

"No. Daddy keeps those because he runs the foundation now. Vic may have copies of them, though."

"Do you think your father would let me see them if I asked him? So I could learn about the family foundation."

"No. I think he'd probably say not to bother your pretty head with his business."

"What if you asked him for me?"

"He'd say, 'Mind your own damned business, Sophie.'"

"I think I'll ask him anyway," Katherine said, wondering if she could muster the courage.

"If you're interested in the foundation, I can tell you what I know. One thing I've learned working in the development office is that without the Driscoll Foundation the zoo wouldn't be able to grow. We get some gifts and loans from other zoos and an occasional small grant from a donor, but the foundation money is the zoo's lifeblood. You know that Gram set up the foundation and ran it for hundreds of years. Daddy has done it for about two or three years, I think." She put her head close to Katherine's and lowered her voice. "Here's something. The foundation charter says the foundation has to be run by a member of the Driscoll family. So when Daddy's not around anymore, that would be you or me."

Katherine looked up in surprise.

"But it won't be me," Sophie said with a shrug, "'cause Gram thinks I'm a drunk and Daddy never has thought much of my abilities, so even though you come from a black-sheep branch of the family, that leaves you. Anyway"—she laughed the first artificial laugh Katherine had heard from her—"you're older than me."

Katherine took another big bite of her sandwich and a potato chip. She followed it with a sip of Diet Coke. "What's she like?"

"Who?"

"Anne Driscoll."

Sophie groaned. "Gram is like no one you've ever known. She's tough and opinionated and stubborn, but she can be fun. She's the kind of woman you might want to be, but you wouldn't choose her as a mother or a grandmother. All my life it's been 'Don't do this' and 'Don't do that' because Gram won't like it. And if she doesn't like it, she won't leave us her money." Sophie's fair skin began to show pink underneath. She moved her head closer to Katherine's. "Here she gives fabulous amounts of money to the zoo, but she won't . . . well, I know Daddy's made some dumb investments and all, but she could help him if she wanted to.'' She looked directly at Katherine. ''She could help you if she wanted to, but she won't do that either.'' Sophie paused and lowered her eyes. ''You've escaped some things by being separate.''

Katherine nodded. ''But I want to see her, Sophie. I need to see her. Your father was discouraging about it, but I want to see her.'' She sat up straighter. Stiffen the sinews. ''And I'm going to.''

Sophie shrugged. ''I don't know, Katherine. I haven't seen her myself for a couple of weeks. Daddy says she hates people to see her looking so weak and helpless. Vain at eighty-one.''

''I'd like to see her anyway. Do you think it would help to write or call her?''

''No,'' Sophie said, ''but you can try.'' She looked up suddenly over Katherine's shoulder toward the window. ''Don't look now, but the world's shortest police lieutenant is trying to get your attention out there. I thought they had some sort of height requirement in the police department.''

Katherine turned and saw Sharb standing at the window motioning to her. ''Oh. He said he might come by this afternoon. I better go see what he wants.''

As she stood to leave, she put the last potato chip in her mouth and dropped the uneaten brownie, still in its plastic wrapper, into her pocket. ''In case of low blood sugar this afternoon.''

She wasn't quite sure how to say the next thing. She cleared her throat first. ''Sophie,'' she said, ''maybe I could be interested in getting to know Vic. If he asks, tell him to speak for himself. He knows where to find me.''

Sophie opened her eyes wider. ''Sudden change of heart, huh? Okay. I'll tell him.''

THIRTEEN

KATHERINE STOPPED at the entrance to the reptile house and stared down at Lieutenant Sharb in astonishment. "A widow in a wheelchair?" Her voice rose.

"Yup."

"Let me see if I've got this straight. My father sent the checks to Travis Hammond, who deposited them into the account of a Dorothy Stranahan at the Bank of Belton. Every month for—how long?"

Sharb blew his nose into what looked like the same crumpled, gray handkerchief from last week. "The payments go back farther than the records you showed me—thirty years, plus a few months." He tilted his head backward and squeezed a spray from a round plastic bottle into each nostril. "Damn these allergies. I'm here for a few minutes and I can't breathe. The dust, the dander."

Katherine was having shortness of breath, too, but it was from surprise. "And Mrs. Stranahan is an elderly woman confined to a wheelchair, and she lives alone."

"Lived," he said, head still hanging back. "She died August twenty-nine at the age of sixty-two. Heart attack."

Katherine's mouth formed a perfect circle. "Oh. Nearly two months ago. That's why he didn't send a check for September or November. Because she was dead."

"I suppose. The bank notified Mr. Hammond of her death because he was a signer on the account. He might've told your father. Hammond was her executor, though there was nothing much to execute. She lived cheap in a rent house, off what your father gave her and some small disability each month. Left nothing behind except a son who grew up and left home years ago."

"A son?" Katherine said. "My father supporting this woman—I wonder if my father could have..."

"Yeah," Sharb interrupted. "It's what you think of right away. Maybe he fathered the kid and was paying for it. Her neighbors say she didn't talk much, this Dorothy Stranahan, but she did say she lived in Austin before moving to Belton thirty years ago. So she could've known your father then. But why keep on paying long after the kid is on his own?''

"Because she was handicapped?'' Katherine wondered out loud.

Sharb lifted his head and inhaled deeply, making a wet, snuffling sound deep in his sinuses. "Maybe. I showed Lester Renfro's picture around to the neighbors in Belton, but they never saw him. They say she never had any visitors except the Home Health Care people, who came to help her three times a week, and the pastor of Bethel Baptist Church.

"But here's something that works against the love-child theory. Her doctor in Belton says she was afflicted with MS for the thirty years or so she lived here. He thinks she had it at least ten years before that. The son is thirty-nine, according to school records in Belton. This doesn't rule it out, but it's hard to imagine a man having a wild love affair with—well, someone who's crippled. It doesn't track. But the doctor said sex was possible and it didn't stop her from having a kid, so..." He threw his hands up.

Katherine's imagination was running wild now. Solving this riddle was suddenly of primary importance to her. "Have you found out where she lived in Austin or anything?''

"No. We're working on it, but nothing so far. If she did live in Austin thirty years ago, she didn't have a phone, wasn't registered to vote."

Katherine leaned back against the rail that circled an empty display area in front of the reptile house and looked up at the mosaic set into the tan brick. On a background of gold tiles, pterodactyls, alligators, cobras, dimetrodons, salamanders, and frogs coexisted in garish colors. Next to the mosaic a big iron plaque said in deep relief, GIFT TO THE PEOPLE OF AUSTIN FROM THE A. C. DRISCOLL FOUNDATION, 1960. Sharb was looking up too, his nose wrinkled in distaste—at the plaque, the mosaic, or the dust and dander, Katherine wasn't certain.

"Have you located the son?'' she asked.

"No. No one in Belton knows anything about him. After high school he went into the service, they think, around the time of the Vietnam war. He never came back there to live. We're trying to trace him, but none of the armed services shows records under his name."

"What is his name?'' Katherine asked, wondering if she had more relatives than she knew.

"Donald Stranahan, Junior. Donald Senior was out of the picture when Dorothy arrived in Belton. She said he was dead and never gave any more information. So there we are."

"Yes," Katherine agreed. "There we are."

She glanced at her watch. "Hey, I'm late. I need to get back to work."

"I'll come in with you," he said, following her through the door. He smiled his rare smile showing his small crowded teeth. "I'll give you an excuse."

They walked through the two-story entrance hall, where a group of children in navy-blue school uniforms were shrieking and sticking their hands down one anothers' backs. "How do you like it here?" he asked.

"I like the zoo a lot. But I'm a little jumpy around the snakes," she admitted, shrugging toward a display full of yellow-and-green baby tree boas looped around little perches.

"Well, damn. I don't blame you," he said. "You couldn't pay me enough to get me to work here. I hate snakes. They make me want to puke."

"Yeah," Katherine said, leading the way through the staff-only door to the hallway that ran behind the exhibits.

Alonzo Stokes, Wayne Zapalac, and Iris Renaldo were there, gathered around the open door of one of the exhibits. A large plastic garbage can sat open next to the door. Totally engrossed in their task, they didn't even glance up at Katherine and Sharb. Wayne and Iris each held a long snake stick through the open door.

Wayne said very quietly, "Good, Iris, keep holding that bugger down. Yeah, now I've got him." Wayne pulled his stick out quickly. Hanging over the hook was a thick-bodied, dusty-colored snake about four feet long; it writhed desperately and buzzed its tail angrily. Wayne slung it into the garbage can with a thud. Alonzo clamped the lid on and they all looked up and smiled at one another, as the noise of the snake thrashing and rattling against the sides echoed inside the can.

"My, God," said Sharb. "They like doing that. Why are they doing it?"

"To clean the exhibit," Katherine explained. "Usually they can clean with the animal in, but not with the venomous species."

Alonzo Stokes caught sight of them and called out, "Katherine, you're late. We wanted you to get some practice on removals. Come on over here." Katherine had been expecting this; it was the next step in her education. She sighed once and approached, but Sharb stood where he was, as though rooted to the floor.

"Hello, Lieutenant Sharb." Alonzo wiped his hands on his pants and stretched one of the wiped hands out, so Sharb had to take several steps forward to take it. "I'm glad to see you're still on the job. You got any news for us?"

Sharb took the hand and dropped it quickly. "Miss Driscoll was detained on police business," he said stiffly. "Otherwise she would've been back on time."

Katherine felt pleased to be defended. She looked back and forth between Sharb and Alonzo Stokes. Alonzo was a full foot taller than Sharb and probably weighed about the same. The two of them facing each other reminded her of some grade-B horror movie— Aspman meets the homunculus.

"So," Alonzo repeated, "what news have you got?"

"None really," mumbled Sharb, eyes fixed on Wayne, who had put his hook back in the exhibit. "We're working on it. Hey, those are rattlesnakes, aren't they?"

"Yes. Western diamondback rattlers, Lieutenant Sharb, one of our local varieties." He started to drag the garbage can toward the policeman. "Would you like a closer look?"

"Hey, no." Sharb raised a palm in protest and backpedaled toward the door.

Alonzo pushed the can back where it had been and followed. "Lieutenant Sharb, wait a minute. I've been wanting to ask you a couple of things." He lowered his voice. "Couldn't you trace the arrow that was found in the deer that Travis Hammond...uh, tangled with? I've been wondering ever since I read about it in the paper. Used to do a little bow hunting myself and thought maybe you could find where the arrow was bought."

Wayne lifted another squirming snake through the door and said, "Katherine, lid, please."

Katherine walked way around so she would not have to pass near the squirming snake. Then she leaned forward and lifted the lid off, keeping one ear tuned to the conversation between Sharb and Stokes.

"No, Mr. Stokes. We've drawn a blank on that one. Only thing we know is it's an old arrow, eight to ten years old, made by the Sequoia Company, but there's just no way to trace it. Any more ideas for us?"

"No, sir. But—"

"But what?"

"Well, you feel pretty sure the same perpetrator did both these murders?" Alonzo asked.

"Absolutely. I know it."

"Have you got a motive in mind?"

"Not yet. Do you?"

Alonzo licked his thin lips. "No. But them both being connected with the zoo made me wonder if there's some animal-rights zealot out there who hates the idea of caging animals or some such." He tried an approximation of his usual sardonic smile, but it died halfway and became a grimace.

"Well, I suppose it's possible it could be a crazy with a general beef like that," Sharb said, "but I believe it's more personal, Mr. Stokes. I believe the murderer had some sort of personal grudge against the victims, felt they had wronged him in some way."

Alonzo's voice had shrunk to a whisper. Katherine had to strain to hear. "Why do you think that?"

Sharb leaned his shoulder against the staff door and glanced at the garbage can as if to make certain the lid was still on. "Because of the notes they both got. The threat sounded like a cold avenger doing what he had to do."

"And what did those notes say, may I ask?" Alonzo said.

"You may. They said the end was near, that it was a matter of an eye for an eye." As he said the word, "eye," he looked directly into Alonzo Stokes's colorless ones.

Alonzo swallowed hard, his prominent Adam's apple bobbing in his scrawny neck. Katherine was surprised to see in him an emotion that looked a lot like fear. Maybe he was worried that his snakes were the next target.

"So you aren't any closer to catching him than you were last week?" Alonzo asked, recovering his lazy drawl.

"I wouldn't say that, but there's nothing I can talk about," Sharb said, hiking up his shoulders for some more height. His eyes widened as Iris and Wayne lifted yet another snake through the door.

"Okay, take it off," Wayne said to Katherine. She lifted the lid and held it in front of her like a shield while they dumped the snake in with the other two.

The three snakes inside the can sounded like a hive of irate bees. Sharb's face had lost all color. His black hair and omnipresent stubble looked very dark in contrast to the pasty skin. He put a hand on the doorknob as if to make a break for it.

Alonzo strode to the garbage can in two long-legged steps and gave the can a little kick. "Quiet, in there," he said. "You're scaring Austin's finest." The noise in the can escalated to a furious buzzing.

Then Alonzo clapped his hands once. "Okay, Katherine. This last one is small, barely out of infancy. Let's see you hook it. Iris'll help."

Wayne whirled around and fixed Alonzo with a long hard glare, but Alonzo just stared back until Wayne reluctantly handed his stick over to Katherine. He gave her an encouraging pat on the shoulder as she turned to face the open exhibit door.

Katherine leaned forward with the stick in front of her to peer inside the exhibit. The little rattler was in the far corner, pressed against the glass. She held the stick at the very end and poked it in the direction of the snake.

"It's hard to control when you hold it so far at the end," Alonzo said.

Katherine could feel that it was true.

"Look at the way Iris holds hers."

Katherine looked. With her right hand, Iris gripped the stick about halfway down the four-foot handle. Katherine choked up on the stick and found it easier to maneuver as she neared the snake, but the hook on the end was shaking wildly nevertheless. Wayne stepped over behind her and reached around to put his hand on top of hers and guide the stick toward the snake. "Okay," he said in a calm low voice, "now we're going to slide it under him, around the middle, yeah, like that. It's not sharp enough to hurt him, don't worry, now we've got him, whoops!" The snake made a sudden quick lurch forward in an attempt to strike at Iris's hook. Katherine tried to jerk the stick back, but Wayne kept a tight hold on her hand so she couldn't. "Easy. We'll get him. Once you've got the feel, it's pretty smooth."

"Actually," Alonzo said, "that one's a little nippy, has been since birth. You've got to be quick and decisive with him."

Katherine's knees felt rubbery, but Wayne moved a step closer to give support, bracing his chest against her back and keeping his hand tight over hers in control of the stick. "We'll get him this time," Wayne said easily. He guided the stick under the snake and lifted it in a quick motion. Iris pressed her hook down on top of the snake to hold it in place as they lifted it out the door. Alonzo hurried over and removed the lid so they could toss the snake in with the other three. Its tail was rattling ominously.

Alonzo secured the top on the can. "Good," he said. Then he looked up at Wayne. "But don't baby her, Wayne. Just because she comes from a high and mighty family doesn't mean she can't carry her load here."

Wayne spun around to face Alonzo, his skin suddenly mottled with angry red patches. "I'm not babying her and I don't know anything about her family. She hasn't even been here two weeks and you have her doing dangerous things already. When I was new here you didn't have me doing things like that for more than a month."

Katherine felt her face fill with hot blood. She didn't know what the precipitating emotion was—embarrassment at being fought over or the fear making itself fully felt.

"Well, I expect big things from her," Alonzo drawled. "She comes from zoo stock. Her gramma could handle a snake with the best of 'em." He stopped and got a faraway look in his colorless eyes. "So could her daddy," he said. "She needs to learn."

Sharb and Iris were watching the exchange silently.

"Thanks, Wayne," Katherine said with her eyes lowered. "I think I have the feel of it now."

"Okay," Alonzo said. "Iris, show Katherine how to clean the bushmaster room in back. It will be her responsibility from now on. The female's starting to shed, so we want it ready right away. If she's finished we might put them in on Friday, see if we can get some action. Wayne, let's get that rattler exhibit spotless and change out those silk plants. They look pretty chewed up."

Turning toward Lieutenant Sharb, he said, "Anything we can help with before you go, Lieutenant?"

Sharb, still looking pale and uneasy, was leaning over and scratching his ankle furiously. "No," he said. "I'm gone."

As he opened the door, he looked back over his shoulder at Katherine. "Take care, Miss Driscoll."

"Be sure to rinse the Lysol off real good," Iris Renaldo advised Katherine. "We don't want any smells interfering with the pheromones the female gives off. Mr. Stokes says we don't want no competing odors."

They had been scrubbing the olive-drab walls in silence for ten minutes. Katherine straightened up from her squatting position and winced as her head came within an inch of hitting the low ceiling. Damn. One more thing she would never get used to.

The small breeding room was hot and stuffy. The only window was a fixed five-by-ten-inch observation slit high on one wall. Iris had propped the door open with a bucket to give them some air, but there was no circulation that Katherine could discern.

Katherine wanted to rest for a minute, to shake out her arm and let the blood flow back into her hand, but she didn't want to appear lazy to Iris, who never seemed to stop working. She was a machine, Katherine thought, glancing over at the stocky, squat figure with her pants worn low on her wide hips. Her powerful brown arm made big circles with the sponge, her ropy tendons bulging out.

"Mr. Stokes wants things just so for his bushmasters," Iris said suddenly.

"Yeah. I've noticed," Katherine said. "Too bad he doesn't feel that way about the people who work here."

"Oh, he don't show it," Iris said, "but he cares about the people here. I can tell he likes you. And you can learn more about herps from him than anyone in the business. This is one of the top five reptile collections in the whole world, right here. Didja know that?"

Katherine didn't answer. She really didn't give a damn.

Iris went on. Since she had not spoken ten words to Katherine in the past two weeks, it was a surprise to hear her talk. "This is a great facility even if it is almost thirty years old, and we get almost any species we ask the Zoological Society for. But it takes more than money to build a great collection. It takes someone like Mr. Stokes, who's so dedicated."

Katherine couldn't deny that he was dedicated. "Is that how new species are acquired? You just ask the Zoological Society?"

"Usually, yeah. How it works is we ask and the society decides if it's reasonable and then the Driscoll Foundation coughs up the money. Sometimes we acquire through trades or gifts from other zoos. And breeding loans, too. Like those cobra eggs we're incubating are on loan from Detroit."

"How come when money's so tight at the zoo, this department can get anything it wants?" Katherine asked, something she had been wondering as she heard about the need for austerity, but witnessed row after row of cages and aquariums filled with new specimens shipped in from all over the world.

"I dunno. I suppose Mr. Stokes has been here so long he knows how to ask. Also, the herps are the biggest draw. People come to see them."

"Really?" Katherine asked, raising her eyebrows. "More than the other animals?"

"Oh, yes. A fact," Iris said. "The development office does these studies and the snakes and the big cats are the main draws."

"I didn't know people liked snakes that much," Katherine said.

"Oh, they don't like them. But they come to see them. You know, the girls giggle and talk about how slimy and dangerous they are and how awful it'd be if they got loose, and the guys tap on the glass and make like they're big macho men."

Katherine hated to be included in the same category with those girls, but she couldn't deny that she was. "I wish I could like them better," Katherine admitted. "I've worked with dogs all my life, but I can't seem to work up any warmth for snakes, or even much interest. How did you get so—comfortable with them?"

"Oh, I been keeping snakes since I was nine years old." Iris stopped sponging for the first time and turned toward Katherine. Her black eyes, which Katherine had thought dull and hostile, began to glitter as she spoke. "That's when I caught my first indigo. Chico. A sweetheart, so tame, real easy to live with. My mom was against it at first, but when she saw how easy he was, she decided it was better than some smelly flea-bitten dog who'd crap up the yard or a cat who'd be all the time clawin' at the furniture. At one point in high school, I had eleven snakes and two lizards, won the city Science Fair award with my project on shedding. It was so great 'cause Chico was right in the middle of a shed when the judges went by."

She dipped her sponge in the rinse bucket and swirled it over the area she'd just washed. "Maybe it would help if you got one as a pet. A milk snake or an indigo's easy to start with. They eat good. You don't wanna get stuck with no fussy eater. But you're into dogs, huh?"

"Yes. I've been training and breeding retrievers for twenty years. But it seems so natural and instinctive to love dogs. You see a puppy and you want to cuddle it and soon he gets to understand what you say and you can work together on training. I can't see how that happens with snakes; I mean, I wish I understood what the appeal is."

"Lemme see if I can explain it," Iris said, stopping her work again. Her greasy short black hair glistened in the fluorescent lighting of the small room. She stood up and hooked a thumb under the wide brown belt with the brass snake-head buckle, and tilted her head while she thought.

"When I first saw Chico, I just wanted to watch him all the time. He was so clean and smooth. You know indigo snakes? They got these dark-blue scales, shiny, and this easy way of moving, like it's just no sweat, you know? Even the way he ate I liked. People think it's all disgusting the way snakes eat, but it seems to me somehow pure."

She laughed here to shake off the almost mystical expression on her dark face and went back to her vigorous scrubbing. "No chewing or fuss, just take the whole thing in and use every part of it. When you feed a snake you get to feeling how efficient it is. With Chico, it was a lot like you and a puppy really. He loved to curl up with me. Snakes can't control their body temperature, you know, so they love to be next to warm things."

"Do you still have him?" Katherine asked, surprised at how voluble and animated Iris was once she got talking.

"No. He died. I don't have snakes of my own now. I keep some of the snakes from here that need special attention. In my living room."

Katherine stopped sponging. *Snakes at home. In the living room. Oh, my God.* She remembered now. *The glass boxes in the living room. My father brought them home from the zoo. My mother and I were scared to go near them. We hated them. "They can kill you," my mother said. And she was right.*

Katherine shuddered.

"You all right?" Iris asked.

"Oh. yes. I just remembered that when I was little, my father kept snakes in our living room."

They scrubbed in silence for a while.

Finally, Iris said in an uncertain voice, as if she were venturing into a dangerous area, "Funny thing, you having a father who's a keeper like me, then having this rich grandmother who gave the money for this building and for most of the animals in it. I mean, it's so...oh, you know, different worlds." She looked up at Katherine trying to gauge her reaction.

Katherine nodded.

"This is none of my business," Iris continued, "so you just tell me go stick it if this bugs you, but if your grandma's so rich, how come you have to work a job like this? It's not society-lady work like that cousin of yours in the front office, but real, shit-shoveling work."

Katherine smiled at Iris, beginning, to her astonishment, to like her. "I don't even know my grandmother," Katherine admitted.

"I'm working here for the money, just like everyone else. My dog-training and kennel business in Boerne is way down and I've got a lot of debt, so I need to earn money."

Iris nodded vigorously. "Yeah, I know how that goes. It's buying on credit that gets ya. You buy a TV or a VCR and think paying it off'll be a snap, then first thing you know you can't make a payment and they take it back and you lose all the payments you already put into it. And the damn thing don't work right, anyway."

Katherine thought about the stack of unpaid bills on her desk at home. "No shit!" she said.

Iris laughed and turned to look at Katherine, who was surprised to see two big dimples appear in Iris's cheeks.

They worked for a while in companionable silence, two women who knew firsthand the pitfalls of borrowing money.

Finally Iris said, "But since you feel the way you do about herps, I wonder why you weren't assigned to one of the other vacant jobs."

Katherine stopped scrubbing. "What other jobs?"

"Oh, Yolanda over in birds says they need someone there. And I hear they need someone for the hoof stock."

"Do they? How long have they had openings, I wonder?"

"Coupla weeks, at least."

"Hmmm," said Katherine, picturing Sam McElroy looking over the folder on his desk and telling her the only opening was in reptiles. She remembered the surprise on his face when she jumped at the job. She wondered why he didn't want her around.

"Of course, they're gonna need someone in cats, too, now, to replace your dad," Iris said. "Not that he's replaceable really," she added quickly. "But they'll need to hire or promote someone to the head job over there. Danny's real conscientious. And he's got the desire. He begged your father to take him on, but he just don't have the experience yet to be permanent head." She shook her head sadly. "He was so good with them big cats, your dad, and he loved them. He was as good in his way as Mr. Stokes is in his."

Katherine digested that for a while. They had been working in opposite directions around the small room and now they met and finished off the last section of wall, Katherine doing the top part, Iris scrubbing down low.

"Now the floor and we're finished," Iris said. "Let's start in the back corners." She dropped to her knees and began scrubbing the rough cement floor with one of the two brushes she'd brought in.

Katherine marveled at what an efficient work machine Iris was. By the time Katherine had the other brush in hand and was on her knees, Iris had already completed a large part of the corner and was rinsing it with the sponge.

"I never knew my father," Katherine said. "Tell me about him."

"I didn't know him that good, but I admired him. He was real kind to me when I was a kid working part-time for Mr. Stokes while I was still in high school. I guess that's why I still call him Mr. Stokes and always called your dad Mr. Renfro, 'cause I started doing it so young and never could switch when I got older."

"What did you admire about my father?" Katherine asked.

"Oh, I guess it was mostly how strong in his opinions he was. When he thought something was right for the animals he wouldn't let nothing sway him. And he had a real temper. Like I remember Vic was going to put down this old lion, Simbaru. He suggested it as humane, you know, 'cause Simbaru was blind in one eye, had this painful growth on his rear and had lost all his teeth and everything and was stinking up the lion wing. But your dad was against doing it—he thought the lion had some good years left. He really went all out to try to save that lion. I guess what I really admired was his sticking up for his animals like that."

"What happened with the lion?" Katherine asked.

"Oh, in the end, they didn't put him down, but they did get rid of him, so I guess Vic won out. After that your dad was so mad he tried to stop Vic from getting the head-vet job, but he did anyway. I always like when someone, oh . . . you know, stands up to everyone and don't back down.

"That and him being so nice to me when I was young. You remember those things. It makes me want to help you when I see how hard it's been for you."

It brought a catch to Katherine's throat—the idea of kindness coming full circle, but if she were to respond, it would bring on tears again, so she returned to the subject. "His strong-mindedness seems to have got him some enemies, though."

Iris, on her hands and knees, glanced over, then shook her head vigorously. "Oh, sure, but these aren't the kind of things people get killed over, if you're thinking that. Not Anglos, anyway," she added under her breath.

They bumped feet when she reached the open door. Iris first, they crawled backward, scrubbing their way out. They stood up to survey their work.

"Looks pretty good," Katherine said, gazing down at her shriveling hands and vowing to buy some good rubber gloves before the next time. "How often does this need to be done?"

"This thorough, each time a new pair goes in," Iris said.

"Will it meet Alonzo Stokes's standards, do you think?"

Iris studied it. Then she sniffed the air and wrinkled her nose. "Too much Lysol smell. We'll leave the door open to air it, and if there's still some smell tomorrow, we'll put a fan in." She smiled at Katherine, showing her dimples again. "Then it might pass inspection."

Iris looked at her big Timex. "Quitting time. Tuesdays Wayne and Harold and Irv and me go out for a beer after work. Wanna come?"

"Oh, I'd love to," said Katherine, pleased to be asked, "but I promised myself that today was the day I would go to visit my grandmother, whether she wants to see me or not. If I put it off, it might be another thirty years before I get up the nerve again."

Iris laughed, picking up her bucket and starting for the service area. "I know what you mean. Well, maybe next week. You'll like getting to know the guys better. We really got a great group here."

"Yeah, seems to be. Why isn't there a head keeper here?" Katherine asked, throwing her sponge and brush into the other bucket and picking it up. "The other departments all seem to have one."

"Yeah, they do," Iris answered, walking ahead, "but not here. Mr. Stokes is curator *and* head keeper. He needs to keep a hand in everything. I guess he can't trust anyone else to do it right."

When Iris got to the sink, she hoisted her bucket and dumped out the dirty water. "I've been here longer—nine years, and sometimes I've, you know, hoped he'd settle on me, but..." She shrugged her shoulders in resignation. "Anyway, good luck with your grandma," she said. "Maybe she'll like you and leave you her millions and you'll end up the boss of us all."

Katherine laughed and dumped her bucket into the sink. "And maybe Alonzo Stokes will decide we did such a good job scrubbing that he'll retire and make you head keeper."

Iris flushed under her dark skin and then smiled, showing the dimples again.

FOURTEEN

KATHERINE TOOK one more look in the mirror hanging on the back of her locker door. There really wasn't anything more she could do—she'd brushed her straight chestnut hair so it looked shiny and neat. She'd washed her face and added a touch of color to her cheeks and lips. But she kept staring at her face. What would her grandmother think of this face when she saw it for the first time in thirty-one years? Would she see there some trace of the five-year-old child she had known? Would she see in the gray eyes and straight nose some small reminder of Leanne, her only daughter? Or would she see a thirty-six-year-old woman who looked in no way familiar, an utter alien?

Although she had brought some other clothes with her, Katherine decided not to change out of her zoo uniform. She liked the dark-green cotton shirt with the zoo logo on the left sleeve and the patch over the right breast saying, "Katherine, Reptile Keeper." And she liked the comfortable green pants with the big pockets. She thought it might be helpful somehow for her grandmother to see her wearing the uniform, to see that she was involved in the family endeavor.

She slung her big canvas tote over her shoulder, shut her locker, and walked out the back door of the reptile house into the cool air of late afternoon. Her heart was beating quick and light as she headed toward the parking lot. She had endlessly imagined what this day would be like, had envisioned scenarios of everything from being ejected bodily from the house to being enfolded in loving arms. But it didn't matter, she told herself. She was going to drive to her grandmother's house, and this time, instead of slumping down in the car to watch the house, she was going to walk up to the door, ring the bell, and identify herself. Stiffen the sinews; summon up the blood.

Driving up MoPac toward the Windsor exit, Katherine admired the subtle change of color in the leaves. It must have happened since she'd been in Austin, because she hadn't noticed it on the drive from Boerne two weeks ago, and she had been so preoccu-

pied since then that she hadn't even looked. The sumac, brilliant
red at the side of the road, leapt out from its background of rust
and yellow.

The pasture behind her house would be softened by fallen leaves
now and the grass would be turning brown. If she were at home,
by now she would have chopped and stacked enough mesquite at
the back door to fuel a winter of fires in her big stone fireplace.
Thinking about that familiar landscape caused an actual pain at the
center of her body, somewhere under the heart. Seven more days
and it would belong to someone else. And Ra, too. It was still intolerable to think it, but she saw no way out.

Turning onto Woodlawn, she slowed down to give herself time
for a few deep breaths. Then, out of old habit, she pulled into her
accustomed place across the street from the stone mansion, and
parked. No, she told herself, not this time, not anymore. She re-
started the engine and turned into the circular driveway, stopping
directly in front of the door.

Before getting out, she lifted her face to the rearview mirror and
smoothed her hair behind her ears. Then she slid out and slammed
the door. It was too late to turn back now. She felt dramatic and
silly at the same time, like a character from Dickens—the orphan
being reunited with the matriarch. Even this stone mansion was
Dickensian.

She walked the stone path to the massive carved oak door, lacquered to a high sheen. She pushed the bell and listened to its
chimes echo through the house. But there were no answering footsteps, no sounds at all in the house. She rang again, leaning into it
for a long, insistent ring. Again she heard the chimes filling the
house. This time, after a few seconds, she caught the distant thud
of soft-soled shoes descending stairs. The sound got louder, but
slowly, as if the person were crossing a vast space.

Katherine crossed her arms over her chest, fortifying herself. A
woman's voice, harried and annoyed, called through the door,
"What is it?"

"It's Katherine Driscoll. I'm here to see Anne Driscoll."

That was met with silence. Then came the sound of a chain rattling and a lock being turned. The door opened and a small woman
in a nurse's uniform stepped outside. Katherine caught only a
glimpse of glowing dark wood floors and a curving staircase inside before the woman eased the door shut behind her, holding on
to the knob so it didn't click shut.

Katherine looked down at her. She was a woman of around fifty, compact and neat with dyed black hair bent into a tight page boy. Her tiny bow of a mouth was outlined with vivid red lipstick. "Now," she said with a minuscule spreading of the lips, "what was it you wanted?"

"I'm Katherine Driscoll. I'd like to see my grandmother. Who are you?"

The woman nodded her head once, as if she recognized the name. "How do you do, Miss Driscoll. I'm Janice Beechum, Mrs. Driscoll's nurse. I'm afraid it's impossible for you to see her now. She's not up to receiving visitors. Sorry."

"Well, when could I see her?" Katherine asked.

"I wouldn't know that, miss. I'd have to ask my employer."

"You mean Mrs. Driscoll?"

"Well, no. I suppose she is technically my employer. No, I mean the person who hired me and really is responsible for Mrs. Driscoll's welfare—Mr. Cooper Driscoll."

Katherine stuck both hands in her pockets. She had a sudden urge to push the smaller woman down, race into the house, slam the door behind her and find her grandmother. She took a breath to remind herself of her adult status. Maybe she had come at a bad time. "Well, okay. Will you call Mr. Driscoll now and ask him when I might come back?"

"Yes. I'll ask him," Janice Beechum said through closed lips.

"Good. Shall I wait here or may I come in?"

"Oh, I don't advise you waiting. It may take some time to reach a busy man like Mr. Driscoll. Why don't you telephone in a few days?"

"A few days! I just want to drop in and pay my respects to my grandmother."

"I'm sorry you're upset, Miss Driscoll, but my job is to do what is best for the patient." She lowered her voice to a professional intonation. "She's a very sick woman. We don't want anything to upset her unnecessarily, do we?"

"No, we don't want to upset her, but we do want to see her."

Janice Beechum turned toward the door. "Well, I'll see what I can do, Miss Driscoll. I need to get back to the patient." She opened the door just wide enough to slip back inside.

Katherine did something she wouldn't have believed herself capable of: Before the nurse could shut the door, she put her foot in the opening to block it. "If you could just give me a time when it would be convenient for me to come back," she said.

Janice Beechum looked out through the narrow opening with widened eyes, as if she were frightened that Katherine was going to barge in. "Please don't make this difficult, Miss Driscoll. I'm just doing my job. You need to talk to Mr. Driscoll." She looked down at Katherine's foot on the threshold as if it were a dead rat.

Slowly Katherine withdrew the foot.

The nurse shut the door, locked and chained it without another word.

Katherine felt her face flush with the sudden shame of rejection. As if she were a poor relation not worthy of entering the house, she had been turned away again. Again? she asked herself. Why do I feel I've been turned away from here before when I haven't? And why should I feel ashamed? When she and her mother left Austin it had been like this, as if they had done something so terrible that they were banished forever. They pretended it was because they chose to live apart, but really they had been banished and, in spite of all Leanne's protestations, Katherine had always sensed that.

Katherine stood there on the step, breathing hard, staring at the wood door and the polished brass knocker with "A. C. Driscoll" engraved on it. Anne Cooper Driscoll—the name was everywhere—on the foundation, on the reptile house, on this door, on plaques all over the zoo, but the person was hard to locate.

Katherine walked back to the car slowly, hoping a window would open upstairs and a voice, old and cracked, would call her back. But she reached the car in utter silence.

As she got back on MoPac and headed south toward her father's house, she felt she was in full retreat, with her sinew shriveled and her blood too timid for the task; the excitement she had felt, the growing resolve to act, had fizzled into dejection.

She turned on the radio to fill in some of the empty spaces. As soon as the music boomed through the speakers, she switched it off.

Damn it to hell. Was she going to retreat with her tail between her legs at the first rejection? Or was she going to treat this like all-out war and imitate the action of the tiger? She began to ponder the next step. Certainly she had to call Cooper Driscoll and find out what the story was. She had every right to see her grandmother. She would insist on it. Nothing was going to stop her. If she heard from Anne Driscoll's own lips that she didn't want to see her, then she would stop trying, but not until then.

Her resolve was stiffening.

Even before Katherine opened the car door, Belle had launched into her usual baying from inside the house. Unlocking the front door, Katherine murmured reassurances to the dog and the noise abated.

As she stepped into the front hall, Belle was waiting, as she did every day, with a rawhide bone in her mouth. The dog pressed one end of the bone against Katherine's hand, trying to entice her into a tug-of-war. This had started the first day Katherine had come home from work, clearly a carryover from a routine her father and Belle had enjoyed. Visualizing the sixty-year-old man playing with his old Lab always made her smile and she usually accepted the invitation to play, but today she refused. "Not now, Belle," she said. "I've got to make a phone call while my resolve is firm."

She bent down to pick up the mail that had fallen in through the slot and carried it to the kitchen. Without looking at it, she tossed in onto the kitchen table and opened the back door to let Ra in. She had settled on allowing Belle to stay inside during the day to nap, and Ra to stay out in the fenced backyard, because he was accustomed to being outside.

Ra burst in, first dancing circles around her, then sniffing both ends of Belle in their ritual greeting. She threw each dog a Milk Bone and headed for the refrigerator where she kept a jug of Almaden Rhine wine. She unscrewed the top and poured herself a large glass over ice cubes—a reward for getting through another day in the snake pit, she told herself. And a bracer for being assertive with her uncle.

Sipping her wine, she sat down at the table and made the phone call.

"Katherine, how are you?" Cooper said when he came on the line. Then he lowered his voice to a tone of unctuous concern. "Any news on the investigation front?"

"Not that I know of," she said. "Uh, Coop. I stopped to see my grandmother after work today and Janice Beechum said I'd need to check with you on a convenient time to visit her."

There was a silence. Then he said, "Well, Katherine, you should have let me know you were planning to stop by, saved yourself some time. Let's do this. Next time the doctor comes I'll check with him on it, see if she's up to... oh, someone new. She's very weak and sedated much of the time. So let me make a note here to ask him."

Katherine unclenched her teeth so she could respond. "When will he come by?"

"Let's see—Thursday or Friday, I think. I'll let you know when I talk with him."

"But if she's sedated, she wouldn't even know I was there. I just want to look in on her. I wouldn't stay long."

"Well, I'll pass that on to the doc. He really makes the decisions about your grandmother. Don't you worry. I'll take care of that. It's nice of you to stop by to see the old girl. When you coming to see us, Katherine? You never got that dinner we promised you."

Katherine could still smell the beef tenderloin she missed. "Well, thanks. There was another thing I wanted to ask." She took a deep breath. "I've gotten interested in the Driscoll Foundation and I wondered if you'd fill me in about it. I'd love to look at some of the records and—"

"Well, finally. I've been waiting years for someone in this family to take an interest. I'm not going to live forever. I always tried to get Sophie interested, but she never would listen. Sure, I'd like nothing better. Probably talk your ear off." He laughed a jovial bark. "Make you sorry you ever asked. Uh, what records would you like to see?"

"Well, I was wondering about acquisitions and—"

"Sure. I'll tell you everything you ever wanted to know, and more, probably. Of course, the records are confidential, but you don't want to get into that level of detail, anyway. So...Miss Katherine, what else can I do for you today?"

He was trying to brush her off. She knew the tone of voice.

When she hung up the phone, she took a long sip of wine. He really didn't want her to see Anne Driscoll. Why not? And why didn't he want her to see the foundation records? Did he have something there to hide? She suspected he did. And she was going to find out what that something was.

Reluctantly, she began to leaf through the mail. It had been nothing but bad news lately. There were two bills for her father, which she would pass on to Travis Hammond's partner, John Crowley, who had taken over the settlement of Lester's estate. The big envelope from Joe she had been dreading—he'd told her about it in their phone conversation yesterday. It contained mail he was forwarding: lots of bills she couldn't pay, another letter from the bank, a note from Hester Kielmeyer, and a plea from George Bob Rainey for her to come to the bank to sign some papers. She hadn't been home to Boerne once in two weeks, in spite of George Bob's rantings and Joe's pleadings; every day she made a new excuse why she couldn't go. She wasn't sure why she didn't want to, but it had something to do with trying to disengage herself from the place.

On the bottom of the stack was a small blue envelope addressed to her at her father's address in dark, smudged pencil printing.

She worked her index finger under the flap and ripped it open, pulling out a small piece of flimsy light-blue stationery. She unfolded it. The second she caught sight of the heavy penciled block letters, even before she read the words, she felt a chill of recognition. It said, "Katherine, put your father's house in order. Justice is nigh. An eye for an eye, a tooth for a tooth. Pointman."

She dropped the note on the table, stood up, and walked to the front door, slowly, calmly, so as not to alarm herself, and locked it, even though she knew no one could approach the house without Belle making a racket. Her chest felt tight and her fingers cold and prickly. She rubbed her hands together to get the circulation going as she walked back to the kitchen. Ra was standing alert and trembling, staring at her with raised ears and bright eyes. She wasn't fooling him.

Without touching the note again and without sitting down, she read it once more.

Then she leaned over to the wallphone and dialed the police headquarters number from memory. It took several minutes to locate him, but Lieutenant Sharb finally came on the line with a croaked, "Sharb."

"This is Katherine Driscoll. I just got in today's mail a warning note, like the ones my father and Mr. Hammond got."

"Read it to me."

She read it slowly, feeling the malice in the print, in each bold pencil line.

"Is it written in pencil on thin blue stationery?" he asked.

"Yes."

"I'm coming over to get it. Put it down and don't touch it again. We'll try for prints. Are you okay?" he asked.

"Sure," she said.

"I'll be there in a few minutes. We'll talk about it."

Katherine hung up and let her hand fall to Ra's head. He licked her hand and leaned into her leg. She stroked the silky ears and bent down to kiss him on the muzzle. "Don't worry, you baby," she said. Still standing, she lifted the wineglass to her lips and started to think about an eye for an eye, and a tooth for a tooth. It was revenge in kind that was being promised—biblical, savage, and implacable. But revenge for what? What had she done to this pointman, whoever he was? What had her father done? And Travis Hammond, what had he done?

EIGHT MINUTES LATER Sharb arrived in a patrol car with its light flashing. When she saw the whirling light through the kitchen curtains, she was aware for the first time of panic rising in her from her chest into her throat. She took another sip of wine to wash it back down.

Belle fell into a frenzy of barking at the approach of the police car. Katherine put her out in the backyard before she went to the front door to admit Lieutenant Sharb and a young uniformed officer.

"This is Patrolman Rogers, Miss Driscoll. Let's have a look." She led them back to the kitchen and pointed to the note on the table. When Sharb saw Ra sitting under the table, brushing the floor with his swaying tail feathers, he stopped dead in his tracks and sucked his breath in.

"It's okay, Lieutenant Sharb," Katherine said, "he's tame. And I put the other one out."

"Good," he said. He studied the note without touching it, pulled a large Ziploc bag out of his pocket, and nudged the note into it with his pen. He took out another bag and nudged the envelope into that.

"I don't want to alarm you, Miss Driscoll, but this is identical to the one we found in your father's pocket—except for two words: 'Katherine' instead of 'Lester' and 'your father's house' instead of 'your house.' I'm not a handwriting expert, but I've looked at that other note a bunch, and I'll wager it's the same handwriting, same pencil, same stationery...same killer. And young Susan Hammond says her grandfather's note was the same."

He sat down at the table. "Sit down. Drink your drink," he said. "Let's brainstorm."

Patrolman Rogers remained standing at the kitchen door, politely looking off into space.

Katherine stayed standing and dumped her wine into the sink.

Sharb didn't seem to notice. "What do Travis Hammond, Lester Renfro, and now Katherine Driscoll, have in common?" he asked. "Let's see...Travis was Lester's attorney. They both were involved deeply with the zoo, and they shared the secret of the payments to Dorothy Stranahan. But what about you? Where do you fit in?" He looked at Katherine for an answer.

She spoke slowly, trying to think it out. "I'm involved in the zoo now. I'm my father's daughter. And I know about the payments, but the only person I've told about them is you, Lieutenant, I have a feeling it may turn out to be discreditable to my father, so I haven't told anyone else. I've been standing here wondering if this pointman is someone I know and what I could have done to him."

"Any hunches?"

"Do you think he could be someone who works at the zoo?"

"Yes, I do," he said. "I've thought all along that Lester's death was arranged by an insider, someone with keys and knowledge of the routine."

Katherine nodded. She thought so, too.

"You got any candidates?" he asked.

Katherine thought for a while, as she ran through her head the people she knew at the zoo: Sam McElroy, Alonzo Stokes, Iris Renaldo, Wayne Zapalac, Danny Gillespie, Hans Dieterlen, Vic Jamail. "No," she said.

"There were quite a few folks there didn't get along too good with your dad. He was somewhat combative."

"Yes, I know. Who are you thinking of in particular?"

"Sam McElroy, for one." He looked at her for a reaction. "Sit down," he said, "my neck's getting stiff."

Katherine lowered herself onto one of the bentwood chairs.

Sharb continued. "Several people heard him threaten Lester with firing if he didn't mind his own business and stay out of the confidential records in the office. You know anything about that?"

"No," she said, thinking fast to separate what she could say from what she couldn't, "but I think Sam really didn't want to hire me and I've wondered why." She told him about Sam's reluctance and Iris's telling her there were several job openings besides the one in reptiles. "I think he was trying to frighten me off."

"Hm," Sharb said. "I wonder what confidential records your father was getting into. My sources didn't know that."

Katherine decided to add some candidates of her own. "Iris Renaldo told me Vic Jamail, the head veterinarian, had a fight with my father over euthanizing an old lion and that my father tried to block his promotion after that."

Sharb looked in his notebook and wrote a few words. "I heard that, too. Your father's described to me as a dignified and conscientious man, who could have a big temper when crossed. But none of these tiffs comes close to being a motive for murder. I have to tell you I'm stymied."

There was a long silence during which the only sound was Belle's barking in the back yard and Ra's heavy breathing under the table. Sharb studied a page in his notebook while Katherine stared at the window.

"Well, okay," Sharb said, snapping his notebook closed, "we need to talk about how we're gonna keep you from getting knocked off by this pointman, who seems to be batting a thousand so far. I don't want to have to take on another of these animal things—you getting swallowed by a boa constrictor or torn up by an alligator. So first off, you need to quit the zoo, as of now."

Katherine's first thought was, here's an honorable way out of the snake pit. Her second thought was that she was no quitter. She had started this job for good reasons and she was going to finish it. "No," she said. "I don't think that's necessary. I'm hardly ever alone at work. And I'll be very careful."

He waited until she looked at him, then fixed her eyes with his beady black ones. "Miss Driscoll"—he patted the pocket he'd put the note in—"I believe this. You should believe it, too. I think you need to stay away from danger for a while, until we catch this wacko."

"Lieutenant Sharb, if I go back to my house in Boerne, I'm alone in the country; I'll be thrown out in a week anyway. If I sit around this house all day waiting for you to catch him, I'll be a nervous wreck, not to mention totally broke. I need to work."

Sharb sighed. "Reconsider."

"No," Katherine said.

"How about going to stay with your cousin, the other Miss Driscoll, so you don't have to be alone here?"

Katherine thought about being in the same house with her uncle. "Oh, no. I've got a great watchdog here. I'll be okay."

"If you insist on staying here, I can have a regular patrol come by often and keep an eye on you—here, and at the zoo. We don't have the manpower for any more than that. I wish we did. Do one thing to humor me, though. At least get your cousin to come over here and stay with you. Call her now."

Katherine opened her lips to refuse. She couldn't ask someone to share the danger...but—she hesitated. It could be an opportunity. If Sophie were staying here, she could pump her about the foundation and about the family history. There never seemed to be enough time when she was with her cousin to talk about all the things she wanted to discuss. Anyway, it would feel good to have her around. If she'd agree.

"I'll call her," Katherine said. "I'll have to tell her about the note. She might not want to take the risk."

"Oh, she looks like a game girl. Go on and call her," Sharb urged.

"THIS IS LIKE a slumber party," Sophie said, putting her needlepoint down and lighting her tenth cigarette since midnight. She rolled heavily onto her stomach on the narrow cot. "Lord, I'd like to have a drink. I don't suppose you . . . No. Did you have slumber parties growing up in Boerne?"

Katherine did not know how to answer that without portraying herself as the poor little match girl. "No," she said, "there was always work to do at home. My mother and I were sort of a unit, so I really didn't have many friends at school."

"My mother and I never had much in common," Sophie said, taking a deep drag on the cigarette and holding the smoke in for several seconds. "But I would have loved to meet your mother. When she was young." She exhaled the smoke and lowered her voice. "Because she was a bad girl, I think, like me in past years."

Katherine tried to keep her voice light so she wouldn't frighten Sophie away from the subject. "How were you bad and how was my mother bad?"

Sophie rested her cigarette in the ashtray and let her face sink into the pillow, so her voice emerged muffled. "I got pregnant and had an abortion at sixteen; I was already drinking a whole lot at seventeen, smoking pot, skipping school; I barely made it out of high school. I think my father bribed Austin High to give me a diploma. I went to bars, picked up cowboys, you name it. But I've outgrown it now, all but the drinking."

Katherine shifted position in the chair, dangling her legs over the arm. "My mother never outgrew the cowboys. You know anything about that?"

"Well, I don't know the details; no one will talk about it, but every time I did something really bad, so my father had to notice, he'd say, as sort of the worst thing he could think of, 'Just like my sister, throwing your life away. If you go on like this, you'll find yourself chucked out of the family, too.'"

"So what did she do to get thrown out of the family?" Katherine asked. "That was one of the secrets she wouldn't talk about."

Sophie was silent, face sunk into the pillow.

"I've often thought I was probably unplanned," Katherine said to egg her on.

Sophie looked up, pale eyes bright with interest, cheeks flushed pink. "Yeah. I think she got pregnant at seventeen, 'cause Dad said I'd outdone even her on that score. Gram just couldn't accept it. She's a stickler for"—Sophie laid her hand over her heart and gazed heavenward—"the family honor."

"What else?" Katherine asked.

"Well, I think she had affairs after she was married," Sophie said, watching carefully to gauge Katherine's reaction. "But so did I. Doesn't sound so awful."

"What makes you think she did?"

"Well, at one point, after I was married and living in Dallas, when I really screwed up, got into a car wreck with this married man and Dad had to come bail me out of jail, and this man's wife was there yelling at me, Dad said that I was following in Leanne's footsteps and it would lead to disaster like it did with her."

Katherine knew immediately that it was true: Her mother had lived dangerously and something very bad had happened. She felt a prickling at the back of her skull, like a memory trying to form, to get up on its knees and creep to the front of her brain, but it couldn't quite get going. *Whispered secrets in the middle of the night. Then screaming and accusing. It was because of something my mother did. We were driven away by something horrible she did. It happened the night we left. Yes. I felt ashamed, as if we were being driven out of the Garden of Eden, like the pictures of Adam and Eve in my storybook, stooped over in shame, as they were driven away by an angry angel with a sword.*

Katherine glanced up suddenly to see Sophie kneeling in front of the chair, patting her knee. "I'm sorry. Katherine, I'm such a clod. I shouldn't have said that. Sorry."

"Oh, no," Katherine said earnestly. "I asked you. I need to know. I'm just trying to remember what happened, but it was so long ago and I think I've chased it out of my head. Sophie, do you know what happened the night my mother and I left Austin? I remember just enough to know it was something very bad."

"I was just a baby then," Sophie said.

"I know, but haven't you heard anything about it?"

Sophie leaned back against the cot and picked up her needle-point. She worked a few stitches without looking at Katherine. Finally she said, "What I've heard from Mother and Daddy is that Leanne's behavior just got too outrageous and Gram couldn't cope with it anymore. She was worried about scandal, the family name, all that bullshit. She told her to go away and never darken her door again.'' She looked up to see how Katherine was taking it. ''Is this too painful?''

''No. I want you to tell me everything.'' She smiled at her cousin. ''Now tell me what you know about my father. Everything.''

''Not much really,'' Sophie said, stretching out on the floor in her green silk pajamas. ''I liked him. He was so nice to me when I started at the zoo, acted like an uncle, even though he wasn't anymore. And he was this tall, strong, good-looking man.'' She smiled up at Katherine. ''I always appreciate that. He was standoffish to some of the people there, but he seemed especially to help young women. Not lecherous, just helpful. I wondered if it was because he missed you all those years.''

''What else? Tell me everything you know.''

Sophie thought. ''That's really about it. My parents never had anything to do with him, so the only time I saw him was at the zoo.'' She ran a hand through her hair to try to smooth it down, but the frizzy curls bounced right back to where they had been. ''Oh! But there's one thing: Even though Mother and Daddy didn't have anything to do with him, Gram did.''

Katherine sat up straighter. ''She did?''

''Yeah. I know he went to see her a few weeks ago because I overheard Dad getting into a real snit over it on the phone. He was telling that tight-assed woman who works there that if she let Lester Renfro in again, he was going to fire her. He said she was to check with him before letting anyone in to see Gram.''

Katherine said, ''Well she's taken it to heart. I know because I went to see her today after work and she wouldn't let me in, and she had to check with your father. But why?''

Sophie shrugged and yawned. ''I guess 'cause she's so fragile. God, though, with Daddy it could be anything. Maybe he's afraid she'll leave you some money or her house or something if she sees you. He's desperate to inherit before he has to declare Chapter Eleven. But if you want to see her, you should be able to.'' She yawned without covering her mouth.

Sophie looked down at her watch as she stubbed out her cigarette. ''Three A.M. God. I'm beat.'' She pulled herself up onto the cot and let her head drop to the pillow. ''Don't you have to get up in three hours? Let's go to sleep. Or are you scared to?''

Katherine unfolded from the chair, reluctant to stop the conversation, but barely able to hold her eyelids open. She stood up and stretched. "Yeah, a little scared. But I'm so tired now it won't matter. Sophie, thanks for coming. It really helps."

Sophie rested her head on the pillow and waved a hand in the air, wiggling her scarlet fingertips. "Oh, actually," she said into the pillow, "the invitation came in the nick of time. I hate to think it took a death threat to get me out of the house, but I was stifling there and I can't afford a place of my own yet. I'll stay as long as you want me." She dropped her hand down and patted Belle's head where she slept next to the cot.

Katherine switched off the light at the door.

Sophie squealed in surprise. "Oh, leave it on tonight. Okay?"

Katherine switched it back on. "Night."

Ra got up and followed her, but Belle stayed where she was. Katherine looked back and saw that Sophie was gripping the dog's collar.

FIFTEEN

AFTER THREE hours of sleep, Katherine woke to the alarm and sat up in bed. *Damn.* The first of November. Only six more days until the auction.

As she drank her strong coffee in front of the kitchen window, a police car cruised by, slowing as it passed the house. Sharb keeping his word. She wondered at her own absence of fear. Maybe the two weeks of steady apprehension she'd felt in the snake pit had built up an immunity. But it was so unreasonable. Why should her fear of a caged reptile transcend her fear of a death threat? She thought about it on the drive to the zoo. Lots of people were afraid of snakes, but her fear seemed to be deeper and somehow more personal. Maybe it had originated with those snakes in the glass boxes in their living room. And they had left that house, she and her mother, before she had had a chance to work the fear out.

As she entered the keepers' area, Danny Gillespie, Wayne Zapalac, and Vic Jamail were leaning against the counter, gathered around a fat, rust-colored blood python. Danny was restraining the thick body on the stainless-steel counter while Wayne held its head up, his fist wrapped around it just under its black-and-gold eye. Vic manipulated with both hands several metal rods and a hypodermic, all stuck into the snake's gaping mouth. The blood python was a friendly, sluggish, non-venomous snake, so Katherine moved in closer to see what they were doing.

Danny looked up at her. "Intestinal problem," he said. "Amebiasis, Vic thinks."

Slowly Vic drew out a long-handled curette and scraped the contents into a piece of foil. Then he pushed the plunger of the hypodermic. The snake writhed powerfully, but Danny held the coils down calmly, his sinewy arms showing the strain as the tendons bulged out and the muscle flexed.

"Why don't you use a snake tube?" Katherine asked.

"Too much trouble for such a nice guy as this," Vic said, drawing out eight inches of hypodermic tube. "You obviously haven't tried to persuade a snake into one of those. It's like trying to stuff a limp noodle into a drinking straw." Both Danny and Wayne laughed, nodding at the analogy.

Vic put down the hypodermic and reached for his coffee cup on the edge of the sink. He took a long drink, his eyes studying Katherine over the rim.

Wayne held on to the python's head while Danny looped the coils around his arm and with his other hand pinched the head right behind the eyes, taking it over from Wayne.

"It should go in Quarantine F," Wayne said, pointing to one of the white fiberglass isolation cages along the wall. He looked up at Katherine and said, "How're you doing, Katherine? You look like you had a big night."

"Do I?" she asked, amazed at his perception. She'd thought she looked pretty normal. "What are you doing over here, Danny? How's Brum?" she asked as he opened the door and threw the big snake in.

Danny turned and slicked his thinning blond hair back from his forehead with a delicate hand. "He's okay. I'm taking your place today. Sam decided the cats don't need round-the-clock baby-sitting anymore, so Salvador is feeding them and I'm here."

Then she noticed that her clipboard with her schedule and notations was out on the counter. "Taking my place? Why?" she asked.

"I don't know." He pointed at Vic. "Vic just told me to report here and take over your chores for the day." He picked up her clipboard. "But I need you to go over some of your notes with me. What's this about the bushmasters? You're moving them today?"

"Tomorrow, I think, or whenever the female's shed is finished. That's the big female in the exhibit and the male in the quarantine box—they're supposed to go into the breeding room together. Blind date."

Wayne pulled a newspaper from the counter and looked at it. "Long, dark South American male," he pretended to read, "one of the smoothest of his species, two penises, seeks cool female who's into mice and long snoozes. Purpose: Courtship behaviors leading to copulation and eventual clutch of vipers."

Katherine laughed and was surprised to see Danny's smooth peach skin coloring to red. He looked down as he chuckled.

"So, if you're taking over for me, what am I supposed to do?" Katherine asked in Vic's general direction.

"I need some consultation with a canine expert," Vic said. "I hear you've had a bit of experience. Ever trained a wolf?"

She looked up at him in surprise. "Tried to once. A hybrid, half-wolf, half-husky. This rancher had set his heart on having it as a family pet." She shook her head, remembering the man's disappointment when the wolf-dog killed and ate his wife's elderly poodle. But she *had* taught him to sit and heel.

"You can tell me about it on the way over to Wolf Woods," Vic said, gathering up his instruments and loading them into his battered backpack. "I've got my Jeep outside. Anytime you're ready. My assistant is down with the flu, so I hoped you'd fill in for the day after we finish with the wolves." He stopped in the doorway to wait for her.

Katherine felt flustered and apprehensive. Any one of these men could be the pointman and she was being coerced into going off alone with a man she didn't know. To stall for time, she picked up her clipboard and glanced at her notes for the day. Danny looked over her shoulder. "Well, first I need to check on the Gaboon vipers. We're supposed to do a fecal check on the young male. He's been losing weight, Alonzo tells me, so we isolated him to get a sample today."

"I can do that," Danny said. "I worked here before and it's more pleasant to do a reptile fecal than a tiger fecal, believe me." He took the clipboard out of her hands.

"Be sure to air out the bushmaster room," she said. "Maybe with a fan. I think there's still some Lysol odor." She was surprised to hear in her voice the beginning of a proprietary interest in her responsibilities. She would still be meeting commitments in hell.

Danny nodded. "Bushmasters, yeah. Don't worry about it. Hey," he said, turning to face Vic, "I better be careful with those characters. Wasn't it a bushmaster involved in that fatal snakebite here a long time ago?" His eyes were shining with interest behind his thick lenses.

"Yes, I think so," Vic said. "It was way before my time." He glanced at his watch.

"Well, it wasn't before Alonzo's time," Danny said. "I've asked him about it, but it's a real sore subject. He doesn't want to talk about it at all."

"Yeah, I know," Vic said. "I asked him once, too. He hates to be reminded. This has always been his bailiwick and he feels responsible for everything that happens here."

"I don't know why he'd feel responsible," Danny said. "Everybody knows that accidents happen when you work around these venomous species. Actually we've got a great safety record here."

Vic headed for the door, looking at his watch again. "That's true, as those things go with herps. One fatality and two bites that didn't amount to anything in fifty-six years is pretty damn good."

"Not if you happen to be the one fatality," Katherine said, busying herself with some index cards on top of the gecko cage.

Vic stood in the doorway watching her. "Well, are you coming, Katherine?"

She looked at him, then around the keepers' room. Oh, hell, she'd take her chances. She followed him out the door.

Wayne laughed and called after them, "Watch out for those wolves!"

The open Jeep was parked on the sidewalk right outside the front door of the reptile house. Like all zoo vehicles, it was painted forest green and sported an official decal on the door. Katherine inhaled the crisp morning air and felt like a schoolgirl about to play hooky. She had been sprung from the pit, from its sour smell and overheated air, from the constant supervision of Alonzo Stokes and her own incessant fear.

Vic vaulted over the door into the driver's seat and opened her door from the inside. She got in without looking at him—an overbearing, macho sort of man; she knew the type. In her work she dealt with them all the time—hunters, good ol' boys who brought their retrievers to her to train, and never stopped expressing their surprise that a woman could do the job. But he was offering her some freedom, and the chance to pick his brain about recent zoo acquisitions if she played her cards right. And there was a bonus: He seemed to be offering wolves. She loved wolves.

Vic revved the Jeep engine and smiled at her, showing all his glossy white teeth. She looked away without smiling back. He drove on the sidewalk, heading toward the far end of the zoo, away from the main gate. As they sped past the pachyderm complex, she noticed that the morning sun was bathing everything in rosy gold; the two rhinos, Teddy and Ursula, were transformed from dirt-colored clay into massive golden statues stretching their horned snouts over the stockade fence that separated their pens. The giraffes at the African Pavilion glittered like towers of reticulated gold. The sprinklers had just finished soaking the oak and mountain laurel leaves so they glistened in the sun. It was a paradise. She felt like a woman emerging from her cave at the dawn of time.

They rode in silence for a while until Vic said, "In the morning light it looks like Eden, doesn't it?"

Katherine turned her head and looked at him for the first time. "I was just thinking that."

"I thought so," he said.

She studied his profile for a moment. He was clean-shaven for a change, his dark skin looking a little raw from the scraping. His thick black hair grew long on his neck, curling slightly under his ears. His nose had the fierce curve of a scimitar and his hairy hand on the wheel was huge, the skin on the fingertips cracked and callused. She looked away so he wouldn't catch her staring.

"Tell me about the wolf-dog you trained," he said.

"I said tried to."

"Okay. But don't tell me they're not trainable."

"Oh, they are, with some hard-nosed conditioning—up to a point. It depends what you want them to do. You can certainly condition them to do certain things, but they'll never retrieve and they'll never make pets or guide dogs."

"What I have in mind is much more modest than that. We just want them to come into their holding cages at a certain signal."

"Why?"

"Well, of all the animals here, the wolves have always been left most alone. They stay outside in all weather, rarely enter their shelter. The keepers just throw them some bones and meat once a day and that's pretty much it.

"But now we've got a problem. The bulldozers and landscapers are coming next week to do some work in their enclosure and it'll take maybe two weeks to complete. We want to get the wolves into their holding cages during the part of the day when the workmen are there and let them out the rest of the time, but they won't go into the enclosure. The keeper's been able to get one or two in at a time, but not all six."

"Have you tried feeding them inside so they have to come in to get it?" she asked.

"Jerry says he's tried that, but it doesn't work." Without slowing down he bumped across the tracks of the little train that girdled the zoo and pulled up to the fence enclosing Wolf Woods—a long narrow strip bordering the extreme west end of the zoo grounds. The area was sparsely planted with a few bushy pines and some large boulders were scattered around.

There were six of them lying in the shadows at the back of the exhibit, long-legged and bush-coated, positioned almost exactly ten feet apart from one another. Dogs would be lying together in an indiscriminate heap, but wolves needed some distance. Four of them were solid gray, one was a gray-and-cinnamon mix, and one was off-white. Every time Katherine saw a wolf she was reminded that in their anatomy wolves were almost indistinguishable from dogs. But, what a difference in temperament there was between *Canis lupus* and *Canis familiaris!*

Vic pointed at a small flat-roofed hut at the south end of the exhibit. "That's the shelter. They don't like it, but the workmen say they won't work here while the wolves are out. Even though we tell them it's safe."

"I don't blame them," Katherine said. "Wolves have a bad reputation."

"Yes, they do," Vic agreed. He hoisted his backpack out of the rear of the Jeep and started walking along the fence. He led the way to the far end, near the hut, where a huge hollow Gunite boulder concealed the gate. He dropped his bag to the ground and pulled out a crumpled coverall. He stepped into it and pulled it on over his zoo uniform. "They tend to jump," he explained. "Muddy paws." He smiled down at Katherine as he zipped the fly. "And they could get hurt by my belt buckle. After we solve this first matter, maybe you could train them not to jump."

"No problem," she said.

He pulled a jangling key ring from his pocket and unlocked the gate. Instead of entering, he bowed and swung his arm toward the pen for Katherine to precede him. She stepped in, keeping an eye on the resting wolves whose erect ears were turned in their direction. Vic entered, closed the gate and was about to lock it, when he saw a man trotting toward them. "Here comes Jerry," he said to Katherine. "While we're here we'll do a little howling. Socialize. And it'll give me a chance to look the pack over. I don't get here often enough and Sterling, that's the alpha female, had a tumor we removed several months ago. I'd like to check the site."

A burly red-haired man opened the gate. "Morning, Victor." He nodded at Katherine. "Is this the trainer?"

Vic locked the gate. "Yes. Katherine Driscoll, Jerry Waters."

Vic jogged toward the wolves, who looked up at him with glowing eyes. He went right to one of the grays, leaned over, buried his hands in her thick fur, and rolled her onto her back. Jerry did the same with the white one. To Katherine's surprise, both men scratched the wolves' bellies and began to howl, throwing their heads back, trying, unsuccessfully, to imitate the deep, mournful howl of a wolf. The two wolves writhed on their backs emitting whines and playful yips, appearing to be in ecstasy as the men rubbed them and gained volume with their caterwauling.

Katherine stood watching with interest. It was impossible not to smile.

Vic moved on to another wolf who'd been jumping on him and whining for attention. He flipped it over and gave one pathetic yowl, then looked up at Katherine. "It's important to get them on their backs right away."

Katherine understood what he meant. Wolves respected height. They had a highly structured hierarchy and you needed to establish dominance right away if you were going to head the pecking order.

"Why the howling, though?" she asked.

"Oh, this guy, an ethologist who bred these wolves, Ernst Klinghammer, says anyone who needs to interact with wolves should do some howling with them every once in a while." He bayed to illustrate and moved on to another wolf. As he was scratching his stomach, he said to Jerry, "How come this female doesn't have an ISIS number?"

"Oh, she arrived after the others. Remember? We'd already tattooed them."

Katherine leaned over and asked, "What's an ISIS number?"

"Look here," Jerry said, pointing to the place where the hind leg connected with the groin. "We're marking all our animals with numbers. International Species Inventory System numbers, to help monitor breeding. All zoos are doing it."

When the two men had played with all six wolves, and Vic had examined the healed scar of the female who'd had surgery, they brushed themselves off and headed toward the hut. Three of the wolves frolicked at their feet until they got close to the building, then fell back.

Inside were eight large cages and a small kitchen corner with a sink and refrigerator for preparing food.

Vic turned to Katherine. "This is where we want them to come, all at the same time. Have you been thinking about it?" he asked.

"I have," Katherine said. "Jerry, what's your procedure for feeding them?"

"Around noon every day, I just toss them some raw meat, about three pounds per animal. I try to spread it out around the enclosure, so the dominant animals can't keep the others away. Last week I tried putting it in the cages, but they weren't having none of it, went on strike. All but one refused to come in."

"How long do you have to accomplish this?"

"The workmen are supposed to start on the thirteenth, so twelve days."

She nodded. "It might work if you did it in increments, a small step at a time. Today you could put the food near the hut, a little closer than the place they stopped when they were following us just now. Spread it out, so they all have a chance at it. Then tomorrow, put it a little closer, the next day right at the door. The third day, you could put it down at the door and then drag it inside, some into each kennel, so it leaves an irresistible trail. And I'd get a dog whistle and blow a few blasts just before putting the food out every day. Then they'll start associating the sound with food coming and they'll go where they're expecting it to appear. Especially if you condition them to come immediately when the whistle blows by removing the food if they don't come within five minutes. The next time they might remember they have to hustle."

Jerry was nodding.

Katherine thought for a minute. "The problem is the time crunch. We could certainly do it if we had several weeks, but twelve days isn't much—with wolves. It might speed things up if they're hungrier than usual. You could cut down the rations today and tomorrow, to motivate them." She pointed at the water trough in the center of the enclosure. "You could also empty that and move the water inside tomorrow so they get more accustomed to the cages."

Jerry was nodding at her. "Sounds sensible. What do you think, Vic?"

"Try it."

"With wolves, the key is steady, incremental conditioning. If the old male and the alpha female do it, of course the others will," Katherine added.

"Yeah. Well, we'll try it. Maybe you could come back in a few days and see how it's going," Jerry said. "I hear you're in reptiles with Alonzo Stokes."

Katherine nodded. She felt so good right now she didn't even want to talk about it. "Your wolves are beautiful. I'll be interested to see how they respond to this."

They walked to the gate. Jerry let them out and relocked it. "Vic, when are you going to look at that lame muntjac?"

Vic glanced at his watch. "Not now, possibly this afternoon. It's a pretty full day."

"Okay. He's real skittish, so be sure you bring your dart gun." Jerry looked at his watch and said, "Got to run. I've got a group coming." He jogged off toward the plains exhibit.

As they walked back to the Jeep in silence, Katherine looked back wistfully at the wolves, who had settled back down into their places.

Again Vic jumped into the Jeep without opening the door, but this time Katherine was too quick for him. Before he could lean over to open the door for her, she stretched a leg over the door, anchored a foot on the seat, and hoisted herself in, feeling smug that she could do it so easily.

Vic started the Jeep and headed back the way they had come.

They bumped along in silence while Katherine racked her brain for an innocent way to bring up the subject of acquisitions. Here she was wasting this golden opportunity about the subject. She needed to get on with her inquiries. Maybe she should just ask directly. Before she could think of an approach, they had pulled up in front of the pachyderm complex where the elephants, rhinos, hippos, and tapirs were housed.

"Ever see rhinos mating?" Vic asked as he turned off the engine.

Katherine glanced over at him to see if he was serious. "No," she said.

"Me neither. Not many people have. Today we could be among the select few. I hear it's awesome."

Katherine looked across the road to the reptile house and felt a tug of anxiety. "Is it okay with Alonzo for me to be gone all day?"

"Oh, yes. I already arranged it with him." He looked at her for a reaction. "Is that all right with you, Katherine?" For the first time she thought she heard in his usually assured voice a note of uncertainty.

She glanced back once more at the gaudy mosaic set into the expanse of the tan brick reptile house. "Yes. It's fine."

"It'll give you a chance to see more of the zoo. Actually, it wasn't easy to arrange. Alonzo didn't leap at the idea of exchanging you for Danny." He vaulted out of the Jeep. "He thinks Danny is excessively rough with the herps and he thinks once you get over your—initial reluctance, you could be a competent keeper. That's high praise coming from him."

Katherine climbed out and walked along beside him, taking bigger steps than usual to keep up with his rapid, long-legged pace.

Three men were clustered at the entrance to the fenced-in side yard. Katherine recognized Hans Dieterlen, the dour senior keeper, who seemed to be involved in everything that happened at the zoo. He was engrossed in conversation with two old men who would have to be the legendary Traeger Brothers, who had been in charge of the pachyderm house for thirty years. Katherine had heard they had been trying to retire for years, but had been unable to since no one else could handle the five elephants they had raised.

They had clearly been waiting for Vic because as soon as he arrived, the group moved into the stockaded yard where bales of hay were stacked and several bushels of apples waited for feeding time.

Vic introduced her around as Katherine who was filling in for his missing assistant. The two brothers were Manuel and Luis Traeger. Katherine had only seen them from a distance before. Up close, they looked every bit as tough as they were reputed to be.

"Are we certain she is in estrus?" Hans Dieterlen asked, looking at Vic for the answer.

"Luis says she's jumpy and hasn't eaten in two days. These are the usual signs. The keepers usually know." Vic looked to Luis for confirmation.

Luis scratched at a wormlike raised scar that ran from his earlobe down the neck and disappeared into his shirt collar. "Well," he drawled in a low, rumbling voice, "this morning she squirted some urine on the dividing fence and Teddy made a flehmen response." He pulled his lips back from his teeth and wrinkled his long nose to show how Teddy had looked. "He's interested. And her behavior's weird. I think we have a real good chance here for a mating."

His brother, leaning against a stack of bales picking his teeth with a piece of straw, nodded his head in agreement. "Yup. In heat."

The two brothers looked at one another and smiled.

Vic said in a low voice that barely contained his excitement, "Let's open the door to the bridal chamber. What do you say, Hans?"

"Okay," Hans said to Manuel and Luis. "If you're ready, open the gate. We don't want to upset them, so the rest of us will go around to the front and keep quiet."

The two brothers disappeared through the door while Hans, Vic, and Katherine walked around to the visitors' viewing area at the front of the outdoor pens. The zoo hadn't opened yet, but already a group of about twenty zoo staffers had gathered at the rail, watching Teddy stand at the fence that divided him from the only female of his species he had ever seen. Apparently word had gotten out.

The group contained mostly keepers and maintenance crew, plus a few people from the front office. Iris Renaldo was walking over from the reptile house. Sam McElroy stood talking with his assistant, Kim Kelly, who was dressed as usual in safari clothes—today a long khaki skirt and leather boots. As soon as he saw him, Sam beckoned to Vic, who joined them, leaving Katherine and Hans standing together.

Luis Traeger was already in the pen approaching Teddy. He passed by, smacked him on the rear, raising a dust cloud. The rhino's skin looked so much like armor Katherine expected it to clank, but the noise was just like what you'd get if you thumped your hand into a sandbag. Then Luis walked to the gate in the dividing fence. He unlocked the huge padlock, pulled the chain that secured the wooden gate, and swung it open. He propped it open with a rock and walked backward toward the group at the railing, keeping his eye on Teddy whose squat, powerful legs propelled him slowly and inexorably toward the opening.

They all watched with riveted attention as Teddy lumbered through the opening and pointed his worn-down nub of a horn toward Ursula.

Hans stood with his hands clasped behind his back, his face impassive. "I hope these dinosaurs do what they're supposed to," he said in his thick German accent. "Getting the female here has been a major pain in the ass."

"Oh? How?" Katherine asked.

"The paperwork involved in getting her over here you wouldn't believe. She's on breeding loan from the Frankfurt zoo and it took several dozen permits and releases to get her here, as well as two years and a small fortune." He gestured toward Teddy. "All for this moment. I hope he isn't queer."

Luis clambered down into the moat, up the other side, and vaulted the railing as if he were a young man. As he joined the group, his eyes were shining under bushy gray brows and his nervous fingers jangled the key ring hanging from his belt. His brother stood in the doorway of the pachyderm building with a pitchfork in hand. They all watched with an anticipation Katherine found infectious.

"Where does the money for transport and everything come from?" she asked Hans.

"The Zoological Society," he said without looking at her.

"Not the Driscoll Foundation?" she asked.

"No. They pay only for actual acquisitions."

"Hans, do local game ranches ever buy animals at the same time the zoo buys them, like in the same shipment?"

He kept his eyes fixed on Teddy. "How would I know what they do, those places?"

"They don't ever buy animals from the zoo?" she asked.

He glanced at her coldly. "Certainly not. It is against AAZPA regulations."

Teddy was sniffing the air. Ursula tossed her head, shaking the hairy tassels at the end of her silly donkey ears and trotted toward him. She stopped and leaned her massive head against his and rubbed it gently back and forth, waiting for him to make the next move. Teddy endured it for a moment, then trotted away to the other side of the enclosure where some hay was still left. He lowered his head, picked some up and began to chew contentedly.

"That prehistoric dolt," Hans Dieterlen muttered, adding a few guttural words in German. "Doesn't he know a come-on when he sees it?"

"Patience, Hans. He's just a beginner," Luis said. "He's never seen this done by his species, so he's got to work it out."

Ursula was not about to give up so easily. She followed Teddy at a brisk trot and this time she was bolder. She lowered her head to his stomach and dragged her horn along the length of his body. When she reached his groin, she began to lick his belly and then moved on to his penis, which had been hanging down like a useless fifth leg. Teddy let out a squeal. Everyone's eyes were glued to the penis, which immediately started to grow and lengthen until it was about three feet long and pointed forward toward his nose horn.

Iris Renaldo took a few steps to get close to Katherine and whispered in her ear, "Wow. I'm glad I decided to come watch. Isn't that something?"

"It sure is," Katherine said with conviction. The erection continued to grow. Katherine suddenly saw where Asians had got the idea that rhino horn was an aphrodisiac.

Ursula, seeming suddenly nervous by what she had unleashed, ran to the edge of the dry moat between her and the spectators and scrambled down into it.

"Oh, no," Luis said. "He won't be able to get at her in there and I don't know if she'll be able to get out on her own. Come on, let's head her out." He jumped the railing and scrambled down into the moat, with Hans and Vic behind him. They walked up to the female rhino and tried to turn her around with thumps to her flanks, but she refused to budge. She was planted where she stood. When they heard the clop of soft hooves, they looked up to see three tons of rhino bearing down on them. Teddy was approaching. As he slid down the side of the moat, the three men scrambled up the other side, getting out of the way just in time.

Ursula leaned suggestively against the incline and Teddy took the offer. He climbed up on her backside and thrust himself against her, but the observers, craning their necks, could see he was aiming far too low. He got down and looked around bewildered.

"My God," said Sam McElroy, "it makes me want to go down there and put the dong in for him."

"He'll get it," Luis said. "He just needs some practice."

And sure enough, Teddy mounted her again, ramming himself against her. There was a slapping noise, then two simultaneous sighs from the rhinos as he found the right spot. It took only a few seconds of thrusting in and out before he let out a bellow and his pom-pommed tail shot up like a flag. But Teddy didn't move; he stayed in position, resting his head on Ursula's rump.

"It's not over by a long shot," Luis Traeger said. "Rhinos can ejaculate every fifty seconds for several hours." As if on cue, Teddy began thrusting again, and again he bellowed and this time so did Ursula. It went on and on for the next half hour and promised to continue indefinitely. By now the zoo was open and visitors were gathering to watch. Some mothers with small children in tow took one look and dragged the kids away.

"Too bad," Vic said to Katherine. "It's good sex education. Come on. Tear yourself away. We have promises to keep."

As Katherine turned to leave, Iris whispered into her ear, "Whew! I don't know about you, but I could use a cold shower."

"WHAT'S NEXT?" Katherine asked, the wind whipping her hair as they bounced along the rutty road to the Australian Pavilion in the new section of the zoo.

"A bird—her keeper thinks she's egg-bound," he said, pressing on the accelerator. "A cassowary." They screeched to a stop at the side of the pavilion where several gigantic ostrich-like birds stood stamping the dust with their big feet. Gawky and startled, they regarded the Jeep's arrival with heads held high on long crepey necks. Batting their long lashes, they looked like aristocratic matrons interrupted at a tea party.

"There she is." Vic pointed at a lone bird in the corner of the pen who was stomping her feet and shaking her richly feathered tail as if in the throes of some compelling force. A young woman keeper came running toward them, holding on to her hat. "Thank God you're here," she said, breathless. "Matilda's been straining since I arrived this morning."

"How many has she laid already?" Vic asked.

"Nine. And now she gets stuck on what's probably the last egg."

"Okay, Lisa, she's been at it way too long. Let's see if we can give her some help." He pulled his pack from the back of the Jeep and headed toward the gate.

"Oh, boy," Lisa groaned, pulling on some thick leather gloves and pushing down on the bill of her baseball cap. "Oh, boy."

"Here's the plan," Vic said to the two women. "It won't be too hard to catch her, but you two will need to hold her still while I see if I can help her ease it out."

Lisa groaned again and looked over at Katherine. "You got any jewelry on?" she asked.

Katherine shook her head, puzzled.

"Good. This is my least favorite thing to do."

Vic unzipped his bag and slung it over one shoulder. "Be careful. These birds can kick like mules."

"Especially this one," Lisa said, unlocking the pen. "She's the Incredible Hulk of the bird world. We need to get close to her right away so she can't get a good one in."

The cassowaries, except for Matilda, who stayed right where she was, straining and shuddering, ran with a few strides of their powerful legs to the opposite end of their pen. Vic headed toward Matilda's corner, clearly planning to approach from behind; Lisa approached from the front; and Katherine from the flank. Vic moved in first, grabbing her around her muscular thighs, while Lisa threw her arms around the base of the long naked neck, and Katherine grabbed what was left—the bulbous feathered body. She had to bend over and stretch her arms as far as they would go, resting her cheek against the small flightless wing. She was surprised that under the soft plumage, the body was rock hard and trembling.

The bird struggled, stomping and dragging her big feet, raising clouds of dust that Katherine couldn't avoid breathing in. There was also some noisome brown sticky stuff on the feathers that was getting smeared on her cheek and in her hair. She envied Lisa the baseball cap that protected her hair.

"Fine," said Vic squatting down under the bird's rear end and peering up. "Ah, I see it, just a nickel's worth, but there it is. Now...can't you keep her a little steadier so I can get my hand in there without getting it ripped off? Katherine, tighten up."

Katherine hugged harder and gave a little yip of surprise when Matilda snaked her long neck down and grabbed Katherine's shirt collar with her black beak and began to tug at it. "She's trying to rip my shirt," Katherine complained.

"Good," Vic said, looking up into her face, only about a foot away from his. "It'll keep that end busy for a while." He poured some liquid on his hands and rubbed them vigorously, then poured a clear oil onto them and inserted the left hand into the bird's cloaca. Katherine was beginning to feel her wind cut off by the continual powerful yanks on her shirt. More dust was being kicked up, which made her eyes itch and water and her tongue feel gritty. Just as she felt close to strangling, she heard a rip as the collar began to separate from the shirt.

Vic smiled up at her. "Ah, I can get a few fingers around the side. Keep holding—a little tighter if you can."

The beak gave a final tug and pulled off a large part of Katherine's collar.

Lisa called down to her, "Sorry. I can't hold any higher on the neck or I could damage her windpipe. It's very fragile in these birds."

Matilda dropped her head again and nipped at what remained of Katherine's collar. This time she caught a strand of Katherine's hair in with it.

"Ow," Katherine yelled. "She's got my hair now." She looked down at Vic for help.

"Hold on," he said. "It's really lodged tight in there, but I just felt it give a little. No wonder she was having so much trouble. Coosh now, coosh," he said, pulling his hand out and patting the bird on the tail. He poured some more oil on the hand. "Crisco," he said to Katherine, "better than obstetric jelly." He stuck his hand back in as Katherine felt her hair being yanked upward, so hard it jerked her head back and brought tears to her eyes.

"Ow!" She shouted so loud the bird let go of the hair and collar.

"Don't shout," Vic said. "It makes her jumpy."

Then his black eyes opened wide and his whole face took on a rapturous expression. "It's coming," he whispered to Katherine. "I feel it coming." Katherine couldn't take her eyes off his face; it was radiant with pleasure, his usual high color heightened; eyes blacker, lips redder, skin flushed. His eyes looked directly into hers, as if he were waiting for a response.

Slowly he worked his hand from inside the bird, whispering a calming, "Coosh, coosh," and when it emerged with a slurping noise, he held the egg up in his palm for her to look at: a glistening bottle-green orb, pear-shaped and large as a cantaloupe. It looked to Katherine like a piece of the moon, luminous and magical, burnished smooth by centuries of worshipers' touches.

Katherine gasped. "Do they always look like that?"

Vic nodded and said, "Here comes the hard part—letting her go without getting kicked." He backed up slowly with the egg until he was out of range of the long legs. "Now," he said. "Run!"

Lisa and Katherine released their holds and ducked out of the way as Matilda flailed out with one powerful limb. They dashed to the gate where Vic was waiting with the egg. He handed it to Katherine, saying. "We'll take it to the nursery for incubation with the others."

She received it reverently in both hands.

SIXTEEN

KATHERINE LOVED the way the candle backlit her glass of Beaujolais, making it glow a luminous ruby. Listening intently, she turned the glass by its stem and took occasional sips.

Vic was talking about his lonely childhood with his mother in small-town Texas. "The animals seemed to fill that gap," he said. "My mother tolerated them all, but it couldn't have been easy for her."

"I don't think I could have survived my childhood without the dogs," Katherine said, surprising herself with the revelation. She'd never admitted it before. "Does your mother still live in Emory?"

"No, she died a few years ago," Vic said.

They lapsed into a comfortable silence. After a strenuous day in the open air, three hours of animated conversation over a sumptuous dinner, and two bottles of wine, Katherine felt mellow and happier than she had in many weeks. She took a long sip of wine and said, "This is a good restaurant. I really enjoyed my dinner."

"Makes up for the lunch we never got around to today." He looked at her clean plate. "Should we try some of the chocolate intemperance? It's their specialty."

"Why don't you order some and I'll help," Katherine said, thinking she really shouldn't drink any more wine. The warm prickling in the back of her neck alerted her to overindulgence.

"Why is it women like to eat dessert, but never order it?" he asked, rearranging his long legs under the table and pressing his knee against her thigh in the process. Katherine had a sudden image of Ursula rubbing her horn along Teddy's belly and blushed.

"Wasn't that incredible today with the rhinos?" he asked. "I've always thought of Teddy as part of the earth—a mountain—dirt-colored, ancient, enduring. So it was like the earth rising up to renew itself. When his tail shot up the first time, I felt like applauding. I didn't know that would happen."

Katherine laughed. "I liked that, too. It would be wonderful if it produces a baby rhino."

"We'd be one of only a few zoos to have done it." He looked at her over the top of his wineglass for a while, his black eyes reflecting the curve of the glass. Katherine thought that Sophie was right: he did clean up well—in a blue suit, white shirt, and red paisley tie. With his dark skin and curved nose, it gave him the look of something wild temporarily civilized: a Berber warrior come in from the desert for a weekend in the city. She shook her head to dispel the image. Silly. It was the wine. This was just an overworked veterinarian out for dinner.

"Will you be around to see the calf born if Ursula *is* pregnant?" he asked.

She paused, thinking about it. "How long is gestation for rhinos?"

"Seventeen to eighteen months."

"I don't know, Vic. I wish I did. Everything is so up in the air right now. Eventually my father's house will be sold by the bank, so I'll need to find someplace to live. I like the zoo, really like it, but I don't think I'll ever get used to the snakes." She felt an urge to try to explain it to him. "It's almost as if I was born with an aversion so deep and automatic, I can't control it—this instinct to hike up my skirt and run when I see one. So all day my body is producing surges of adrenaline to prepare me to flee, but I have to stay. It makes me feel like one of the silly females Iris Renaldo makes fun of. I hate it, but it won't go away."

Vic nodded and recited in a low voice:

> *"Several of Nature's People*
> *I know and they know me*
> *I feel for them a transport*
> *Of Cordiality.*
>
> *But never met this Fellow*
> *Attended or alone*
> *Without a tighter Breathing*
> *And Zero at the Bone."*

"Zero at the bone," Katherine said. "That's it exactly. A chill so deep it feels as if it's in the bone marrow. What is that?"

"Emily Dickinson," he said. "Even now, when I see a snake unexpectedly, I feel it—the tighter breathing and the cold bones. When I'm expecting them, it's not a problem."

Katherine sighed. "It goes even beyond what I've said. It's as if I have some ancient tribal memory of a bad experience. I can't get rid of the feeling. Maybe it has to do with—" She stopped, uncertain whether she wanted to tell him. She decided she did. "I just remembered recently that my father kept some snakes at home, in the living room, when I was very young. My mother and I were terrified of them."

He nodded slowly. "Would..." He hesitated a minute, then began again. "Would you be interested in another job, like working for a good trainer here in town?"

Katherine glanced quickly at his lowered eyes, then away. "Why do you ask?"

"Well, Sam asked me the other day if I knew a trainer who might need help. He wanted me to suggest it to you, as a better alternative. Actually, he ordered me to suggest it to you."

"I think he's eager to get rid of me," Katherine said, watching his face for a reaction.

He surprised her. "So do I," he said. "I've been wondering why."

"Me, too." They looked at one another over their wineglasses. She calculated that he'd drunk even more than she had, but he showed no effects.

She decided to give voice to her suspicion. "Was it Sam's idea for you to take me around today, try to sell me on the trainer job?"

He looked injured, his black eyes wide. "No. That was all my idea. Of course, I checked it out with him."

Katherine nodded, trying to decide if she was convinced.

"Well, are you interested?" he asked.

"Why? Did you find me a job?"

"Yes. Josh Burton at Circle C Kennel would hire you tomorrow. He says you're the best trainer of retrievers he's ever seen. Says your present dog is so good he's not really a dog at all."

Katherine felt a sudden gush of pleasure spread through her body. It seemed years since anyone had praised her. "Thank you for telling me that," she said. "It makes me want to purr."

"So...what shall I tell him?"

"Tell him thanks, but I plan to stay at the zoo. I'm going to learn to be a credit to Alonzo Stokes if it kills me." She took a big swig of wine and looked away from his puzzled expression.

As THEY FINISHED off his chocolate intemperance and another glass of wine apiece, Katherine took a deep breath and asked the question she had been framing all evening: "Vic, is it possible that a ranch in Kerrville has a bongo and some aoudads?"

He looked up with eyes so wide his forehead wrinkled. "Aoudads, sure. Lots of the game ranches have big herds of them, but a bongo, no. They're on the endangered list, hard even for zoos to get hold of. We were damn lucky to get our young male."

"The one that's over in quarantine?"

"Yeah. He's the only one in Texas. Houston, Dallas, San Antonio—none of them have any."

"How did we get ours?"

"Through an animal dealer who has contacts in the Congo, all over Africa, really. And the Driscoll Foundation was generous enough to put up the twenty thousand dollars for it. Why, Katherine?"

"I saw a photograph of a bongo being unloaded at a ranch in Kerrville on October second."

"October second...that's when we got ours," Vic said. "Are you sure it was a bongo?"

"Pretty sure."

"May I see the photograph?"

Katherine took a deep swig to finish off her wine and pushed her glass away. She'd reached her limit. That reminded her she needed to find the ladies' room. She stood up without answering his question. "I'll be right back," she said.

In the bathroom she splashed cold water on her face to clear her head. She needed to make a decision. Now. If she was going to investigate the documents her father had left her, she had to ask direct questions, take some chances. She was sorely tempted to show them to Vic and get his opinion on how to proceed. But what if he was involved in whatever it was that was going on?

She patted her face dry with a paper towel. She needed help, that was certain. But could she trust him? She pictured the white teeth against his dark skin. God, he looked like a dishonest camel trader. Why pick him to confide in? But who else was there? Sam McElroy? No way. Alonzo, certainly not. Hans Dieterlen? No. Her uncle? Impossible.

She felt a burning need to talk to someone about it. But Vic? Why take the chance? She thought about his knee pressing her leg, the way his hair curled under his ears. Maybe it was just wine and hormones at work here, but she had to take a chance on someone. And even if Vic was involved, at least she would have taken some action that might jar something loose.

She stopped at the pay phone in the hall to call Sophie at her parents' house. They'd agreed to come back home at the same time so neither would be in the house alone. Sophie answered the phone and agreed to meet Katherine at ten-fifteen outside the house, so they could go in together.

As she approached the table, Vic finished signing the bill and rose from his chair. "Hard question, huh?" he asked.

"What?"

"About seeing the photograph."

"Oh, that. Very hard," she said.

"You ready to go?" he asked.

WHEN HE PULLED his old Volvo station wagon into the gravel driveway, he left the engine running and turned to face her.

Before he could say whatever it was he had on his mind, Katherine said, quickly, before she could back out, "Can you come in for a minute, Vic? I want to show you something."

He nodded enthusiastically.

Just as they reached the front door, Sophie pulled her BMW into the driveway next to Vic's car and jumped out. "Perfect timing," she said. "Hi, Vic." She had to shout to be heard over Belle's barking.

Vic looked puzzled. "Sophie," he said.

"Sophie's staying with me," Katherine explained as she unlocked the door, soothing the dog with her voice. "Easy, Belle. Good girl."

As they entered Vic caught sight of Ra undulating toward them. "This must be the dual champion, Amun-Ra," he said.

"Radiant Sunrise's Amun-Ra," Katherine said, scratching the dog on the chest.

Vic stopped as they walked through the dining room-studio to glance at the walls of photographs. He immediately spotted the color ones of Katherine and went to study them. "Very nice work your father did," he said. "Very nice."

The three of them sat down in the kitchen and talked for a few minutes until Sophie said, "Time for me to turn in." She looked

at Katherine. "Late night last night. I don't know how you do it."
She walked out, headed toward the library with Belle at her heels.
They heard her door closing.

"I'm going to get the photograph. I'll be right back," Katherine said, rising from her chair. She stopped in the doorway and looked back at him, on the verge of asking him to take a pledge of secrecy, but she decided it would sound melodramatic, and it would be useless anyway. He was either trustworthy or he wasn't. And she was wagering that he was.

She left without saying anything.

She pulled the envelope from under her mattress and carried it back to the kitchen, her foggy head full of warring emotions. No doubt the wine and lack of sleep over the last twenty-four hours were contributing to this act of indiscretion. But she was going to risk it.

She lay in front of him the page on which she'd copied the four photos that had been marked with the date 10/2/89 and "RTY Ranch, Kerrville." "These are just copies, but you can make them out well enough." She pointed at one of the photos. "This is a bongo, isn't it?"

"Oh, yes," he said. "Even in black and white, there's no mistaking the vertical white stripes on the body and the leg markings and the hunched line of the back. It's a bongo, and not ours." He counted the stripes with his index finger. "This one has twelve stripes; ours has fourteen."

Katherine turned the page over. "This is what was written on the back of each of these pictures," she said.

"October second, 1989," he read, "RTY Ranch, Kerrville. I've been there. About five years ago. It was the first of the big game ranches. Their profit comes from charging hunters immense fees to shoot exotic game to nail up on their walls. I've heard you can even shoot big game there if you have enough cash. This outfit's run by a guy—Robert Yost—whose family owned the ranch for generations. Old Texas money. But they had fallen on lean times until he had the idea of stocking exotic game."

He turned it back over to look at the other photos on the sheet. "This is an aoudad, a Barbary sheep, of course. And look at this, Katherine." His voice rose with excitement. "Here's two greater kudu. What the hell! And an oryx."

He looked up at her. "Your father took these, didn't he? What did he say about them?"

"Nothing. He left them hidden for me. I found them after his death. There are more." She laid another page in front of him.

He stared at it. "A pair of bushbuck! We don't even have bushbuck at the zoo. Well, shit! A sable antelope and an addax!" He turned the page over and read, "August tenth, 1989, PLS, Lampasas." He looked into the distance trying to remember something. "August tenth. We got a shipment August tenth, I think. It was the two wildebeest for our herd."

"I know," Katherine said. She handed him the page listing zoo acquisitions for August. She'd marked the date and the two entries. She watched his reaction carefully. His forehead was crinkled and he looked genuinely perplexed as he studied the record and then the photos.

"There are more," she said, handing him the rest.

He sat in silence for about five minutes, studying them, checking the dates on the photos against the acquisition records. Katherine alternated between pacing the floor and peering over his shoulder. When he finally looked up, his mouth was a tight line and his eyes were unfocused as if he were trying to visualize something but couldn't quite get it in view.

"Well, what do you think?" Katherine asked, waving a hand over the documents on the table. She sat down so she could listen better.

Vic shook his head and rubbed his fingers across his furrowed forehead. "If these photographs are labeled accurately, for the past six months, each time the Driscoll Foundation buys some new animals for the zoo, on that same day, one of four Texas ranches gets a shipment of animals. Some of the animals are illegal by federal and international law. And all of them have no business going to a game ranch to get shot."

Katherine was impatient. "Yeah, I know that, but what does it mean?"

He took a deep breath. "This is hard for me to believe, but it could be that there's some…scam going on and that people at the zoo are involved. Probably your uncle, too, since he's head of the foundation." Vic looked her in the eye. "What are you planning to do about this?"

She shrugged. "My father wrote me that he had something he wanted me to do, something only I could do. Then he left these for me. I want to find out what was going on and do whatever he had in mind for me to do." She sat back in her chair. "I wish I knew what that was."

Vic was silent for a long minute. Then he thumped his knuckles on the pictures. "This scares me. If your father collected this information, it could be the reason he was killed."

Katherine nodded. "If there were something illegal going on at the zoo, can you see how it might work?"

He looked into space. "I've been trying to, but it's so hard to believe that I can't quite imagine it. I know there's big money in the exotic-game business."

She nodded again. "Vic, what might my next step be to find out more?"

He stared at the black window, thinking. "I'm reluctant to tell you because I'm afraid you'll do it and then get into trouble for it."

"Let me worry about that. If you want to help me, give me some advice."

"Do you have access to the Driscoll Foundation records and numbers?" he asked.

"No. Don't you?"

"No. Cooper Driscoll keeps them. Could you possibly get him to let you look at them?"

"No. I've tried."

"Let me think this through," he said. "We could call one of these ranches and pretend to be hunters, say we wanted to hunt a bongo or a kudu or an oryx, but I don't think they'd tell us and it would make them suspicious. No, that wouldn't work. But..." He stopped.

She leaned forward toward him. "What?"

"I can think of only one thing." He pushed the first page of acquisition records across to Katherine and pointed to the column labeled "Source." "The last three shipments came from our main dealer, Max Friedlander. That's what the initials MFWAD stand for: Max Friedlander Wild Animal Dealer. You could ask him what animals were in the October second, August tenth, and April seventeenth shipments."

Katherine drummed her fingers nervously on the tabletop. "Where would I find him?"

"He lives in New York or New Jersey. I could get his number for you from the files, but I don't know if he'd talk to you about his business. The zoo's a big customer. Katherine, maybe you ought to leave this alone. What have you got to gain?"

"My father wanted me to do something about this and I'm going to do it."

He covered her hand with his, stilling the movement of her fingers. "Okay, but will you promise to keep me in the picture here? I don't want you doing this all on your own."

Katherine thought about it. "Yes, if you continue to be useful."

He laughed, loud. She put a finger to her lips in warning to keep quiet. "Sophie doesn't know about these. It's touchy."

"Yeah, I can see that." His hand pressed down on hers.

She looked away from him and stifled a yawn.

"Time for me to go?" he asked.

She nodded. "Thanks for dinner...and the day. Can you get that number for me tomorrow morning?"

He rose. "Okay. Against my better judgment."

She stood up, too quickly, and felt a wave of dizziness. Vic wrapped an arm around her shoulders. "You okay?"

"Just tired . . . and drunk. That was great wine."

He slid his hand from her shoulder to the back of her neck, underneath her hair. "It was." He bent down and kissed her softly on the lips, lingering just long enough for her to taste the Beaujolais, the chocolate intemperance, and the tang of something unknown.

When he took his hand way from her neck she could still feel the imprint of it and the heat.

THE POINTMAN slipped his hand into the neck of his shirt and held on to his lucky charm for a moment. He clenched his teeth and tried to regulate his breathing, but the anger would not stay down; it kept churning up into his throat, spewing bile and acid into his mouth.

He'd had it all planned out to perfection, just like he'd done with the others. But, fuck, this goddamned woman was so changeable. She just had to foul everything up. Thinks everyone should jump just because she says so. Even though it ruins everybody's plans.

He watched the bushmasters through their exhibit window. The big female lay next to the log in the back corner. Her old skin, looking like cloudy cellophane, was caught on the rough bark and she was slithering out of it. But it was glacially slow. Like a woman with no arms trying to wiggle out of a tight nylon stocking by rubbing against a tree trunk. The beadlike scales of her freshly molted front half glistened in the fluorescent light; they formed a dark pattern—lateral triangles of charcoal outlined in yellow—distinct and handsome. The pattern and colors of the unmolted back half were cloudy and dull.

The snake looked listless now, but just wait until she finished getting rid of that old skin. Then her aggressiveness would emerge, especially after he had a go at hurting her enough to bring out the meanness. She was seven feet long and when he was finished with her, every inch would be aggressive.

Touching the charm helped calm him. He was doing fine. This delay was nothing. After all, he'd waited so long. One more day wasn't going to make any difference.

He smiled. Actually, the delay wasn't such a bad thing at all; it gave him more time to anticipate her punishment. Because, really, he'd discovered that most of the enjoyment was in the planning and anticipating. After it was over, there was a letdown that felt like falling into a deep well.

Until he got involved with the next one.

Strange. Maybe his mother had been right. "Sonny," she used to say, "happiness lies in keeping busy."

Well, he'd been keeping very busy lately and there were times he felt almost happy.

SEVENTEEN

IT WAS MADNESS, absolute lunacy.

As the plane circled LaGuardia, Katherine opened her eyes and felt the flush of incipient panic start in her cheeks and spread down her neck. Worse, it was lunacy on borrowed money and borrowed time. The money—$384 for a round-trip ticket, coach class—she'd borrowed from Vic; and the time—his day off today in exchange for her working for him on Saturday—from Danny Gillespie. They'd both been generous and willing to accommodate her, but they didn't know what she knew—that this was probably a wild-goose chase.

When she'd called Max Friedlander yesterday at his office in Manhasset, he had flatly refused to discuss his business dealings with her. Brusquely, he'd told her in his harsh Dutch accent that his affairs were confidential. When she'd tried to tell him about the unusual circumstances, he had cut her off mid-sentence to say it was impossible for him to discuss it with her. Then he'd hung up.

So what did she do? She had booked a reservation, borrowed the money from Vic, arranged to trade days off with Danny, lied to Sam and Alonzo, telling them her best friend had died in New York. Then she'd persuaded Sharb she'd be safer in New York than in Austin, borrowed a jacket from Sophie, and finally caught the 6 A.M. flight, exhausted from all the arranging. Now she had no idea how she was going to persuade this unpleasant Dutchman to talk to her. Maybe the simple desperation of her coming all this way to see him would sway him.

She'd planned to spend the flying time plotting a strategy, but the early hour and the vibration of the engines weakened her will. She'd put her head back, lowered her lids, and drifted into reverie. She replayed her dinner with Vic the night before last, imagining a different ending to the evening. Instead of poring over pictures of animals in the kitchen, she leads him to the bedroom and slowly peels off his clothes, taking hours to do it. Before unbuttoning his shirt, she slips her hands underneath and feels the texture of the skin on his back.

It had been almost a year since she had broken her engagement to John Rehnquist, and in all that time she hadn't felt the stirrings of passion for anyone. She had thought, with some relief, that perhaps her capacity for passion had withered away from disuse. But now here was lust reasserting itself, alive and well at a most inappropriate time. Well, she had a date with Vic tonight, if she got back as scheduled, so she could test it out—see if it had atrophied or not.

As the jet bumped down and taxied to the gate, she dragged herself up from the fantasy and began to think of how she could get Max Friedlander to talk to her. Vic had said he was a crusty old Dutchman who'd been dealing in animals ever since the end of the Second World War, when he'd emigrated to the United States. He was one of three big animal dealers in the country, generally reputed to be the best. Vic had met him several times and had the impression that he was an honorable man, unlikely to be involved in any illegal dealings.

Driving the rental car to Manhasset, she watched the dying foliage of early November speed past her window. It reminded her of what she had chosen not to think about: November seventh was only four days away. There wasn't a chance in the world now that she was going to save her home from that auction on the courthouse steps. She needed to face up to it.

When she finally located Max Friedlander's office address in Manhasset, she parked three blocks away and walked through the cold wind, aware suddenly of how meagerly she was clothed. It seemed that every time she came north, she was unprepared for the weather. It was thirty degrees and she was shivering in her lightweight silk slacks and blouse, with only the thin jacket she'd borrowed from Sophie.

She stood on the filthy sidewalk, staring at a decrepit dark-red-brick building. The sign on the building said LENNY'S HARDWARE and the streaked window displayed a few dusty tools and kitchen gadgets. But the address was right. Near tears, Katherine looked up to the second floor and saw painted on the window in black and gold, "Max Friedlander, Wild Animal Dealer."

She let out a long breath, which appeared as a puff of smoke in front of her. To the left of the hardware store, a door with peeling black paint seemed to be the only way to get to the second floor. She opened it and climbed the dark wooden stairs, still trying to perfect the lie she would tell. The door at the top had a small brass plate with his name, but she didn't know whether to knock or just enter. After a minute of hesitation she knocked and waited, glancing at her watch. It was eleven thirty-five.

Please be here.

There was no answer, so she knocked again. The door jerked open. A rotund elderly man with a fringe of flyaway white hair and a well-trimmed white beard stood there, looking angry. "I called, 'Come,' but you stay out here." He glowered at her. "So? Now I'm here, say what you want."

"Mr. Friedlander?" Katherine asked.

"Yes. Yes. Who else? You see the name on the door." He pointed to the plate.

He made her feel like a naughty ten-year-old. "I'm Katherine Driscoll. I talked with you yesterday, but I—"

"You called me yesterday. From Austin, yes?"

"Yes. But it's so important I flew up today so I could see you in person."

He clasped his hands behind his back and rocked back on his heels, as if her impertinence had knocked him off balance. "You thought maybe I was kidding you yesterday? That I would talk private business with just anyone who calls?"

"But I'm not just anyone." Katherine squared her shoulders and stood up straight.

"Oh?" he said, throwing his head back and sticking his paunch out. "And who might you be, then?"

This was perhaps her only chance and she was going to go for it. "I'm the granddaughter of Anne Driscoll who set up the foundation that has bought millions of dollars' worth of animals from you. I'm the daughter of Lester Renfro, who was killed eighteen days ago by a tiger who was sired by a tiger the Austin Zoo bought from you. I'm a reptile keeper at the zoo... but I'm really a dog trainer," she finished lamely.

He stood in the door, his head still back, his mouth rounded and puckered as if he were expecting a kiss. He stood silent for a long time, looking at her. Finally he spoke. "Your grandmother I know well and your father I read in the paper about. My condolences." He stepped aside for her to enter and made an elegant bow from the waist.

Katherine entered feeling like a beggar who had suddenly turned into a princess.

"My office is ahead on the right," he said, stopping to flip the switch on an answering machine sitting on a metal desk near the door.

She walked through an ultra-modern reception area full of computer equipment, telexes, faxes, and phones, into a dark, smoky, book-lined room with a huge mahogany desk and an old Victorian love seat. Stepping through the door was like going back a century to a slower, more comfortable era.

"Please," he said, pointing to the love seat.

She sat and felt the panic reasserting itself. How was she going to approach this?

Watching her intently, he walked to his desk and picked up an ashtray with a smoking cigar in it. He lowered himself painfully into the seat next to her, rested the ashtray on his knee, and stuck the half-smoked cigar in his mouth. "Tell me," he said.

The lies and subterfuges she had cooked up evaporated into the smoky air. She pulled the copies of the photos and zoo records out of her bag and spread them on the small table in front of him. Then she told him everything: the letter from her father, his death, how she found the envelope containing the photographs, her getting a job at the zoo so she could investigate, and, finally, Vic's suggestion that she talk to him. She ended with a sigh of relief and leaned back into the seat feeling fully relaxed for the first time in weeks.

By that time, he had smoked his cigar down to a nub. He stubbed it out, picked up the pages, and carried them to the desk. Switching on a reading lamp, he sat down and pulled a magnifier from his drawer. He spent the next twenty minutes in silence, bent over her documents, then studying entries in a ledger of his own. He got up once to pull a folder from his file cabinet. They were the longest twenty minutes Katherine had ever experienced. She tried to occupy herself with surveying his books, a huge collection on exotic animals, the African section alone filling an entire wall.

Finally he looked up and said, "You must be thirsty after your journey. I have some sherry I have been saving. Will you join me in a glass?"

"Yes, please," Katherine said.

He pushed himself up out of his desk chair with difficulty. As he squatted to open the credenza behind the desk, he said, "In the days when all of us were much younger, Anne Driscoll was one of the liveliest and most charming women I have ever known. Right after the war, this is before you were born, we went with a group of zoo people on safari in Kenya and Tanzania, then Tanganyika. She was fearless. Like a man. I have always been a little in love with her."

He stood, a bottle in one hand, two glasses in the other. "And, of course, after that we did business, which turned out lucrative for me, very lucrative. Her foundation was my first big customer." He put the glasses of heavy cut crystal on the desk, uncorked the bottle, and poured from it. Shuffling carefully so as not to spill the amber liquid, he carried the glasses toward the love seat. Katherine leaned forward to take hers.

He sat and raised his glass toward Katherine. "To not harming the people we have loved." He touched his glass to hers and took a long sip.

Katherine had never liked sherry—too heavy and sweet—but this she enjoyed. It tasted perfect for the environment. They both sipped in silence.

"For the past two years," he said, "I have dealt with Cooper Driscoll, you know. Your uncle. Not Anne. To him I have no attachment."

Katherine nodded.

"I have not spoken with her in that time. Cooper tells me she is . . . dying."

"I don't know," Katherine said. "He won't let me see her, but that is what I hear, too."

"I am uncertain what to do here. Very uncertain. It is unusual for me to be uncertain, but in this case . . ." He shrugged and finished off his glass.

"Mr. Friedlander, the last thing I want to do here is hurt any member of my family, especially my grandmother in her fragile condition. If you give me the information I am looking for, I promise I will use it responsibly. I will not do anything detrimental to Anne Driscoll. You can count on that."

He sighed and rose again to fetch the bottle from the desk. He filled Katherine's empty glass and his own. "You are working in reptiles at the Austin Zoo?" he asked.

"Yes."

He shook his head. "I don't deal in reptiles. They have never appealed to me. Birds either. I deal in mammals, only mammals." He pointed at one of the photographs on the only section of wall not covered with books. There were three photographs: a large male orangutan with swollen cheek flanges, an okapi, and a baby gorilla. "These are some of my best finds. Cheops, the orangutan I caught wild in Borneo. He died last year after twenty years in the Detroit Zoo. Now everything is computers and ISIS and red tape. Ninety percent of my time is doing paperwork and keeping up on the regulations for importing exotic species. I may retire. Especially now." He pulled a fresh cigar from his shirt pocket and waved it at the papers on his desk. "I should go to the authorities with this. You know that."

Katherine decided not to argue or push him. She had the feeling it would not help her case.

"Tell me," he said, "why you are a dog trainer."

Katherine reached over and put her empty glass on his desk. "I think it's because I love talking with another species. It's a privilege. Like being one of the few to walk on the moon or to visit some foreign country that other people haven't seen. I've just always known that working with animals was what I was supposed to do."

He sat back and closed his eyes. " 'They are not brethren, they are not underlings; they are other nations, caught with ourselves in the net of life and time, fellow prisoners of the splendor and travail of the earth,' " he recited.

"Henry Beston," Katherine said, pleased to recognize a quote she had always loved.

He opened his eyes and smiled at her. "If I give you the information you want, you will promise me not to let your grandmother get hurt? This involves her son, and sons are of great importance, even bad ones. More important than granddaughters."

Katherine raised her right hand and said, "I promise."

"And you will promise me that this will come to an end, what is going on in Austin?"

"Oh, yes."

He nodded. "Then I tell you this and I can document it all." He smiled at her and added, "In triplicate. On October second, I shipped by air freight to Dallas seven animals destined for the Austin Zoo: two bongos from San Diego, both mature males; three aoudads; two greater kudu; and one scimitar-horned oryx. They were paid for from the Anne Cooper Driscoll Foundation, half in advance, half when they arrived safely. That was done. The checks were signed by the foundation director, Cooper Driscoll." He tapped the cigar he'd been holding on the table. "Now I see from the zoo records you brought that only one of the bongos and two aoudads actually reached the zoo."

Even though it was what she had suspected, Katherine was shocked, so shocked she had to concentrate on her breathing to regulate it. She had been slow, but she was beginning to see the big picture.

He put the cigar in his mouth but didn't light it. "The same thing with this shipment in August. Only the two wildebeest arrived at the zoo, but I sent also two bushbuck, an addax, and a sable antelope. Also, on April seventeenth, animals I sent did not get acquired, according to your records."

"Who took charge of these animals in Dallas? Do you know?"

"Yes. Because I get the shipping orders back. They were all signed by Hans Dieterlen, your head keeper."

Katherine tried to picture it: The animals arrive by air freight. Hans Dieterlen signs the shipping order. He directs one or two of the animals into the zoo van and the others go into vans headed elsewhere. Cooper Driscoll and Hans Dieterlen were nothing less than bandits, or rustlers. And the penalty for rustling in Texas was traditionally death by hanging.

"What about Sam McElroy?" she asked. "Do you think he's involved in this?"

The old man shrugged and said, "It's hard to think he wouldn't know."

They sat in silence for a minute.

"So, Miss Katherine Driscoll. What will you do about this?" he asked.

"Is there any way to prove the animals, if we can find them, are the same ones you shipped, the same ones that were paid for out of foundation money?"

He smiled at her and nodded his head, as if she were a cleverer child than he had suspected. "Sure. Some of them, the ones I bought from other zoos, had already been tattooed with their ISIS numbers."

Katherine's heart gave a little leap. "Inside the left thigh?" she asked. She remembered Vic had told her that most of the animals and all the highly endangered ones were tattooed with the International Species Inventory System number.

"Yes. The bongos were both tattooed and..." He struggled to his feet and reached for his ledger and magnifying glass on the desk. He opened the book, found the entry. "Also the oryx, and, in August, the wildebeest and the sable antelope."

"Could you write those numbers down for me?" Katherine asked.

"Yah." He struggled to his desk and carefully recorded for her the animal, date shipped, and the ISIS number. He handed her the paper, then looked at his watch. "It is almost one o'clock. May I take you to lunch at the best restaurant in Manhasset?"

"I would love it, but I need to get back as soon as I can. Will you give me a rain check?" She turned to walk to the door.

As he was letting her out, he said, "May I give you some advice?"

Katherine nodded.

"It is this: The October shipment was worth one hundred five thousand dollars. The August shipment, seventy-four thousand dollars. And this is with discount for the zoo. Game ranches in Texas expect to pay more for these rare antelope. I know from seventy-four years of living that when that kind of money is loose and when murder has already been done, there is danger. I think I will take a vacation until this is done. You should maybe do the same." He put his hand out to her.

She took his hand in both of hers and held it. His fingers were very cold at the tips. "Thanks, but I can't do that yet," she said.

As she promised, Katherine called Sophie from the Austin airport at 6:15 P.M. and told her not to worry about meeting her at the house; by the time Katherine got back, Vic would be there to pick her up. But, with no luggage to collect, she arrived home in record time—fifteen minutes. Good. It would give her time to wash her hair and spruce up before Vic picked her up at seven.

She wasn't sure if it was the anticipation of being with Vic or the weight of the information she carried, but she felt almost feverish as she walked to the front door.

She had slid her key into the lock before the sense of something being wrong stopped her from turning it. What was it? She stopped and listened. She could hear the traffic from the highway three blocks away and the wind rustling the treetops. Never before had she approached this door in silence. Always, every single time, the racket of Belle's barking had accompanied the unlocking of the door.

She jerked the key from the lock and took a step back.

Something was definitely wrong.

She turned and ran down the steps, back to her car. As she opened the door to get in, she saw a blue-and-white police car cruise past. With a cry, she bolted out of the driveway into the street, waving her arms to flag it down.

The car squealed to a stop and Patrolman Rogers jumped out. "Miss Driscoll? Just driving by to check."

Katherine grabbed his arm. "I just got here and the dog's not barking. She always barks when someone approaches the house. Always. There's something wrong."

"Hold on," he said. "Let me call this in." He pulled the radio from his belt and spoke into it in a low voice. Then he touched the butt of his pistol. "You stay here while I take a look."

Katherine handed him her key with a shaking hand. "I'm coming with you," she said. She stayed close behind him up the steps, holding her breath as he inserted the key and turned it in the wrong direction. "No." She barely had the breath to get the word out. "The other way."

He twisted the key the right way and the lock clicked. The door swung open. He stuck his head in first, then flicked the light switch at the door. He looked inside for a few long seconds. Then he stepped back outside. He drew his pistol.

"You stay right here," he ordered. "Don't come in."

He entered the house, leaving the door open.

Katherine felt her systems shut down. Her heart stopped pumping blood; her lungs shut off the air. Her body remained in suspension as she waited.

When he didn't return after a minute, she leaned her head in the door and looked.

Her throat closed and stuck.

On the hall floor lay a black heap.

Belle.

Blood had blackened the brick floor and pooled around the dog's head. The smell told her the dog had been dead for hours.

The scene dislodged a memory. *My mother drags me out the door, but I break away. I run back into the house. To say good-bye to Pasha. But he's lying on the bedroom floor. Even at five, I know he's dead.*

She jerked her head back and tried to call for the policeman, but her throat was still stuck.

Ra.

Where was he?

She had left him in the backyard early this morning.

EIGHTEEN

THE FOUR OF THEM had been silent for several minutes as they listened to the clatter of the police packing up their gear.

Cooper Driscoll stood behind his daughter, scowling so that his mouth was stretched into a pencil-line slit. His hands rested on his hips, holding his suit jacket back to reveal his massive torso. As he looked down at Sophie, who sat weeping at the kitchen table, his mouth stretched even thinner, sinking into his face.

Katherine sat across from Sophie, studying the pattern of blotches that reddened her cousin's fair skin. She refused to meet Cooper's eyes. If she did, she knew he would read in her eyes the suspicion that was almost a certainty now. She glanced over at the door where Vic stood, his back turned to them as he watched Sharb's team finish dusting for prints in the hall.

When would they all get out? She couldn't tolerate sitting here much longer. She was impatient to talk to Vic alone, to tell him what she'd learned from Max Friedlander today, and to enlist him in her plan to finish this off.

Since the moment she had seen Belle lying dead with her throat cut, she had felt hardened, crusted over. She had surveyed the ransacked house coolly. It had been ravaged—drawers dumped out, closets emptied, beds cut open and pulled apart, pictures and mirrors pulled down and smashed, furniture slashed, bookcases upset, books thrown everywhere. The wreckage of the kitchen lay all around them—piles of food from the refrigerator and freezer, broken dishes, cans, cutlery, pans, and, on top of it all, a layer of garbage already beginning to smell. She had barely glanced at it.

But under the table she pressed Ra's big head against her leg, her fingers stroking the silky expanse of ear. Finding him unharmed in the backyard had brought her to her knees, for a long, desperate hug of relief, but even then her eyes had stayed dry.

If this had been done to frighten her, it had succeeded. She was frightened. But she was damned if she'd show it or give in to it.

Sophie broke the long silence. "How could they do that to an innocent creature? Why would anyone do all this?" She gestured at the ravaged kitchen. "I really need a drink," she said in a low voice. "Do you have anything, Katherine?"

Katherine had thrown out the white wine and the one old bottle of Scotch her father had kept in the cupboard when Sophie had come to stay—to eliminate temptation. "No. Nothing," Katherine said.

"Now, darlin'," Cooper said to his daughter, patting her shoulder with thick fingers, "you just be glad you and Katherine weren't here. Letting you two gals stay here alone with this maniac on the loose was real bad judgment on my part." He looked at Katherine's lowered eyes, willing her to look up at him. "You can't say you weren't warned."

Vic turned around looking puzzled and opened his mouth to say something when Lieutenant Sharb appeared in the doorway, his face tight and angry. Vic stood aside to let him in. "Just about finished," Sharb said, facing Katherine. "You know you can't stay here tonight. You either," he said to Sophie. "Back door's splintered, needs replacing, and this mess is just too depressing."

From his place behind Sophie, Cooper Driscoll strode around the table toward Katherine, stepping over a pile of smashed crockery, his high-heeled boots striking the linoleum with such force it made the floor shake. He rested a heavy hand on Katherine's back. "My niece is coming home with us as soon as you're finished with her, Lieutenant," he said. "It's clear she needs some rest."

Katherine came to attention with a flash of panic. She hadn't thought about needing a place to stay, but she certainly couldn't stay at the Driscolls'. It would be like going from the frying pan into the fire.

Sophie lifted her head. "Please come, Katherine."

"Thanks," Katherine said, directing her words to Sophie, "but I've already made arrangements with Vic to stay at his house."

She glanced at Vic's face to catch his reaction to this lie. He nodded, his face calm.

Cooper raised his chin and looked down at Katherine with deep-set navy eyes. "That doesn't seem really...appropriate, does it? Katherine, I insist. Lucy's expecting you. I already called her to get the guest room ready. You can keep the dog with you in there. No problem."

Katherine still didn't look at him. "Tell Lucy thanks, but I've already accepted Vic's offer," she said. "I'll be fine there for tonight."

Cooper raised his voice. "But, Katherine, this—"

Sharb interrupted him. "Miss Driscoll, have you been thinking about what I asked you? This house was searched like nobody's business, turned inside out. What do you have that someone would go to all this trouble to find?"

Katherine concentrated on keeping her voice low. "I told you I don't know."

Cooper, his scowl now a deep gash in his face, turned to face Sharb. "Lieutenant Sharb, you've already been over this and Katherine says she doesn't know. Surely that's enough for now. It's pretty clear this . . . pointman, who sent her that threatening note, is just escalating his threat."

"What?" Vic asked, taking a step forward. "What threatening note?"

Katherine groaned inwardly. She hadn't told Vic about the note yet.

Cooper answered before she could find the words. "On Tuesday my niece got one of those notes like her father and Travis Hammond got. And that's why she should—"

Sharb interrupted again. "This does look like a threat, Mr. Driscoll—the dog killed like that, the house tossed way beyond what was needed. But it doesn't look to me like the pointman's style. He's already made his threat." He shook his head. "This is too messy. Not his MO. Could I see you in private for a minute, Katherine?"

It was the first time he had used her given name. Katherine rose from the table quickly and patted her leg for Ra to heel. She followed Sharb through the hall, where they skirted the chalked outline of a dog's body on the floor.

Sharb was silent for several minutes, leaning against the sofa arm and looking down at his small, scuffed shoes. Katherine recognized his technique and remained silent, too. She discharged her nervous energy by kneeling down and rubbing Ra's ears more vigorously than he liked. He walked away from her and settled down under the window.

Finally Katherine was unable to endure the silence. "Lieutenant Sharb, have you found out anything more about Dorothy Stranahan?"

"Nope," Sharb said. "We've drawn a blank so far. No Donald or Dorothy Stranahan owned property or were registered to vote or had a telephone in Austin in the late fifties. And zero on the son, too. If Donald Stranahan, junior, was in one of the armed services, it was under another name."

Abruptly Sharb looked up, his tiny black eyes intense as a raptor's. "What the hell is going on here, Katherine?"

Katherine wanted to turn and run. She hated lying to him; during the last two weeks she had come to feel some admiration for his persistence. But she couldn't tell him. It was a family matter, not her secret to tell. Before she could tell anyone, she needed to discuss it with Anne Driscoll, and before she did that, she wanted an incontrovertible piece of proof to present to her.

"I don't know what's going on," she said. "Someone ransacked my father's house and killed his dog and I don't know why."

"Oh, hell! You know why they killed that damn dog. It never would shut up, so they killed it."

"Probably."

"It was also a good way to let you know how serious they are. Katherine, if there's something you haven't told me, please tell me now."

She sighed and looked down at the threadbare carpet. Lying was exhausting. When she finally looked up, she said, "What's your first name?"

"Bernard," he said with a shrug.

"Okay, Bernard. I don't know. When I do know something, I'll tell you. We all need to get to bed. May I go?"

He let a puff of air out through his nose and shook his head. "Why don't you want to stay at your uncle's?" he asked. "It was real obvious you didn't want to go there."

Katherine jerked her head up. Lying to him had made her angry. "Where I stay really isn't any of your business, is it, Lieutenant?"

He flinched as if she'd hit him. Then he squared his shoulders. "It certainly is my business. You're right in the middle of this case. You've gotten a warning from a murderer who's killed twice. Your house has been tossed, one of your dogs butchered. Unfortunately, it's all my business." He was breathing hard when he finished. Then he waved a hand of dismissal at her. "Go on. We're finished for tonight. Sergeant Lomas is coming to board up the back door. I'll wait for him. If I was you, I'd tend to that first thing tomorrow."

WITH RA IN THE BACK along with a suitcase containing her two zoo uniforms and a few personal items she'd salvaged from the chaos of the house, Katherine followed Vic's car to a rutted road in Westlake. He turned into a winding driveway at the end of which a small stone-and-glass house nestled in the middle of a large wooded lot.

Vic pulled her bag from the car and unlocked the front door. He switched on the lights and stood aside. Katherine and Ra entered a living room in which there was a leather sofa and nothing else. "I never seem to get time to shop for furniture," he apologized, dropping her bag at the door. "For the past eight years I've been saying I'll do it on my next day off, but then something happens and I never get around to it."

Katherine shrugged.

Turning to lock the door, Vic said, "I'm glad you're staying here and not at the Driscolls'." His back still to her, he said, "Why didn't you tell me about the note, Katherine? Sharb knew about it. Sophie knew. Even that asshole Cooper Driscoll knew. Why keep it secret from me?"

"Cooper knew about it because I asked Sophie to come stay with me. I just didn't think about telling you, Vic. I've been preoccupied with the photographs, and the note just seemed like another issue. I wasn't keeping it secret."

He turned around to face her. "Another issue, shit! Your father gets killed. No one knows why. Then his attorney gets killed. You inherit these photos. You start asking around and then you get a note just like the ones they got, threatening death. And the house you're living in gets ransacked. Surely they were looking for the photographs today."

Katherine nodded. "I think so."

"But you took the copies to New York with you?"

She nodded again.

"What about the originals?"

"They're in a safe-deposit box at a bank," she said.

"So they didn't get anything?"

Katherine shook her head. "Not that I know of."

"Good." He collapsed on the sofa and patted the place next to him. "Who might have known about the photos?"

She sat down to think it over. "Damned if I know. You and Max Friedlander are the only ones I've told. But on Wednesday I asked Hans Dieterlen some pretty direct questions about game ranches." She put her hands to her cheeks. "That was a bad mistake. He's certainly in on this with Cooper. But I don't know how they could have known about the photos.''

Vic moved closer to her on the sofa. "Tell me what Max Friedlander told you. I could see in your face the whole time over at the house that you have news.''

Katherine began to talk. She told him everything Max Friedlander had told her. "And the shipping orders were all signed by Hans,'' she finished.

Vic gasped and hit his forehead with the heel of his hand. "I'm so fucking dense. When you showed me the photographs the other night, I just couldn't believe what they seemed to say. But for the past year I've wondered. Every damn time a shipment comes into Dallas, Hans Dieterlen insists on going personally to collect them instead of sending one of the animal maintenance people. And he has stopped asking me to go along. This has been going on right under my nose and I've been so stupid. I just thought the guy was a glutton for work.''

He shut his eyes and squeezed the bridge of his nose between his thumb and index finger. "I just can't believe Sam is in on this. At the very least, he must be deliberately ignoring it.''

His voice grew in volume, echoing around the bare room. "And that goddamned, overbearing Cooper Driscoll, the big philanthropist, standing there tonight with his belly hanging over his belt, pretending innocence. God. I'd like to see that pretentious son of a bitch go to Huntsville for this.'' He lowered his voice. "And maybe for murder, Katherine.''

"I've been thinking about that," Katherine said, leaning back in the deep sofa and closing her eyes. "What I'm pretty sure about is this: Cooper buys the animals with foundation money, pretending to the dealer that they're for the zoo, then he resells them to the game ranches and keeps the money, or shares it with Hans Dieterlen, maybe others. My father finds out somehow, follows them, takes the photographs, and copies the zoo records.''

Vic leaned back and stretched his legs out, his foot coming to rest touching hers. "Let's take it further. Cooper finds out your father knows and arranges for him to be killed, probably has Hans do it. But it's too late; your father has left the photographs hidden for you.'' Vic reached over and picked up both her hands in his. "Katherine, why not call Sharb right now and tell him? This may be just the piece of information he needs.''

She was silent.

"Why not, Katherine?''

She opened her eyes and looked at him. "I can't tell him yet and there are some bothersome things you don't know."

"What things?"

"I'll tell you in the car," she said, jumping up. "Everything. I'll bare my soul."

"The car?"

"Yeah. On the way to Kerrville."

"Now? It's almost nine."

"Yeah. That's good because it's dark. Vic, I can't think about anything else. It's urgent. I can't stand not doing anything. I want to tell my grandmother all this, but I need some proof to convince her. Let's go right now." She reached down, took his hand, and pulled on it.

He nodded and a small smile spread into his big flashy display of teeth. He looked like a buccaneer or a highwayman—a perfect companion for the task she had in mind. "I suppose you want me to bring my tranquilizer pistol," he said, squeezing her hand and letting her pull him up so he stood close to her.

She smiled back. "And your camera. If it weren't for the problem of getting a bongo to lie down and spread its legs, I could do it myself."

KATHERINE THOUGHT that Texas highways at night were the darkest places in the world, and the loneliest. Highway 16 was an inky ribbon undulating through total blackness, pulling the car around its smooth curves at a relentless speed.

Vic woke up just as they crossed the Pedernales, fifteen miles outside of Fredericksburg. He'd fallen asleep on the outskirts of Austin after she'd told him all about her father's payments to Dorothy Stranahan and he had slept soundly through Dripping Springs, Johnson City, and Stonewall.

He jerked his head up suddenly and said, "What was the name of the woman again? The one your father was making those payments to?"

"Dorothy Stranahan," Katherine said.

"Stranahan." He shook his head hard, like a dog with an earache. "It's familiar, but I can't quite place it." He stretched his legs and brought his seat back up.

Katherine took her eyes off the road for a minute to look at him. "Familiar how?"

"Oh, somehow the name rings a bell." He looked around and said, "Boy, is it dark! Where are we?"

"About ten miles from Kerrville. You don't have to do this, you know. You could just fix the dosage now and show me how to use the dart gun. I'm a good shot. You could wait in the car."

"Hell, no. I need the exercise. But, Katherine, you know this is a wild-goose chase, don't you? I don't want you to get your hopes up. The bongo's been here for a month now. Chances are it's been shot already. In which case it's stuffed and hanging on some elegant wall in Rover Oaks. And even if it's still there, odds are we won't find it. I was at the ranch about ten years ago to vaccinate their aoudads. It's a huge place. Needle in a goddamned haystack."

"I know, Vic, but I've been thinking. If it's still there, they wouldn't let it out with the other antelopes, would they?"

"No. It's too valuable. They'd have it confined somewhere."

"And I don't think they'd risk having it out in the open, do you?"

He thought for a moment. "Probably not."

Her voice was getting animated as her excitement grew. They were only a few miles away. "So we're looking for a shelter, a barn maybe. Vic, if we can find that bongo and get a picture of his ISIS number, then I can go to my grandmother with conclusive proof that some of the animals bought with foundation money are ending up at game ranches. I know you think I ought to take this to the police now, but—"

He broke in. "Just for the record, yes, I do. I think we should stop right now and call Sharb."

"I know. But I can't do anything without Anne Driscoll's go-ahead. It's her foundation. Her money. Her son." She glanced over at him again. "And I keep wondering why my father didn't go to the police."

"Maybe he got killed before he had the chance to," Vic said, "like we're going to, if we wait too long."

THE WROUGHT-IRON ARCH over the stone gateposts said RTY RANCH in letters so ornate they looked more like Arabic than English. The heavy gate was closed and locked. That Katherine had expected. What she hadn't expected was the fourteen-foot-high chain-link fence with a barbed-wire crest running behind the gate and encircling the entire property. She looked at it and sighed.

"It has to be that high to keep the deer in," Vic said. "Must have cost a fortune. At least it isn't electrified." He reached to the back seat and hauled into his lap the knapsack he'd packed before leaving the house. "Keep driving. We'll have to find a weak spot."

As Katherine drove, he drew out of the pack a long pistol that looked like a toy. He pulled an aluminum dart with a yellow tuft at the end from the bag and fitted onto it a needle with a small barb on the end. Then he stuck it into the barrel of the pistol until it clicked. "It's got a dose of M-99 big enough to bring down a bongo in a few seconds," he said, "bigger dose than I'd usually use, but still in the safe range." He stuck the pistol in his pants pocket. "In the unlikely event we find a bongo."

When they came to the corner of the property, Vic said, "Can you switch this to four-wheel so we can turn off the road here?"

Katherine shifted and turned left onto a dirt track that ran parallel to the fence. They bounced along for about a mile before he said, "Whoa. Look at that big old tree. That's what we're looking for." It was a towering oak on the opposite side of the fence, several of its gnarled branches spreading over the barbed-wire top. "Could you turn around and park the car so we're right under it? As close to the fence as you can get."

Katherine made a circle and maneuvered the car so it was directly under the main branch and almost touching the fence.

"I'm going to show you the only useful thing I learned in the army," Vic said. He opened the door quietly, dragged his pack out, and began to unload it. First he pulled out a black leather jacket which he threw in to Katherine. "To cover your white blouse." As she was putting it on, he handed her a flashlight. "For emergency use only." Then he took out a neatly coiled rope and laid it on the roof of the car. "Ready?"

Katherine took a deep breath and slid out the passenger door, zipping the heavy jacket and slipping the car keys under the floor mat.

Vic slung his pack over one shoulder and climbed onto the hood of the car, and from there to the roof. He picked up the rope and stood on top of the car so his eyes were level with the barbed wire at the top of the fence. When he reached his arms overhead, he was able to grab the branch with both hands. He tested it by gradually putting his weight on it. Then he stretched one leg over to the fence, finding a toehold for his tennis shoe, and hoisted himself up, putting the other foot into the mesh and walking up the fence as he hauled with his arms. When he was high enough, he pulled himself onto the branch and threw a leg over it, careful to avoid the barbed wire.

Katherine, standing now on the car roof, looked up into the darkness. The figure in the tree, dressed all in black, dark skin and hair disappearing in the night, showed suddenly a flash of white teeth. Like the Cheshire cat, she thought.

He wrapped one end of the rope around the branch, tied a loop in the other end, and dropped it to her. "Around your waist," he whispered. "Then do what I did. I'll help."

She slipped the loop around her waist and grabbed on to the branch, which she could just reach. She stuck a toe into the fence and began to climb. Vic tightened the rope and supported part of her weight as she walked up the fence and pulled herself up on the branch. As she did it, she thought that her three weeks in the snake pit had yielded some benefits; the heavy lifting had definitely improved her upper body strength.

Getting down the tree was much easier because there were several low branches on that side of the fence. Once on the ground, inside the ranch property, Katherine's legs shook violently. Exertion. Fear. Anticipation. She wasn't sure which.

Vic left the rope hanging from the tree branch and led off in the direction of the front gate. The sliver of moon gave just enough light for them to see major obstacles in front of them—mesquite clumps, trees, and an occasional prickly pear. When they had walked in silence for about ten minutes, Vic stopped and took hold of her arm. The lights of a building complex appeared through the trunks of a peach orchard. He knelt down and Katherine hunkered close to him. A big two-story house showed several lights inside. A huge flood illuminated the area in front. Behind it loomed a garage and some other small outbuildings. About a quarter of a mile back from those was a horseshoe-shaped complex of what looked like motel cabins.

He leaned over to her and whispered, his lips grazing her ear, "If I'm remembering right, most of the livestock's in corrals and a barn back of the cabins. Let's look."

He rose and led the way, skirting the lighted area and heading toward the back of the complex.

In the dark they could just make out a long low building with a fenced-in area at one end. Katherine smelled the horses before she saw them standing in the corral. There was a lot of snorting and stomping of hooves as the horses caught their scent. Vic gave them a wide berth. "I think there's a barn back here," he whispered.

After a few minutes of walking along an unpaved track, a huge barn loomed against the dark sky. "In here," he said.

They approached silently. The big double doors were latched but not locked. Vic lifted the latch and dragged the door open a crack so they could squeeze through. Inside was total darkness. The warm rich smell of manure engulfed them. Vic switched on his flashlight and shone the beam around. Stalls around the sides contained cows and a few horses. In one large stall, a flock of sheep looked back at them with sleepy eyes. Not an exotic animal in the place.

"Strike one," Vic whispered in her ear.

They closed the door behind them and headed back toward the stable they had already bypassed. "I don't like this," Vic whispered. "The horses are jumpy and it's close to the house. But these stalls are a possibility."

They walked along the row of stalls built of rough, weathered boards. Dutch doors opened at the tops. They glanced in each door. Most contained a single horse. One held a goat which let out a loud *maaa* as they passed. When they got to the end, they circled the corral. A few of the outdoor horses jumped and whinnied as they passed.

They stopped to listen. Nothing.

They walked down the other side of the long stable, looking in each stall. As they approached the last stall, a distant barking started from the direction of the house.

"Oh, shit," Vic said. He grabbed Katherine's arm and headed back toward the barn at a fast walk.

The barking intensified. It was coming toward them.

Katherine couldn't see them in the darkness, but she could hear. Thudding paws. Panting. Baying. "There are two of them," Katherine whispered, "and they're big—Dobermans, I think."

She looked around for a tree. Anything they could climb. But the landscape was bare. And the barn was too far.

Vic broke into a run. Katherine reached out for his arm. "Don't run, Vic. Makes it worse."

The barking was just yards away now.

They turned and saw the two dark shapes hurtling toward them, baying and slavering. Vic pulled the dart gun from his pocket. "I can only get one; takes several minutes to reload."

Katherine unzipped the jacket, ripped it off, and wrapped it around her left arm as she turned to face the two dogs bearing down on them.

Vic moved forward a step. As the first dog lunged at him, he stepped to the side and fired. The dart hit flesh with a soft, *pfut*. The dog yipped and swerved. As it turned to attack again, it staggered and collapsed to the ground. A large rottweiler with a thick studded collar.

The second dog flew at Katherine. She extended her wrapped arm in front of her body and said in her trainer's voice, "Release, sir." It didn't work. With a growl, the dog grabbed the padded arm in his teeth and clamped down. Then he shook his head from side to side, snarling with fury, as if he were trying to rip her arm from its socket. Katherine needed all her strength to keep holding the arm in front of her. She'd been attacked by dogs before and had the scars to prove it, but never like this, in the dark. She knew the teeth would soon penetrate the thick leather and pierce the flesh of her arm. She glanced desperately to Vic. He was digging in his back pack, scrambling to reload the dart gun.

A door slammed in the distance. A man's voice called, "Diablo! Jeff! Come here, you clowns."

The dog dragged down on Katherine's arm with all his weight, snarling and whimpering with the effort. Just as she felt the prick of a fang through the fabric, she was pulled to her knees by the dog's weight.

The man's voice called out again, "Who's there?" Another door slammed. Two more voices spoke.

Then she heard the *pfut* of the dart pistol. The dog released its grip on her arm. A blessed reprieve. She felt she could float off the ground now, run forever without that weight dragging her down.

Vic grabbed his pack and they sprinted away from the approaching voices. They streaked past the barn and turned into the woods. Toward the car. Vic ran at full speed. His knapsack bounced on his back. The dart gun was still in his hand.

Katherine kept up, but barely. Her lungs burned with the effort. Her eyes stayed glued to the ground.

She heard the cry of surprise when the men found the sleeping dogs. Then she heard nothing but Vic's labored breathing ahead and her own gasps. After a few minutes, she fell behind. Vic glanced back and slowed down to a trot, waiting for her to catch up. After another minute they slowed to a walk and listened for the sounds of pursuit.

Nothing. No voices behind them. No barking. They'd gotten away.

Now all they had to do was get back over the fence.

But they'd failed. She should have known it was impossible. They were just lucky to get away unhurt.

"Katherine," Vic whispered, through his gasps for breath, "let's get out while we can."

She nodded her agreement, too short of breath to speak.

They picked up their pace, heading back to the fence.

A minute later, Katherine glimpsed a dark shape off to the left. She pointed. "Look."

It was a small structure standing by itself.

Vic put his sweaty cheek down close to hers. "Want to check it out? It's taking a chance. They'll try to find us."

"Let's just look," Katherine rasped.

He turned to glance behind. "Okay. A quick one."

As they approached, the structure took the shape of a small aluminum siding barn with a corral at the back.

They tried the door, but it was locked tight with a huge padlock. "Let's go," Vic said, pulling her back the way they had come.

"Wait." She ran around to the side. The only break in the aluminum wall was one small window, five feet off the ground.

Katherine put her head close to look at it. It was open a crack. She stuck her fingers in and lifted. It opened smoothly.

Vic handed her his pack. "Pass this through when I get in." He hoisted himself up to the window and squeezed through. As he dropped inside, he let out a gasp of alarm or surprise. Katherine held the backpack up to the window. Vic pulled it through.

Katherine hoisted herself up into the window frame. It was so dark inside she could see nothing. She hesitated.

Vic switched on his flashlight. The beam illuminated one large amber eye, which repelled the light, casting it back off an opaque, reflective disk that glowed chartreuse behind the amber lens. The face around the eye was scarred and mangled. On the broad, flat nose and under the closed eye, dozens of black scars striped the tawny fur. Half of one ear was ripped away. The black mane was patchy and littered with wood shavings. The old lion looked placidly at Vic and tried to stand up, but the cage was so small, he had to crouch. He rubbed his side along the wire and purred as Vic pressed his hand against the wire mesh.

Vic spat out one word: "Bastards."

Then he stood and played his light slowly around the enclosure. Sacks of feed and wood chips were stacked against the far wall, a wheelbarrow, an empty cage, and several crates took up the middle. In the corner near the door was a large metal stall. Inside it, watching them with gentle dark eyes, stood a quivering mahogany-colored antelope. Twelve white stripes ran down its side.

"Eureka!" Vic whispered. "Let's do this fast."

In a rage of excitement Katherine wriggled through the window and dropped into the barn.

Pfut! The sound of the dart pistol broke the stillness. The bongo fell to its knees. It lay with its head drooping for a few seconds and then fell over heavily on its side.

"That stuff really works," Katherine said, rushing to help.

"Help me roll him over," Vic said. He propped the flashlight against his pack and they both shoved until they had positioned the bongo on its back with its legs sticking up in the air. Vic took his camera from his bag and straddled the animal. Katherine held it in place by the rear legs.

There in the groin where the rear leg met the belly, on that hairless blue skin, was the black tattoo—its ISIS number—11-3881. Katherine knew it by heart. It was one of the bongos Max Friedlander had shipped.

The flash was an explosion that blinded her in the darkness. Vic took five more pictures from different angles. Then he pulled a hypodermic from his bag and injected it into the bongo's haunch. By the time they were out of the stall, the animal was already struggling to its feet.

Vic stopped at the window. He aimed the camera at the old lion and took five more snaps.

As Katherine was struggling through the window, she heard him whisper, "I'm sorry, boy, so sorry." She stopped and looked back, not sure she'd heard him right. Vic gave her a shove through and tossed his pack to her.

"Vic, you know that lion," she said.

He dropped to the ground next to her. "Damn right. Let's go." Katherine leading, they ran toward the car.

They'd done it. Home free. She saw the fence in the distance.

Then she heard the voices off to the side. And behind them. Lights flickered through the trees.

"Goddammit," Vic whispered. "They're right here."

They sprinted now, crashing through bushes. Only fifty yards to the fence.

A voice behind them shouted. "Halt! I'll shoot."

They ran faster than Katherine knew she could.

When she heard the first shot, she accelerated. Her lungs burned with the effort.

As they neared the fence, she cried out in disappointment. No tree. No car. Just a long expanse of sturdy chain link. Fourteen feet straight up.

They'd misjudged the car's location.

A spray from a shotgun pattered into some mesquite trees just behind them.

Vic grabbed her hand. "Come on. It's this way." He made a sharp right turn. They ran along the fence for what seemed like an eternity.

Another shot hit the ground between them.

They ran bent over. Katherine's lungs felt wrung out.

She looked up. Thank God. The tree. Its branches seemed to reach toward them.

Vic grabbed the trunk and stood aside. He pushed her up into the lower branches and followed close behind. She climbed as if there were a fire licking at her feet.

Two shots thudded into the tree trunk. The rough bark scraped her hands and arms. She reached the top branch as the men broke through the bushes into the clearing. She dropped down onto the roof of the car.

She slid down the side of the Jeep to the ground and crouched behind the car. Vic dropped down next to her, panting and dripping sweat onto her as shots pinged into the other side of the Jeep.

Two men were climbing the tree. Two more approached the fence.

Katherine opened the door and grabbed the keys from under the mat. Vic was right behind her. She scrambled into the driver's seat and hunched over the wheel. She fumbled with the keys, trying to find the right one.

The car rocked as a man dropped on top of it.

She found the key. It took three tries to get it in the ignition.

Vic was struggling now to close the door. An arm from above held it open.

Katherine started the engine and revved it. Another heavy thump on the car. Two up there!

"Go! Go!" Vic yelled.

She stepped on the accelerator, jerking the car forward. Then she hit the brake abruptly, throwing a body off the side. The other rolled onto the hood, blocking her vision. Vic slammed his door. "Again!" he shouted.

She stepped on the accelerator again and spurted forward. Again, she slammed on the brake. The man on the hood flew off and hit the ground in front of the Jeep. She swerved to avoid him.

"Fast," Vic shouted.

She drove as fast as the terrain permitted, punishing the car by bouncing over ditches, low bushes, and cacti. When they got to the road she increased her speed to ninety and maintained it all the way to the highway.

The only sound in the car was their labored breathing as they tried to suck in enough air.

Then Vic began making a low rumbling noise which turned into laughter as they raced along the highway. He tried to speak but couldn't get the words out. Finally he slid closer to her and conquered his laughter enough to say, "That was incredible. We actually did it. At the end there, I didn't think we would." He put his arm around her shoulders. "Are you okay?"

"I think so. My adrenaline is pumping so hard, I'm not sure. How do you feel?"

He took her right hand off the wheel and pressed it between his legs. "Carnal in the extreme."

She felt the hardness stir under her touch.

"Mmmm," he said. "How fast can you drive this car?"

NINETEEN

KATHERINE TOOK a long time washing the dust and sweat out of her hair. Then she let the hot jets sting her skin alert. It was 2:30 A.M., but she had never been more awake.

It wasn't just the delicious buzz of excitement and relief that had charged the air in the car all the way back from Kerrville. It wasn't even the tingling anticipation of knowing Vic must be waiting for her now in his bedroom. It was the sense she had of being on a quest.

It reminded her of fairy tales where the youngest child was given a task to perform, a difficult task that only she could accomplish. Her father had given her this mission and she was close to the end; she could feel it. She had followed the clues he left for her, discovered what he had intended she should. What remained was for her to make the correct use of the discoveries. Today she would do that; she would finally meet her grandmother, confront her with what she had discovered, show her the proof. Surely this must be what her father had wanted her to do.

She stepped out dripping onto the bathroom floor. As she toweled her hair, she remembered she had nothing clean to put on except her zoo uniform. She wrapped the towel around her waist and looked into the bedroom, half expecting Vic to be waiting there. The room was empty, so she threw off the towel and walked to the closet naked. Inside hung a few old shirts and jackets. One was a long white T-shirt. She pulled it on over her head and inspected herself in the mirror on the door. The shirt hung to the top of her knees and clung to every curve of her still-damp body. Perfect. She smiled at herself, tucked her wet hair behind her ears, and let a tiny shiver ripple down her body.

She stepped into the hall to listen for sounds of life. A refrigerator door closing at the other end of the house brought her stomach to life; she followed the sound, trying to remember the last meal she'd had. It was probably the rubbery turkey sandwich on the flight from La Guardia yesterday.

The kitchen was dim, only the small light over the sink turned on. Vic stood at the counter spreading peanut butter on a piece of toast. Ra sat at attention at his feet, gazing up hopefully.

"Beggar," she said.

They both turned her way. Vic wore a short blue terry-cloth robe and his hair was dripping wet. He studied Katherine for a moment in silence, his face in shadow. Then he held the piece of toast out to her. The aroma of hot toast and melting peanut butter filled her mouth with liquid and made her stomach contract. She took a few steps forward, but just as she reached out to take it, Vic put it behind his back. She smiled, really wanting it, and reached around him with one hand. Looking down at her, he brought his left arm around behind her back and slowly drew her in close until her breasts just touched the rough terry cloth covering his chest. Now the clean fragrance emanating from his skin and hair merged with the rich peanut butter to create a scent that instantly filled every cavity of her body with wet desires. She looked up at him and said, "Peanut-butter toast must be the human pheromone."

He brought the toast forward and waved it gently under her nose; then he held it to her lips. She took a bite, scattering crumbs between them. The toast was thin and crisp and the peanut butter was chunky, whole peanuts crunching between her teeth as she chewed. He raised the toast to his mouth, took a big bite, and offered her the rest. She took it in her teeth. Never had she eaten anything so profoundly delicious.

"How soon can you get the pictures developed?" she asked.

He used the back of her shirt to brush the crumbs off his hand and encircled her now with both arms, gradually tightening them so she could feel the contours of his body against hers. "The one-hour place opens at ten," he said in a hoarse voice, "so I should have them back by noon."

She felt the solid musculature of his chest, the hollow of his flat stomach, and the hardening pressure of his groin asserting itself. "I want to show them to my grandmother as soon as possible," she said, her breath becoming ragged. "Can you bring them to me as soon as you get them?" God, they hadn't even started yet and already she couldn't breathe.

Remembering yesterday's fantasy of exploring his bare back, she pulled away a little so she could slide her hands inside his robe and move them around under his arms to his back. As she did it, the robe fell open. Now nothing but her flimsy, damp shirt separated them.

"Yes," he said. "Oh, yes."

Starting in the small of the back, she inched her hands upward, savoring the smooth skin stretched taut over the hard muscles underneath. "I'm working on a plan to get in to see her," Katherine said, glancing up at his face. His eyes were closed and his lips open. "Do you have any ideas?"

He pulled her tighter against him. "I have lots of ideas."

She moved both hands up to his neck, the place where his hair curled under his ears, and traced it with her fingertips. The hair was wet and cool, just beginning to curl, the skin warm and smooth.

He leaned over and found the same place on her neck with his mouth and kissed it, lingering over it, tasting the skin. Then he lifted his head and found her lips. First he just touched them with his, licking off the crumbs and traces of peanut butter. Then he took full possession of her mouth, occupied it, explored it, made it the center of his attention. She held on to him now for support because her entire body was liquefying like peanut butter on hot toast.

When he spoke he was breathless, as if he'd just raced up twenty flights of stairs. "Let's go to my room. Okay?"

She nodded into his chest.

AT SIX WHEN the alarm went off, she was already awake, watching his bare back and doing the most recent version of her countdown: three days left until the auction, until she had to deliver Ra up to the highest bidder. It was her first thought every morning, even this morning when her head was brimming with other issues.

Vic reached up an arm to shut the buzzing off and turned to face her. "What are you thinking about?" he asked.

"That I was never much interested in sex before," she answered.

He laughed with pleasure and put his index finger on her forehead, drawing it slowly down the center of her body. "Neither was Teddy," he said. "It just takes the right combination."

She glanced at the clock and sat up.

He reached for her bare shoulder and said, "What's the hurry?"

"I've got to be there on time today. I swore Danny an oath I'd work for him today since he filled in for me yesterday."

He pulled her down. "Katherine, I can make an excuse for you. You don't have to go."

She sat up again. "Yes. I do. Today especially. There's that famous herpetologist coming this morning. They've all been looking forward to it; I'm the only one who's willing to hold down the fort. You won't have the photos ready until noon anyway. Then I'll take a long lunch hour to visit my grandmother. Today's the day."

She swung her legs out of bed and felt suddenly shy at her nakedness. Noticing her discomfort, he found the shirt she had borrowed at the foot of the bed and tossed it to her. She flushed when she caught it and slipped it over her head, remembering how a few hours before he had lifted it up one inch at a time, taking an excruciatingly long time to remove it.

He jumped out of bed naked and disappeared into his bathroom.

SHE SHOWERED QUICKLY and dressed for work.

In the kitchen, Vic had already fed Ra an old hamburger and let him out. "We need to get dog food today," he said, not looking up from the orange juice he was pouring.

She watched the top of his dark head and felt an undulating contraction move down her abdomen. This was going too far too fast. "I'll need to start the cleanup on my father's house after work and get the door fixed," she said.

He handed her a glass of juice and looked directly into her eyes. On his chin was a small bloody cut where he'd nicked himself shaving. "Katherine, please don't go back there alone. Stay here for a while, at least until this is over. I like having you here."

The concurrent rushes of pleasure and apprehension made her scalp tingle. She liked being here, too, but she needed to get some distance from him. He had been invaluable last night in Kerrville. Too valuable. There was no way she could have done it without him. She was already becoming dependent on him. "Thanks. Let's think about it today," she said.

"And, Katherine, please let me in on your plans. I want to help and I don't want you to be anywhere alone. At work this morning, manage to be with someone else all the time—Iris if possible. She's got a good head."

He downed his juice in one big swig and poured another glass.

"What worries me, Vic, is what will happen to them now?"

"Simbaru and the bongo?" he guessed.

She nodded, sipping her juice.

In the car on the way home from Kerrville he had told her the story. The old one-eyed lion in the barn was Simbaru, the lion he and her father had fought over several months before. Vic had decided he was so old and decrepit that even if he recovered from his pneumonia, he should be euthanized; Lester maintained he still had some good years left and was a good draw. Finally, Hans Dieterlen had intervened with a compromise: They would give the lion to a private zoo he knew of in west Texas where he would be cared for. He had sold them animals in the past, he said, and knew it to be a first-rate operation.

But Simbaru had ended up crammed into a tiny cage waiting for a hunter who would pay thousands of dollars for the privilege of shooting a lion.

"I've been thinking about them, too," Vic said, a muscle at his jaw twitching. "I'm really responsible for Simbaru's plight. Your father was right. After you've talked with your grandmother, I think we'll send the U.S. Fish and Wildlife agent over to pay them a visit."

ALONZO STOKES hadn't liked Katherine's taking the day off.

"Have a nice day yesterday, Miss Driscoll?" he asked without looking in her direction as she entered the keepers' area. He was leaning against the counter using a toothbrush to clean dried blood and tissue off a tiny skull. Iris was sitting on the counter working on an even smaller skull. "Thank you for gracing us with your presence this morning." He glanced at his watch. "Even though you are nine minutes late." He looked up at her. His pitted skin tightened across the sharp cheekbones so that she could see underneath the shape of his skull as clearly as she saw the reptile skull in his hand.

"I had some pressing family business to take care of," she said.

"Well, we have some pressing business here, too, and we're behind. First item is the rocks in the crocodilian pool. They've grown an unpleasant algae that needs scrubbing off. It's pretty resistant stuff, so it needs some real elbow grease. It's too much for Harold alone, so you and Wayne have volunteered to help him. Pool's almost drained now, so you can get busy." He stuck the toothbrush under the running faucet to wash it off, then went back to the delicate job. "You're in luck, though," he added with a stretch of the lips, "Wayne and Harold have already removed the caimans."

She turned to leave, but he called her back. "Second item, Katherine. You'll be glad to hear the female bushmaster has finally got around to finishing her shed. You can move her and the quarantine male into the breeding room today. But dammit, Katherine"—he held the skull under the faucet—"there's some loose slivers of wood on the west-wall baseboards. Big sharp ones. Didn't you notice that? They could get cut or ingest those sharp splinters. You need to sand them down real smooth and clean up all the dust that results. Can you manage that on your own?"

"All but moving them," Katherine said. "I'll need some help."

"Definitely," Alonzo said. "Bob Jacobs, relief keeper over in birds, is coming to help this morning. He's experienced with snakes. The two of you should be able to handle it, but be careful. They're often nippy right after they shed." He set the dripping skull on a paper towel to dry and left the room.

Katherine watched him go, struck by how loosely his pants hung on his gaunt frame. He had lost weight in the nineteen days she had been watching him. And the dark circles under his eyes were black now.

"Don't pay no attention to him," Iris said. "He's just nervous because his hero is here—Cyrus Harrison-Jones—and the big man's going to come back here after the lecture, so Mr. Stokes is jumpy. He wants everything more than perfect today."

Katherine nodded as she picked up a sponge and helped Iris clean the scales and bits of flesh off the stainless-steel counter. She had been hearing for two weeks about the impending visit of the world's foremost expert on Lacertilia, the author of the definitive work on skinks. He was speaking in the Ambrose conference room for all staff members who were interested.

Katherine stopped at the supply close for a bucket, a stiff scrub brush, and a pair of high rubber boots. She headed toward the rock pool that usually displayed six or seven dwarf caimans that drifted around all day with only their wicked-looking eyes and the tips of their snouts above water. Now the pool was almost drained, only a small puddle of water left in the bottom. Harold Winters, the crocodilian specialist, and Wayne Zapalac were standing in the pit with their rubber boots on, looking it over. The rocks were covered by a bright green slime that smelled like spoiled fish. She turned her head away, took a deep breath, and stepped into her boots. Then she climbed down into the empty pool.

"Join us in the pit," Wayne said. "We missed you yesterday. Did the funeral go okay?"

Katherine looked up at him. "What? Oh, yeah. It went fine." She bent down to feel the algae. It was slimy and stuck fiercely to the rocks.

Harold, a tiny man who always wore a red bandanna tied around his head, said, "This is going to be a son of a bitch. We try everything to discourage this stuff, but it grows anyway. Let's get to it." He began scrubbing in silence.

Harold rarely spoke and Wayne was unusually silent this morning. Katherine was grateful. It left her mind free to range.

Every time she thought ahead to the meeting with Anne Driscoll, her imagination began to run wild. How she would get in the house with Janice Beechum on guard she didn't know yet. Maybe she'd have to do it by brute force, just push in and dash up the stairs. Once in, she was certain she could convince Anne to listen. She would show her the photographs, her father's and the ones Vic had taken last night. Her grandmother would be shocked, of course. It would be difficult for her to believe that Cooper was doing this, but eventually she would be convinced.

Katherine tried to stop the fantasy here. It was best to enter with no expectations, so the disappointment wouldn't be too severe. But her fantasy was irresistible. Her grandmother would thank her for revealing this. She would hold her hand and then they would talk for hours and hours about Katherine's childhood—all the things she didn't remember. It was silly, she knew, but her hunger to fill in those blanks that were her first five years had been growing. The tiny snatches of memory she had retrieved since she'd been in Austin had only fed it.

She had to admit it: She was in need of a past.

Finally she let herself linger on the night before with Vic. Blood rushed to her face and she looked up to see if anyone was watching. Wayne. He had stopped work and was looking at her in puzzlement. "Penny for your thoughts," he said.

"Oh," she mumbled, "nothing really. Just thinking about the bills I haven't paid."

"You, too, huh?" He started to scrub again, vigorously, with both hands on the brush, sending the slime flying. "It's sure hard to live on a keeper's salary, isn't it? I don't know how I'd make it if I didn't have some disability payment from the Marines."

"Disability?" she asked, staring at his powerful arms and hands.

"Yeah. You can't see it by looking, but it's there. Goddamned Vietnam."

It took more than two hours for the three of them to clean all the slime off the rocks, then hose them down and drain out the rest of the water and residue. When they began refilling the pool, Alonzo arrived and examined the rocks, indicating his approval with a single nod.

Katherine stretched her cramped legs and climbed out of the pool. She stepped out of the rubber boots that had made her feet feel like boiled potatoes and looked at her watch. It was now a quarter to eleven. Vic would be getting the developed photos soon. God, she hoped they'd turn out. He would come around twelve and arrange for her to take two hours off.

She picked up her boots in one hand, the bucket in the other, and carried them back to the keepers' area. She rinsed the brush and sponge in the sink, leaving them out to dry on the draining board.

Then she went back to the supply closet and looked through the neatly labeled plastic boxes that were stacked on the shelf. She pulled out the box labeled "Sandpaper" and removed two new sheets. She also grabbed a pair of shears from the hook.

At the entrance to the breeding room, she switched on the overhead light and unlocked the door. Inside, she ran her eyes around the baseboard of the empty room. Sure enough, on the west wall were three angry-looking spikes of wood protruding from the cedar baseboard. Damn. How could she and Iris have missed that when they cleaned this room four days ago? No wonder Alonzo was annoyed. It did look dangerous.

She knelt down on the floor and felt the huge jagged splinters. She snipped the large pieces off with the shears, eager to erase this evidence of her negligence. Then she began sanding the rough wood, keeping her head up as high as she could so she wouldn't breathe in the fine dust. She jumped when Iris stuck her head in the open door and called, "We're off. You need to come mind the store until Bob gets here."

Katherine twisted around to look at her. "Okay. I'll be right out. Enjoy."

"Thanks for staying. I'll take notes for you."

Katherine noticed Iris had applied a tiny coat of lipstick and had fluffed her hair up. She smiled up at her. "Yeah. Everything you ever wanted to know about skinks but were afraid to ask."

She turned back to the baseboard. One area was still rough. She wanted to get it a little smoother before she stopped. She intensified her efforts, sanding furiously and coughing as the dust reached her nose. She had it almost smooth now. Just one small area of roughness remained.

She heard a footstep at the open door and said, "*Okay*, Iris. I'm coming." But she didn't turn around until she heard a noise that sounded like some heavy coils of wet garden hose hitting the floor just behind her.

She spun around on her knees and caught a glimpse of the two shining dark coils, already unwinding. She had just enough time to note the beadlike texture of the black inverted triangles.

Bushmasters.

Then the lights went off.

The door slammed shut, throwing the room into total blackness.

The click of the bolt shooting home on the outside of the door entered her heart like a dull cold arrowhead. From that frigid center an icy chill radiated out through her body, reaching down into the marrow of her bones.

Zero at the bone. Frozen. Iced. From the bone it crept outward, a glacier filling her body, chilling the blood in her veins and the moisture in her eyes, stinging her skin and numbing her toes and fingertips. She moved not a muscle, unable to rise or even blink an eye. She had become a kneeling ice sculpture.

The room was utterly silent. How loud the hum of the fluorescent lights had been! She yearned to have that noise back in her ears. Just a tiny hum, a vibration, some tickle in the ear to keep her company while she waited.

She was so alone. Never before in a life of being alone had she felt so completely forsaken.

Eyes wide open in the pitch-darkness, she imagined she could see them—the female seven feet long, heavy-bodied, her freshly molted scales shiny and distinct, slowly uncoiling and raising her spade-shaped head, darting her black tongue in and out to smell the air. The male, nine feet long, more slender, stretching himself along the floor to feel for vibrations. Had they seen her before the lights went off? If they hadn't and if she stayed frozen, maybe they wouldn't know she was there. Maybe they would just remain where they were. They couldn't see in the dark any better than she could. Maybe it would be all right.

Then she felt a dull cramp of despair.

Fool.

Those snakes don't need to see. They're pit vipers.

She could hear Wayne explaining the cavities under their eyes. They were infrared heat receptors that would register the presence of warm blood in the room. A bushmaster could find a mouse and strike it accurately in total darkness.

She heard now the tiniest noise—the whisper of a scraping—and she knew what it was: the ventral scutes of a large snake pushing off against the floor.

She should at least stand up, get her face out of striking range. But the muscles of her legs were frozen brittle, her feet stuck to the floor. It was a state of terror she couldn't have imagined.

Yet there was something familiar about it. As if she had once before, long ago, felt this same arctic terror.

Yes, I remember. I'm so scared I can't move. It feels just like this—the frozen bone marrow, the blood chilled, thickened.

And there's a snake, too! In the house I live in with my mother and father. It must be a nightmare. Yes, a nightmare. I'm just five years old, and I have trouble separating dreams from reality.

I dream of being awakened by loud noises, shouting. It's hot. Very hot. My nightgown is wet, stuck to my body. I'm frightened. I get up to find my daddy. I open the door of their dark bedroom and walk in. Some light from the hall spills in. I see they aren't there. Pasha comes in. Big warm Pasha. I feel better with him close. I love him. He whines and sniffs around the room.

A noise—that same tiny scraping—comes from under the bed. I am curious. I lean over to look. A dark head, a monster's head with a darting tongue, appears from under the bed. Then the long body slowly emerges, undulating forward. I'm frozen, mesmerized by the sinuous movements. My feet stick to the floor. If I move I will rip the skin off the soles of my feet.

Pasha growls. He barks and jumps forward.

The snake curves its way toward me, closer and closer. Until the head with the flickering tongue almost touches my bare foot and bony shin. Now Pasha barks again. He snarls and snaps at the snake. Fast as an eye blink the snake strikes. The dog yips in pain.

I scream and scream.

Now Katherine heard the sound again. That tiny scraping. It began, then ceased, and began again. They had moved closer. She listened intently. Yes. They were moving again. This way. Both of them.

The ice that had contained her and numbed her body began to thaw. She was suddenly unprotected.

In panic, she tried to visualize the room, seeking a place to escape. She recreated it exactly: a rectangle with a low ceiling and nothing else. Except her. And the two snakes. And two pieces of used sandpaper. And the shears. Where were the shears? She had put them down to sand, but where? Did she dare feel around on the floor? Or would the vibration attract the snakes to her? What would she do with the shears if she had them when she couldn't see? If she reached for them, the snakes might be there. They'd feel threatened and they'd...her heart was beating so hard it was rocking her body. She tried to stop it, to reduce the vibrations.

Oh, God. Please. Let someone come and unlock the door.

Vic. He was coming. But not until noon. An hour away.

Bob! Yes, Bob What's-his-name. From birds. He was coming. But he would not know to look here. The others were gone. For hours.

She couldn't live that long. The panic was growing and taking hold now. The intermittent scraping, the rustling of scales were coming closer. If only they could bite her without touching her; then it wouldn't be so bad. The ice had all melted and now she felt herself a great meaty body, reeking hot blood, like an overthawed steak, calling them with her heat. They would find her. They couldn't miss.

The sound again—a rustle, like tissue paper being blown by a faint breeze. This time almost at her feet.

She threw her head back and remembered that other time, the nightmare she had forgotten until now. She had screamed and screamed.

The snake rears up again, bent into an S. I watch the flickering tongue. The blunt nose. The black stripe running back from the eye. The mouth opening wider. The fangs.

My screams tear at the tissue of my throat, suck at my lungs, stab into my eardrums. A dark shape fills the doorway behind me. The light comes on. My father. Yes, he's there. He bellows in fury and despair. Kate, oh, no. He throws himself forward, lifts me up in his arms. He sweeps me from the room.

Then they all come running—the others. What are they all doing here in the night? Their faces are white masks of fear and anger, as if the worst thing in the world has happened. As if there is no going back.

That was the night her mother had dragged her out to the car. The night they had left forever.

Her raw throat felt bloody and torn. Slowly she contracted the muscles in her thighs and stood up. She took a step back, right into the wall. The wall! She would climb it. That was it! She would climb the wall. She turned and tried to dig her fingers into the plaster, clawed them into the wall trying to get a grip. She pressed her cheek against it and pulled, scrabbling her feet against it to boost herself up.

When the pain came, finally, it was in her left ankle.

Like prongs of fire. A burning so intense she gasped.

It was sharp, fiery, excruciating—and a relief. She could lie down now and it would be over. She sank slowly to the floor and curled up tight. It was so long since she'd had a good sleep. She abandoned herself to the dream.

WHEN THE LIGHTS came on, she was dreaming of a voice. It whispered in her ear, "No. Please, no. This can't happen. Not again." She dreamed of strong arms lifting her. "It was supposed to be me this time. I got the warning. I was ready." A door slammed and the voice cooed on and on: "Don't worry. We'll get this fixed up. It's my sin, not yours. The Stranahan business, what we did. Oh, Kate. Don't worry. We'll take care of this. Don't worry."

She heard the shrieking of an alarm and some shouting.

Then she remembered something.

That old dream—it wasn't a dream at all. It had really happened.

TWENTY

THE BLOOD THAT KEPT oozing from between her teeth tasted like thick rusty salt water.

Katherine sat up in bed, spat into the plastic basin, rinsed her mouth out again, still awed that those two tiny red pinholes in the back of her ankle could cause such devastation throughout the body. Why should a snake that needed to kill only rodents have venom toxic enough to kill a human being? Nature's death force seemed charged with a power far greater than needed.

She held the basin under her chin, trying to decide if she was going to throw up again. No, she decided, her stomach was certainly empty by now; and since she planned never to eat again, that, at least, was finished.

The doctor had assured her that all her symptoms—nausea, kidney pain, extreme swelling in the limb, bleeding gums—were typical of hemotoxic envenomation. She'd like him better if he would speak plain English and say snakebite. But he seemed to know what he was doing.

She pulled the sheet away from her left leg and forced herself to look down at it. Not so bad. It was still puffy, but nothing, thank God, like the shapeless mass that had swollen up on the first day. And the color was better now. During her twenty-eight hours in the hospital, the leg had darkened from its usual tan to an angry puce, but now it had faded back to yellow-brown, like an old bruise.

The pain had also subsided. After beginning as an intense burning at the bite, it had erupted into fiery shooting pains the length of her leg. But now it had settled down into a mild, throbbing soreness. She could shift around in bed and hobble to the bathroom by leaning on a cane. The worst of it was behind her, she hoped.

Katherine sighed as she settled back onto the pillow.

"Jesus," Sophie said, looking up from her needlepoint. "If I'd known what it was like getting bit by a snake, I would have been a lot more scared than I was. And growing up in Texas I've always

been plenty scared, made it a point not to go anywhere a snake
might be. Wise.''

Katherine loved hearing Sophie's voice, knowing that she was
sitting there at the foot of her bed. All her life Katherine had preferred being alone in times of trouble or sickness. She had deliberately isolated herself to get through whatever it was on her own:
Chicken pox, her mother's absences, failed romances, business
problems—she had navigated them all alone.

Until now.

Something had shifted when she was in that dark room. She
didn't want to be alone anymore. She wanted people around her.
The closer the better.

Throughout the emergency-room ordeal yesterday and the tests
to see if she could tolerate the antivenin, Sophie had held one hand
and Alonzo Stokes, very tenderly, had held the other. It amazed her
that she wanted them there, that they were a comfort. It was as if,
with the venom, she had been injected with the capacity to feel the
comfort other people could provide.

And the comfort came from many sources. All yesterday afternoon people had stopped by her hospital room, and with each visit
her spirits had risen. Lieutenant Sharb had come first, looking totally out of place in the cool white room with his shiny black suit
and stubbled face. Vic had come, bringing perfect photographs
from the night before, promising to take good care of Ra while she
was in the hospital. Sam McElroy had come, assuring her the zoo
insurance would cover all her expenses. Danny Gillespie had come,
trying to smile and bearing a huge bouquet of fresh flowers he
surely couldn't afford. Wayne had come with the news that the
bushmasters had done nothing but copulate since one of them had
bitten her; they'd have to remember this aphrodisiac, he said, next
time they had trouble getting snakes to breed. Iris had come hoping this wouldn't discourage Katherine from working with herps.
Cooper and Lucy Driscoll had come to present her with an immense basket of fruit.

She turned her head on the pillow to look out the window. The
sky was a deep, pure blue, with luminous clouds floating through
the window frame. It was Sunday afternoon and the auction was
scheduled for Tuesday. She'd be lucky to be released from the
hospital by then. It might have to go on without her, but maybe
that wasn't such a bad thing. After it was all over, she could go
clean out the house and deliver Ra. She had a valid excuse for not
having to face the day itself.

"Thank God for Alonzo Stokes's perfectionism," she said aloud.

"Amen," Sophie said, reaching out to rest a hand on Katherine's good foot.

Alonzo had repeated his story like an incantation yesterday as they waited for the ambulance and then as they rode to Brackenridge. Waiting for the lecture to begin, he had gotten worried about the splinters and the moving of the bushmasters. He'd had a bad feeling about it, he said, and since the lecture was delayed ten minutes, he had run back to check. Thank God. When he turned on the light and lifted the shade on the observation window, he had seen her curled up on the floor. The snakes were in the other corner copulating. Thank God.

She had been bitten only once, in the left ankle. It was bad, but it could have been fatal if they had continued to bite her. Apparently they had lost interest in her after one bite.

Saved by the power of sex.

In the ambulance, when the world began to come back into focus, she had looked up at Alonzo's face. The intensity of his concern seemed to be melting the flesh right off his narrow skull. He had refused to let go of her hand, insisted on riding in back with her, the antivenin buttoned in his breast pocket.

When she remembered what he had whispered as he carried her out of the breeding room, she had reached up and pulled his head down close to hers, so no one else—the attendant on her other side, or the driver—could hear. "Alonzo, you said something about Stranahan back there. Did you know Donald Stranahan? What does he have to do with all this?"

He pulled back slightly and shook his head gravely.

"Alonzo, you said you'd been warned. Did you get a note from the pointman? Did you? I did, too. What happened to Stranahan? This is important. Please tell me."

Again he shook his head, not as if he were saying no to the questions, but as if he could not think about it now, or ever. "I was upset," he said. "It was just ravings." He squeezed her hand in both of his. "Thank God I came back. That's the important thing. This is going to work out just fine. I promise. I can tell. I've seen lots of snakebites and this'll give you some pain, but you'll be dandy. Especially once they start the antivenin." He patted the vial in his breast pocket.

So he refused to tell her anything. Looking up at his ravaged face, she was certain that he knew the whole story. But he would never tell. Perhaps he had gotten so accustomed to keeping the secret after thirty-one years that his ability to tell the truth had atrophied. Whatever valve it was in the human spirit that allowed the free passage of honesty had been rusted shut.

She would have to reconstruct the story without his help.

If she wanted to reconstruct it.

Even without her willing it, part of the story had begun to spin itself inside her head. She thought she knew now what had happened thirty-one years ago. The ugliness of it made her cringe.

When Sharb arrived at her hospital room, just as they were bringing her up from emergency, she had asked to speak to him alone. Quickly she told him what Alonzo Stokes had murmured in her ear. Then she gave voice to some of her suspicions. She suspected Donald Stranahan had worked at the zoo, in the reptile house, when her father worked there, when Alonzo Stokes was the new head keeper there. She had a feeling it was very important. Would he please check it out? Right away?

He sure as hell would. Did she feel up to a few questions? Sharb pulled out his notebook and asked the inevitable. Had she seen the person who'd thrown the snakes in and locked the door? Who else had keys? Whom had she seen that morning? Did she have any hunches?

None of her answers gave him much help.

Finally he had left, posting a uniformed man outside the door of her room. Now that she'd had a day to think about it, she could see that that might be a problem. She'd have to get rid of him.

The nurse with the yellow smile button pinned on her belt entered on soft feet and once again wrapped the blood-pressure sleeve around Katherine's arm, gravely watching the gauge rise and fall. She picked up Katherine's limp wrist and felt her pulse while looking at her watch. She checked the IV bag of antivenin, held the tube up to see if it was dripping just right. All the comforting rituals they had been enacting every hour.

Katherine accepted it all with a mellow sense of well-being. The sheets felt cool and smooth to her skin, and she was comforted to see the dogged persistence of her vital functions.

When the nurse readjusted the swathed foot on its pillows, Katherine flinched.

"Still pretty tender?" the nurse asked. "Want something more for the pain?"

"Will it make me sleepy again?" Katherine asked.

"Probably. But it won't hurt you to sleep a little more."

"No." Katherine said. "I need to be alert for a while and I'm really not having much pain now."

"You need to rest. It's the best thing for snakebite, slows down the envenomation."

Katherine looked at the IV bag. It was almost empty. "When this is finished, is that it?" she asked.

The nurse looked at the label on the bag. "Probably. That's the recommended dosage—five ampoules of Soro Anti-Laquetico. But Doctor says we need to keep you under observation for another twenty-four hours, at least—perhaps several days—to observe the site. With hemotoxic venoms, there can be some tissue damage. Do you need to urinate yet? We need another sample for the lab when you do."

Katherine shook her head.

The nurse adjusted the pillows under Katherine's head and picked up the basin, looking into it without the slightest appearance of repugnance. "Well, want to change your mind and have a little dinner? If your stomach's still queasy we could bring Jell-O and soda crackers."

"No, thanks," Katherine said, her stomach heaving at the thought.

After the nurse left, Katherine felt sleep pulling her down again. Against her will. She was so tired. It wasn't just the pain medication. She tried to recall the last time she'd had a full night's sleep. In the five days since she got the note from the pointman she had slept precious little, and during the last forty-eight hours, even less. Two days ago she had flown to New York to see Max Friedlander. Her father's house had been ransacked and she and Vic had driven to the ranch in Kerrville. And escaped gunfire. And made love. And then... Her lids flickered. So much happening in such a short time. She let her eyes close. No wonder she . . . just a short nap.

WHEN SHE WOKE, the window that had been filled with blue sky was a black square and Sharb was standing next to her bed, staring down at her, willing her to wake. She sat up with a start. Sophie's chair was empty.

"I told your cousin to grab a bite," Sharb said. "Don't worry. She'll be back."

Katherine lowered her head to the pillow and looked up at the black beadlike eyes, so close together she wondered if he had any peripheral vision at all.

"You were right," he said. "Donald Stranahan, the husband of the woman your father sent money to, did work at the Austin Zoo. For two years, up to July 18, 1958." The black eyes glinted in the dim light. Katherine knew him well enough now to recognize the signs of excitement. "Until he was snake-bit. By a bushmaster. Same species that nailed you. But Mr. Stranahan died from his bite."

A tiny smile on his lips, Sharb waited for her reaction.

Katherine just nodded once. She wasn't much surprised. She'd been expecting it. It fit right into the story that was telling itself in her head. "So he was the one fatality at the Austin Zoo."

"Yup. There have been a few other snakebites, but this is the only one that ended in death. It was before they had a specific antivenin, like that one they dripped into you. But it wouldn't've made any difference anyway."

"Why not?" Katherine asked.

"Seems he was drunk, fooling around with the snakes late at night after the zoo closed. May even have had a woman there, showing off for her. Stokes says he was a cowboy type—wild, macho womanizer, big drinker. Snake bit him square on the cheek right next to the nose." Sharb rubbed his stubby fingers on that area on his own face.

"This much I got from Alonzo Stokes. I also looked up the old ME's report. Stranahan died real fast. He was drunk, blood alcohol level of point twelve, and alcohol speeds the progress of the venom, they tell me. Even so, strange he never managed to push that emergency button or do anything to save himself. Alonzo Stokes says"—here Sharb tried to imitate Alonzo's twangy drawl— " 'It's one of those things that just happens sometimes when you let impetuous or intoxicated folks around dangerous reptiles.' " He took a piece of Kleenex from his pocket and blew his nose. "Makes you wonder, don't it?"

It made her do more than wonder; it drove home the certainty. His gaze was making it difficult for her to maintain her mellow calm. The more she tried not to show emotion, the harder it was to keep the skin under her eye from twitching.

"What'ya thinking?" he asked. Without taking his eyes off her, he dragged Sophie's chair up to the head of the bed and sat down on it.

What she was thinking she could never tell him. The description of Donald Stranahan's type was all too familiar to her. Now the story in her head was pushing into some very tender areas.

She looked up. Sharb was waiting for her to say something.

"My father was a co-worker, maybe a good friend," she said. "When Donald Stranahan died he must have felt in some way responsible for the crippled widow and young son. So he helped support them after the accident. That would explain the payments." She watched his face to see if he was buying it.

Sharb snorted. "Yeah? Policemen get killed all the time and sometimes it's because of some mistake another policeman makes. But he doesn't give up his salary for the rest of his life because of it. He donates a coupla hundred bucks to the Police Benevolent Fund, he goes to the funeral, and that's it."

Katherine shrugged and looked at the ceiling.

"I've got this theory. Wanna hear it?" Sharb asked. Without waiting for an answer he said, "Donald Stranahan, Junior."

Katherine felt herself tense.

"Look. Alonzo Stokes is as slippery as one of those snakes he's so crazy about. But we finally leaned on him so he admits he got a note from the pointman, too. More than a week ago. So we got notes to four people: your father, Travis Hammond, Stokes, and you. What do you four have in common? Well, Stokes and your father worked in the reptile house, which, by the way, was just a wing on the bird house then, when Donald Stranahan was killed there. Wow. Some coincidence, huh? And Hammond, well, he passed your father's payments on to Stranahan's widow, so he's connected, too. Then there's you, Katherine. Let's suppose it's a sins-of-the-fathers sort of thing and young Stranahan sees you as responsible because you're your father's daughter."

He looked over at her trying to get an expression. "Are you with me so far?"

She nodded.

"Now. Doesn't it seem strange to you that of the four people who received these threatening notes, you were the only one to report it to the authorities? You gotta ask, why didn't the others report it? Alonzo says he didn't take it seriously enough to report it. Now, that's bullshit. Right? The only answer is they've all got something to hide. I don't know what it is, but I know I'm right.

"Okay. Now we're going to make a leap. I told you I've been bothered by the fact that we haven't been able to find any trace of Donald Stranahan, Junior. Neighbors in Belton recall his leaving home right after high school to join the service, but we can't find a record of him in any of the armed forces. And they keep damn good records. So this is bothersome. Also, there's something about the pointman notes: this eye-for-an-eye stuff. It's about vengeance. He blames all of you for his father's death. And then he kills with animals: a tiger for your father, a deer for Travis Hammond, and he tries to kill you with a snake." His voice was rising with excitement. He got off the chair and perched on the edge of the bed, leaning his head down close to hers. "And here's what really does it for me, Katherine: He uses the same kind of snake to go for you that killed his father."

He stopped for a few seconds to let this have its impact, then continued, swept up in his narrative. "Why wait so long to get his revenge? you might be asking. Well, maybe he had to wait for his mother to die. But he planned it long ago, when he changed his name and entered the service with a new identity. So when the time is right, he comes to work at the zoo so he can get at your father and Alonzo easily. This has to be the work of an insider. Only someone who has keys and knows schedules could have done that to you today. Someone who knows how to handle deadly snakes." His mouth puckered in distaste. "Whether I'm right about Stranahan I don't know, but it is certainly an insider at the zoo doing these things."

He stopped to take a breath and looked to Katherine for a response. But she'd let her eyes close. "Say something. You're not asleep. Am I off track or does it makes sense?"

She tried to picture the white faces surrounding her in the dream. "Go on," she said. "I'm thinking about it."

"Yeah. Well, don't knock me over with your enthusiasm. Donald Stranahan, Junior, would be thirty-nine now. I just sent a man to Belton to get a description of him, a yearbook picture, anything he can get from twenty-one years ago when he left town. Of course he was an eighteen-year-old boy then. But a good photograph could crack this case for us. I looked at the zoo's employment roster. Of the seventy-six employees, there are twenty-one men between the ages of thirty and forty-five. But let's get serious here. Of those who have the keys and the knowledge, it narrows down to four, doesn't it, Katherine?"

She still didn't speak.

"You could be helpful here," he said. "You've had more chances to observe them than I have. Come on. Open your eyes and work with me on this."

Katherine kept her eyes shut.

"Let's think about them for a minute," Sharb said. "The four men in that age range who have full sets of keys for the reptile house and who have the know-how, and, listen to this—all four of them served in Vietnam. I've thought all along that a guy calling himself 'the pointman' must've been in Nam." He pronounced the four names, pausing after each one: "Wayne Zapalac. Danny Gillespie. Harold Winters. Vic Jamail. They were all near the scene at eleven o'clock yesterday. All four were there at the beginning of that lecture before the alarm broke it up. Any of the four could have tossed the snakes, locked you in, and gotten to the lecture in time. It started a little after eleven and people were going in and out."

"Was Danny there?" she asked in surprise, opening her eyes.

"Yes. He had the day off, but came in for the lecture. He says he's eager to broaden his knowledge so he can work in reptiles. There's no accounting for taste, is there?"

"A description would help," Katherine said finally. "Those four men are very different physically."

Sharb nodded. "You've been working with them. What do you think of them?"

In her mind Katherine lined up the four men in front of her. "Harold I barely know. He doesn't talk much. Danny...well, he's high-strung and so eager to ingratiate himself, you want to hit him. You know he asked to work with my father in cats and he's been trying to get into the reptile house, but Alonzo doesn't want him."

"He is a nervous little bugger," Sharb said, "And a picture that's bothered me from the start is him arriving first on the tiger scene that morning after Dieterlen's call for help. Here's a guy who was a sharpshooter in the army. He's got a gun and he sees that poor devil in there at the mercy of—" He stopped and looked at Katherine for the first time since he began the speech. "Oh, sorry. Well, you know. Your first impulse would be to shoot. Unless he knew already that the guy was dead."

"Yes," Katherine said. "I've wondered about it, too."

"How about Wayne Zapalac?" Sharb asked. "You tell me your impressions first. Then I'll tell you what I know."

"Wayne...well, he's interesting—very sensitive, different from the way he looks, but it's hard to figure him out."

"Sensitive, huh?" Sharb snorted. "He's got a record for assault and battery. Psycho release from the Marines. Expert in silent killing in Vietnam. A real strong suspect, I think. We're checking his credentials, seeing where he really came from. This guy could be the one."

"Maybe," she said, looking up at the blank television screen on the wall. "He wanted to work with my father and when that didn't work out, he chose reptiles."

Sharb sat forward on his chair. "How about Vic Jamail?" He looked at her intently. "Is this a hard one for you?"

Katherine sighed. Hard? It made her heart shrink to think he might do anything to harm her. Of the many things she did not want to believe, this was one of the most powerful. She thought of the pleasure of lying close to him, running her hands down his back. "I trust him." She turned to meet his eyes. "I know it's not him."

Sharb held his palms up toward her. "Well, he battled publicly with your father and he has access to every area in the zoo. You just need to stay away from him until we work this out."

They both looked up as Sophie entered the room with a steaming cup of coffee in her hand. Sharb stood up and pushed the chair back into its former position with a screech.

"When are you likely to get the description from Belton?" Katherine asked.

"Could take a while. Twenty-one-year-old info takes time. My man didn't start until six tonight. He may not have anything until tomorrow."

Katherine yawned.

"Guess I should go," he said, sticking his hands into his pockets. "How do you feel? I forgot to ask."

"Oh, I feel . . ." She paused to decide how she really did feel. "I feel free from fear. You know, when you're terrified of something and then you come face-to-face with that very thing and the worst happens, you don't have anything to be afraid of anymore. I feel good."

He nodded in such a vigorous way she knew he understood.

"Well, I'll let you know when I hear anything." He turned to leave.

"Lieutenant Sharb," she called. "Bernard. Your man outside the door. Please take him with you. The security is plenty good here."

"And I'm staying the night, anyway, Lieutenant," Sophie said.

He turned around and planted his feet firmly. "Someone tried to kill you yesterday."

"Please. It will help me relax. Take him with you. We'll be fine." He hesitated.

"It makes me feel like a prisoner. I can't stand it. Please."

He looked at Sophie. "No one comes in but the doctor and nurses. Right?"

"Right," Sophie said, blowing on her coffee.

Katherine lifted her head. "Call when you get the information from Belton. Even if it's the middle of the night. Will you?"

He nodded and left.

"What information?" Sophie asked. "I've been pretty good about not bugging you, haven't I? But now it's time to tell me."

Katherine held up five fingers. "Give me just a few minutes to think something out, Sophie. Then we'll talk."

She closed her eyes and watched the speckles of light on the inside of her lids. Sharb was pretty good. He was using the facts creatively to reconstruct an old story, an old crime probably. But he could only see part of it. Because he didn't have the memories.

But she did have the memories.

Some lines of poetry she had been forced to memorize in the eighth grade kept intruding into her head. What was it? *The Ancient Mariner.*

> *Like one, that on a lonesome road*
> *Doth walk in fear and dread,*
> *And having once turned round walks on,*
> *And turns no more his head;*
> *Because he knows a frightful fiend*
> *Doth close behind him tread.*

That's exactly how she felt. She didn't want to turn around to face the fiend that was treading behind her.

Well, why should she? Life was difficult enough.

She could adopt Sharb's limited version. She could dismiss her memories and adopt a version that fit the known facts.

It would be so much easier.

On everyone.

Now was the time to decide. Was she going to go after the truth no matter what damage it did? Or was she going to contain the damage? Hell, people edited the truth all the time for comfort's sake. It was a reasonable survival technique. They chose condensed versions that would be easier to live with. She had that option now—to ignore, bury, deny the memories that had come back to her. Hadn't she been doing that all her life, really? Suppressing painful memories?

If Sharb could make an acceptable picture from the puzzle pieces he had, she could just throw away those painful extra pieces. Why not? Like that snake in her parents' bedroom, she could banish all the other memories right back under the rock of obscurity where they'd lived for thirty-one years.

She could wait until tomorrow and see what Sharb came up with on the pointman. That was the sensible approach. If he managed to identify the pointman and arrest him, then she could just leave it at that. She did not have to tell the other things to anybody, or even think about them.

Alonzo Stokes knew, but he would never talk, even if he died for his silence. Even if she died for it.

And anyway, all she had were bits and wisps of memory. Nothing solid. It was not up to her to do this.

She clenched her fists and felt knots of tension throughout her body. The problem was she couldn't stand this incompleteness, this not knowing. It felt as if the story had germinated and was growing through her body like a bean stalk, pushing its way relentlessly up and out. It demanded closure.

And if this story was true, Anne Driscoll knew it all.

Katherine couldn't wait any longer. She had to find out.

Now.

Tonight.

SHE OPENED HER EYES and smiled at Sophie, who had let her needlepoint drop into her lap and was staring into space, her eyebrows squeezed together. Katherine shifted over on the bed a few inches and patted the space she'd made. "Sophie, let's talk."

Sophie rose and perched very gingerly on the edge of the bed, trying not to rock it. "So. Are you going to tell me all of it, or an abridged version?"

Katherine smiled. "I'm going to tell you everything I know. Some of it is going to be hard for you to hear. And some of it is going to be hard for me to tell."

Sophie crossed her arms over her chest. "Go ahead. I can take it if you can."

Katherine began with Cooper Driscoll's misuse of foundation money. Step by step she led Sophie through the evidence. "So," she summarized, "with the photos my father left, and with Max Friedlander's records, and with the photos Vic took in Kerrville last night, it's pretty conclusive that your father's been looting the foundation for some time."

Sophie sighed and let her head droop forward. She ran both plump white hands through her frizzy hair, then massaged the back of her neck. "Well, it doesn't really surprise me. He's been so desperate." She glanced up at Katherine without lifting her head. "I suppose he was behind that mess at your father's house, looking for the pictures?"

Katherine sighed and nodded.

Sophie closed her eyes. "And Belle. What are you going to do, Katherine?"

"I don't know. Before I make up my mind, I'm going to ask Anne Driscoll what she wants done."

Sophie lifted her head. "Yeah. I can see that. It's her money. It's really her decision. But with her, the family name and reputation is everything. I don't think she'll want you to go public with it. She'll be mad. God, she'll be mad." She thought about it for a minute, then looked up. "My father may be a real sleaze, a money-grubber, a blow-hard, but I don't believe he's killed anyone."

"No. I don't think so either. I don't think his swindle is related to the killings at all. Sharb thinks the murderer may be the son of a man who was killed at the zoo thirty-one years ago and that he's doing it for revenge."

Sophie's blue eyes rounded with interest. "Revenge for what?"

Katherine told her about the payments Lester Renfro had made to Dorothy Stranahan through Travis Hammond. She continued with Alonzo's revelations yesterday and Sharb's information that Donald Stranahan had been killed by a bushmaster.

Then Katherine took a deep breath and told her about the dream that was not a dream and how it felt to be locked in the room with the bushmasters. "Sophie, I'm not sure why, but it's so liberating to discover that this terror of snakes comes from what happened that night. Now I have to know the rest of it."

Sophie's eyes were wet with empathy when she finished, which made Katherine's eyes mist over. "So," Katherine said, blotting her eyes with her hospital gown, "Sharb is waiting for a description of Donald Stranahan, Junior, from Belton. He's sure it'll turn out to be Vic, Wayne, Danny, or Harold Winters. And I agree with him. I think some old injustice is coming home to roost."

Sophie looked stunned. "Oh, Katherine. I hope for your sake it's not Vic."

This was one thing Katherine was not prepared to discuss yet. "What time is it?" she asked.

Sophie glanced at her watch. "Almost ten."

"Sophie, I need to talk to Anne Driscoll now. Tonight. I have this sense of urgency, that if I don't do it now, I'll never have another chance. It'll be like what happened with my father. I can't stand the uncertainty. Let's drive over there now."

Sophie's mouth fell open. She snapped it shut. "No way. No damned way."

"Please just hear me out. You heard the doctor say it all looked good and the treatment was complete."

"Yes, ma'am. And I also heard him say you were to stay in the hospital, in bed, another few days to ensure a good recovery."

"Yeah, but if you drove the car around to the front door, I'd hardly have to walk at all. There's a cane in the closet so I wouldn't have to put much weight on the leg. And if I wore your raincoat, I wouldn't even have to get dressed."

Sophie stood up and went back to her chair. She picked up her needlepoint. "No. It's a dumb idea. You can go in a few days." She sat down hard on the chair and studied her canvas.

"I have to go now. Please, Sophie. Just a half hour alone with her would do it. Then I can come back here and be a good patient. I'll sleep and eat and make a good recovery. But I have to do this first. Please."

Sophie pushed her needle in and jerked it through the canvas.

"Sophie," Katherine pleaded, "we'll be back here before they even miss us. Come on. Let's just wait until the hall is empty and go."

"Oh, there's no problem getting out of here," Sophie said, "but how do you plan to get past Janice Beechum?"

Katherine smiled. She'd hooked her. Her heart began to pound with excitement. "We're resourceful. We can cook up a plan together. You know her, Sophie, and she wouldn't be suspicious of you. Could you distract her somehow? Keep her downstairs. So I could slip upstairs. Maybe you could excuse yourself to go to the bathroom and leave a door unlocked for me?"

Sophie rubbed her chin for a minute. "Well, she's a passionate needlepointer. She works at it in the kitchen at night. Maybe I could get her to show me a stitch or something and you could sneak up to Gram's room." She threw her canvas onto the floor and stood up. "Oh, God this is absurd, Katherine. We sound like kids at summer camp. We're grown women. We can't do this. If she sees you, she'll call Daddy and he'll be furious."

Katherine looked her steadily in the eye. "Well, that would be just awful—to make Daddy mad."

Sophie stared back angrily, then let her face relax into what was almost a smile. "Just awful," she said. She walked to the small closet next to the bathroom and rummaged around in it. She pulled out a heavy aluminum cane and her wrinkled trench coat.

Katherine stifled a groan as she sat up and swung her legs off the side of the bed.

Sophie turned around and tossed her the coat. "I know I'm going to be sorry for this," she said. "Hell, I'm already sorry."

THE POINTMAN HAD been slumped down in his car watching the hospital for hours. His head was still hot with shame. "If it's worth doing, sonny, it's worth doing well," his mother had always said. He should have taken the antivenin from the refrigerator and thrown it away. No. They would just have flown some in from Houston or Dallas. Snakes were too unreliable, insufficiently aggressive.

Sluggish creatures really.

From now on he'd use a more certain method. No more trusting to chance. He fingered the .45 automatic tucked into his belt, under his leather jacket. Enough fooling around. The remaining three he'd waste the way he knew best—efficiently, with a bullet to the brain.

At least he'd given her a good scare, a few nightmares, locked in there with the bushmasters. And her afraid of snakes anyway. He smiled thinking about it. She wasn't going to die from the snakebite the way he'd planned, but at least she'd had a little taste of what it felt like.

It was important she should know how it felt. It was her family that had treated his daddy like some dead dog to put out with the garbage. He'd make her see how wrong that had been, make her admit it.

He couldn't be bought off like his mother. No way. He was a man who carried out his threats. Not some little weasel who backed off when the going got tough.

And no little setback was going to stop him. No sirree. He was a force of nature. Like Brum.

"When you fall off a horse, sonny," his mother had always said, *"get right back on so you don't lose your nerve."* Well, there wasn't much chance he was going to lose his nerve. He was getting right back on.

He should do it right now. Just go up to her room and do it. If the cousin was still there, waste her, too. She was part of that family. It would serve her right, the fat bitch.

He pulled his lucky charm out from under his shirt and ran his fingers lightly over the flat head. He needed to calm down. He was a good worker. He wouldn't fail. But he was hyped up from all the waiting. He needed to do something, to get rid of the tension.

He pulled the door handle and started to push the door open when he saw something that made him shrink back and slump down in the seat again.

Un-fucking-believable. There she was right now. Coming out the main door. What the hell! She was wearing a long raincoat and limping with a cane. How could she be out so soon? God, she must be tougher than she looked. Who would think it to look at her? Looks so hoity-toity and self-satisfied, but there she is. And there's that cousin of hers picking her up. In a BMW. Look at that. You can see she hurts the way she gets into the car.

Hell, I wonder where they're going.

When the BMW headed west on Fifteenth Street, he started the car and followed them, staying far enough behind so they wouldn't notice. The BMW took MoPac north and exited on Windsor. When it turned right on Woodlawn, the pointman began to feel an excitement in his loins. God, they're going to the old crone's house. Sure they are. This is too good to be true. He could get two at the same time. What a break!

Then only one to go.

His work would be done.

His duty fulfilled.

TWENTY-ONE

It was a blessing she hadn't been able to get a shoe on her swollen left foot. Socks made for greater silence on the uncarpeted wood stairs. Leaning her weight on the banister, she climbed painfully, one step at a time, the cane stuck under her arm. Slow progress, but quiet. One slip and Janice Beechum in the kitchen would hear, even though the television was on and Sophie was fulfilling her part of the bargain by talking loud and steadily.

Before she was halfway up, her arms and shoulders shook with the strain. Each time she bent the left knee, a stab of hot pain shot through her leg, up into her hip and abdomen. She gritted her teeth and kept climbing. Thank heavens it was just one floor.

This was certainly not how she had fantasized her first visit to her grandmother—sneaking in at night dressed in a wrinkled trench coat and dirty socks. But she was going to meet Anne Driscoll, finally.

For better or worse.

At the top of the stairs, a tiny cloisonné lamp on a mahogany table lit the landing. Katherine stopped and leaned against the wall, panting and trembling. When she'd caught her breath, she turned right, and supporting her weight on the cane, hobbled along the hallway. First door on the right, Sophie had told her.

The door was open.

The large bedroom was dark except for the glow of a single night-light and the meager rays from the hall spilling across the hardwood floor. In the center of the room stood a hospital bed like the one Katherine had just gotten out of. A rolling tray-table next to it was covered with bottles and vials, a pitcher and some glasses.

At first Katherine thought the bed was empty. But when she looked again, she saw that a very thin body, covered only with a white sheet, lay there, so still it made Katherine hold her breath. As she stood in the doorway, she sent up the first prayer she'd said since she'd stopped going to Sunday school at age nine. Please don't let her be dead. If I don't get to talk to her, I'll never know for sure. And please don't let her be comatose. More than anything in the world I want to talk to her. Just a half hour of lucidity. That's all I ask. It's my history and I have a right to it.

She entered the room, one tiny step at a time, careful to make no sound that might be heard below. The room was overheated and smelled strongly of furniture polish. Leaning on her cane for support, she walked slowly toward the bed.

When she was about six feet away she caught the glint of light on an open eye, large and luminous. She stopped, suddenly panicky. What if she's frightened and she screams? What if the shock brings on another stroke? In her haste to get here, she hadn't thought it through.

Katherine raised her index finger to her lips and held it there as a plea for silence and calm.

The head on the pillow turned slowly in her direction until both eyes were visible in the glow of the night-light. There was no trace of fear or panic in the eyes; they studied her, fixed her, absorbed her into their depths. Then they narrowed slightly, as if displeased with something.

Keeping her finger to her lips, Katherine took one step forward. Then another. And another. Until she was looking down on the very alert, sharp-chinned face of an old woman. The left side of the woman's mouth drooped slightly. Her thin white hair was drawn back tight into a hair net, and the skin was blotched and wrinkled, but Katherine recognized the straight, delicate nose and the large gray eyes. Just like her mother's.

The gray eyes continued to assess her.

The sheet moved and an arm, thin and trembling, emerged and crept slowly upward. A long index finger extended and pressed against lips in an exact replica of Katherine's gesture.

Katherine closed her eyes. *Thank God.* This was Anne Driscoll and she still had her wits about her. Katherine leaned her cane against the bed and lowered herself to sit on the edge. There was so much she wanted to say that for a moment she couldn't speak at all.

"I'm Katherine Driscoll," she whispered finally.

"I know." The voice was faint but surprisingly firm, coming from such a frail body. "I can see. You look exactly like your mother. Why did you take so long to come? Every night I spit out the sleeping pill she gives me and wait." She spoke out of the right side of her mouth; the left was immobile, frozen into a downward arc. "Are you hurt?" she asked.

"I was bitten by a venomous snake yesterday at the zoo. A bushmaster."

The gray eyes closed for several seconds, then opened wide. "We need to get out of here. Cooper hired Beechum to keep me from seeing you or making the changes I planned to..." Here she had to stop and draw some long shuddering breaths. She lifted her hand to ask for time, then let it fall weakly to her chest. Talking was clearly a strain.

Katherine filled in the silence. "Cooper has been misusing foundation money, too," she said as she reached into her coat pocket for the photographs to prove it.

Anne Driscoll stared at her as if she were a slow child. "You mean that thing about selling zoo animals to the game ranches?" The hand that rested on her chest raised slightly in a dismissive gesture. "I know all about that."

Katherine sucked in her breath. Nothing could have surprised her more. "You know?"

"Of course. Your father told me and showed me the photographs the day we made the bargain about you." Her words were clipped and businesslike, even though the voice was weak.

"Bargain about me?"

"Of course. You've come for the money, haven't you?"

Katherine felt her head spinning. "What money?"

"The hundred-thousand-dollar advance. For you to run the Driscoll Foundation. Your father must have told you about our bargain."

"My father's dead. He was killed at the zoo three weeks ago. Murdered. *Before we had a chance to talk.*"

Anne gasped and tried to sit up, but the energy required seemed too much for her. Her head fell back to the pillow as if it were too heavy a weight for her to lift.

"Tell me about the bargain with my father," Katherine said.

"He agreed not to make a scandal with the pictures he'd taken if I would agree to fire Cooper and make you foundation director. And pay you a hundred thousand dollars—as your first year's fee. He insisted that you get it in advance. Your father thought he was blackmailing me, but I liked the idea."

She stopped to catch her breath. "I've been waiting for him to come back. Lying here wondering all this time. He was going to bring you along so we could discuss foundation plans. I should have known something had happened to him. He said he'd be back in a few days and he's—was—a man of his word." She stopped and gasped for air.

Katherine felt like a cartoon character with a light bulb suddenly flashing above her head.

Of course. I've been so slow.

It all fits.

The money. In his letter he wrote that it was available immediately, not that he had it. He didn't have any money to give, so he blackmailed Anne into giving it. And what she would do in return—the thing that only she could do—was to be director of the Driscoll Foundation. Because it had to be headed by a family member.

Anne was talking again. "My mistake was telling Cooper what I intended to do before I did it. He hired Beechum and they stopped letting anyone in to see me and they won't bring me the newspaper or let me use the telephone. He thinks I'm dying. This medication they force on me is supposed to help me along, I suppose, keep me drugged up until I die." Her nostrils flared. "But I'm not going to. We're going to get out of here." She stopped and studied Katherine's face for a few seconds, breathing deeply, her thin chest rising and falling under the sheet. "Cooper didn't kill him, did he?"

"I don't think so. I don't think it has anything to do with Cooper and what he's been doing at the foundation. Travis Hammond was murdered, too, the day after my father."

Anne flinched as if she'd been slapped. "Travis, too," she murmured.

"And someone tried to kill me yesterday at the zoo by locking me in a room with the bushmasters. And there have been warning notes—to my father and to Travis, to Alonzo Stokes and to me." She lowered her head closer to her grandmother's. "The notes speak of revenge—an eye for an eye. I think it's because of what happened thirty-one years ago, the night my mother and I left Austin."

Anne turned her head away and stared at the wall. She locked the fingers of both hands together over her chest, as if she could prevent some secret of the heart from escaping.

Katherine pushed on. She *would* dig it out now. "It's important for me to know what happened. I've lived with these secrets all my life. I know it must be horrible for you to remember, but please talk to me about it."

Anne kept her eyes fixed on the wall and tensed her fingers.

"I think I already know most of it, anyway," Katherine said. "About Donald Stranahan. All I need is for you to confirm it. And to fill in some of the blank places."

Finally Anne turned to face her. "Katherine, there is no good to be gained from going into this. It seems we've all been punished adequately already for old sins. This is best left alone."

"No. It's past the point where it can be left alone." Katherine's voice shook in spite of her efforts to control it. "Alonzo Stokes is in danger. And I am. Goddamn it, my father died for this. Travis Hammond died for it. I'm in danger of dying, too, and I want to know why."

Anne looked her in the eye. "Not now. The best thing is to get out of here. I want to be admitted to a hospital tonight, get the drugs out of my system. Then we can talk. I need to be alert." Her voice swelled into the authoritative tone of a woman used to giving orders. "And I want to talk to an attorney. Immediately. Since Travis is dead, John Crowley will do. I'm going to make sure Cooper doesn't get another cent from me and has no power over my affairs. He will regret this every minute of his life."

Katherine was amazed at the strength of will in such a frail body. She had no doubt Cooper would regret it all.

"Yes. Of course," Katherine said. "I'll arrange it right now. But first I want to know what happened. Some of it I remember. And some of it I've worked out. Let me tell you what I think happened." She tried to engage Anne's eyes, but the old woman refused to look at her.

"My mother was having an affair with one of my father's co-workers, Donald Stranahan, wasn't she?"

The right side of Anne's mouth trembled. The other side remained frozen in its downward curve. "Your mother..." she began. "Your mother..."

"Was promiscuous," Katherine finished for her. "I know. I lived with her for eighteen years. And Donald Stranahan sounds like the kind of man she never could resist—an irresponsible, hard-drinking cowboy. I think maybe my father came home and found them together. And something very bad happened." She looked at Anne for confirmation, but Anne's face remained blank.

"I think Donald Stranahan got bitten at our house, not at the zoo. And I think you persuaded Alonzo Stokes to cover it up. In return he got a curatorship. A new reptile house. And unlimited funds to build his collection. Right?"

Anne shook her head. "Katherine, there's no point in going on with this."

Katherine was unable to stop. It was rolling now and she was aboard. "Am I right? Did it happen at our house?"

Anne said, "It's all just speculation. Why dig—" She stopped suddenly and her eyes grew wide with alarm.

Katherine thought she heard it, too—a creak on the landing.

They both turned to face the open door.

A dark shape blocked the doorway.

A guttural whisper filled the room. "For Christ's sake, tell her, you old crone. Tell her what she wants to know. She's going to die for it, she should know why."

The man wore jeans and a black leather jacket, open over a white shirt. Something dark hung around his neck. Strands of blond hair surrounded his head like a spiky halo backlit by the lamp in the hall. He closed the door behind him quietly and stepped into the glow of the night-light. Katherine saw the glint of glasses and the thick lids magnified into sleepy folds. He held a big gun close to his body.

"Danny," she said in astonishment. It was as if the obsequious family lap dog had suddenly turned into a snarling mastiff.

He shook his head hard, as if he were trying to dislodge something. "No. Not that weakling sycophant. Sycophant." He repeated the word slowly as if he were savoring the syllables. "Call me by my rightful name. Donald. Donald Stranahan, Junior. Or pointman. Take your choice." He pointed the gun at Katherine. "Come on. Take your choice."

Katherine whispered it. "Donald."

"That's good," he crooned. His lips pulled back from his teeth, baring them to the gum line. It was the first time Katherine had

ever seen his teeth. She had thought he kept them covered because
they were bad, but now she saw that they were perfect—beautiful,
even, white teeth.

Quickly, as if he had suddenly realized he'd revealed something, he pressed his lips shut and started toward her.

Katherine leaned on the cane and struggled to rise. But in two
long strides he was behind her, digging the pistol hard into the back
of her neck, pushing up as if he were trying to shove it into her
skull.

He stretched his head down close to the woman in the bed. "Tell
her, you old bitch, or I'll splatter her brains all over you. Tell her
now," he said.

Katherine squeezed her teeth together to refrain from crying out
in pain. She stared down at her grandmother. The face showed no
emotion, not even a flicker of fear.

"I said, tell her." His voice rose to a shrill pitch. "Now do it."

Anne Driscoll opened her lips. She spoke calmly, her enuncia-
tion exaggerated, as if she were addressing a servant who spoke
only rudimentary English. "I can see how you would blame me,
Donald, but why her? Let her go and you and I will discuss this."

In his fury he drilled the muzzle even harder into Katherine's
neck. It felt as if her head were being impaled on a dull stake. "You
bitch. You think that I've-been-to-college-and-you-haven't voice
is going to stop me? She was there," he hissed, "and she's going
to pay for it. Her slut of a mother died before I could get to her, so
she can take her place."

Anne spoke again, in measured, even words. "She was a child,
sleeping in her bed when it happened. Settle with me. Let her leave.
She doesn't even remember."

"Oh, she remembers. No one could forget that night. She's got
most of it right, doesn't she? Since you won't do it, I'll help her fill
in the blanks."

He pressed his cheek against Katherine's and dug the gun deeper
into her skull so that she had to press back. "Don't you remember, little Katie? One of the most important things about that
night? I was there. Eight years old, and I saw it all. We'd come to
your house before. Often. My daddy brought me because Mother
was sick. He'd leave me to play with you while he went into the
bedroom with your mother. Only this time, it was different be-

cause your father came home. Uh-huh. You got it right, Katherine Driscoll. He caught them in the act.''

His voice began to rise in pitch again. "Oh, I was there all right. I was in the living room watching the snakes in the glass boxes like I always did. After he looked in the bedroom, your daddy closed the door real quiet and came and knelt next to me and he watched the snakes, too. Then my daddy opened the bedroom door. I remember he stood there doing up his belt and laughing like it was all a joke. And you know what he did, your father?'' Now his voice was almost a shriek. "He grabbed up that big black snake and slung it at my daddy. Right in his face. Daddy had to pull it off him, tore a chunk out of his cheek doing it.''

He took some deep breaths and lowered his voice. "You've never seen anyone die so fast. I guess it was because he was drunk and the snake got him in the face.''

Katherine didn't know she was going to speak. It was as if the memory were speaking through her. "But the snake was alive in the bedroom. I woke up and saw it there.''

The pointman smiled, showing his perfect teeth. "Yeah. They closed it in the bedroom after it bit him. You found it. It would've killed you, too, but for that great dog you had. The dog got it. And then it got the dog.''

Yes. She remembered. *Pasha was bitten. He yowled and jerked back. The snake rose again, curved into that deadly S. Pasha attacked again. This time he snapped and caught the snake. He crushed it in his jaws. The snake struck again, but Pasha held on. Even in death he held on.*

The pointman withdrew the gun from her neck and pushed it slowly down her backbone, bruising each vertebra on the way. Katherine closed her eyes, waiting for the bullet that would sever her spine.

But he took the gun off her and shoved it against Anne's cheek. "Then you came into the act, old woman, when your daughter called you screaming and blubbering. You came running. By then my daddy was dead and you bribed Stokes to cover it all up, like my daddy and me were some filth to be swept under the carpet. Just like it never happened. Isn't that right? Isn't that what you did?''

Katherine winced as she saw the gun press into the delicate skin of her grandmother's cheek.

"Answer me when I ask you a question," he shouted. "Isn't that right? We were so unimportant compared with you Driscolls that you just pretended it didn't happen. Isn't that right?"

Katherine wished Anne would answer. She wished they would hear downstairs and call the police. She wished she were back in the hospital with her leg propped up and with the cool sheets against her skin.

"I told my mother what happened, but she pretended he'd really died in a zoo accident. When Lester Renfro started sending her money, more money than my daddy ever brought home to her, she didn't want to make trouble. We moved to Belton. She wouldn't let me do the right thing, so I had to wait all those years until she died.

"But I don't have to wait anymore, do I?" He pushed the gun so hard against Anne's cheek that Katherine saw the skin tear. "Do I?" he repeated.

Anne remained silent, her eyes looking back into his unblinking.

"I'm going to blow your head open. But first you're going to answer me once." His voice crescendoed to a scream. "Do I?"

From downstairs, a quavering voice called out, "Who's up there? Are you all right, Mrs. Driscoll? I'm going to call the police."

He straightened up in alarm and turned his head to glance at the door.

Katherine groped for the cane she had left leaning against the bed and wrapped her right hand around it.

He turned back and grabbed her hair with his left hand, jerking her to her feet and away from the bed, spinning her around to face him. His face had darkened and the eyes were just slits beneath engorged lids.

"Say good-bye to your grandmother, Katherine." He released her hair and leaned toward the bed, raising the gun to Anne's face.

A roar filled Katherine's head. *Enough, goddammit. Enough. Stiffen the sinews.* She reached her left hand across her body and gripped the cane in both hands. *Summon up the blood.* Taking a step back to give her range, she whipped the cane upward with all her strength into his outstretched right arm. The force of the impact stung her hands. The gun flew into the air, clattered to the wood floor and slid out of sight into one of the dark corners of the room.

He bellowed and clutched his arm.

Katherine threw herself forward onto the bed and scrambled over her grandmother. She rolled off the other side onto the floor, crashing into the tray table. She scuttled across the floor on her belly toward the corner where she thought she had heard the gun come to rest. She expected each second to feel him grab her. Where was he?

She glanced back over her shoulder and gasped. Anne Driscoll was gripping his open jacket with one hand and she had managed to hook the other elbow through the thong around his neck. He was trying to pull away, but she was hanging on.

Katherine turned and groped desperately in the dark corner for the gun. Where the hell was it? She wished she could smell it, like Ra could. She imagined he was there and threw her arm out straight as if to give him the line for the retrieve. Her middle finger touched smooth metal and bumped it out of reach against the wall.

She looked back. Now he was leaning over the bed pressing down on Anne's neck and grunting.

Katherine pulled herself forward. Her hands hit the wall. She felt along the baseboard. There it was! She picked it up with both hands and sat up, turning and pressing her back against the wall to steady herself. He was still bent over Anne, shaking her by the neck.

Katherine closed her eyes and pictured a blue sky with a covey of quail overhead. The gun felt heavy and comfortable. Slowly and evenly, as she had done many times before, she aimed the gun and squeezed the trigger.

The explosion rattled the windows of the closed room and thundered in her ears. He stood up straight, as if he'd been startled by the noise. Then, as the echoes died, he made the tiniest sound, like a pigeon cooing in the distance, and crumpled to the floor.

Still holding the gun in front of her, Katherine struggled to her feet and approached the bed. "Anne? Anne? Are you all right?"

Anne Driscoll coughed. Then she croaked out two words. Katherine wasn't sure, but she thought they sounded like, "Yes. Thanks."

Anne raised one hand to touch her neck. Then she fumbled at the side of the bed, found the remote control hanging there, and switched on the light.

Katherine limped around the bed and blinked down at the heap on the floor. It was just Danny Gillespie, his glasses broken, his heavy-lidded eyes closed, his mouth open in surprise. On a thong around his neck hung a snake head, the gaping mouth revealing two sharp fangs. A splotch of red was spreading across his shirt.

"Turn it off," Katherine said. "It hurts my eyes."

Anne switched the lamp off, returning the room to shadows.

Katherine took a step and groaned. There was no part of her body that did not hurt. Her entire left side was on fire. Her scalp felt raw where he had pulled her hair. She located her cane on the floor and used it to hobble over to the door. She opened it and called, "Sophie!"

A tight voice answered from the foot of the stairs. "Oh, Katherine, thank God. What's happened? We didn't know what to do. The police are on the way. Was that a shot?"

"Yes. We're all right. I just—"

Behind her, Anne spoke in a weak, raspy voice. "Tell her to wait. We need to talk."

"Sophie, will you give us a minute?" Katherine called down. She limped to the bed and sat down on the edge. Anne shifted over slightly to make room. Katherine picked her leg up with her hands and hoisted it up to the bed. Then she stretched out next to her grandmother. They both listened to the wail of sirens in the distance.

Anne turned her head so her mouth was about an inch from Katherine's ear. When she spoke, it was in a croaking whisper. "We did it."

"Yes," Katherine said, "we did."

"I plan to honor the agreement I made with your father," Anne whispered. "When the banks open tomorrow, I'll write a check for a hundred thousand dollars. Your fee for the first year. Will it be in time?"

Katherine couldn't remember what day it was. Sunday still? The auction was on Tuesday, she thought. She nodded.

"Good. Will you take over the foundation? Do you think you could do it?"

Katherine nodded again and turned her face toward Anne. "I know I could."

Anne looked directly into her eyes and nodded back. "I believe it. As for what happened here tonight," she whispered, "We'll say we don't know anything. There's no way for them to find out."

Katherine's head throbbed. "But it is true, isn't it? My father did kill Donald Stranahan and you did get Alonzo Stokes to cover it up?"

The sirens were getting closer.

Anne didn't speak. Her eyes closed in exhaustion.

"It is true," Katherine said.

"True?" Anne said in the faintest voice and sighed. "Who cares? Ancient history."

Katherine sat up. "But all this death and violence happened because a crime was covered up. Secrets like this fester! I don't like them." Her voice was shaking and she was close to tears. She felt like a hysterical child. The sirens were right outside the house now. They could see lights flashing through the shades. The phone was ringing downstairs. "I don't like them," she repeated.

"You're hurt now. Upset," Anne said. "Don't say anything yet. Wait until you feel better."

Katherine was silent. Anne was right. There was no point in rehashing ancient history. It would label her father as a murderer, her mother a whore, her grandmother and Alonzo Stokes as accomplices to murder.

And it was clear what was being offered here.

All she had to do was stay silent now and she would have the money to pay off the loan. She'd keep her home and her business and Ra. And she'd get to run the foundation. She could have it all. Anne was right. It was over. There was no point in opening this can of worms.

But all these secrets were corrosive. Secrets had created the pointman. Secrets had kept her from her father. She was tired of secrets. She wanted to expose them all to the air, to drain them of their power.

Doors slammed and police radios crackled outside the window.

"They're here," Anne said.

Katherine took a deep breath. "If I tell it all to Lieutenant Sharb, then your offer to me is withdrawn?"

Anne sighed. "You won't do that. It wouldn't make any sense."

The door opened downstairs. Men's voices rumbled up the stairs. Sharb's voice called, "You all right up there, Miss Driscoll? We're coming up."

Heavy feet pounded the stairs.

Katherine closed her eyes and tried to concentrate on stiffening the sinews and summoning up the blood.

The hardest part was coming up.

TWENTY-TWO

KATHERINE LAY HUDDLED with her back to the window. She didn't want to look at the overcast sky. She didn't want to pack her few possessions in the shopping bag Sophie had brought. She didn't want to see anyone, or talk to anyone, even to say good-bye to the nurses who had been so kind to her. She would just stare at the white wall until the doctor came to discharge her.

She had put on the long blue Mexican dress Sophie had brought her and the clean white socks. Her foot was still too swollen for a shoe. She'd showered and washed her hair, hoping it would make her feel better, but it hadn't.

A profound hopelessness had settled on her. All human effort seemed so futile.

She had made her choice and told Sharb everything she knew about Donald Stranahan, Junior, and what had happened that summer night when she was five years old. He was interested, very interested, but after questioning Alonzo and Anne, decided there wasn't enough evidence to reopen the case. Anyway, the perp was dead and the others merely accomplices.

She had told the truth, aired the secrets, and it really hadn't made any difference in the outcome. The official report released to the news media had said simply that it appeared that Donald Stranahan, Junior, had killed out of resentment over the accidental death of his father at the zoo three decades earlier.

The Stranahan case would end in a week with the grand-jury review of the shooting death of Donald Stranahan, Junior. Katherine would need to appear, but it was just a formality, Sharb assured her.

The case was closed, everything tied up neatly.

It should feel good to have done the right thing, but Katherine didn't feel good at all.

The future looked bleak.

What was she going to do now? She could get a room somewhere. Or share an apartment with Sophie, if Sophie ever really got around to moving out of her parents' house, as she had been threatening. Vic had been persuasive in his invitation to have her stay with him, but it was too soon to think about that. She needed a place of her own, a home base.

Tomorrow she'd have to go back to Boerne and make plans for moving her furniture out and putting it in storage until she decided what to do.

And she'd have to deliver Ra to his new owner. She didn't know who that was because they hadn't called her yet. She'd expected the call around noon yesterday, right after the auction, but it hadn't come. George Bob was probably being kind and waiting until she got out of the hospital. She'd call him this afternoon, get it over with.

She missed Ra, hadn't seen him in four days. Well, maybe this was helping her get ready for the big separation. Maybe she should just ask Vic to deliver him to his new owner and not see him again. No good-byes. No tears.

She couldn't go back to working at the zoo. Alonzo hadn't called or been in to see her. She could understand that. He must be furious. And even if he would let her come back, Anne Driscoll would surely not allow her to work there, or be anywhere in her sight. Anne hadn't called or sent a message to Katherine in the two and a half days they'd both been in the hospital. It was perhaps the worst blow.

She'd have to start job hunting. Maybe that trainer friend of Vic's still had a job available.

She sighed and curled up tighter.

When the phone rang, she almost didn't pick it up. But after the fifth ring, she reached over and lifted the receiver. "Hello." The sound of her own voice repelled her. It was a zombie voice, dispirited and dead.

"Kate?" The lusty twang was a voice from home. "This is Hester Kielmeyer here. How are you, dear? I read in the paper about the difficulties you've been through."

"I'm okay, Hester. Getting out of the hospital in a few minutes, so I can't really talk," Katherine said, trying to inject some animation into her voice.

"Well, I won't keep you. We just wanted to congratulate you. We're so pleased."

"Huh?" Katherine said.

"About your property. Judith and I felt all along it would work out somehow."

"What do you mean?" Katherine asked.

"Well, that you were able to pay off the loan and keep your place. I know what it means to you and it means a lot to us, too. You and Ra have always been our favorite neighbors."

Katherine knew Hester would not be deliberately cruel, but this was almost too much to endure. "Hester, I didn't pay off the loan. My property got sold yesterday at auction."

There was a long silence.

"Kate, I just saw George Bob Rainey. He said he'd never been so surprised in his life as when that lawyer of yours from Austin showed up at ten yesterday, in the nick of time, and paid it all off in cash."

"My lawyer from Austin?" Katherine echoed.

"Sure. John Crowley of Hammond and Crowley, George Bob said. Kate, are you all right, dear? You poor thing. You don't sound like yourself at all."

"And he paid off the whole loan?" Katherine said, her voice cracking.

"Yes. Kate, is there something we can do to help?"

"No. I'm fine," she said, tasting the tears on her lips. "How are you and Judith? I miss you."

"Oh, that's nice of you, Kate, but with murders and viper bites and all, goodness, I don't imagine you've had much time for missing. Listen, dear, I hope you don't find us interfering old busybodies, but we paid Joe his wages for the last two weeks. We knew you didn't want to lose him. He's a gem really, keeping the place so nice and keeping the boarding business going for you. When I was over there, I noticed he'd even chopped your mesquite for you and stacked it at the back door the way you always do in October. The nights are cool enough now for fires. And, Kate, that yellow viguiera is everywhere this year. Best fall for it I ever did see."

Katherine sat up on the bed. "Hester, I'll pay you back. Tomorrow. Is Higgins okay?"

"Oh, my, yes. His hair has grown back over the shaved place and we're still practicing his sits and downs. I think we need to go on to heel and stay. When do you think you'll have time to work with him?"

Katherine was crying so hard she could barely answer. "Soon. Very soon. Thanks for everything, Hester."

"Well, I know you're in a hurry, dear. Take care. Bye now."

Katherine hung up the phone, then pushed the button for the nurses' station and asked for Anne Driscoll's room number.

She got up from the bed with the help of her cane, her lucky cane, and headed slowly toward the elevator. Her grandmother was just one floor up.

In the elevator, she blotted her face on her dress and pushed her damp hair behind her ears.

She knocked on the closed door of room 511.

"Come," said the voice, authoritative and clipped.

Anne was propped up in bed dressed in a quilted peach satin bedjacket. Her hair had been done in a smooth chignon and she was wearing tiny diamond hoops in her ears. She had managed a spark of glamour in spite of the purple bruises on her neck and the cut on her cheek.

Katherine opened her mouth. The words were difficult. First they stuck in her throat and then tears threatened to overwhelm them, but she finally managed. "Thank you," she said. Then, meeting her grandmother's steady gray eyes, she said it again: "Thank you."

Anne waved a hand in the air. "Oh, it's just a cash advance on your salary this year. You'll earn it. But it was a very close thing yesterday. Wasn't it, John?" She glanced in the direction of an elderly man in a gray three-piece suit sitting in a chair next to the window and reading some papers. He looked up at Katherine and rose to his feet.

"We just made it, Miss Driscoll. The bank had a buyer lined up. Local rancher. I think he was disappointed mainly because of the dog. Mr. Rainey at the Bank of Boerne would like you to stop by at your convenience to pick up the canceled mortgage and sign some of his paperwork."

Katherine's heart fluttered. It was really true. "Thank you, Mr. Crowley."

He started to respond, but Anne interrupted. "Well, I'm glad you're here, Katherine. We need to get to work on the foundation. You're well enough for this, aren't you?" She didn't wait for an answer. "Sure you are. Cooper's left things in quite a mess, so you've got your job cut out for you. Pull up a chair and let's start with signing some papers. John, give her that foundation con- tract, please. At the hourly rates you're charging me, you could move a little faster. Sit down, Katherine. We need to decide what to do about Sam McElroy and Hans Dieterlen."

Katherine remained standing. "How about tomorrow, Anne? Right now I'm getting discharged and I haven't seen my dog in four days. Also, I need to drive to Boerne to attend to my own busi- ness, but I'll be back tomorrow, ready to go to work." Katherine looked at John Crowley. "What would be a good time for you to- morrow, John?"

He was trying to suppress a smile, but it broke through into a radiant display of perfect dentures. "How about after lunch, Miss Driscoll? Two o'clock." He looked over at Anne and raised his eyebrows. "Mrs. Driscoll?"

Anne was staring hard at Katherine, her eyes cold slate, lips straight and tight. It was a long thirty seconds before she said, "Two o'clock tomorrow suits me fine."

Katherine limped to the bed, leaned over, and kissed her grand- mother lingeringly on the cheek. She smelled of talcum powder and mothballs and Shalimar, old and rich and very complex.

"Is Alonzo Stokes angry with me?" Katherine asked.

"No. He's humiliated that you know all about it. He feels you must despise him. He said he hoped you would come back and spend some time in the reptile house."

"Oh, I plan to," Katherine said, walking to the door. "I need to complete my education." She paused in the doorway. "We need to find a mate for the bongo, and there's an old lion in Kerrville we need to make space for. I can't wait to start. This is going to be so much fun. We'll be good partners." She smiled at her grand- mother.

Anne Driscoll smiled back with the half of her mouth that still worked. "We've proved it."

Katherine hobbled down the hall toward the elevator. She couldn't stop grinning. Tonight she and Ra would go home. Maybe she'd invite Sophie and Vic to come along. If it got cold enough, they would pile some of the mesquite in the fireplace. Then they'd sit around the fire and tell secrets.

First Time in Paperback

A
JOHN
COFFIN
MYSTERY

Gwendoline Butler

MATTERS OF THE HEAD

Life was good for Detective John Coffin—he'd earned a promotion and had just moved into a new home in the tower of a renovated church-turned-theater. True, he now headed his own force and was no longer a street detective, but his business was still crime and there was plenty in the Docklands.

And then a severed human head was found in an urn on the church steps. A hand turned up in a freezer upstairs. It was one of those cases that stretched out long fingers to touch many lives...or, rather, deaths.

"Butler pens a superior procedural."   *—Publishers Weekly*

Available at your favorite retail outlet in June, or reserve your copy for May shipping by sending your name, address, zip or postal code, along with a check or money order for $3.99 (please do not send cash), plus 75¢ postage and handling for each book ordered, payable to Worldwide Mystery, to:

> **In the U.S.**
>
> Worldwide Mystery
> 3010 Walden Avenue
> P.O. Box 1325
> Buffalo, NY 14269-1325

Please specify book title with your order.
Sorry, this offer not available in Canada. Available in U.S. only.

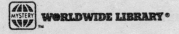 **W⊕RLDWIDE LIBRARY** ®

COFFINM

The Hour of the Knife

SHARON ZUKOWSKI

First Time in Paperback

A BLAINE STEWART MYSTERY

A SUSAN WREN MYSTERY

First
Time in
Paperback

THE WINTER WIDOW

CHARLENE WEIR

SHE'D BEEN ONE OF SAN FRANCISCO'S FINEST—SEMI-HARD-BITTEN, CYNICAL AND HAPPILY UNATTACHED...

Until Daniel Wren blew in like a tornado, sweeping Susan off her feet and back home to Hampstead, Kansas, new bride of the small town's police chief. Ten days later Daniel was killed by a sniper.

Susan was an outsider—a city slicker, a woman, and worse, personally involved in the case. She was also Hampstead's new police chief...hunting for her husband's killer.

"Nonstop action and harrowing suspense." —*Publishers Weekly*

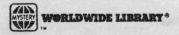

WORLDWIDE LIBRARY®

WIDOW

Death DOWN HOME

First Time in Paperback

EVE K. SANDSTROM

A SAM AND NICKY TITUS MYSTERY

MURDER IS A FAMILY AFFAIR

Reality was a far cry from the posthoneymoon bliss Nicky Titus envisioned. First came the frantic call, then the flight from Frankfurt, and finally the arrival of Sam and Nicky down home in Holton, Oklahoma, where Sam's father, big Sam, lay in a coma after an "accident" on the ranch.

Convinced that somebody had tried to kill his father, young Sam Titus plunges into his own investigation and soon it's clear that no one in the Titus family is safe—not even its newest member, Nicky!

"A crackerjack new series."

—*Kirkus Reviews*

 **WORLDWIDE LIBRARY®**

DEATH

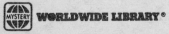